Dear Reader,

Welcome to another ~~n~~ of exciting romances from
Scarlet. From your letters to date, for which I thank
you, it seems as though you are enjoying my monthly
choice of new novels.

I wonder, have *you* ever thought of writing a romance?
We are always looking for talented new authors here at
Scarlet. Do you think you could produce 100,000
words of page-turning storytelling which readers such
as yourself would enjoy? Don't worry if you're not a
professional author, as we're happy to help and advise
you if your work shows promise. If you *are* interested in
trying your hand at writing for *Scarlet*, why not write
to me at Robinson Publishing (enclosing a stamped
addressed envelope) and I shall be happy to send you
a set of our guidelines?

Keep those letters (and manuscripts!) pouring in!

Till next month,
All best wishes,

Sally Cooper

SALLY COOPER,
Editor-in-Chief – *Scarlet*

ELIZABETH SMITH

NOBODY'S BABY

Enquiries to:
Robinson Publishing Ltd
7 Kensington Church Court
London W8 4SP

First published in the UK by Scarlet, 1997

A copy of the British Library Cataloguing in
Publication data is available from the British Library

ISBN 1-85487-931–6

Printed and bound in the EC

10 9 8 7 6 5 4 3 2 1

For Don, Felicia and Lesley

CHAPTER 1

'See? I told you!' The woman's voice was strident and echoing in the early morning stillness of the airport.

Shrouded in white and stilled by freezing temperatures, Denver International, with its hundreds of weary, stranded passengers, had been transformed into a slumbering giant. Outside, it was strangely quiet. The turbulent winds of the night before had subsided, but the startling effects of the sudden storm lay just beyond the snow-crusted windows.

'That's not him,' replied a weary male voice.

From his place on the floor Joe Devlin, still feigning sleep, opened his eyes slightly and was greeted by the sight of four feet firmly planted no more than twenty-four inches from the tips of his shoes. One pair of feet was encased in tennis shoes, the other in cowboy boots. He should have known things were too good to last. Continuing his pretense of sleep, he shifted slightly, turning his head to the side.

'I would know him anywhere,' the plump woman in tennis shoes announced.

'I'm tellin' you, you have the wrong man. Look at the way he's dressed,' the man in cowboy boots insisted.

The woman scrutinized Joe's beige slacks and the navy sweater that covered a white Oxford shirt. 'It's a disguise,' she announced, pleased at her astuteness.

Next to Joe, a young woman with tangled blonde hair slept soundly. He didn't remember her from last night, but it had been late when his flight from Nashville had landed. The only thing he had been interested in then was finding a vacant spot on the floor so he could get some sleep.

'C'mon,' said the man who had been watching Joe intently. He tugged at the woman's arm, but she shook his hand off.

'No, I'm not leaving until I get his autograph.'

Joe nearly groaned aloud. Every bone in his body ached from sleeping on the cold, hard floor, and he was in no mood to be civil. The last thing he wanted was to be recognized.

'For cryin' out loud, Janie, the guy is sleeping,' protested the man.

'Then I'll just wake him.' The woman stepped forward.

Joe flinched and knew a moment of panic. Under different circumstances, he would have gladly given this woman his autograph, but not now, not here. Not when there was little chance to escape the crowd that would gather once his presence became known. Frantically his mind raced, running over a list of possible diversions.

When the woman in tennis shoes stepped forward, his instincts for preservation kicked in, and he deliberately rolled against the sleeping woman next to him. She stirred, sighed, but did not wake. Impulsively, Joe leaned over her and kissed her slightly parted lips. They

2

were soft and warm, and when her lips moved against his in response he was pleasantly surprised. Encouraged, he continued his charade with more enthusiasm.

She moaned softly in approval.

He forgot about the threat of discovery and began to kiss her in earnest.

'That's not him, Janie,' the man declared with certainty. 'Joe Devlin wouldn't be layin' on the floor of the Denver airport kissin' some gal. For once in your life, use your head.'

'That's him,' insisted the woman over her shoulder as she was pulled away from the couple on the floor.

'I don't know what gets into you,' the man said, 'or why I bother listenin' to you. It's just like that time you and that half-wit sister of yours told everyone you were in K-Mart and . . .'

Their voices drifted off. The impulsive kiss had served its purpose. Joe supposed he could stop now, but he was concentrating on the business of enjoying the sweet, moist mouth under his. Slowly, the woman's hand crept around his neck, her fingers tangling in his dark hair. In return for this unexpected pleasure, he wrapped his free arm around her and pulled her easily but firmly against the length of him.

It was a long time since Stevie Parker had been in that pleasurable state of suspension, somewhere between sleeping and waking, that blissful time where the most surprising erotic dreams can surface. So it seemed perfectly natural when she pulled her leg up and laid it across the hard male thigh that was pressing against her. Joe's physical reaction to this move was so immediate that Stevie emerged from her dream state as

3

abruptly as if ice-cold water had been thrown over her. Her blue eyes opened wide before she realized that this was no dream. This was real and the man who was kissing her was serious about it.

Joe pulled back, amused at her reaction. 'It's about time you woke up,' he said in a husky voice. 'Things were about to get out of hand. Pretty soon we would have had a crowd around us.'

'What is going on here?' she demanded indignantly, pushing her hair out of her eyes and raising herself up on her elbow.

'I think that's pretty obvious, don't you?' he replied, dropping his eyes to where her leg lay.

Stevie glanced down. A bright red flush crept from under her sweater and spread upward. She jerked her leg away from him and scrambled up to a sitting position, trying her best to keep her eyes averted from the area where her leg had been. She wasn't about to take any responsibility for this situation, but at that moment it was a toss-up as to whether she should be outraged because this stranger had been kissing her, or embarrassed to death because she had thrown herself all over him.

'God, what were you doing?' she asked, pushing her tangled hair away from her face.

'I wasn't doing anything but enjoying what you were doing.' Joe grinned, and stretched for a moment, rubbing the back of his neck, then stood slowly and reached down to pull her up beside him.

She ignored his outstretched hand, coming to her feet without his help. 'I didn't do anything,' protested Stevie with a shake of her blonde curls, not quite believing what had just taken place.

4

Like hell you didn't. Joe ran his hands through his dark, rumpled hair.

Stevie pulled at the sides of her khaki slacks, then tried to smooth out the creases in her sweater. She could not bring herself to look Joe in the eye, so she kept her head bent and reached down for her jacket and purse. She decided a quick exit was in order.

As if he could read her mind, Joe said, 'You can't leave now – not when we were just getting to know each other!'

Straightening, Stevie forced herself to look up at him. She studied his face, the laughing brown eyes that seemed to know more than they were telling, the disturbingly sensual half-smile. A funny little ripple snaked through her stomach. 'I ought to call Security on you,' she announced with her usual candor.

'I'm Joe Devlin,' he said impulsively, surprising himself. He watched her eyes closely to see if the name would mean anything to her. It didn't. On one hand, he was relieved; on the other, he wondered what planet she had been visiting. Lately, it was difficult for him to go anywhere without being recognized. Last week in Dallas he had spent two hours signing autographs, something he never minded doing under the right circumstances. Early on in his career, he had decided that when, and if, success came to him, he would never shortchange the fans who made it possible.

Stevie hesitated for the space of a few seconds, knowing he had no intention of moving out of her way until he was good and ready. 'Stevie Parker,' she responded.

5

'Stevie?' he repeated, not sure he had heard her correctly.

'Short for Stephanie,' she explained.

He nodded. 'Look, I'm sorry, Stevie. There were some people I was trying to avoid and, ah, well, there you were,' he finished cheerfully.

'How convenient for you. I bet you never even stopped for a moment to consider what you were doing.' The small insincere smile she pasted on her face, accompanied by exaggerated squinting of her eyes, only accentuated her intentional sarcasm.

'Sure I did, but I did it anyway. Are you hungry, Stevie?' he asked quickly, switching gears, then without waiting for an answer he continued. 'I'm starving. Let's go find a restaurant and get some breakfast.' He had taken six or seven steps before he realized she was not following. He retraced his steps. 'Come on, Stevie, I'll be a perfect gentlemen. I owe you something for being so accommodating.'

A look of annoyance crossed Stevie's face, causing her small straight nose to wrinkle in disapproval. So far, his actions had been anything but gentlemanly. While she was not immune to his looks, her reaction to him was tempered by the smug assurance that was written all over his face. Clearly, he was a man who was used to getting his way with women.

'I was not "accommodating",' she protested, throwing her purse over her shoulder. '"Accosted" was more like it.'

Her first impulse was to refuse his invitation, but then she wavered. Shrugging her shoulders and shaking her head, she gave in to the smile that had been tugging at the corners of her mouth. Last week, she had complained to her friend Beth about how boring her life was. Beth, always straightforward, reminded Stevie that she, and she alone, was responsible for that situation. At twenty-eight, Stevie purposely avoided any situation that might result in romance. Well, this boldly executed, six-foot specimen of masculinity was definitely not boring. Besides, what could happen with all these people around? Better not to dwell on that, she decided.

'You don't have to . . .' she began, wanting to let him know that he was not under any obligation to her.

'But I'd like to, very much,' said Joe, smiling. With one finger he reached down and tipped her face up, forcing her to look him in the eye. 'In fact, I'm looking forward to it.'

Stevie was pretty sure he wasn't talking about having coffee together. 'I'd better go clean up,' she said, flustered, as she moved away from his touch.

Inside the rest room, Stevie splashed cold water on her face, combed her hair and applied fresh makeup. She paused in mid-motion while putting on lipstick and searched the reflection in the mirror. She had been awakened by a stranger's kiss this morning, and no matter how indignant she might appear to be, the truth was that she was fascinated.

John Joseph Devlin frequently had this effect on women. His appeal was difficult to describe since he wasn't exactly handsome in the traditional sense. But there was a ruggedness about him, a sense of restrained power that seemed to lie just beyond the surface. The sensuality that played about his full and well-defined lips was jarring, and definitely at odds with the laughter in his eyes.

Upon closer inspection, it would seem his brown eyes had a look of anticipation, as though they knew something special that was about to happen that no one else knew. His hair, which was thick and dark and curled slightly over the collar of his shirt, was not as long as his manager wanted it to be. His voice, full and husky, was tempered by the southern accent that made every phrase sound almost like a caress.

Joe was leaning against the wall waiting for her when she came out of the rest room. 'Ready?' he asked with an approving smile as he looked her over and noted that, while she was of medium height, she still gave the impression of being petite. It was her face, he decided after a moment; heart-shaped, with incredible blue eyes that managed to be both innocent and mischievous.

Their choice of restaurants was limited to one of the many self-serve places that lined the concourse. 'Which one?' he asked Stevie as they walked in the direction of the main terminal. From the corner of his eye, Joe saw a young woman in jeans and a black leather jacket stop suddenly about ten feet from them and grab the arm of the man she was with. She pointed excitedly toward Joe.

Stevie turned and was about to answer that it didn't matter to her where they went, when without warning Joe grabbed her arm and pulled her into the cafeteria-style restaurant to their left. 'Let's try this one,' he said hurriedly.

How ironic that only a year ago he and his band had struggled for whatever recognition they could get, playing any club that would hire them. His rise to stardom as a country music singer had been nothing less than meteoric, or so the media had proclaimed. The reality was a ten-year struggle and unwavering determination. Out of the dozens of songs he had written and performed during those years, one of them, 'Lonely Nights', had finally propelled him from being a nobody straight to the top of the country music charts.

'I was still making up my mind,' Stevie protested, pulling her arm from his grasp.

'You took too long thinking about it,' he teased. 'A guy could starve.'

The restaurant was crowded and the line moved slowly. Joe watched as Stevie loaded her tray. When they reached the cashier Joe paid for their meals, then followed Stevie to a small round table in the far corner near a window. They sat across from each other and Joe, eyeing her heaping plate, wondered how anyone that slender could eat that much.

'Umm, thanks,' she said between bites. 'Airport food is not the best, you know. That is, unless you're hungry.' Stevie looked down at her plate, then up at Joe. 'I skipped dinner last night,' she explained, her eyes wide.

'I could tell,' he said.

After a few bites she asked, 'Are you in Denver on business or on vacation?'

'Business,' he answered truthfully. 'Public relations for a Nashville company.' It was a half-truth. He was here to finalize a contract for three performances the following summer.

'What about you?' he asked. 'Are you on your way in or out of Denver?'

'Out. I was leaving on vacation to Florida. This is not what I had in mind,' Stevie said with a wave of her hand toward the huge drifts of snow outside the window. 'Tell me about public relations. Do you like your job?'

'Most of the time I do. It gets hectic and sometimes I get tired of traveling. When the hotels start to look alike, and I wake up and can't remember what town I'm in, I know it's time to take a breather. What about you?'

'I'm a writer,' answered Stevie.

Joe watched with interest as Stevie ate. While they talked, she picked up one of the two muffins on her plate. A moment later the entire muffin had disappeared.

'What do you write, Stevie?' asked Joe, puzzled. *How in the world had she eaten an entire muffin that fast?* Now he watched her even closer.

'All kinds of things, but I make my living writing non-fiction,' Stevie answered, hoping he wouldn't ask her who she worked for. After seven years with *The Denver Mountain Times*, she had learned that some people acted strangely when they found out she wrote for a newspaper. Maybe it was a fear of seeing something about themselves in print.

Stevie felt Joe's eyes on her. How was she going to get that other muffin off her plate and into the waiting napkin in her lap? What she needed was a diversion. Suddenly, she knocked her fork from the table to the floor. It landed on the terrazzo floor with a clatter. 'Ooh, I'm sorry,' she said with as much sincerity as she could muster.

Joe bent down to retrieve the fork. 'I'll get you another one,' he said, rising.

Taking advantage of his absence from the table, Stevie scooped the second muffin into a napkin and slipped it into the side pocket of her bag. It was an old habit and she knew it was silly, but the muffins would be tonight's snack or tomorrow's breakfast.

Joe returned with a clean fork, but before he sat down he asked politely, 'Can I get you anything else?' He looked down at her plate, astonished. The second muffin was missing. 'Another muffin, perhaps?' he asked with a perfectly straight face.

Stevie's face turned the same bright red as her sweater. 'No, thank you,' she replied primly.

Joe sat down again and studied the pretty woman who shared his table. 'Are you from Denver?' he asked with interest.

'No, I'm from a little town in Wyoming, just a few miles north of Cheyenne.'

'A cowgirl,' he concluded.

'Hardly,' Stevie answered with a wry smile. 'It's one of the reasons why I left Wyoming and came here to Denver. I always felt like a fish out of water at home. I don't like anything about cowboys, or horses, or ranches . . .'

'Not even country music?' he asked quickly with a grin. He waited, his eyes firmly fixed on hers, curious as to what her answer would be.

'Especially not country music,' she answered disdainfully.

'Why not? What's wrong with it?' Joe leaned forward.

'It's all about losers,' answered Stevie, her blue eyes sparkling as she warmed to her subject. She remembered the constant blaring of the radio in the kitchen of the trailer where she had had spent her lonely childhood. The memory of hour after hour of country music, interspersed with farm reports and those awful commercials from local businessmen, was still vivid. 'It's nothing but whining from guys who have lost their horses, their pickups and finally their women. And that's usually the order of importance,' she concluded.

Now it was Stevie's turn to study Joe. In addition to his compelling looks, his clothes were expensive and conservative. 'You don't look like the country music type,' she announced.

His music was so much a part of his life that her words took him by surprise. 'What type do I look like?' Joe asked as he leaned back in his chair, careful to keep his voice even.

Stevie rested her elbow on the table and propped her small chin on the palm of her hand. 'Definitely *not* country music.' She leaned forward now, her tone almost confidential as if she were sharing a secret. 'For one thing, you're not dressed right. Country music guys have a different kind of look. I can spot them a mile away,' she concluded smugly.

This time Joe didn't just smile. He laughed out loud.

'What's so funny?' asked Stevie, suddenly uncomfortable.

'You,' he answered, not taking his eyes from her face.

Stevie sat up straight, annoyed. He wasn't laughing because he thought her reply was humorous or clever. He was laughing at her.

12

'That's a great system you have, but it doesn't work,' he said as he turned slightly in his chair and stretched his long legs out. 'Tell me, Stevie, do you just sit back and look people over, check out their fashion choices, then neatly file them away under suitable categories?'

'I don't do any such thing,' answered Stevie defensively with an emphatic shake of her head that sent her blonde curls bouncing. 'I consider myself very open-minded.'

'I'm sure you do,' drawled Joe as he finished the last of his coffee, 'but you just did it to me. You decided I wasn't the country music type because I wasn't dressed in Wranglers, a plaid shirt and boots.' He leaned across the table and pointed his finger playfully at the tip of Stevie's small straight nose. His brown eyes had that knowing look as he said, 'Well, you're wrong, babe. I'm *crazy* about country music.'

After a moment of surprised silence, Stevie sighed dramatically. 'Too bad. I like rock. There's something so primitive about it. When you're out on the dance floor moving to the beat . . . it's sexy.'

'And you don't think country music can make you feel sexy?' Joe leaned back in his chair.

'Well, I suppose. With the right person,' she added grudgingly.

'With me,' he stated confidently. While his egotistical statement served to annoy her, his probing eyes demanded the truth.

'When hell freezes over,' she lied.

A slow, lazy, suggestive smile made its way from his sensuous lips to his eyes. 'You're a lousy liar, Stevie,' Joe said softly.

The blood zoomed from Stevie's toes to the roots of her hair. She shifted in her seat uncomfortably. Since this morning, she had tried to ignore what he did to her, but the truth was the excitement she felt when he had kissed her just wouldn't go away.

Stevie groped for something clever to say to fill the awkward gap, but for one of the few times in her life she was at a loss for words. In college she had worked diligently to cope with her shyness and now this stranger was causing her to both blush and stammer. All her old insecurities surfaced, leaving her feeling vulnerable.

His smile lingered. The silence, coupled with the knowing look in his eyes, made Stevie more uncomfortable than ever. Joe Devlin was having a great time. Today he was an ordinary man enjoying the company of a not-so-ordinary woman. He could be himself. How long had it been since he had spent time with someone who didn't want something from him?

He pushed his chair away from the table, hooked his arm over the back of the chair next to him and propped his right ankle on his left knee. His eyes narrowed as he studied her, much the same way a predator studies its prey.

'Don't jump to any conclusions,' stammered Stevie nervously, unable to stand the silence between them any longer.

'I'm not,' he said. A smile played around his full lips, but his voice was even, revealing nothing.

'Good,' said Stevie quickly. 'I mean, I just met you.'

'Yes, you did,' agreed Joe.

She glanced out the window, hoping he would take the hint and let her off the hook, wishing he would quit looking at her that way.

14

But Joe wasn't going to do anything to alleviate this tension between them. He was enjoying himself immensely.

Stevie pushed her chair away from the table and stood. Joe Devlin had managed to shake her confidence thoroughly. She thought about the months she had gone out with Michael Baldwin, moving in social circles she had only read about until she met him, and not once had she felt as rattled as she did right this moment. 'Thank you for breakfast,' she said primly, anxious now to break things up.

'Don't you want to find out?' he asked.

She opened her mouth, but nothing came out on the first attempt. 'I should be going . . .' Her voice trailed off. *Who am I kidding? The man is sexy beyond belief. And he knows it.* Stevie nearly groaned aloud at the thought.

'I don't have any other plans,' he said, as a lazy smile revealed his even white teeth. 'Do you?' He stood and came around the table to join her. 'We'll go sightseeing first, then we'll decide how to spend the rest of the day,' he said, as they left the restaurant.

A protest rose to her lips. She wanted to tell him to leave her alone, that she didn't want to be around a man whose look could cause shivers down deep in her stomach. Then she saw the unspoken challenge in his brown eyes. And Stevie knew she couldn't let it go unanswered.

CHAPTER 2

Before they had gone very far down the concourse, Joe stopped to make a call while Stevie sat down across the way to wait.

'Hi, Lorraine,' he said to his secretary when she answered.

'Joe, are you okay? I saw on the news last night that Denver was shut down by a blizzard.'

Joe smiled into the receiver. 'It was, still is, actually. I spent the night at the airport.'

'Well, Jeannie is stuck in Memphis. Her flight was delayed. She left three messages on my answering machine since she found out you went on without her – she's not a happy traveler, Joe.'

'I'm sure she's upset at having her schedule altered.'

Lorraine smiled with satisfaction, positive she detected a touch of sarcasm in Joe's voice. During the year she had worked for Joe, she had taken on the role of confidante, protector, and stage mother. She never made any effort to hide her disapproval over anything that wasn't beneficial to him, including Jeannie Williams. From the very beginning Lorraine had no trouble recognizing Jeannie for what she was – greedy and manipulative. Why, Lorraine wondered, was it taking Joe so long to figure it out? She cleared her throat and relayed the messages from Jeannie.

'Thanks, Lorraine. I'll talk to you later.' With a frown Joe replaced the receiver and digested the messages Lorraine had just passed on to him. Jeannie had worked hard to ensure his success, but she kept pushing at the boundaries Joe had set. Theirs was a professional relationship, nothing more. Except for that one time.

It had been his anniversary, his and Kathy's, and he had celebrated it alone like he had for so many years, his bitterness increasing as the hours passed. Life had cheated him: It had given him success but not happiness. That night, the more he had drunk, the less it had seemed to hurt. Then Jeannie had knocked on his door. What was it she had wanted? He couldn't remember except that she was there and willing, and he was lonely. By the time they had undressed, he had had enough booze to convince himself that what they were doing was okay. And for a little while, it was. He could forget about everything.

It had been a stupid, stupid thing to do. The next afternoon he had talked with Jeannie, hoping to set things straight between them, to make her understand that he had acted irresponsibly. No matter how much she might wish it otherwise, Joe had no interest in her except as his manager. It was a concept that seemed to elude Jeannie, and she continued to act as though there was something between them. God, how he wished he had never slept with her. Except in business situations, he now tried to avoid her, but it was almost impossible given the fact that they frequently traveled together. He had thought about replacing her with another manager, but that would be unfair and unwise. He had been equally responsible for that one unfortunate lapse of good judgement.

Without moving from the phone booth, Joe studied Stevie speculatively as she pursed her lips and watched the people around her. It was so liberating to spend time with someone who didn't want something from him and who was not fawning over him. If anything, Stevie seemed to antagonize him at every opportunity. It was then that he realized this pretty little blonde had, in a matter of only a few hours, argued with him, pissed him off, made him laugh, and aroused him. It was this last that most intrigued him.

Across the way, Stevie watched Joe as he ambled toward her. His slow, easy gait drew admiring glances from the women he passed. The sight of him made her tingle all over.

They spent the rest of the morning exploring the airport, talking to weary airline personnel and anyone else who had an opinion as to when the airport would open.

When Joe confessed to Stevie that afternoon that he had never built a snowman because it rarely snowed in the South, Stevie insisted they go outside immediately and build one.

'But we're not dressed for it,' he protested as she led him to the exit.

'Can't let a little thing like that stop you,' she countered. 'You may never see this much snow again.'

'But it's freezing cold out there,' Joe reminded her.

Stevie halted and turned toward Joe. 'I always did think you Southern boys were a little on the wimpy side,' she replied with her hands on her hips. 'It must have something to do with the way you talk.'

A few minutes later, with plastic bags from one of the shops on the concourse tied over their shoes and their hands, Stevie and Joe went outside to build a snowman. It didn't take long in the freezing temperatures for Stevie to suggest they build a smaller version, thereby shortening the length of time they would spend outdoors. Joe agreed. They worked quickly, stopping at brief intervals to warm their hands. When they had completed their task, they stood back to survey their creation – a snowman, which stood no more than three feet tall, complete with gravel eyes and a cigarette in his mouth.

'I wish we had a picture,' Joe said.

'Wait!' said Stevie as she looked around, then dashed back inside the glass doors. She emerged a few minutes later with a tall, gangly young man in tow, handed him the camera that she had taken from her purse, then ran to stand on the other side of the snowman.

'Okay, shoot,' she said with a grin.

The young man aimed the camera.

'No, wait!' she called, then turned to Joe. 'We can't just stand here doing nothing. It'll look silly. We've got to pose or something. Come here.' She tried several poses. When she got one she liked, which involved both of them sitting in the snow, she instructed the young man to take the picture.

As soon as the picture was snapped, Stevie scrambled to her feet and stepped toward the reluctant photographer to thank him and retrieve her camera, but Joe grabbed her hand, pulling her back against his wide chest. He wrapped both arms around her and leaned his cold, rosy face down against the top of her head.

'Just one more picture, okay?' he asked the photographer.

'Sure,' said the young man, tucking a strand of hair that had escaped his ponytail behind his ear. 'Just say "Freezing my ass off", and smile when you're ready.'

Their burst of laughter was accompanied by the sound of a click and whir as the young man took the picture and the film advanced.

By mid-afternoon one runway was opened and Stevie rushed to find out which flights were leaving. By five, she had given up on her trip. Things were moving slowly and only a few flights were scheduled for departure that evening and the following morning.

Finally, she called Beth, knowing that she would have to make arrangements to get home from the airport, but not wanting her time with Joe to end.

'Stevie? Where are you?' asked Beth.

'Not in sunny Florida like I'm supposed to be. I'm stuck here at the airport.'

'Oh, Stevie, I'm so sorry. I know how much you were looking forward to this trip.' Beth Carr had been Stevie's roommate in college, and they had remained best friends.

'What are my chances of getting home?' asked Stevie.

'I'm afraid you're out of luck. The storm has shut down the entire city. The news reports say that snow-plows have begun to clear Broadway and Colfax down-town, but there's more than twenty-seven inches of

20

snow on the ground. The drifts here are so deep I can't even see my car. As a matter of fact, I can't see anyone's car. I'm afraid we're going to have to wait it out.'

'But that could be days,' wailed Stevie.

'You might as well be in Kansas,' said Beth. 'The airport is so far away from everything. If anything changes I'll have you paged.'

Stevie hung up and dialed *The Denver Mountain Times*. When she answered, Carrie Phelps told Stevie much the same thing. 'If you do get out of there, Stevie, don't bother to come to work. We shut down at ten last night. Even if we had gone to press, there's no way to deliver the paper.' Carrie sighed. 'I was supposed to get off early last night. I had a date. What a difference a few hours could have made in how I waited out this storm.'

Stevie hung up a few minutes later. Joe was waiting for her with two styrofoam cups. Steam rose from each cup along with the aroma of freshly brewed coffee. 'This is the best I could do,' he said as they walked slowly toward a frosted window.

Outside, the snow was falling once more, but aside from the steadily falling flakes there was no other movement. From inside the airport it was impossible to discern the shape of any of the objects that lay idle on the field except the planes, which stood reverently like silent, frozen monuments stilled by a force greater than man's mechanical genius. Carefully she took the cup from his outstretched hand.

'I thought you might be hungry, but the restaurants have sold out of everything,' said Joe. 'They couldn't get supplies delivered in, so there's nothing left to eat.' He looked over his shoulder, then leaned over and

21

whispered in her ear, 'Don't make any sudden moves. Word is spreading that there's no food left and I think the natives are getting restless.'

Stevie giggled. 'Wait,' she said as she reached into her bag. With a flourish she drew out two small bundles wrapped in napkins. Her lips curved in a broad smile as she folded back the napkins and held out her offering to Joe.

Fighting to keep a straight face, Joe took one of the muffins from her and held it up for inspection. 'Umm . . . these look familiar.'

'I saved them from breakfast this morning,' explained Stevie shyly.

'Well, that solves the case of the disappearing muffins. Do you do this often?' asked Joe teasingly.

'No,' lied Stevie, unwilling to tell Joe that it was an old habit. 'It just seemed like a good idea at the time.'

She broke off a piece of the muffin and popped it into her mouth, suddenly reminded of her unhappy childhood, of taking food to her room in case she got hungry later, mindful of her mother's warning not to get up in the middle of the night while her mother had 'company'. She had been scared of the dark then, and at night she would pull the covers close to her and bury her face in the soft, rounded tummy of the little stuffed bear she kept with her. Through the thin walls of the trailer she would hear her mother's voice, then the deep voice of the man her mother had brought home. Laughter would follow and other muffled sounds Stevie couldn't identify.

Outside the wind would howl, causing things to slam into the trailer. Tumbleweeds gathered in large clumps, making scratching sounds as they shifted back and forth along the metal skirting. The noise would frighten Stevie, and the wind never seemed to stop. Not even in the summer.

In the mornings Stevie would sit solemnly at the table, her wide, unblinking blue eyes solemnly studying the men who stayed around for breakfast. The silence in the tiny kitchen was broken only by the woeful sounds of KTRE, a country music radio station in Cheyenne. From behind her bowl of cereal, a watchful Stevie learned not to react to hushed morning conversations punctuated with secret smiles, or the fact that some of the men talked about her as if she wasn't in the same room, sitting right across the table from them.

A few of them treated her mother nice and bought her pretty things, and some of them were even kind to Stevie, but most of them considered her a nuisance. So she learned to make herself as scarce as possible when there was a man in the house. On those mornings when her mother's friends left before daylight, she was relieved.

Joe watched as she chewed, her thoughts clearly somewhere else, then ran her tongue over her lower lip to retrieve a crumb. When he bit into his muffin he found it to be crusty on the outside, but soft on the inside. A little, he suspected, like the petite woman beside him.

'As soon as the snowplows can get out on the streets things will begin to move again,' said Stevie after a minute as she warmed her hands on the steaming cup.

'What are you going to do then?' asked Joe.

Stevie shrugged her shoulders. 'I don't know,' she answered. 'I guess I'll wait until I can get a ride home. What about you?' she asked.

'I'll be in town for a few days,' answered Joe truthfully. 'A business associate is joining me here for a meeting, then it's back to Nashville.'

A sudden sadness at the thought of not seeing him again washed over Stevie. He teased her and he infuriated her, and with his laughing brown eyes he had made her feel more alive than she had in a long time.

This was unfamiliar territory to Stevie – not that she would admit to it, but it had been a long time since she had spent time with a man. Since her relationship with Michael, she had managed to avoid anything more than casual friendships. She supposed she should tread softly in this new territory, but the attraction she felt for Joe had caught her off guard.

During the course of the afternoon they talked, and Stevie learned that Joe was from Piney Creek, Georgia. His parents still lived there. It was his job that took him to Nashville.

He learned that she was from Eagle, Wyoming, a small town just north of Cheyenne. She had left at seventeen to attend college at Colorado State University in Fort Collins, then moved to Denver after graduation.

He had traveled extensively in the United States, and would be making his first trip to Europe in the spring.

She had never been anywhere outside of Wyoming and Colorado. This trip to Florida would have been her first real vacation.

He loved all the traditional Southern, calorie-laden foods his mom fixed.

Unless Stevie went out to eat, which was usually something healthy like salad or pasta, she ate TV dinners from the microwave.

She loved romantic old movies. 'But I never cry,' she assured him.

His idea of a great old movie was *Lethal Weapon*, and he didn't believe her.

He kept reminding himself that he was only going to be here a few days.

She had already thought about that.

She didn't know that Joe was a celebrity.

He didn't want her to.

And then there was Kathy to consider.

Joe wanted to kiss her again, slowly and thoroughly, just to make sure it was as good as he remembered.

Stevie wondered if he would ever get around to kissing her again – the way he had this morning.

It was heady stuff.

Outside it was already dark and it made Stevie sad to think this wonderful day was almost over. She could still feel the heat of his lips on hers, and the look in his eyes and she knew wouldn't be able to forget Joe Devlin for a long, long time.

For the last half-hour Stevie had been playing cards with seven-year-old David and his ten-year-old sister, Megan. When Stevie had suggested to the kids that they sit next to her so they could think up a game to play, the children's mother had smiled gratefully. Restless, and anxious to hear the latest updates on the storm, Joe had gone to listen to the news on television and then to baggage claim to find his and Stevie's luggage.

'Cash your chips in, Stevie, we've got to go,' Joe said with a grin when he returned with his bag in hand.

'But finally I'm winning,' she protested, looking up at him and indicating the pieces of paper she and the children were using as poker chips. 'It's time for revenge. David almost cleaned me out.'

David giggled.

Joe reached down and rumpled David's dark blond hair. 'Sorry, kids, but Stevie has to leave now.'

David and Megan protested, then at their mother's urging they thanked Stevie for playing with them.

'Hey, where's my luggage?' asked Stevie.

Joe took Stevie's arm and guided her toward the escalator. 'Couldn't find it. They said they would call as soon as they located it.'

'Where are we going?' asked Stevie breathlessly as she rushed to keep up with Joe's long stride.

'Downtown. I've arranged for transportation. It will be slow going, but we should be able to get through'

Stevie came to a skidding halt. 'Joe, wait.'

He turned. 'What's wrong?'

'I can't go. I mean, I just can't take off and go with you. I don't even know where you're taking me.'

His smile was speculative. 'Adventure is not your thing, is it, Stevie?'

'Adventure has nothing to do with it.' Her blonde curls bounced as she shook her head. 'I don't know you.'

Joe raised his brows, the humor in his eyes shining.

'At least not well enough to go anywhere with you,' Stevie clarified seriously.

Joe reached for her hand, and continued to pull her along toward the exit. 'These are not ordinary times, Stevie. We're going to my hotel. We can get something to eat and you can stay there until you can get home.'

'But I . . .' she began to protest.

Joe dropped her hand and wrapped his arm around her shoulders, hugging her to him. His brown eyes danced as he looked into her upturned face. 'So you're an old-fashioned girl. That's okay with me, but being foolish is not okay. Your chances of getting home are a lot better from downtown Denver than they are from here.'

Stevie realized he was right, but rather than acknowledge it she muttered, 'I am not old-fashioned.'

'Here's the car,' he said, smothering a chuckle, as they stepped outside into the icy darkness. At the curb he opened the passenger door of the waiting four-wheel drive.

CHAPTER 3

At the hotel, Stevie stood just inside the doorway to Joe's suite. 'Wow,' she said under her breath as she surveyed the room before her.

The bold, deep yellow-and-rose flowered chintz that covered matching love seats and the striped moss green of the side chairs gave the large living room the look of a cheerful English country garden. Across the rear wall were three floor-to-ceiling windows. An oval cherry table and four chairs occupied the space in front of them. In the corner, concealed by a half-wall, was a wet bar and a small refrigerator. To the right of the living room was a spacious bedroom and an adjoining bath. Soft yellow carpeting covered the floors. It reminded Stevie of the color of pale butter.

'What did you say you do?' Stevie asked as she wandered from the spacious living room into the bedroom. Without waiting for an answer she took in the desk, the queen-size bed and the *chaise longue*. Here the colors of the living room were repeated, but the hues were softer. Next she stuck her head in the bathroom where deep green marble and gleaming gold fixtures greeted her. It was also about the size of the living room in her apartment.

Joe walked up behind her. 'Public relations,' he answered. 'For JJD Productions.'

'Not bad, not bad at all,' she said, missing entirely the important piece of information he had just revealed. If she had had any knowledge at all of country music, she would have recognized the name of his production company.

'For a country boy from Georgia,' added Joe.

Stevie laughed appreciatively and marveled at the elegance around her. Anyone who traveled for the newspaper was asked to do so as economically as possible. She had never stayed in a place like this; she had never even seen a place like this except in magazines.

When they had finally arrived at the hotel, Stevie had insisted on a room of her own, but because of the weather and a convention group that was unable to leave the previous day, nothing was available.

She went to stand at the windows, gazing at the twinkling lights of the city spread before her. Now that she was here she was beginning to have second thoughts.

Joe reached for his briefcase. At the table he spread some papers before him. 'Make yourself at home. I've got some things to look over,' he said as he glanced at his watch. 'Then we'll have dinner.'

Stevie turned from the window to face him. 'Joe, I . . . I don't think I can stay here with you.' Stevie swallowed, her mouth suddenly dry.

'You can have the bedroom, if that's what you're worried about.' He leaned back in his chair, amused.

Bright pink colored Stevie's cheeks. 'It's not that,' she protested.

'Okay, I'll take the bed, you can have the sofa.'

'No, it's just . . .'

'Not proper?'

'That, and . . .'

'You hardly know me?' supplied Joe, with a mischievous grin. 'Didn't we just go through this at the airport? I promise you, Stevie, I am completely trustworthy and very discreet. I'll never tell a single soul that we're spending another night together.'

'We're not spending *another* night together!' she protested, spinning around to face him. 'We never even spent the first night together.'

'Technically, you're right. Okay, you win. Tonight will be our first night together and I promise I'll make it very special for you.'

Stevie sputtered at his audacity. 'Will you stop? I'm just not sure I should have come here with you. Maybe I should call someone to come and get me,' she bluffed.

With a sweeping hand Joe gestured toward the phone. 'You can try, Stevie, but you saw the streets earlier. You know how long it took us to get here.'

He was right, of course. She plopped down on the sofa and leaned her head back and closed her eyes. After a few moments she said, 'I just feel . . .'

'Strange?' supplied Joe.

'Strange,' agreed Stevie.

'Surely this isn't the first time you've spent the night with a man? In a hotel room?' teased Joe.

'Yes, it is.' Stevie's blue eyes were sincere, as she straightened and turned to look at him.

'Which one?' At her puzzled look, Joe restated his question. 'Which haven't you done before? Spent the night with a man, or spent the night in a hotel with a man?'

Stevie blushed and looked down at her hands. 'Uh, the hotel,' she mumbled.

'Ah, the hotel,' mused Joe and wondered how many men there had been.

She stood suddenly, anxious to change the direction this conversation had taken and to escape his scrutiny. 'Well, if I'm going to stay, I could certainly use a bath,' she announced impulsively. 'I can't believe how grimy I feel.'

'Right through there. Wait.' He went to the closet in the bedroom and took out a white terry robe. 'Here, you'll need this,' he said, handing it to her.

Stevie nodded, her complexion suddenly rosy. This is all make-believe, she reminded herself as she grabbed the robe from his outstretched hand.

Heavenly, thought Stevie a few minutes later as she slid into the huge tub that could easily have accommodated more than one person, and reached for the shampoo. After lathering her hair, she leaned back in the tub and let the water lull her into a relaxed state.

A knock at the bathroom door a half-hour later brought her back to reality and she sat up straight, spilling water on to the marble floor.

'Stevie, hurry up, will you? I want to take a shower before dinner.'

'Sorry, Joe, I'll be right out.'

A few minutes later Stevie opened the bathroom door a crack and looked around. The bedroom was empty. With a sigh of relief she stepped out. Her doubts about about this whole arrangement surfaced again. It was too intimate. Just being here in the same hotel suite with him was overwhelming. It made her nervous. As she had confessed to Joe, it was a brand new experience; one she had never shared with Michael.

Stevie shuddered. It was inevitable that she would think about Michael. Today was a milestone. It was the first time she had allowed herself to show any real interest in a man since she had discovered the truth about Michael Baldwin.

No wonder Michael had never suggested they move in together. It would have changed the special relationship they shared, he had insisted, then he would kiss Stevie quickly on the tip of her nose and nuzzle the back of her neck, as if that would divert her attention. Even though she was never able to pinpoint Michael's reluctance to move on to the next plateau in their relationship, she had never suspected his duplicity. Stevie shook her head now as if to chase away the unpleasant memory. Michael was part of the past.

The terrycloth robe was much too large, she decided as she studied her image in the full-length mirror.

'Are you decent?' asked Joe from the doorway.

'I'm afraid so,' she answered with a smile as her heart tripped with unexpected anticipation.

Joe made his way across the bedroom, his eyes traveling the length of her. First the corners of his mouth twitched upward, then he began to laugh out loud. Great big sounds from down deep. The kind of sounds that her grandfather would have described as a belly laugh.

Stevie watched him first in amazement, then in agitation. 'What's so funny?' she asked, her hands on the bunched fabric at her hips.

Realizing that he had hurt her feelings, Joe took her into his arms and pulled her against him in a bear hug. With her face pressed against his shirt, Stevie could feel his chest. It was heaving with silent laughter.

'What are you laughing at, Joe?' Her question was muffled against his shirt.

'You,' he answered, biting his lip to keep his merriment under control. But it was still there, in his voice. He pulled back to look down at her upturned face. The smell of soap and water combined with the scent of her shampoo was nothing like the cloying perfumes that most women wore. Joe inhaled deeply, then spoke. 'I was sitting at the table envisioning you all warm and steamy from your bath, wearing this robe and looking tousled and sexy.'

'Well?' she asked in a hurt tone.

'Well, instead of tousled and sexy, you look like a kid in someone else's clothes. This robe is at least three sizes too large and it's definitely not sexy.' With his hands on her shoulders, Joe turned Stevie around and gently pushed her toward the closet. 'C'mon,' he said, 'we'll find something that fits you better.'

'Joe,' began Stevie, 'I don't know . . .'

'Just until they locate your bag, Stevie, then you can change into your own clothes.'

Together they stood in front of the open closet while Joe flipped through his clothes. He pulled a garment

33

out and handed it, still on its hanger, to Stevie. 'Here, put this on while I take a shower,' he said as he disappeared into the cavernous bathroom.

Stevie stood where she was and listened for the sound of running water. As soon as she heard it, she held up the garment in her hands for inspection. It was one of Joe's shirts, a soft blue cotton. Absently, she ran her hand over the fabric, then held it against her face. It smelled clean and masculine. She had never worn a shirt or anything else belonging to a man. Not even something that had belonged to Michael. He wouldn't let her, explaining that he was very particular about his clothes and they never looked the same after they had been worn by someone else.

The white terry robe fell around her feet as she stepped out of it and slipped into the blue shirt. Standing in front of the mirror, a small shiver of excitement ran through her. As she turned slightly in each direction, then twisted to catch her reflection from behind, she wondered what Joe would think of her now.

Absently, she ran her fingers through her hair. Deciding that she looked much too wholesome, she bent over and shook her hair to make it appear fuller. Then she unfastened one button, then another. She peered anxiously into the mirror. The soft cotton fabric of the shirt felt good against her bare skin. The front and back dipped above her knees, but the sides curved up to expose the upper part of her legs.

Aimlessly, Stevie wandered through the living room, then decided to explore the contents of the bar. In the refrigerator were several bottles of wine. She selected one, then rummaged through the drawers in search of a corkscrew.

She had just opened the wine when there was a knock at the door. It was too early for room service, thought Stevie as she looked down at her shirt. Deciding that she was adequately covered, she crossed the room. Before she could open the door, the doorknob was torn from her grasp. She jumped back to keep from being hit.

A tall woman with dark red hair and green eyes that flashed with surprise, then anger, pushed her way through the door into the suite. 'Where's Joe?' she demanded, looking Stevie over. 'And who are you?'

Stevie stepped back and looked at her, speechless. At five feet ten inches, Jeannie Williams towered over Stevie. But it was not her height that startled Stevie into silence, it was the way the woman was dressed. Heavy, large turquoise and silver earrings dangled against her shoulders. Around her neck hung a jumble of necklaces. Multiple bracelets of silver, copper and turquoise clanked and shimmered up and down her arms. With every movement her rings flashed in the lamplight – at least seven of them. Against the white knit dress she wore everything about her seemed to shimmer and dangle and clank.

Recovering her powers of speech, Stevie pointed to the bedroom. 'Joe's in the shower.'

'I'll wait,' said Jeannie as she walked over to one of the love seats and sat down. From her purse she took a pack of cigarettes and a lighter. With narrowed eyes she studied Stevie as she lit her cigarette. Through the haze of exhaled smoke she spoke. 'I'm Jeannie Williams, Joe's associate.' To her credit, Jeannie was careful not to reveal Joe's identity.

35

From her place near the door, Stevie assessed the woman who had blown in with the force of a hurricane. She appeared to be in her late thirties. Aggressive and tough were two words that popped into Stevie's mind.

'Where did Joe find you?' asked Jeannie as she waved her cigarette in the air.

'I'm Stevie Parker. Joe and I met in the airport.'

Jeannie raised her eyebrows and looked pointedly at Stevie's attire. She exhaled, sending a stream of smoke in Stevie's direction.

How dare he! thought Jeannie, angered by the fact that Joe had interfered with her plans for this trip, but she could have worked around that. What she hadn't counted on was Joe picking up this bimbo. She wondered if this girl had any idea who he was. Most of the girls who managed to attract the band's attention were groupies. If this one didn't know who he was, she would probably find out soon enough. As soon as they found out, they always seemed to get greedy. Jeannie had seen it happen before.

Stevie blushed and her hand flew to the opening of her shirt. 'Oh! My clothes . . . well, you see, I don't have any,' she began to explain with a nervous laugh, then stopped, realizing how that must sound.

Without waiting for Stevie to finish, Jeannie jumped up from the sofa and walked though the bedroom to the bathroom door. She knocked. 'Joe? It's Jeannie. I want to talk to you.' Her voice was loud and demanding.

There was a pause before Joe answered. 'I'll be out in a minute, Jeannie.'

Stevie couldn't help but notice that Jeannie's expression was tense when she returned to the living room. By now Stevie had figured out that this woman was greatly disturbed by her presence in Joe's suite.

When Joe appeared, leaning indolently against the framework of the doorway between the living room and the bedroom, he was wearing a pair of soft, faded jeans that molded themselves to every curve and indentation of his muscular body. His white shirt hung loose and open. His feet were bare, his dark hair damp and curled from the shower.

Across the room Stevie sat with her feet curled under her, prepared to enjoy the fireworks. What she was not prepared for, however, was the sight of Joe half-dressed, still damp, and sexy beyond belief. She drew in her breath sharply.

'Hello, Jeannie. How was your flight?'

At the sight of Joe, Jeannie switched gears, her voice becoming softer, her anxiety diminished. 'My flight was fine, darling. I thought you were going to meet me in Memphis,' she said as she rose from the chair and crossed the room. With a deliberate show of intimacy, she pressed her body suggestively against his. 'I missed you,' she whispered in a sultry voice.

Joe stepped back. 'Have you met Stevie?' he asked with narrowed eyes.

Jeannie ignored his question and said instead, 'I need to talk to you in private. Let's go downstairs and have a drink.'

From over Jeannie's shoulder, Joe looked across the room toward Stevie. He couldn't help but notice the quizzical look on her face that seemed to mock the scene she was witnessing. Her eyes were wide and blue and definitely enjoying his moment of discomfort. He knew she was waiting to hear his answer.

'Not tonight, Jeannie. Stevie and I have our evening planned. I'll meet you for breakfast tomorrow, then we can go from there to our meeting.'

Inside Jeannie was seething, but outside she remained composed. She knew the raging jealousy she felt right now would just turn Joe off. She would bide her time. Women like Stevie would come and go. Sometimes they lasted a night or two, sometimes longer. They were a diversion to break the monotony of touring and the long hours spent in strange hotel rooms.

It never surprised her when she found out that one of the others in Joe's group had picked up a girl along the way, but she was surprised that Joe had brought this girl here with him. Not that he was a saint. She knew from firsthand experience he wasn't. It was just that he usually didn't have much to do with the women who chased after him. She might not like Stevie's presence, but Jeannie knew that when Joe was done with her, he would send her on her way. She could wait.

Taking a deep breath, Jeannie backed away from Joe and grabbed her purse. At the door she paused. 'See you in the morning.'

Joe stood where he was, his jaw tightly clenched.

Stevie remained in her chair, her expression amused. 'You and your associate seem to be on very friendly terms,' she remarked.

Joe flashed her a look of annoyance. 'That's what she'd like you to think.'

'Are you?' persisted Stevie.

'No, we're not, but one night we nearly were, because I failed to exercise good judgement. It's a long story – '

'And it's none of my business,' finished Stevie.

'Your powers of perception amaze me,' retorted Joe.

'Me, too,' Stevie agreed brightly. 'So, is it over between you two?'

'It was over before it even began. Why are you so interested?'

'I'm not interested,' Stevie replied quickly. 'Just curious. Writers are supposed to be curious.'

'Are they supposed to be nosy, also?' asked Joe with a crooked grin.

'Of course,' Stevie replied and gave him a dazzling smile, uncurled herself from the chair and went to the bar.

Joe knew that Jeannie was furious. He had seen it in her eyes. He would have liked to have seen the expression on her face when she had entered the suite and seen Stevie dressed only in his shirt.

He hoped that Stevie's presence would send the message loud and clear to Jeannie that he wasn't interested in her. What Joe hadn't counted on, though, was the fact that Stevie's presence here in his hotel room was causing him some problems. The sight of her shapely bare legs as she rose from the chair and went to the bar, and the thought of what else the loose-fitting shirt was hiding had caused his temperature to rise more than a few degrees.

As she poured wine into two glasses, one side of the blue shirt curved to reveal the rounded contours of her bottom and the smooth length of her legs. He fought the sudden urge to pull her tight against him, to let her feel what she was doing to him, to bury his face in her soft fragrant hair. *Stop it, Devlin. You're trying to discourage one woman, not get involved with another.*

With a glass of wine in each hand, Stevie turned to face Joe. Slowly, he went to her, took both glasses from her, placing them on the table, then reached out and ran both his hands over her shoulders and arms, smoothing the soft blue fabric of the shirt.

Stevie was powerless to tear her eyes from his. She could feel the heat of him through the shirt. Unconsciously, she ran her tongue over her parted lips. All day long she had waited for this moment, knowing it would happen, wanting it to happen. She stood very still, afraid to breathe as his lips captured hers in what was the beginning of long, slow, drugging kiss.

Stevie stood on her toes and pressed her body against his, as if she couldn't get enough of his warmth. When Joe probed her parted lips with his tongue, she felt a slow heat radiate through her. Then she felt her insides begin to melt.

Deliberately Joe unwrapped his arms from around Stevie, then put his hands on her shoulders to put some distance between them, his eyes moving slowly over her face. Then he kissed her once more.

Pulling back to look down at her, Joe inhaled sharply. There was no doubt in his mind where this was going to lead. Her response had convinced him that she was willing and, as evidenced by his physical condition, he wanted her. So why wasn't he doing anything about it?

Stevie's eyes searched his in confusion. In a consuming flash of desire, she knew without a doubt that she wanted him to make love to her, slowly and tenderly.

Instinctively Stevie knew that was the kind of lover he would be. So why had he stopped? And why was he looking at her with regret in his eyes?

'Come on, honey,' Joe said in a husky voice as he put his arm around her and lead her to the sofa.

'Joe?' she whispered against his shirt and the sound of his name held a thousand unanswered questions.

'Look at me, Stevie,' Joe commanded softly.

She did, and her confusion was evident.

'You are very beautiful and very desirable and I would like nothing better than to keep kissing you.' Joe took a deep breath and ran his hands up and down her shoulders. 'But I can't.'

Stevie searched his face.

'The shirt looks very good on you,' he said, absently fingering the fabric. He hesitated, taking a deep breath. 'I'm afraid if I continue, I won't want to stop.'

Embarrassed at her blatant invitation to him, and confused at his response, she stood suddenly, but before she could take more than a few steps Joe caught her by the arm, swinging her back to face him. There was a shimmer in her blue eyes that hadn't been there a moment ago, and he knew she was close to tears.

'I . . . I'm sorry,' she stammered. 'I guess I just misread some signals here.'

'No. You didn't misread anything, Stevie.'

'But you just said – '

Joe nodded wearily, and watched helplessly as a lone tear ran down her face.

When would she learn that no one wanted her?

He pulled her to him and she could feel his strength as her tears blotted themselves on his shirt. He didn't

41

speak, he just held her, his strong hands caressing first her hair, then her back.

Stevie couldn't look up. With great effort, she blinked away her tears. She swallowed hard. She pushed at his restraining hands, freeing herself from his grasp, unwilling to have him see her like this, embarrassed and hurt. She had gambled with her emotions, willing, for the first time in a long while, to take a chance with this man.

'I'm sorry, Joe. I . . .' she said, stepping back from his touch . . .

'I didn't mean –' he whispered.

'It's okay. It's just . . . my luck.' She tried her best to laugh, but it came out more like a sob. How could she explain that she had been rejected by everyone she had ever cared about? Just now, Joe couldn't even bring himself to pretend that he wanted her. *Why was it so hard for her to realize that no one was ever going to love her?*

He retrieved their glasses from the table, while a million reasons why he should make love to her danced in his head. But the one reason why he shouldn't outweighed all the others. Stevie Parker wasn't like the others. He had a feeling that if he made love to her it would not be a passing thing. And when it was over, he knew he would never forget her. It was too high a price to pay.

Joe drank from his glass, then handed Stevie hers before he spoke. 'It was a mistake.' He deliberately kept his voice even.

'A mistake?' she whispered.

Joe looked away, unable to bear the hurt and confusion in her eyes. 'Stevie, I didn't bring you here for that reason. It won't happen again.'

He put his glass down on the coffee table that separated the two love seats, then stood. He wanted to say more, but the words weren't there. Instead he disappeared into the bedroom. When he reappeared, he carried a jacket over his arm. 'I'm going downstairs for a while,' he said without looking at her as he slipped his wallet in the back pocket of his jeans. 'I have a key.'

CHAPTER 4

Downstairs in the hotel bar, Joe watched the ice cubes float aimlessly in his drink. The scene with Stevie kept replaying itself in his mind. Bringing her here was a bad idea.

That he couldn't keep his hands off Stevie was only a small part of the problem. Making love to her would be disastrous. After a few days he would be leaving Denver to return to Nashville, and in the end Stevie would be the one who would be left behind. She deserved better than that.

But there was no place in his life for someone like her. He lived a gypsy life without the adventure. Boredom made it difficult when, from day to day, for weeks on end, only the names of the cities and the colors of the bedspreads in the hotel rooms changed. But it was more than the fact that he traveled constantly. That was only an excuse he used. The events of that terrible January night seven years ago had seen to that. He couldn't afford to care about anyone.

Joe finished his drink and signaled the bartender to bring him another one. Maybe it would help him forget the feeling of Stevie's body, her soft inviting lips and the desire he had read in her eyes. Tomorrow, he decided, he would find a way to get her home.

The next morning bright sunshine streamed in through the drapes in the bedroom as Joe slipped into his jacket. In the living room, Stevie was still asleep on the sofa. Silently, he crept past her. With her blonde hair in disarray she looked young and vulnerable. Remembering the night before, Joe swore under his breath. Thank God she had been asleep when he had finally returned. He would talk to her today when he returned from his meeting. Then he would find a way to get her home before his resolve weakened, before he found himself in a situation where he couldn't resist making love to her.

Jeannie was waiting at the hotel restaurant when he arrived. 'Well, well,' she drawled as he pulled out a chair and sat down. 'How's lover boy this morning? Tired, honey?'

'Cut it out, Jeannie,' Joe said irritably as the waitress filled their cups with dark steaming coffee. When he thought of what he had to face when he went back to his suite, he sure wasn't in any mood to listen to Jeannie's innuendos.

'I can wait,' said Jeannie with the self-assurance that made her so valuable as a manager. Her green eyes narrowed as she lit a cigarette.

'There's nothing to wait for, Jeannie,' answered Joe, knowing that she was talking about him.

'Sure there is, honey. You'll get tired of her. These things never last more than a few days, and I'm a patient woman.'

'Look, Jeannie,' said Joe, 'if it wasn't for your help I doubt that I would be where I am. You have a special talent for opening doors and I appreciate everything that you've done.' Joe paused and took a deep breath. He wanted to do this as quickly and painlessly as possible. 'But there is nothing between us.' Joe watched as Jeannie brought her cigarette to her lips and inhaled. Her expression didn't change.

'How can you say that, Joe? The night we spent together was good.' Jeannie smiled suggestively. 'Very good, as I remember it.'

'Then you probably remember more than I do, Jeannie. I had too much to drink and we had sex. That's all it was, and it should have never happened. It was my fault.'

'But, Joe . . .' protested Jeannie. Her composure slipped.

'There's nothing between us, Jeannie. There is not going to be anything between us in the future. It was one night and it's over. If you can accept that, then we can continue with our professional relationship.'

Jeannie idly ran one finger around the rim of the saucer that held her cup as she considered this ultimatum. 'And if I can't?'

Joe took a deep breath, but before he could answer she spoke. 'Okay, Joe, we'll do it your way.' Leaving her coffee untouched, she grabbed her purse and stood up to leave. 'I'll meet you in the lobby in a half-hour.' For now, Jeannie knew she had to go along with whatever Joe wanted.

After he dumped this girl, she would begin a new campaign. To jeopardize her business relationship with

46

Joe now would be foolhardy. With his talent, his looks and charisma, Joe Devlin paid off like a slot machine. He had been a nobody when she found him in that dump of a club outside Nashville. As his manager, she was making more money than she had ever dreamed possible.

'Are you ready to order, sir?' asked the waitress for the second time.

'No, uh . . .' said Joe. 'Just a refill on the coffee, please.' He felt relieved that he had finally gotten things out in the open with Jeannie. Now if he could just send Stevie on her way without hurting her, everything would be okay.

'Any messages for me?' asked Joe when he and Jeannie returned from their meeting late that afternoon. Over lengthy negotiations that had included lunch, the terms had been hammered out and the contracts signed. Joe Devlin would do three shows in Denver this summer.

'Just one, I believe, Mr Devlin,' said the clerk.

Joe took the note from the clerk and stuffed it into his jacket pocket without looking at it.

'I've decided not to stay,' announced Jeannie as they crossed the elegant lobby. 'There's a flight out late this evening. Under the circumstances I think that would be best.'

Joe nodded, relieved. He couldn't agree more.

Jeannie turned toward the elevators. Joe reached into his pocket and withdrew the message. It was from Stevie. He read the brief note, then crumpled it in his hand.

'How long ago did Miss Parker leave the hotel?' asked Joe, returning to the front desk.

'Miss Parker?' asked the desk clerk uncertainly.

'The young woman who left this note,' explained Joe.

'Just before you returned, Mr Devlin. She can't have been gone more than five minutes.'

The words were hardly out of the clerk's mouth before Joe turned and ran out of the hotel toward the Sixteenth Street Mall one block away. At the corner Joe stopped. Stevie was nowhere in sight.

He shivered. In spite of the weak afternoon sun, the temperatures hovered around zero. The snow from the blizzard was piled high everywhere, a silent testimonial to nature's fury. He had to find Stevie, talk to her. He couldn't let her go like this. In spite of his decision to send her on her way, Joe needed to explain things to her. He didn't want to hurt her. Besides, he had been the one responsible for bringing her to the hotel.

By the time Jeannie was ready to leave for the airport an hour later, she had a satisfied grin on her face, like a cat who had just caught a mouse. She knew that Stevie had left the hotel and that Joe had gone after her. In a few days, when Joe got back to Nashville, things could proceed just like she had planned.

Outside the sun had set and it would soon be dark. Once the sun disappeared behind the Rocky Mountains, the temperature would drop even more and darkness would set in. There were no long, lingering twilights.

Joe knew Stevie was still out there with no way to get home. Except for the central part of the city, most of the streets remained closed. He had to find her. There were too many unanswered questions between them.

48

'Damn,' swore Joe as he made his way toward Six-teenth Street. Why couldn't he just let things be?

The streets were nearly deserted and only a few people turned to look at the tall, good-looking man as he checked every doorway and alley, calling aloud for someone, but the name was muffled. The collar of his jacket was turned up against the bitter wind. His hands were jammed in his pockets.

You're a sucker for anything that tugs at your heart-strings, Devlin. Warm puppies, little kids, Stevie Parker.

In the commuter bus terminal, Stevie huddled in her coat, shaking from the cold. She felt so alone and she had no place to go. She couldn't get home. The buses weren't running. She should have thought about that. Actually, she hadn't thought about much of anything, except that she needed to get as far away from Joe Devlin as she could before she made a fool of herself again.

She had spoken briefly with Beth, who was still snowed in. Bill Schaeffer, another friend and photo-grapher for the paper, told her the same thing.

Neither of them had asked where she was, and she was reluctant to tell them. She had thought about going back to the hotel, but it was too humiliating. How could she go back to a man who had made it so clear that he wasn't attracted to her?

Stevie was contemplating that thought as she watched the reflections of the street lights through the glass doors. A sadness seemed to descend over the city with the deepening shadows.

Joe saw Stevie through the brightly lit glass before she saw him. At that moment she looked so forlorn and sad that he knew he had been right to come after her. For whatever reasons, he needed to have Stevie with him.

A blast of ice-cold air followed Joe through the doors. From her place on the bench, Stevie looked up and her eyes widened in disbelief at the sight of him while her heart took this opportunity to pause before it resumed its normal rhythm.

'Stevie, where the hell have you been? I had almost given up on you.' Joe held her by her shoulders, fighting the urge to shake her. 'I've been so worried about you. Are you okay?'

Stevie nodded, unable to speak, incredibly happy to see him. With one arm wrapped around her shoulders, he led her out of the bus terminal toward the hotel. By the time they reached the entrance to the Hyatt, she was shaking uncontrollably from the cold.

'Why did you leave this afternoon?' Joe looked down at Stevie as he led her to his suite.

'After last night, I thought it was best,' she answered from between chattering teeth.

He guided her into the bedroom to the edge of the bed. 'Sit here,' he directed. 'You have every right to leave if you want, Stevie, but why didn't you call someone to come and get you? You could have frozen to death.' Without waiting for an answer Joe went into the bathroom and turned on the shower. Hot steam began to fill the bathroom.

In the bedroom Joe pulled Stevie to her feet. 'Come on. You need a hot shower to warm you up.'

'I can't,' she said. 'I'm too cold.'

Joe reached for her coat and began to slip it off her shoulders.

Stevie wrapped her arms tightly around her torso. 'I'm really cold, Joe.'

Gently, he took hold of Stevie's wrists, unwrapped her arms, then slipped off her coat. Next he reached for the waistband on her sweater and began to pull upward, forcing her to hold her arms over her head. The sight of Stevie standing before him with the soft creamy swell of her breasts accentuated by her white lacy bra was too much for Joe. He wanted to run his hands back and forth over them, to fill his palms with their softness. All he had to do was reach out and . . .

Joe pushed her toward the bathroom. 'You do the rest, honey,' he said in a raspy voice. 'It's safer that way.'

In spite of her chilled state, Stevie agreed. The feel of Joe's hands brushing against her cold skin had sent tremors through her. She had not been mistaken about the desire that she had seen in his eyes a few moments ago, but she had learned her lesson last night. He had made it clear he wasn't interested.

Billowing clouds of steam enveloped Stevie as she stepped into the bathroom. A few moments later she began to warm up as the hot water cascaded over her.

After Stevie had emerged from the shower, she peered around the door, wrapped only in a towel. Outside on the bathroom doorknob Joe had hung the same oversized bathrobe that she had put on the night before. She reached for it and wrapped herself in its warmth and comfort.

'Here, drink this,' said Joe as he looked up and saw Stevie standing hesitantly in the doorway between the bedroom and the living room. Slowly she crossed the room, feeling unsure, waiting to gauge Joe's mood. She took the steaming mug from his hands, then seated herself on the sofa, her feet tucked under the folds of the terrycloth robe.

'Drink,' Joe ordered.

Stevie obeyed, raising the mug to her lips. She was pleasantly surprised to find that it was coffee flavored with Irish Cream.

Now that Stevie was here with him and safe, Joe was relieved. He was also angry that she would do something so stupid. He stood a few feet away with his feet spread apart, his body taut. 'Who takes care of you, Stevie?'

Her head jerked up at his odd question. 'What do you mean?' she asked, a puzzled look on her face.

'I want to know who takes care of you. Somebody must, or should, because it is obvious that you don't have enough sense to take care of yourself.'

Stevie began to rise from the sofa. 'I have always taken care of myself – '

'Sit down,' commanded Joe in a harsh tone. 'What were you doing tonight? Where were you planning to go? Tell me the truth. What would you have done if I hadn't come after you?' Joe spit his questions out rapidly, not giving Stevie a chance to answer. He ran a hand through his dark hair, the gesture reflecting the frustration he felt.

'God, Stevie, do you have any idea how frantic I've been since I discovered you had left? You could have at least told me that you were planning to leave. Don't you think you owed me that?'

'I left you a note, Joe. I thought it was best if I left before you returned. Especially after last night,' she added in a whisper.

'What about last night?' demanded Joe, knowing exactly what she referred to, but wanting to hear the words from her lips.

Stevie was silent, then cleared her throat, not sure what to say to him. 'Well, we . . . things got a little heated between us.' She stumbled over the words. 'And you made it clear that you weren't interested.'

Joe's eyes narrowed. There was nothing he would like better than to carry her to bed right now and make love to her all night long. 'Are you in the habit of going to bed with men you hardly know?' he asked, his words terse.

Stevie's head jerked up at his question and their eyes locked.

'No,' she answered vehemently, 'and I had no plans to go to bed with you.'

'The hell you didn't.'

'You can think whatever you need to satisfy your ego, Joe. But you're wrong. Besides,' she added, 'you have no business asking me a question like that.'

'About sleeping around?' Joe paused and raised his mug to his lips, but not soon enough to hide his smile. 'Sure I do, because you were more than ready to sleep with me last night.'

'That's ridiculous. All we did was kiss and . . .'

Joe stopped her with a look that said she was lying. 'There was more to it than that, Stevie, and you know it.' His words hung suspended in the silence between them.

Stevie remained quiet, knowing that there were things better left unsaid. There was a lot more to it. The intensity of her feelings for Joe had caught her by surprise, and her willingness to make love to him could only be explained by these incredible things he did to her when he looked at her, when he touched her. Disconcerted, she reached for her coffee from the table in front of her; as she did so, her robe gaped open, revealing the roundness of her breast.

From where he was, Joe was privy to the sight and with each moment that passed he was having regrets that he had not sent Stevie on her way as he had intended. Right now all he wanted to do was run his hands and lips over every inch of her until she cried out with wanting. He ran his eyes over her, remembering how she had looked earlier when he had started to undress her.

Stevie fiddled with her cup, feeling his eyes on her. He was making her nervous. 'I know what you're doing,' Stevie announced anxiously.

'What?' Joe's eyes locked with hers. It was impossible to misread the challenge in them.

'You are testing me,' she snapped. 'You're doing this deliberately.'

Joe laughed derisively. 'Tell me what I'm doing.'

'You want to see if I'll make a fool out of myself like I did last night. You're deliberately trying to provoke me and I want you to stop it.'

Now his brown eyes danced at her accusations. 'Provoke, hmm . . .' he said thoughtfully, then, 'No, I definitely did not intend to provoke you. I would know if I was. Provoking is something else entirely.' Joe came around the sofa to sit beside her.

'If I was going to provoke you, I'd probably do something like this.' He lifted his hand to her face

54

and ran his index finger over Stevie's full lower lip. 'Or like this,' he said as he let that same finger trail lightly from her lips to her cheek, then down the soft curve of her neck to the rounded top of her breast.

Stevie caught her breath.

'Maybe,' continued Joe in his husky whisper, 'I'd even do this.' He reached down to her ankle, then ran his hand under the robe up the length of her leg until he found the softness of her thigh.'

Stevie's insides quivered. She was helpless to stop this sensual assault.

'Then,' he whispered as he bent his head toward her, 'I'd definitely do this.' The last word was muffled as he moved his lips lazily across hers, then more urgently as his tongue invaded her warm mouth, heating her blood and sending it rushing to every part of her body.

Without warning, Joe's lips left hers and sought the taste of her skin, traveling downward, following the same path his finger had taken earlier. Only this time he didn't stop until he had pushed her robe from her shoulders and captured her breast in his mouth.

Stevie gasped, powerless to stop this onslaught as Joe's tongue found her nipple and moved back and forth across it, causing it to harden.

With his free hand, Joe tugged at the tie belt that held Stevie's robe, but before he could untie it, Stevie grabbed his hand and stilled it.

Joe straightened, startled.

'I don't sleep around, Joe. Not with you; not with anyone. And, as you reminded me last night, you're not interested.'

Joe cursed under his breath.

Stevie sat up straighter and pulled her robe close around her. 'How much longer are you going to be in town?'

This time it was Joe who was taken aback at her question. 'Why?'

'Just answer me,' she commanded.

'Until Sunday.'

'And then?' asked Stevie.

'Then I go home.'

'So I probably wouldn't see you again?'

'Ahh . . .' Joe now knew where this line of questioning was headed. He leaned back against the sofa and ran his hands though his dark hair. Sooner or later they all got around to the same subject. 'No, you probably wouldn't see me again,' he answered truthfully.

'So there's not much of a chance that this would develop into something more than a one-night stand or, at best, it wouldn't last more than a few days.'

'Probably not.' Joe sighed.

'I'm not looking for that kind of thing. I don't believe in one-night stands,' said Stevie. 'I want more than that.' She took a deep breath. 'I want a relationship.'

Nothing about Joe moved. Not the flicker of an eye or the twitch of a muscle. It was almost as if he hadn't heard her.

Stevie took a deep breath and plunged ahead, 'Isn't that exactly what happened between you and Jeannie?'

Joe moved now, stretching his legs out in front of him, opening his eyes. Why couldn't she have just kept her mouth shut? 'I don't want a lecture about my sexual activities, Stevie,' said Joe tersely. 'Least of all from you.'

56

Stevie shook her head from side to side, her blonde curls shimmering in the lamp light, her expression remorseful. 'Oh, Joe,' she whispered softly, 'I'm so sorry if I managed to *provoke* you.'

Angrily, Joe jumped to his feet and marched to the door.

'Where are you going?' asked Stevie innocently.

'None of your goddamned business,' he answered as he slammed the door behind him.

CHAPTER 5

Stevie was sitting cross-legged on the sofa with a magazine open in her lap, feeling that maybe that had been a crummy thing to do. No, she decided a few seconds later, he deserved it. She was merely repaying him for what he had done to her the night before.

Then why do I feel so awful?

Joe Devlin did the most incredible things to her. With a look he could send a surge of excitement through her. When he touched her she never wanted him to stop. And when he kissed her she wanted it to go on forever.

She wondered what would have happened if she had just let him make love to her tonight, then shivered at the thought. What she didn't know was that Joe Devlin had this same effect on thousands of women every time he appeared on stage.

Restlessly, she shoved the magazine away. For a while she tried watching television, but she couldn't concentrate. From the bedroom closet she pulled a pillow and a blanket and threw them on the sofa in the living room with a grin that bordered on fiendish.

58

She had slept there last night. Tonight it was Joe's turn to be uncomfortable. She snickered at the thought of him trying to crowd his six-foot length on to that cramped love seat, then pulled the door to the luxurious bedroom closed behind her. *I hope he has a miserable night.*

With the covers pulled up around her chin, Stevie lay in Joe's bedroom, still wrapped in the oversized robe, waiting for sleep to come. Mentally she reviewed the days since she had met him. Never in her life had she experienced such roller coaster emotions as she had in the last thirty-six hours. Last night he had rejected her and tonight he had expected her to let him make love to her.

Just who in the hell did Joe Devlin think he was?

Because of the snow it was a slow night in the hotel bar so Charlie Collins was glad to have someone to pass the time with. Other than a few scattered patrons seated at the tables along the far wall, the place was empty. 'Back again?' asked Charlie from behind the bar as he dried the glass he was holding, then inspected it in the dim light.

Joe looked up from his stool at the far end of the bar, his thoughts still on Stevie. For a moment he looked blank.

'You were here last night,' said Charlie by way of explanation. 'Just about this time.'

'Yeah,' answered Joe as he ordered a Miller Lite. When Charlie set it on the glossy bar top, Joe pushed the accompanying glass aside and drank from the chilled brown bottle. Absentmindedly he twirled the bottle around on the bar and reviewed the events of the last hour.

I went out of my way to find her and bring her back, and here I am again, sitting out the night in the bar, knowing I can't get within two feet, no, make that the same room, or even the same city, without wanting her.

'You look to me like a guy with a problem,' said Charlie cheerfully. His Irish face was round, his complexion ruddy. He was ready for some conversation. He liked the bar best when it was full of chatter and laughter; tonight, it was too quiet.

Joe nodded. 'Same problem, different night.'

'This is about a woman, right?' asked Charlie from a few feet away.

Joe looked up in surprise, then grinned reluctantly. 'Is it that obvious?'

'From the moment you walked in. Last night, too,' said Charlie. 'I've been a bartender at this hotel since it opened. After a while you start to analyze the customers, especially on a slow night. It helps pass the time. Pretty soon you get good at it. Most people don't mind telling a stranger their problems 'cause they know they'll never see them again.'

Joe nodded and took a long swallow from the bottle. Why was he in such an uproar over that pint-sized woman? Most of the time he couldn't shake women off. They followed him, sometimes from city to city. They gladly offered their bodies just to be able to tell everyone that they had had sex with someone famous. It was the mark of a successful groupie. But Joe thought that messing around with groupies was bad business, so instead they usually settled for one of the band members or one of the production crew.

And now he had found someone he really wanted, but she wasn't buying, at least not tonight. But then, she wasn't a groupie. And then there was that damn conscience of his. It wasn't buying this deal either. He wondered if it would make any difference to Stevie if she knew who he was. After studying the silver-foil label on his beer, he decided that it probably wouldn't matter in the least.

Joe shifted and leaned one elbow on the bar. 'What's your name?'

'Charlie,' answered the bartender.

'Charlie, I'm Joe,' he said, reaching across the bar to shake the bartender's hand.

It was on the tip of Charlie's tongue to tell Joe he already knew who he was. The hotel employees reported all the activities of celebrity guests. It made for good break-time gossip. Most of the things celebrities did were outlandish and demanding by normal standards, but the consensus seemed to be that Joe Devlin was a regular guy. It was a compliment.

'Tell me, Charlie, what do you think a woman means when she starts talking about a relationship?' Joe asked, shaking his head. 'Just what kind of word is that? And what exactly does it mean?'

Charlie chuckled as he shook his head. 'I've got five sisters, a wife and two daughters. Now, I figure that makes me an expert of sorts, or at the very least a survivor.' He paused, then leaned against the bar. '"Relationship" is a woman's word,' Charlie answered. 'It's the kind of word they use to sucker you

61

in. You think it's going to be nothing more than a few laughs, a good time in the sack, then they start talking about a relationship.

'Now all this takes some time, mind you. Maybe a few weeks or months. But you can be sure that by the time they get around to using *that* word, they usually figure they got you by the balls.'

Joe smiled wryly. 'This one is talking about a relationship and we haven't even made it to the sack yet,' he said. 'I've only known her for a few days.'

'Man,' said Charlie, shaking his head and chuckling as he reached for another glass, 'this one may be trouble. It doesn't sound to me like she's the kind of woman you want to mess around with, Joe. Chances are she's not looking for a relationship. I'll lay you odds she's looking to get married.'

Charlie raised his index finger as if to warn Joe to give his next words special consideration. 'Uh huh. She's gone and given you a warning, Joe. That's what she's done. Announced her intentions. I suppose that's an honorable thing, in a way. But it sure does screw up things for you. The way I see it, anything that happens between the two of you from now on is strictly your fault. And if you mess up, she's gonna get you good.'

Joe's head jerked up at Charlie's words as he sat up straight, his grin replaced with a startled expression. 'That's not funny,' said Joe.

'Not tryin' to be,' answered Charlie, grinning and shaking his head. 'No, sir. What this girl is about to do ain't funny at all. Especially if you're the guy it's being done to.'

Joe finished off his beer and asked for another. 'Thanks for the advice, Charlie.'

Charlie wiped at the dripping ice-cold bottle with a cloth and set it before Joe before he moved toward the opposite end of the bar. 'Anytime, man. I'm here every night except Sunday and Monday.'

'Aw, shit,' muttered Joe as he held the brown-glass bottle up in a mock toast and tried to laugh off what the bartender had just told him, but in his gut he knew that Charlie Collins was right.

Joe stared at the beer bottle as though it would provide all the answers to his questions. Then with precise motions he made a series of tangent circles with the beads of sweat that had slowly trickled to the bottom of the bottle. He was about to reach for a napkin to wipe up the watery design on the surface of the bar when he heard a voice at his elbow.

'Excuse me, but me and my friends have a bet going and I wonder if you could help me.'

Joe swung around to face the young dark-haired woman at his side. 'What's your bet?'

'I bet them that you're Joe Devlin, the country music singer,' the girl said quickly.

Joe considered denying it then changed his mind. He smiled. 'You win. I'm Joe Devlin.'

The young woman laughed nervously. 'It took a lot of nerve for me to come over here and ask you that,' she said. 'But since I've come this far, can I please get your autograph?'

Joe nodded and reached for a napkin from the bar, then asked Charlie for a pen. 'Are you a student?' he asked with interest.

'No,' she answered. 'I graduated from college last May, but I'm still unemployed. It's the economy. Without any experience it's really hard to get a job.'

'What's your name?'

'Karen,' she answered.

Joe took the pen and began to write, then he handed it to the young woman. 'You'll succeed,' he said sincerely. 'Just keep trying.'

'Thanks so much, Mr Devlin. I really appreciate it.'

Joe stood and laid some bills on the bar. 'This ought to be enough to cover the kids' tab,' he said to Charlie, 'and your professional counseling fees.' He shook hands, then turned and waved to Karen and her friends in the corner.

When she read what Joe had written on the napkin, Karen smiled. *Don't ever lose your nerve*, it said, *you can't be successful without it*. Below that was Joe's signature.

Damn good advice he gave that girl, thought Joe, as he left the bar and headed for the elevators. Advice he should follow. He had lost his nerve with Stevie. She had affected him as no other woman had, and he had not been prepared. Never before had he had trouble facing facts, but what he felt about Stevie bothered him. He cared what happened to her and for some reason he couldn't fathom, he had a primeval urge to protect her. He also had a powerful urge to make love to her.

By the time Joe had unlocked the door to the suite he felt a renewed sense of purpose. He had summoned the same kind of nerve the young woman in the bar had summoned when she had approached him. It filled him with confidence. He should tell Stevie how he felt about her.

What good would that do? No matter what, I'll only end up hurting her. Quickly Joe shoved the thought aside. He would deal with his conscience when the time came. But not now.

Only one lamp next to the sofa was lit. Joe looked around in confusion. Stevie was not on the sofa where he had expected to find her. It was empty except for a pillow and a blanket.

Suddenly he realized that Stevie had put the pillow and the blanket there for him. Did she actually expect him to spend the night on the sofa? All six feet of him? On that puny love seat where everything from his knees down and elbows up would dangle in the air?

Never in a million years would he allow Stevie Parker to kick him out of *his* bed in *his* hotel suite.

Just who the devil does she think she is?

CHAPTER 6

The powerful stride that carried him across the living room and into the darkened bedroom had the all the impetus of a diesel-driven rig. When he reached the bed, Joe halted. By God, there she was, looking sleepy and sweet in his bed with the covers tucked up around her chin.

In one swooping motion Joe reached down and picked Stevie up, covers and all, and threw her over his shoulder like a sack of potatoes.

Startled, her blue eyes flew wide open, but before she could voice her protest Joe carried her into the living room and dumped her unceremoniously on the love seat.

'What are you doing?' yelled Stevie angrily as she scrambled to her feet and tried to free herself from the jumble of covers that were twisted and tangled around her.

'Removing your sweet ass from my bed.' Joe backed away from Stevie, satisfied now that she was where she was supposed to be.

'Hah!' Stevie shouted through clenched teeth as she wrestled with a sheet that was trapped under her feet.

'That's one for the books! I could have sworn that was exactly where you wanted me to be.'

'It is,' Joe shouted back, 'but not without me. Did you actually think I was going to sleep on *this*?' he asked with a dramatic sweep of his hand toward the love seat.

'Yes, I did,' she answered sweetly. A sarcastic smile accompanied her words. 'After all, I slept there last night. Tonight it's your turn.'

Joe ran his hand through his hair in frustration. Why were they arguing about who slept where when all he wanted was to make love to her? 'It's my hotel suite, Stevie. I can sleep wherever I want. Do you understand that?'

With each word Joe had advanced toward Stevie, who was standing on the very edge of the love-seat cushions. Now they had squared off, taken each other's measure and positioned themselves to do battle. They stood eye to eye, nose to nose, their hands clenched tightly at their sides.

'Fine,' shouted Stevie. 'You take the bed, your highness, and I'll take the sofa, okay?'

'No,' answered Joe, 'it's not okay. I don't want the bed to myself, I want you in it with me!'

'Too bad,' said Stevie, shaking her head. 'Who do you think you are, Joe Devlin? Royalty or something? Do you always get what you want?' Stevie's blue eyes sparked with anger as she delivered her questions with rapid-fire precision.

'Usually,' said Joe, his voice quieter now. 'But I'm not usually attracted to stubborn, bad-tempered women. I like my women sweet. The soft, agreeable kind.'

'The kind that just takes one look at you and falls right into your arms.'

'Into my bed,' corrected Joe.

'I suppose you expect me to do the same. Well, you . . . you egotistical hillbilly, you picked the wrong woman!'

'Not necessarily,' said Joe. His eyes were now speculative and narrowed.

With each exchange Stevie had leaned closer and closer to Joe, so close, in fact, that Joe didn't even have to take a step toward her when he reached out and wrapped both arms around her. But she still drew in her breath in surprise as Joe lifted her from her perch on the love seat, bringing her into his arms.

'Put me down,' commanded Stevie. She pushed against his broad chest with both hands.

'Nope,' said Joe, his eyes now teasing and filled with amusement. 'Nobody calls me a hillbilly and gets away with it.'

'Hillbilly!' she taunted, her face only inches from his. 'Redneck! Georgia cracker . . .'

Joe silenced her taunts with a hot, searing kiss. His lips, firm and hard, moved back and forth across hers, insistent and demanding, and at the very moment she thought she really shouldn't let him get away with this, she realized that he was doing exactly what she had wanted him to all along.

An eternity later he pulled away from her and silently rested his forehead against her fragrant hair. When he spoke his voice was hardly more than a ragged whisper, his brown eyes intense. 'This time let's not play games with each other, Stevie.'

Her heart skipped a beat and for a moment time seemed to stand still. Slowly, tortuously, Joe loosened his grip on her and let her slide down the length of his body until her bare toes touched the floor.

Somewhere in the distant recesses of Joe's mind, as he searched her heart-shaped face, was the nagging thought that he had not been truthful with her. He had deliberately kept his secrets to himself. But how good it felt to know that now, this moment, this woman desired him for who he really was, and not because he was rich or famous.

Still nestled in the warm protective circle of his arms, Stevie was sure that this was as close to heaven as she would ever get. She could feel Joe's hands moving slowly, powerfully over her back until finally, he reached down to pull her hips against him, making sure she was aware of his aroused body.

'Can you feel that?' His whisper sounded ragged. 'This is the kind of power you have over me.'

Stevie nodded, unable to speak.

Every contour of his seemed to have a place where it nestled and matched to her. The heat of him threatened to brand her through her robe, but that wasn't enough. She wanted more. Stevie fumbled as she reached for the buttons of his shirt. Then she stopped, as if she suddenly realized what she was attempting to do. Then she began again, but this time Joe's hands followed hers, surely, swiftly undoing the clothing that separated them. When he stood with his broad chest bare, Stevie lightly ran her hands over the tanned skin and through the dark hair that grew there. Then, with shaking hands and downcast eyes, she reached for the buckle of his belt.

Joe inhaled sharply and captured both her hands with one of his, stopping her. With his other hand he tilted her chin toward him, forcing her to meet his gaze. The passion that he saw there told him everything he needed to know. She wanted this as much as he did. He kept his hand there under her chin, as he leaned down and kissed her. This time it was tender and soft, like the tentative kiss of two people who are new to each other, and it lingered only a moment on her lips, but its message was powerful and sure.

With a quick and sweeping gesture, Joe laid Stevie down on the soft carpet. His breathing was heavy, not from her slight weight, but from the anticipation of the pleasure that was yet to be had. For the second time that night he reached for the belt that held her robe together. With a gentle tug he loosened the robe then pushed the white terrycloth from her shoulders and unfolded the fabric from her body.

He inhaled sharply and he felt himself grow even harder. Like this, she was even more beautiful than he had imagined. Discarding the remainder of his clothes, he slowly covered her with his body. Raggedly, he whispered her name as his lips found the sweet-smelling hollow just beneath her ear. She was so small, so perfect.

Lightly he tasted her skin, beginning with her parted lips then working his way down. When he reached her breasts he ran his tongue over each nipple, then took each one in turn in his mouth.

Stevie didn't even realize the purring sounds were hers until she felt first a fluttering excitement deep from within, then a kind of pressure, dull at first then stronger, demanding, until it made her arch her hips against the hard, angular planes of his body. Whatever it was that Joe Devlin was doing to her, she wanted more.

Slowly, surely, Joe began to explore every inch of her with his hands and with his mouth. He caressed her, teased her, licked her, then he loved her until he captured her mind and her heart, and made her body his slave.

Stevie was sure he'd found places where she had never been touched. Never had she felt so willing to give into the sensations she was feeling. So skilled a lover was he that he branded her body with his desire while he marked her soul with his passion. With each touch he set Stevie on fire; with each response the same fire blazed through Joe.

Never had he imagined that the taking of Stevie Parker would so consume and overwhelm him. Never he had imagined that he in turn would become a slave to his need for her. His desire raged, tearing through him as nothing else ever had and now, before he lost control, Joe spread her legs wide and sought her wet, waiting warmth. When he had filled her, he paused and reached upward to smooth her hair from her forehead, then swiftly he captured her parted lips once more in his.

Knowing now that he could wait no longer, he began a rhythmic assault, the slick, pulsating drive of flesh meeting flesh. And when the mounting friction caused them to suddenly explode, then shatter and convulse, there followed mutual waves of pleasure that caused them to rise and fall, to shudder, to finally exhale and resume the ritual of breathing.

Exhausted, their minds soared while their bodies were left glistening with the sweat of their shared, shocking passion. For long moments neither Stevie or Joe could move. Shaken, neither could speak of what had transpired between them. Expressions of feelings were beyond their power.

Slowly, Joe rolled to his side, pulling Stevie with him. Tenderly he caressed her face as if to reassure himself that she was real. And Stevie, unused to this gentle, reassuring attention, marveled at this moment.

Much later, after they had moved into the bedroom, Stevie roused. 'Joe,' she whispered against his broad warm chest. But Joe never let Stevie finish what she was about to say, as he began to caress her. After a while she couldn't even remember what it was she had been about to ask him.

It seemed like hours later when Stevie stirred, then sat straight up. Slowly she moved out of Joe's reach, slipped her arms into the shirt he had worn earlier and padded across the soft carpet into the living room and behind the bar. With both hands on her hips she stood, her shape outlined by the glowing light of the open refrigerator door.

'Just what do you think you're doing?' The quiet, unexpected sound of the deep voice behind her caused her to jump with fright.

'Oh! You scared me,' she answered, turning to wrap her arms around his bare torso and bury her face against his warm chest.

With the slightest force, Joe took Stevie by the shoulders and set her far enough away to look into her eyes. 'What were you looking for, honey?'

'I'm hungry.'

Joe wrapped his arms loosely around her and nuzzled her hair with his chin. 'What do you want? I'll call room service.'

'Pizza,' replied Stevie, her blue eyes wide and excited. 'but not from room service. I want the kind they deliver hot to your door. I don't think you can get it delivered to a hotel like this.'

'If I arrange for pizza to be delivered, you're going to owe me. Are you prepared for that?'

'Umm,' replied Stevie thoughtfully, then, 'And I suppose you'll expect a tip.' She looked up at Joe and her expression was mischievous as she stepped out of his arms and turned away from him. 'Will you wear a uniform?' she asked, her eyes dancing. 'I always was a sucker for a guy in uniform.'

He tried to let her comment pass, but there was no way he could. The temptation was much too great. Joe reached for her, bent his head and whispered something low and seductive in her ear. Stevie blushed immediately and reached out playfully to punch him. 'That last comment was X-rated, Devlin.'

Joe grinned and walked toward the phone. 'I know. Do you like pepperoni?'

Stevie nodded, then added, 'You'll never get pizza delivered here this time of night.'

'Watch,' answered Joe.

A half-hour later, Stevie and Joe sat in the middle of the rumpled bed, eating pepperoni pizza. For all his trouble, the manager of the nearest pizza establishment and the person who delivered the pizza were well-compensated. And for all his trouble, Joe was sure he would also be compensated. And when he could wait no longer, Joe took the last piece of pizza out of Stevie's hand, put it back in the cardboard box, and rolled her on top of him.

She could feel him grow hard against her stomach. 'You're insatiable,' she giggled into the dark wiry hair on his chest.

'It's the secret ingredient in the pizza that makes me that way. Now,' he said, his voice low and teasing, 'since I arranged for your midnight snack, I'm ready for mine.'

Before Stevie could respond Joe was kissing her, teasing her senses with his tongue and once more she was lost to the magic of his lovemaking.

When the first sign of daylight streamed through the crack between the curtains and laid a stripe of light across the bed, Stevie moved against Joe and somewhere in the deep recesses of sleep she knew she was safe as long as he was there.

The sharp jarring sound of the telephone cut through the peaceful silence. Joe reached for it quickly, hoping that the sound wouldn't wake Stevie. She stirred, but he reached behind him to touch her. Stevie sighed and snuggled deeper under the covers.

'Joe, it's Lorraine. Sorry to wake you. I forgot it's an hour earlier there.'

'It's okay,' said Joe. His voice was low and husky. 'Just hold on a minute.' He reached for his jeans and tugged them on, then went into the living room so he wouldn't wake Stevie up.

'You need to hop a plane and get back here as soon as you can,' said Lorraine. 'The people from MultiSound are ready to cut a deal. They want to meet with you today.'

Joe squinted at his watch. The first flight left in just a little over two hours. If he hurried he could make it. Both he and Jeannie had worked hard on this deal and it would have a major impact on his career. 'I'll be there,' he said softly to Lorraine before he hung up the phone.

Carefully, so as not to wake Stevie, Joe made his way through the bedroom. In the tranquility of the darkened room, he studied the face of the sleeping woman. Last night her passion had matched his. She had been everything he had known she would be. This morning she looked like a small angelic child. Her face was sweet and young, her blonde curls tumbled over the pillow in an unruly golden cloud.

For a long moment Joe gazed at the picture before him. He was having difficulty sorting out his feelings for her. Part of him wanted to stay with her and never leave. The other part wanted to run as fast as he could before he became too involved.

In the bathroom he stood before the mirror. The word 'relationship' flashed across his mind as he reflected on his conversation with the bartender last night. Then he thought of the night he had just shared with Stevie Parker. And Joe knew that she had made him feel a lot more than he was prepared to handle. He should have never let things get this far. Guilt washed over him.

Last night should have never happened.

Stevie stirred, turning on her side and tucking her hand under her cheek. She looked so innocent.

What do I do now? If I stay, it will only make things worse.

So Joe Devlin decided he would do what was best. Quickly, quietly, he showered, dressed and gathered his clothes. In the living room he hastily scribbled a note, and put it into an envelope. Carefully, he propped it against a vase on the coffee table where Stevie would be sure to see it. He crossed the room once more for a last look at the small bundle huddled under the covers. The look that crossed his handsome face was one of longing, then regret. He was assaulted by a wave of guilt. He should have told Stevie the truth.

How many other women have you left like this, Devlin? Joe shook his head as if to clear it, but the voice demanded an answer.

Be truthful. It was a command that Joe couldn't ignore.

More than I should have.

So what makes this so difficult?

It's not difficult, Joe answered the question with a touch of bravado.

Then why are you still here? The voice was insistent.

Because she's different.

Not so different. The voice taunted him now. *She didn't waste a lot of time hopping into bed with you. She's just like all the others.*

No, it isn't like that. She makes me feel . . . Joe hesitated . . . *different.*

And what are you prepared to do about it?

Joe turned away from the sight of Stevie sleeping peacefully. The image of Kathy, as she had been the last time he had seen her, silent and distant, crowded out his indecision. 'Nothing,' he replied softly with a groan. 'Nothing at all.'

But deep down in his gut he felt rotten. He knew he should bundle Stevie up and take her with him wherever he went for the rest of his life. Knowing he might never again find what they had shared, he shook his head sadly. As much as he might want to do just that, he couldn't. There was no way he could keep from hurting her.

He cursed under his breath and hated what he was about to do. With his broad shoulders hunched, he picked up his bag and pulled the door to the lavish suite closed behind him.

Now run like hell, the voice commanded. And Joe did.

CHAPTER 7

The room was still dark and warm and private. Neither the sun nor the clatter of the outside world had yet disturbed her cozy slumber. Only a vague recollection caused her to stir. Stevie blinked, then stretched lazily. When she remembered where she was and what happened the night before, she smiled at the memory. Then she turned and reached out for the man responsible for all these wonderful feelings, but the bed beside her was empty. The door to the bathroom was open. The sound of running water absent.

He's probably gone downstairs. He'll be right back, thought Stevie, as she pushed herself up to a sitting position and propped pillows behind her back, then pulled the sheet up around her. For long minutes she waited for Joe to return, but all was silent.

Finally, unable to stand the darkness of the room, she swung her bare legs to the floor and reached for the robe that lay there, a discard from the night before. She stood and pulled it on, then knotted the belt as she padded barefoot first to the window to pull back the heavy draperies, then into the living room.

Here it was just as silent, but light streamed brightly through the windows. Stevie stretched lazily, then ran her fingers through her tangled hair, pulling it up off her neck and securing it with a rubber band. She shivered and moved to stand in the comforting warmth of the sun.

Where is he? Why didn't I hear him get up? The absolute quiet made her apprehensive.

Relief washed over her when she spotted a white envelope on the coffee table. Reaching for the envelope, she let out the breath she had been holding. *For a minute I was afraid that . . .*

Stevie smiled as she pressed the envelope against her forehead, then her heart, as if to chastize herself for her foolish fears. Joe Devlin was the most incredible man she had ever met, and even though she didn't have much in the way of comparison, he definitely was an extraordinary lover. She couldn't help it; just the thought of Joe and the night they had spent together caused her to blush.

I think I'm in love, she thought giddily. *Absolutely, without a doubt, it's love. I've never felt like this about anyone before.* And she twirled herself around at the thought and danced a few waltz steps to a make-believe melody before she plopped down on one of the love seats. In her hand she still clutched Joe's note.

Her heart was pounding with excitement, and her face was flushed as Stevie ripped open the envelope. But her expression changed rapidly, first to confusion, then to something that resembled pain. She stared at the bold, slanted words before her, then read them once more. Slowly, this time. So she wouldn't misunderstand.

Dear Stevie,

I didn't plan what happened between us last night, even though I wanted it as much as you did. But this morning brought a lot of questions that I'm not ready to answer and some problems I'm not ready to face, so I've decided to leave. Actually, I was called back on urgent business, but I'm not sure you'll believe that.

I don't know what to say to you, so I'm doing the only other thing I know to do. This is for you. Just in case you need it.

I'll miss you, Stevie. One of these days I know you'll find someone who will take care of you. You deserve something better than what I can give.

It was signed, Joe.

Stevie stood and let the note drift from her fingers. Then she reached to the floor and retrieved the envelope that had fallen there earlier. She straightened, and turned the envelope upside down. From inside a folded sheet of plain white paper spilled hundred-dollar bills. Stevie watched in horror as they fluttered to the floor along with a business card from JJD Productions.

Angrily, Stevie stared at the money that littered the butter-colored carpet. He had paid her off! She had slept with him and he had paid her off like some common whore!

Wham, bam, thank you, ma'am! Now here's some money to get you out of my life and off my conscience.

How could he do this to her after their night together? Didn't it mean anything to him?

Confused and hurt, Stevie began to cry. Were all men like this? Was she destined to be hurt by every man she cared about? Bitterly, she remembered her joy of just a few minutes ago. She had actually been foolish enough to believe she was in love, and stupid enough to hope that maybe, just maybe, Joe might feel the same way about her.

She had no idea how long she sat there staring at the floor before she reluctantly slid to her knees and began to gather the money along with Joe's card. She stuffed it all into the envelope, then slipped it into her purse. She would deal with it later.

Forty-five minutes later she had showered and dressed. Quicky she searched the bedroom for anything she might have left. In the living room she paused to look around. Bitterness welled up inside her. She shouldn't have been surprised at the turn of events. Once more she had reached for happiness and love and this time she thought she had found it, only to discover it was an illusion. Stevie reached down for her bag and turned. Quietly, she closed the door behind her.

At the front desk she stopped, unsure of exactly what to do. 'Uh, I'm leaving. Mr Devlin's suite is vacant.'

'Miss Parker, isn't it?' asked the desk clerk as he studied her somberly from behind his computer screen.

Stevie nodded.

'Mr Devlin has arranged for you to stay through Sunday. Didn't he tell you?'

Stevie looked up in surprise, then frowned. It was part of the payoff. 'Send him a refund,' she said firmly. 'I won't be staying.'

The clerk watched as Stevie turned and crossed the lobby, her head hanging and her shoulders slumped. She was tired and she was going home.

CHAPTER 8

Stevie let herself into her apartment. Wearily she set her bag in the bedroom closet. She intended to sit on the edge of the bed only long enough to pull her shoes off, but when that simple task was accomplished, she realized that she was too exhausted to move. Instead, she lay back against the pillows and closed her eyes.

Her last thought before she drifted off into a deep sleep was that she should be strong; she shouldn't let the sadness she was feeling steal her away. But her emotions ruled. The tears that were tearing at her battered heart spilled over and ran unchecked on to her pillow.

Helplessly, she sank into a whirlpool of dreams. Once more she was back in Eagle, Wyoming, where she had grown up. It was all there: the sound of the wind; the trailer and the laughing voices from her mother's bedroom down the hall; the loneliness that never went away. She could see herself running from the trailer into the cold night wind. She stood for a moment in the darkness, confused, lost.

It was a dream she had had many times. *Why wasn't someone calling for her? Didn't anyone care about her?*

Tears slipped from beneath her lashes and rolled down her cheeks. Even in her dreams she was alone. No one loved her; no one wanted her.

When she opened her eyes the bedroom was the eerie dark of a cold and gray winter afternoon. Stevie had no idea how long she had slept. The hair around her temples was still damp from her tears and she was shivering. With great effort she pulled herself to the side of the bed and began to undress.

Wrapped in her warmest robe, she shuffled into the kitchen to make some coffee. When it was ready, she poured herself a steaming cup and carried it to the living room. On the sofa with her feet tucked under her and an afghan wrapped around her, Stevie held the hot steaming cup with both hands.

Images of the previous night danced through her head, and in spite of her efforts to put him out of her mind, all she could think about was Joe. In frustration she reached for the remote control from the table beside her and flipped on the TV.

Mindlessly, she watched colored patterns and shapes weave their way across the screen. Sounds danced across the room toward her, but she never heeded them. A knock at the door startled her out of her reverie.

Stevie opened it to find Beth Carr standing there, looking like she had just arrived from the North Pole.

'It's a good thing you're home. If you hadn't been, I was going to call the police.' Beth stomped her feet several times on the porch to loosen the snow from her boots.

'The police?' repeated Stevie. 'Why?'

Inside Beth threw her parka on the sofa and sat down to pull off her boots. Her dark hair fell forward, obscuring her face. 'I tried to have you paged at the airport, but you never answered your page. Then I called here so many times I lost count. I tried to get my car out of the parking lot yesterday, but the snow was too deep. Today, thank God, they finally plowed.' Beth looked up, her dark eyes serious. 'Stevie, I've been worried sick about you since you called. How did you get home? *Where* have you been?

Stevie followed Beth to the sofa. It was a simple question, but the answer was far from simple. 'I met someone.'

It was not the words that halted Beth as she rose to carry her boots back toward the front door, it was the softness with which Stevie answered.

'A very attractive man,' continued Stevie, closing her eyes. 'I thought it was all there, Beth. Joe Devlin seemed to be everything I've been looking for.'

Beth let the boots slide from her fingers and came to sit on the edge of the sofa. Disappointment and hurt were so apparent in Stevie's tone, that Beth didn't need to ask how things had gone. Now she was wrestling with her natural curiosity as well as her loyalty to her friend. Friends were just supposed to be there for one another, weren't they? They weren't supposed to be dying to hear every last detail, but this guy must have been something else for Stevie to have . . .

Beth jerked to attention. From somewhere deep in the recesses of her mind, an alarm went off. It was something Stevie had said. She leaned forward. 'Stevie, what . . . what did you say his name was?'

Stevie sat up straight, smoothing imaginary wrinkles from her robe, then reached for her coffee. 'It doesn't matter anymore, Beth. I just want to forget the whole thing. It was a mistake, a case of a broken heart because my judgement was slightly impaired. Make that greatly impaired. I fell head over heels for this good-looking guy. We had one night together then . . . then he was gone. Didn't even stick around for breakfast. Probably gone in search of his next conquest, I would imagine.'

She inhaled deeply, trying her best to keep from crying, but her voice quivered when she continued. 'Now I know how my mother must have felt when she thought she had finally found the right guy. Lord knows, she tried plenty of them out along the way.' Stevie's bitterness was unmistakable.

'You said his name was Joe?'

Stevie nodded. 'Joe Devlin.'

'Oh.' Beth chewed her lower lip. 'You don't suppose . . . No, it couldn't . . . The odds of that happening would be . . .' Beth threw her hands in the air '. . . maybe a million to one.'

'What?' asked a bewildered Stevie. 'You don't *know* him, do you?'

'Possibly. Well, no, not personally, but it's been on TV all week. Joe Devlin,' repeated Beth in a voice that was tinged with awe. 'Imagine that. The country music awards show is the day after tomorrow.'

Puzzled, Stevie just stared at Beth.

Beth grabbed the remote control and changed the television to another channel. 'Just watch, Stevie.'

'Exactly what am I supposed to be watching?' asked Stevie after a few minutes.

'Joe Devlin. There couldn't be two of them. Wait! Look! There he is!' Beth jumped up from the sofa and ran toward the television set, then sat on the floor.

Suddenly Stevie jumped up, almost spilling her coffee, and followed her. Close up she watched the screen, unable to move, unable to believe what was before her eyes. It was a promo for a country music awards show, and one of the main attractions was Joe Devlin. He was nominated for best new male vocalist of the year.

Joe Devlin!

Stevie sat motionless, stunned. She might have tried to dismissed it as a coincidence, someone with the same name except for the few seconds when Joe's face appeared on the screen. It was obviously a clip from a concert: Joe, handsome and smiling in a black cowboy hat, with his laughing brown eyes, and the sound of thousands cheering; a voice that could reach out and wrap itself around the heart of every woman in the audience, caressing and persuasive.

Stevie pulled her knees to her chest and wrapped her arms around them. *Joe Devlin.* His name screamed through her mind. Shaking her head, she buried her face against her knees. 'I didn't know, I . . . I had no idea. He didn't tell . . .'

'Stevie, how could you not know?' asked Beth in amazement. 'He's the biggest thing going right now.' Beth stopped, suddenly aware of how awful she must be making Stevie feel. 'I'm sorry,' she said quietly, 'of course you wouldn't know. You hate country music.'

Stevie nodded, and bit down on her lip. *He never told me who he was.*

Beth got to her feet and went into the kitchen.

'Here,' she said, refilling Stevie's cup.

'I must be the world's biggest idiot,' said Stevie. 'How could I have been so stupid? I don't *do* things like that!'

'Sometimes, things just . . . happen,' Beth said quietly. 'Some things are not always of your choosing. Do you want to talk about it?' Beth asked, her expression reflecting her concern for her friend. Since Stevie had stopped seeing Michael, she had done her best to avoid any romantic entanglements.

Stevie shook her head. 'Oh, Beth, I can't talk about this now. I'll call you tomorrow. Right now, I need some time alone.'

Beth hugged her, then put on her coat and boots and left.

As if she was in a trance, Stevie watched the same promo three more times that night. Each time the sick feeling in her stomach became more pronounced. Finally, she grabbed the remote control from the table beside her and clicked off the television.

In her head she recalled their conversation at the airport restaurant while they were having breakfast. Joe had told her he was crazy about country music. How he must have been laughing at her!

I am probably one of the few people in America who didn't recognize him. No, that wasn't true. No one else at the airport seemed to know who he was. And he certainly didn't fit her notion of how a country music singer should look.

Suddenly Stevie sat up straight, her back rigid as she remembered last night. There must be thousands of women clamoring for the opportunity to jump into his bed. And she was no different, except for one thing — she had had no idea who he really was.

While she had given herself, heart and soul, to him, he had deceived her the entire time. It was no wonder he packed up and left this morning without saying goodbye. It was probably no different to him than hundreds of other mornings, and she was no different than hundreds of other women he had slept with. She wondered if he made a habit of paying off his partner for the night. Or just her. *Poor, dumb Stevie Parker who had been silly enough to believe she was in love.* She sighed wearily and the pain that surged through her was as fresh and alive as it had been that morning.

It was late that night when Stevie, unable to sleep, her mind racing, recounted the entire time she had spent with Joe. Feeling sorry for herself, she decided, would serve absolutely no purpose except to make her all the more miserable.

Some time just before dawn, just as she drifted off to sleep, she made a decision. Revenge, pure and simple, was definitely in order. She may have been a fool for sleeping with Joe, but she did not intend to take his deceit lying down. She smiled wryly at her choice of words. Tomorrow she would begin to set things in motion.

The following morning Stevie called her editor, Harry Conklin.

'Stevie, hello. How is Florida?' asked Harry jovially. Evidently it never occurred to him that the blizzard might have interrupted her plans. He sounded genuinely happy to hear her voice.

Most likely Harry had a mountain of work piled on his desk just waiting for her return. 'Warm and sunny, Harry, just like it always is this time of year.' *How would I know what it's like? I never even got out of Denver*.

'I met someone while I was on vacation, Harry. A celebrity. I want to do a series of articles on him, but I need time to do additional background research.'

'Who?' asked Harry

'Joe Devlin,' answered Stevie.

There was a long silence. Stevie's heart raced. *Oh, great. He doesn't know who Joe is. Harry Conklin is as big a boob about country music as I am and he's not going to let me do the story*. She could see her entire scheme going down the drain.

'Geez, Stevie.' Harry let out his breath in a rush. 'We've been trying to get an exclusive interview with Devlin ever since we found out he's going to be here this summer for three concerts, but we haven't been able to reach his manager. How in the world did you manage this?' There was genuine enthusiasm in Harry's voice.

'I met him at the airport,' replied Stevie truthfully. *And the rest, as they say, is history*.

'This is great. When can I see something?'

'Monday. And, Harry?'

'Yes?' he sighed. *Dammit. Here it comes*. He should have known there would be strings attached.

'No rewrite. No editing. Take the story as it is, or forget it. Have I got your word?' Stevie held her breath as she waited for Harry's answer.

'Aw, Stevie . . .'

'Take it or leave it, Harry. My way or nothing.'

'It's a deal,' said Harry and felt like he had just put his head on the chopping block.

From the beginning he had known that Stevie had the potential to be a dynamic writer, but today his gut, that same gut that had never lied to him for the past twenty-five years, told him that she had a personal stake in this story. His gut also told him that this whole thing was going to be nothing but trouble.

When he voiced this concern, Stevie smiled as she held the receiver to her ear. The look on her face was positively fiendish, but the words from her mouth were sweet and reassuring. They should have been music to Harry's ears.

'Harry, I promise I will write a true and accurate story about Joe Devlin. Nothing more, nothing less.'

With a familiar gesture, Harry began to pat the pocket of his shirt, then dig his hands deep in his pants pockets. Where were his Rolaids? He had better stock up, because he had a premonition he was going to have a severe case of indigestion by the time Stevie handed over her story.

For the next two days Stevie dug as deep as she could into Joe Devlin's career. He was a relative newcomer to the world of country music, but he had burst upon the scene with an intensity that few stars ever achieve. After years of playing dives and small clubs he was finally 'discovered'. That was a year ago.

His voice and his musical aptitude, deemed mediocre by some of his critics, was thought to be outstanding by everyone else. Unlike many other singers, he wrote most of the songs he recorded. And he signed autographs for his fans. And he appeared at charity benefits for free and visited sick kids. The list of attributes seemed to go on and on, *ad nauseam*. He was, according to one of the major country music magazines, a true Renaissance man.

Okay. So much for the hype. What about his personal life? But here Stevie was disappointed. Her research turned up almost nothing she didn't already know. Thirty-two, single by all accounts, with no shortage of available females. There were pictures of him with many different women, but curiously there was no mention of him dating anyone on a regular basis. The second child of a family of five, his parents and all his brothers and sisters still lived in Georgia. One of his brothers, Richie, younger than Joe by four years, was a member of Joe's band.

While he maintained an office in Nashville, there was no mention of a big house, or any signs of living the good life, so Stevie assumed Joe had been too busy to enjoy all the money he was making.

In disgust she slammed her notebook on the desk. It had been difficult for her to look at the pictures and videos of Joe. It had been even more difficult for her to watch him on the country music awards show. He had clearly been a favorite with the crowd. When they announced his name, he actually managed to look surprised. Stevie wanted to throw something at him when he made his acceptance speech and managed to sound both humble and appreciative of the honor. But deep down she still hurt. His smiling face still caused her heart to ache.

92

And now, after all this research, she knew much more than when she began. By all accounts, Joe Devlin was the kind of guy that all of America could love. All that was missing was a picture of him wearing a halo instead of a cowboy hat, Stevie thought bitterly. Well, when she got though with him, his fans would have a slightly different perspective.

CHAPTER 9

Lorraine Fisher looked up and smiled broadly at Joe on Monday morning. She was always astonished that the sight of him could make her forget that she was fifty-three and a grandmother as well as his secretary. She smoothed her collar and repositioned the strand of pearls she wore. 'How was the trip, and how was the meeting with MultiSound?'

'The deal with MultiSound is a go,' answered Joe enthusiastically, 'and we're set for three appearances in Denver this summer. It was a productive week.'

'And?' prompted Lorraine, sensing there was more.

Joe looked up quickly and laughed. 'And I saw more snow in two days than I'll probably see the rest of my life.' Almost as an afterthought he added, 'I may have to think about hiring a new manager.'

'No kidding,' said Lorraine, hoping he would tell her more. She had never liked Jeannie Williams, but she couldn't dispute the fact that she was a shrewd negotiator.

'What happened, Joe?'

'It's a long story.'

Lorraine didn't probe further. It was Joe's way of telling her that he didn't want to talk about it.

'Any messages?' he asked as he picked up the stack of mail from the week before and began reading through it.

'A few,' answered Lorraine and she began to read them off. 'Paul Caldwell called, wants you to meet him for lunch this week. John Deitz says he has a song that you've got to hear. Written by some kid in Memphis that no one's ever heard of. And some woman named Stevie Parker called.'

Joe's head jerked up, his brown eyes intense. 'What did she say?'

Lorraine paused, noting Joe's interest, then in a dramatic gesture she raised one hand to the bosom of her new pink blouse. 'She said, and I quote, "Tell Joe Devlin he can go straight to hell."'

When Joe didn't respond, Lorraine asked sweetly, 'A fan of yours?'

Joe ignored her sarcasm. 'Did she leave a number?'

'Why?' asked Lorraine, shaking her head. 'Do you want to call her back so you can hear more of the same? Usually they can't say enough nice things about you, Joe. Some of them actually gush. I never really knew the meaning of that word until I started working for you. What in the world did you do to this one?'

It's what she did to me. Joe ignored her question. 'If she calls again, I want to talk to her,' he said as he walked into his office. 'If I'm not here, make sure you get a number where I can reach her. Don't forget.'

Lorraine raised her eyebrows as her hand fluttered upward to adjust her platinum hair. 'I could hardly forget a woman who had guts enough to leave you a message like that. I think I like her.'

In spite of his agitation at Stevie's message, Joe smiled. She had managed to piss him off good. But he would have his turn when she called back.

'Oh, by the way, here's a FedEx delivery for you,' said Lorraine.

'You open it.'

'I already did, Joe, but I don't know what to do with it.' Lorraine held the large purple, orange and white envelope out to him.

Joe took it. Inside was a cashier's check from Stevie Parker for the exact amount he had left with her. Feeling Lorraine's curious gaze on him, his face turned red. Clearing his throat, he said, 'I'll take care of this.' Joe felt a wave of anger surge through him.

'I, uh, couldn't help but notice that it was from that Stevie Parker person. Would that have anything to do with her message?' asked Lorraine innocently.

'Does the word "unemployed" mean anything to you, Lorraine?' asked Joe with no visible sign of his usual good-natured kidding.

Lorraine blushed and, for one of the few times in her life, really wished that she had used her head before she had opened her mouth. 'Sorry, Joe,' she mumbled. 'I was just kidding.'

'Just let me know when she calls,' said Joe as he walked briskly into his office.

As it turned out, Stevie never called again.

'Good morning, Michelle,' said Stevie that same Monday. 'Is Harry in yet?'

'He's in a meeting, Stevie, but he should be through soon.'

Tucked away in a file folder in Stevie's briefcase was the results of three days' labor. At 2:00 a.m. that morning she had finished writing the story about Joe that would be featured in five installments.

Stevie waited only a few minutes before Harry, along with two men that she didn't recognize, left his office and walked down the hall toward the elevators. At Michelle's signal she stood, straightened the collar of her navy silk blouse under her gray jacket and walked into the empty office. Nervously she paced.

At first it was only a distant sound, but with each second the roar in her ears grew louder and louder until she could stand it no longer. Stevie, more nervous at what she was about to do than she had ever been, unzipped her briefcase, slapped a handful of papers on Harry's desk, then fled down the hall to the nearest bathroom.

Once inside, she splashed her face with cold water then stared into the mirror. Did she have the guts to go though with this? Did she have a right to do this? After telling Beth of her plans, even Beth, who frequently acted on impulse rather than logic, had told her to carefully consider what she was about to do, warning her that it could have legal implications.

Stevie took several deep breaths and nodded affirmatively to her reflection. Joe Devlin had hurt her deeply. He deserved to be taken down a notch or two, and she was just the person to do it.

In the hallway outside the bathroom several people stopped her, wanting to know about her vacation. She tried to fix a silly smile on her face, but wasn't sure she succeeded. When she reached her desk she sat down, grateful to give her shaking knees a rest. Stevie was in the act of putting her purse away when she heard Harry.

'Parker! Get in here!' he roared from the open doorway to his office. The menacing baritone echoed in the air.

All heads turned in her direction, most secretly relieved that they were not the target of Conklin's obvious wrath. Stevie stood at attention, the blood rushing to her face. Only Harry Conklin had the ability to make her react like this. With her back straight and her shoulders thrown back, she swiftly crossed the room. The first month she worked for Harry, she had learned never to show weakness or fear.

No sooner had she cleared the doorway of his office than he said tersely,' I ought to fire you for this.'

Instead of her usual denial of any wrongdoing, Stevie nodded in agreement.

'Who do you think you work for? One of those tell-all, no-matter-how-bizarre newspapers?'

Stevie shrugged her shoulders under her silk blouse. 'No,' she answered quietly, hoping that she looked more composed than she felt. 'But if you don't run this story, I could probably sell it to one of those papers.'

Harry stopped pacing and turned, fixing his intimidating stare on her. He had no doubt she would do exactly that. 'What the hell happened to *my* story, Stevie? The *interview* with Joe Devlin? I expected an interview with a celebrity. Standard stuff. Printable stuff. This is not an interview, this is pure sensationalism.' Harry paused, took a breath and shook his head. 'What happened to you, for chrissake?'

'It's all there, Harry, just like it happened. I spent two days with one of country music's biggest stars and I didn't even know who he was.'

'How could you *not* know who Joe Devlin is?' asked Harry, agitated.

'I don't like country music,' Stevie answered simply.

Harry groped in his desk drawer for a new package of Rolaids. 'Well, from the sound of this,' he said as he indicated the pages before him, 'it didn't keep you from liking *him*.'

A wry grin appeared on Stevie's face. *Not at all.*

'I can't print this, Stevie.'

Stevie tilted her heart-shaped face and fixed her blue eyes on Harry. Her chin jutted out just a fraction. 'You have to.'

'Why?'

'Because you agreed to. And everything I've written is the truth.'

Harry shook his head. 'Our readers don't want this kind of stuff; this stuff they can see on television or read at the supermarket, they want news. They want to be informed. Besides, we could be setting ourselves up for a lawsuit.'

'It'll sell papers,' Stevie reminded him. 'It's creative journalism, writing from the heart. It sizzles, Harry. It's my true confession. Do you think there's a woman out there who doesn't get a thrill in the pit of her stomach at the sight of this guy? I know I certainly did, and now I'm ready to share my experience. The only question is, do you have enough nerve to print it?'

Harry didn't doubt for a minute that Stevie's story would sell newspapers. She had done a fine job of writing, but it read like a goddamn soap opera. Handsome and famous man meets pretty woman by accident. Fate, probably. They kiss. They spend time together, she probably fell a little in love with him even though she didn't admit to it in the story, and all the while she's unaware of his true identity. She might have even slept with him, but she leaves the reader guessing.

The story had a fairy-tale quality until the very end, when Stevie pulled the reader back to face harsh reality. The fairy tale didn't have a happy ending. When the famous country music star left the woman without regard for her feelings, he behaved as though money could cure any hurt. Now instead of being admirable and desirable, the man appeared cold and calculating.

Harry unwrapped the foil from the roll of antacids and popped one of the white chalky tablets into his mouth. Clearly, Joe Devlin ended up looking like a real jerk at the end of Stevie's story. He didn't for a moment doubt that the story would spark controversy, and probably a lot more that he hadn't even considered yet.

He chewed the tablet slowly. As he weighed risk against reward, he ran his hands through his thinning hair. From behind his glasses he studied the small woman before him. Years ago, he had concluded that the amount of guts one displayed in this business was directly proportional to one's age.

Somewhere along the line he had lost that edge, that willingness to take risks. He was comfortable in his job, putting in his time until retirement. Suddenly, he had a desire to know that thrill again, that rush that comes with doing something daring that pushes you over the line.

'Okay,' he said, exhaling. 'We'll print it.'

'Exactly as is,' said Stevie. 'No changes.'

'No changes,' agreed Harry, 'except for an editor's note at the beginning.

'It's a deal,' replied Stevie, knowing that she should be elated. After all, it was a victory, wasn't it? But her feelings at that moment were quite different than what she had expected. Where was the exhilaration? The sweet feeling of revenge? In its place there was a curious hollow. From the slump of her shoulders, it was impossible to tell that she had just convinced her hard-boiled editor to do exactly what she wanted. Instead, she felt as if she had sold a part of her soul.

The remainder of the day passed slowly. By that evening she was a nervous wreck, and in spite of the fact that she had slept little the night before, she had trouble sleeping again. Tomorrow the first of her articles would appear in the paper. At least four times during the night, Stevie reached for the phone to call Harry to tell him to kill her story, but each time she hung up without completing the call.

'Joe,' said Lorraine the following morning, 'I thought you told me you didn't do any interviews while you were in Denver.'

'I didn't. Why?' asked Joe absentmindedly.

Lorraine handed Joe the fax she had just received. It was from the group Joe had met with while he was in Denver.

Joe scanned the sheet of paper. His eyes widened. 'What is this? Has Jeannie seen it?'

'No, it was in *The Denver Mountain Times* today.' Lorraine paused, then asked with feigned interest, 'Does the name Stevie Parker ring a bell?'

Joe's head jerked up.

Lorraine smiled knowingly. 'That's the name of the woman who wrote this article. And guess what, Joe?' said Lorraine with fake enthusiasm. 'It's the *first* in a series.'

Before she could gauge his reaction, Joe disappeared into his office. A few minutes later, he burst through the door, all six feet of him charged with the kind of energy that was anything but positive. 'Get her on the phone!' he ordered.

Lorraine reached for the phone and began to dial. It was obvious from the flush of red that had spread from Joe's handsome face to his neck that he was angry. 'Jeannie will just love this,' she remarked as she began to push buttons. 'She's had her hooks out for you for quite a while now and this ought to send her straight into orbit.'

The look that Joe shot Lorraine clearly said that she had gone too far. 'What's taking so long?' he demanded, pacing up and down in front of her desk.

Lorraine looked up at him innocently. 'I know a lot of things, Joe, but the phone number of *The Denver Mountain Times* isn't one of them. I'm calling Information.' She smiled at him, knowing that it would only irritate him more.

When Lorraine was this sweet, Joe never knew if it was genuine or if she was just doing it to aggravate him. He much preferred her when she was sarcastic. At least then he knew where he stood. The pacing finally stopped when he heard Lorraine ask for Stevie.

'She's not taking any calls,' said Lorraine after a minute, her hand covering the receiver.

'Tell the operator it's me.'

'That and a nickel will get you nothing,' she quipped.

Joe gestured angrily for Lorraine to continue.

She shrugged, indicating how futile she thought this whole thing was, then she smiled. Once more she covered the receiver. 'Her orders are not to forward any calls. Besides, she doesn't believe it's really you.'

'Find out who her editor is. I'll talk to him,' commanded Joe.

Lorraine rolled her eyes, then did as he asked. 'He's not in.'

'Then leave a message,' said Joe irritably.

'For whom?' asked Lorraine primly.

'For everybody, dammit!'

With one hip resting on the corner of Lorraine's desk, Joe re-read the article.

How could Stevie do this? It was a precise narrative of their meeting at the airport and a commentary of her initial impressions of him. How far would Stevie go in her exposé?

He had felt lousy when he had left her that morning, and he could only imagine what she must have felt when she awakened and found him gone. Would she dare write about everything that happened between them? It was one thing for his fans to read that kind of stuff in the tabloids. It was quite another to read it in a reputable newspaper.

The next installment of Stevie's story arrived the following morning. Once again Lorraine was unable to reach Stevie. In desperation, Joe had her send Stevie a fax, asking her to contact him about an urgent matter. He waited, but there was no reply.

Now Joe was more frustrated than Lorraine had ever seen him. The cool, controlled performer, who had quite literally taken his enormous success as his due, was rattled. His failure to reach Stevie Parker had taken its toll. And while Lorraine sympathized with him, she was, on an entirely different level, enjoying his discomfort immensely. It was about time some woman got the best of Joe Devlin.

When Lorraine handed him the third day's version of Stevie's story, he slammed his fist on the desk and ordered her to book him on an afternoon flight to Denver.

'But what about the meeting with the Conroy people?' she asked.

'Jeannie can meet with them. She knows what kind of terms we want.'

'How long will you be gone?' asked Lorraine. 'What do you want me to tell the guys? You *do* have a performance with your band scheduled for this weekend in Biloxi, you know.'

Joe glared at Lorraine, certain she was going out of her way to aggravate him. 'I'll let you know. Just get me a seat on the plane.'

Joe arrived in Denver at 4:25 that afternoon, his second visit in less than two weeks. He called the newspaper from the airport, but he was told that Miss Parker had left for the day.

'Could you give me her home phone number? I'm an old friend from out of town.'

I'm sorry, sir. I can't give out that information,' said the operator.

Joe hung up and reached for the phone book that hung nearby. Quickly he flipped the pages to the P's. When he reached Parker, he was amazed at how many there were. He ran his finger down the page, but there were no Stephanies. Only a Stephen. There were twelve listings for S. Parker. Eight were wrong numbers, one had been discontinued and three did not answer. He hung up the phone and resigned himself to the notion that he had spend yet another futile day in pursuit of the elusive Miss S. Parker.

Outside the airport, Joe hailed a cab, but not before he noticed how mild the weather was. Quite a change from his last visit. During the drive to the Hyatt, he pulled copies of Stevie's story from his coat pocket and began to re-read what she had written. He had to admit it was entertaining. Written in a style that was often used in the tabloids, it promised a lot and delivered what it promised. In detail. The writer was a woman who was still smarting from the treatment he gave her, Joe reminded himself.

But why, he wondered, hadn't she used the photo of the two of them and their snowman? Or the picture of the two of them together with his arms wrapped around her? Could it be that the picture meant something to her, or was she saving the best for last? He folded the papers and tapped them against his knee. And *would* she kiss and tell?

She had so far.

CHAPTER 10

Stevie was a minor celebrity. Her columns about Joe resulted in hundreds of phone calls and letters to the paper. Some were from fans of his who wanted to know if what she had written was true. A few were from upstanding and uptight citizens who were outraged that she would admit to going to a hotel with a man she had just met. Others wanted to know how she could not know who Joe Devlin was.

Stevie found out that even if she hadn't known who he was, there were lots of people out there who did. Yesterday she had even been a guest on a local afternoon television show, and tomorrow morning she was scheduled to be a guest on a morning radio talk show.

Stevie had asked Beth to meet her after work to help her select something to wear on the talk show the next day.

'But no one is going to see you on the radio,' reasoned Beth.

'The staff can,' answered Stevie. 'It's also a matter of confidence. If I look good, I'll feel good and I'll sound good.'

'Right,' mumbled Beth.

'A piranha,' said Stevie, once they were inside the store.

'I beg your pardon?'

'You asked me what Gretchen Kirsh, the bubbly hostess of *Denver p.m.* was like yesterday. She's like a piranha.' Stevie pulled a dress off the rack and held it up against her.

Beth shook her head. 'Wrong color. Washes you out.'

'Why do you suppose they call this section of the store "Better Dresses"?' asked Stevie as she made her way through the tightly packed aisles. 'These look worse than the section we just came from.'

'Let's check out the petites over at Harbinger's. They should have a better selection,' suggested Beth. 'So the interview with Gretchen was bad? I'm sorry I missed it, but I didn't dare cancel my meeting. I've been working for over a year to get a shot at this account.'

'It wasn't exactly bad, but the whole time I kept feeling like she was taking bites out of me. Her tone was nice, but some of the questions weren't. Then she would make a snippy comment and smile at the camera just so everyone would know that of course little Gretchen didn't really mean exactly what she said. She was just being a television personality.'

Inside Harbinger's they rode the escalator to the second floor. 'She actually had the nerve to ask me if I knew what they said about blizzards and blackouts.' said Stevie. 'Of course I walked right into that one with my eyes wide open. Like a dummy I said no. So once more Gretchen looked right into the camera and with that toothy smile she said, "Why, nine months later the baby arrives."'

'What did you say?' asked Beth.

'Nothing. Absolutely nothing. I never responded. On the surface her comment sounded innocuous enough, but she was ready to pounce on whatever I would say to her about her little joke. She was just dying to ask exactly what Joe and I did while we waited out the storm, but I wasn't ready to tell just yet, if for no other reason than that it would spoil my future columns. So I just sat there looking as pleasant as possible, as though I hadn't heard a word she said.'

Stevie sighed then continued. 'Dead air time. That's a killer in television. Of course, Gretchen hadn't expected that, so it sent her scrambling to change the subject before she looked like a bigger idiot than she already was. I think it's safe to say I won't be asked to be on her show again, no matter what I do or how scandalous. As soon as the segment was finished, Gretchen stormed off the set.'

Beth laughed as she led the way off the escalator through the lingerie department toward the dresses. 'No goodbye or thank you?'

'Not a word,' giggled Stevie.

And then there were all those calls from Joe. For two days now he had left messages and sent faxes. Stevie had wanted to call him back. Irrationally, she had wanted to hear his voice. But she knew he was only calling because he must have found out about the story. If he had felt anything for her, anything at all, he would have tried to reach her long before now. Still, her curiosity about his reaction to her story lingered. If she were honest, she would admit that in addition to revenge, her desire to do something that would bring him in contact with her again had been just as strong a motivation.

The sun was bright the next morning when Stevie skipped down the front steps of the four-storey red-brick building that housed the KXAM studios and headed toward *The Times*. For this occasion she had worn the new black suit that Beth had helped her select, along with her favorite yellow silk blouse. Her only jewelry was a pair of gold and pearl earrings.

It had gone well, she decided, as she reflected on her ten minutes as a guest on *Morning Talk with Ken Johnson*. At least Ken wasn't like Gretchen. He was funny, though, and his comments were entertaining rather than insulting. Mostly, people who called in were just curious about Joe. In her mind she reviewed the questions asked by the mostly female callers. Mentally, she congratulated herself as she covered the four blocks that separated the radio station and *The Times*. Her answers had been clever, honest and thoroughly entertaining.

Back at work, Stevie had just poured a cup of black coffee to take to her desk when she realized that the usual buzz of voices that was always present in the newsroom was louder than normal. Curious, she set her cup on the drab green Formica counter and left the cubbyhole that housed the coffee pot and the ancient microwave. She peered around the doorway as she turned the corner, then stopped suddenly.

As soon as she was spotted, all pretense of work ceased and an eerie silence settled over the room.

Everyone looked toward her expectantly. Bewildered, her blue eyes widened, scanning the sea of familiar faces before her. She grinned nervously. It wasn't her birthday, so why was everyone looking at her? Only a few seconds had elapsed until she discovered the reason for the group's strange behavior.

Stevie drew her breath in sharply. Shock registered on her face, altering her usually pleasant countenance. There at her desk was Joe Devlin. All glorious six feet of him wearing a black cowboy hat that rode low over his eyes, a denim jacket, and jeans that hugged his hips and long legs all the way down to his black ostrich boots. Casually he rested against the edge of her desk, feet stretched before him, arms folded across his broad chest, looking for all the world as though it was the most normal way for him to begin the morning.

Across the silent expanse of the room their eyes met and held; his intense and unreadable, hers wide with surprise and confusion. For just a moment time seemed to stand still. Then Stevie took a deep breath. Suddenly, it was much too warm in there and, without realizing what she was doing, she slipped out of her suit jacket and laid it across the nearest chair.

Slowly, she began to walk across the room, her eyes locked hopelessly with Joe's. With each step she took, the distance between them seemed to grow instead of shrink. She felt as if she was moving in slow motion. Now her breathing was shallow, her heartbeat rapid. All these things she knew. She even knew the exact moment when she feared her knees would give way, but in spite of it all, she could not tear her gaze away from his.

Even when she stood directly in front of him, the tips of her black patent pumps only an inch or so from the squared-off toes of his boots, she had no idea what to do or say. So when the words shot out of her mouth, her attempt at humor caustic and sharp, she was as surprised as anyone. 'So, where's your horse, cowboy?'

Around the room there was laugher, some of it genuine, some nervous.

'Hello, Stevie,' said Joe in a quiet voice.

Stevie shifted nervously. She had expected anger and could deal with that. She hadn't expected Joe's quiet greeting. He was so damn handsome, so sure of himself. With concentrated effort, she tore her eyes away from his and glanced around the room. Everyone was waiting expectantly, watching to see what would happen next. She turned back to Joe. 'Let's find some place more private,' she said, acutely aware that he was studying her intently. 'There's an empty office over there.'

'This is fine, Stevie,' said Joe evenly. 'We don't really have much to talk about.'

That's what you think, Devlin. 'Did you see the story? I assume that's why you're here.'

'Why didn't you take my calls?' asked Joe, ignoring her question.

'I knew you'd be angry and I didn't want to talk to you,' she replied.

'Why did you decide to write about us, Stevie?' His brown eyes searched her face.

'Why didn't you tell me who you really are?' countered Stevie with a catch in her voice. She raised her chin and was gratified to see something flicker in his eyes. Remorse? Regret?

111

'I could ask you the same question,' he reminded her.

She looked away, feeling a momentary twinge of guilt.

He watched her struggle briefly with her discomfort before he answered her. 'It was easier not to,' he answered honestly.

Stevie raised her eyes to his. 'Would you have ever told me?'

'Probably not,' answered Joe truthfully. 'I didn't plan to see you again.' The words he spoke were quiet, their meaning unmistakable. *But I didn't count on my body betraying me by wanting you, and my mind hoarding thoughts of you.* 'How did you find out?'

Pain that she had carefully hidden rose once more and wrapped itself around her defenseless heart. She swallowed and was sure she tasted bitterness. 'I saw you on television. A promo for some awards show.'

Joe nodded.

Stevie looked toward the glass wall of the office to her left and spotted the reflection of Harry Conklin heading in their direction. 'Joe, please,' she pleaded, 'can't we go get a cup of coffee or something?' The last thing Stevie wanted was to be interrogated by Harry in front of Joe.

Before Joe had a chance to reply, Harry approached them, his hand extended. 'Well, Joe,' he said, his tone a little too jovial, 'have you and Stevie worked out all the details?'

Stevie looked from Joe to Harry. 'What details?' she asked suspiciously.

Joe remained silent, all the while watching Stevie.

'Haven't you told her yet?' asked Harry.

Joe shook his head. 'Not yet.'

112

'Told me what?' demanded Stevie, looking toward Harry, her hands on her hips.

Inwardly, Harry swore. Devlin had no intention of making this easy. Harry attempted a grin and tried to keep his tone light. 'It's a great opportunity, Stevie, and it will work perfectly with your story on Joe.'

Stevie's eyes flew to Joe. His expression hadn't changed. It was still serious and intense.

Harry cleared his throat in the silence and waited, but it was obvious Devlin was leaving it to him to provide all the answers.

Stevie swung to face him. 'What's going on here, Harry?'

Harry looked toward Joe as if for approval, then said, 'Well, Joe has generously offered to take you on tour with him and his band so you can see what his life is really like. You'll be able to – '

'Why?' The word pierced the air as Stevie's voice rose slightly.

'So you can write about how country music performers really –' Harry began.

'*No!*' This time the word rang out, hanging in the charged space between them while her heart beat wildly at the thought of going anywhere with Joe Devlin. She knew she had to refuse. All she could think of was that she couldn't be near him and not want him again. *This is crazy!*

Harry looked from one to the other. Stevie's chin was high with resolve; the intensity in Joe's eyes as he watched Stevie belied his relaxed stance.

'No?' Harry repeated, as if he no longer trusted his hearing.

'You heard me,' said Stevie, her voice shaky. She cursed her lack of self-control as she turned to Harry. 'I'm not going anywhere with him.' Inside her heart was racing and she thought she might pass out at any moment.

'Look, Stevie, just think what we can do with this story,' pleaded Harry. 'We can keep the series going, and Joe is all for it.'

'I'll just bet he is,' said Stevie with thinly veiled sarcasm. 'But the answer is still no.' She looked toward Joe now, wanting to gauge his reaction. There wasn't one.

Harry reached out and laid his hand lightly on Stevie's shoulder, turning her toward him and said in a low voice, 'He's threatened to sue the paper, Stevie. This is a deal I worked out. He said he wouldn't follow through on the suit if we printed a true account of things, if you go with him. So this is your new assignment. You leave today and you'll be gone for two weeks.'

Stevie struggled with a reply, but before the words were out of her mouth Harry added, 'I've got to go along with this, Stevie.'

Stevie was indignant as she turned away from both men. 'Well, I don't, so you can just forget . . .'

She had taken only one step when a strong hand shot out, grabbed her by the arm and swung her back around. Before she had a chance to protest, Joe, with her arm still held firmly in his grasp, swiftly pushed himself off the edge of her desk. With one sweeping motion he bent down, wrapped his free arm around her thighs, then effortlessly heaved her over his shoulder. It

114

all happened so quickly that it took a few seconds for the whole thing to register. The sounds of surprise, then laughter, swept through the room at the sight of Stevie, bent at the abdomen, her head hanging down, riding over the shoulder of Joe Devlin.

'Let me go!' shouted Stevie as she hammered her fists into his muscular back. The laughter grew louder. And if Stevie could have seen Joe's face just at that moment, she would have seen the sparkling laughter that danced in his eyes as he carried her across the room, stopping only briefly to grab her jacket and purse from the chair where she had left them earlier. In the empty corridor Stevie's angry voice echoed. 'I hate you, Harry Conklin! This is the worst thing you've ever done. I'll show you a lawsuit you won't ever forget. I'll sue you and this newspaper, I promise! Do you hear me, Harry?'

Stevie continued her threats as Joe carried her into the elevator. 'I'll never forgive you for this, Joe Devlin! I'll write the truth about you, all right. I'll tell the whole world what a rotten, conniving bastard you are! I'll tell all those insipid, starry-eyed fans of yours everything.'

Outside, Joe unceremoniously dumped Stevie into the back seat of the taxi he had had waiting at the entrance to the building, then slid in beside her.

If the driver was surprised at having a passenger delivered to his vehicle in such an unorthodox manner, he gave no indication. 'Where to?' he asked in a bored voice.

'What's your address?' asked Joe.

'What's that got to do with –?' began Stevie.

'We're going to your place so you can pack some things.'

'I'm not going anywhere with you,' said Stevie stubbornly as she settled back against the seat and folded her arms across her breasts.

Joe studied her briefly then turned to the driver. 'Denver International,' he said. To Stevie he announced, 'We'll forget about your clothes.'

'No,' contradicted Stevie, nervously. It was obvious now that one way or another she was on her way out of town with him.

She refused to look at Joe as she gave the driver the address of her apartment. Neither spoke during the twenty-minute ride. When they arrived, Joe paid the driver and sent him on his way. 'Our plane doesn't leave for several hours,' he explained to Stevie. She did her best to ignore him.

Inside, Joe made no effort to hide his curiosity about her apartment and her possessions. In the living room one wall, made up of a series of paned windows, let the bright sunlight in and seemed to make up for the apartment's lack of space.

Stevie ignored Joe as he walked slowly around the cheerful room, fingering her possessions. The colors were bright, the furniture a mixture of inexpensive painted pieces and antiques. Together they made the room welcoming. It struck him as odd, though, that there were no pictures of her family or friends.

In the galley-style kitchen Stevie took two cans of soda out of the refrigerator and set them on the counter that divided the kitchen from the living room. 'Here,' she said, 'drink this, then you can explain your caveman behavior.'

Joe picked up the can and flipped the tab. 'There's nothing to explain,' he said after he had taken a long drink. 'We're going on tour – you and me. Since you seem to have a burning desire to share my personal life with your readers, I'm going to give you a chance to observe it first-hand, like it really is.'

Stevie leaned back against the sink, her arms crossed defiantly. 'I'm not going with you, Joe.'

'Sure you are. Get your things together.' It was an order.

'No,' she replied heatedly. 'Two days with you was enough.'

'Don't forget the nights, honey.' This he tossed over his shoulder as he set his soft drink on the counter and sauntered from the living room down the short hallway into her bedroom.

Stevie rushed around the counter and followed him into her bedroom where she found him rummaging through her closet. 'What are you doing?' she demanded. 'Get out of there!'

Joe didn't answer. Instead he began to toss a few of her things on the bed.

'Stop it!' ordered Stevie.

Joe paused. 'Would you like to finish?'

'I told you I'm not going. I've had enough of you, Joe Devlin.'

Joe raised his brow as if to question the validity of her statement, then crossed the room to her chest of drawers where he began to sort through the silky contents.

Stevie blushed. 'I would have to be crazy to want anything more to do with you.'

'Did I treat you so badly?' asked Joe as he pulled out a pair of black lace panties and held them up for inspection.

'Yes,' she answered truthfully.

With the panties still in his hands, Joe turned toward Stevie. In his mind he pictured her in the bit of lace. 'You surprise me,' he replied and she wasn't sure if he was referring to her last comment or the panties. 'Is it because I left without saying goodbye?'

'Because you left,' answered Stevie in a husky voice, fighting to keep the hurt hidden. 'And put those down,' she ordered, reaching for the silky garment.

'You knew I was only in town for a few days, Stevie.'

His voice had been quiet, the words as kind as they could be, and now they took on a life of their own as they penetrated first her heart, then plunged clear down to her soul. It was nothing more than a one-night stand to him. Why would she have ever thought it could be more?

Because I wanted it to be.

It was Stevie who moved first, picking up a pair of jeans that Joe had thrown on her bed and returning them to her closet. 'I can't go with you, Joe,' said Stevie, shaking her head. 'It would cause too many problems.'

Silently Joe had to agree. He had no idea what had come over him when he had threatened to sue the paper and then proposed that Stevie go on tour with him. He only knew that he needed to be with her again. 'I won't touch you, Stevie, unless you want me to. This will be strictly business. You just write about your observations.' Secretly Joe wondered if he would be able to keep his hands off her. He hadn't been able to before. Not even the spectre of guilt had stopped him.

'I can't do it, Joe.'

'Well, you have to. Otherwise I'm going to file a lawsuit against the paper,' he bluffed. 'You'll lose your job.'

'Go ahead,' she challenged bravely, sticking out her chin defiantly. 'There are other jobs, and lawsuits take years.'

'They'll fire Conklin the minute the papers are served. That would be too bad. He seemed like a nice guy. Probably getting close to retirement.' Joe could see the stricken look that crossed Stevie's lovely face just before she turned away from him. He had counted on her loyalty to Conklin and he hadn't been wrong. 'Besides,' he added softly, his brown eyes seductive as they roamed over her body, 'I want you to come with me.'

The message was clear. Stevie roused and swung around to face him.

He held up a hand to stall the words that bubbled in her throat. 'Forget I said that.'

How can I? Silently, Stevie walked to the closet and pulled out her suitcase. She was almost certain she would regret her decision, but for now she was going with him.

CHAPTER 11

'Pay attention,' Joe commanded as he nudged Stevie with his elbow.

'I can't get my seat belt to fasten,' she said, tugging at one of the straps and shifting in her seat.

'Watch the flight attendant while she's reviewing the safety procedures,' he ordered.

Stevie looked around. They were aboard the flight that would take them from Denver to Memphis where they would then board a much smaller plane and go on to Gulfport, Mississippi. 'Nobody else is. They're all doing something else,' she replied.

'Very foolish of them,' Joe explained. 'You need to know what to do and where all the exits are in case of an emergency. Then count how many rows there are between you and the nearest exit. A safety precaution.'

After the flight attendant had finished, Joe reached into the pocket of the seat in front of them and handed Stevie a card with all the information she needed. 'Read this,' he told her.

'You are making me nervous,' she whispered, leaning over close to him.

'I am making sure that you're informed,' he whispered back.

Stevie did as Joe directed. This was her first time on a plane and, in spite of the circumstances surrounding this trip, she was eager to experience her first flight.

Joe could hardly keep from laughing out loud when they took off. Her eyes were round as saucers and for once, as the plane roared down the runway and the nose lifted off the ground, she was speechless.

'A thrill,' she announced once they were airborne, 'but I was sure the tail was never going to leave the ground. It took so long.'

Joe was counting on her enthusiasm to continue replacing, he hoped, her anger at being hijacked from her job to accompany him on tour.

Just a few hours after they boarded their flight they caught a connecting flight in Memphis for Gulfport. Joe and his band were booked for a concert the following evening at the Gulf Coast Coliseum which was in Biloxi, a neighboring town. They were met at the airport by Richie Devlin, who not only played lead guitar in the band but was also Joe's younger brother. The resemblance between the two of them was unmistakable, but where the planes of Joe's face were sculptured and defined, Richie's still carried a youthful roundness.

'I thought Jeannie would have come to the airport with you,' said Joe as he claimed Stevie's bag.

'Not a good idea,' replied Richie, his voice lowered. 'She's not real pleased with you, Joe, for leaving town before the meeting like you did, and when she found out you went back to Denver and were bringing the reporter with you that wrote those stories, well . . .'

'And when she finds out that reporter is the same woman she encountered in my hotel room in Denver, all hell will break loose,' said Joe with a devilish grin.

Richie shrugged. 'For a guy who usually keeps his fly zipped, you sure screwed up this time. Jeannie really will be pissed, and this one doesn't look like she's any too happy to be here.' He nodded toward Stevie, who stood a few feet behind Joe. The frown on her face was testimony to Richie's words.

'Oh, that. Well, this was Stevie's first time on an airplane, and she did just fine on the first leg of the trip. It was this last leg that almost did her in.'

Richie laughed. 'I take it Joe forgot to tell you that this plane was slightly smaller,' he guessed, referring to the commuter jet that only carried eighteen passengers.

'I might as well have been flying the thing myself,' Stevie explained. 'I was practically sitting in the pilot's lap.'

Joe reached out and drew Stevie forward. 'This is my brother, Richie.'

'Hi, Richie. Like it or not, I'm going to be part of the group for the next few weeks.'

'So tell me the truth, Stevie. Were you scared on the plane or did you really like it?' asked Richie.

Stevie glanced up first at Joe, then flashed Richie a dazzling smile that lit up her face. 'I loved it,' she confessed. 'I have never experienced anything like it in my life.'

'Boy, she's being a lot nicer to you than she was to me,' observed Joe as they left the airport.

Stevie only glared at him and resumed her conversation with Richie.

At the hotel Richie had made arrangements for a room for Stevie on the same floor with the other band members. After making sure she was comfortable, Joe went in search of the rest of his group.

Inside her room, Stevie opened the French doors and stepped out onto the balcony, marveling at how green and beautiful it was here even though it was December. Everywhere she looked, camelias bloomed with their lacy layers of scarlet and medley of shades of pink. Straight ahead was a perfect and unobstructed view of the beach and the sparkling blue of the Gulf of Mexico.

She sank down on the patio chair, feeling pulled in two directions. Part of her thrilled at the idea of being near Joe. The other part wanted nothing to do with him. *How can I spend day after day with Joe and not let him know how I feel? How will I endure the disappointment when it's time to go?* But she had endured disappointment before; she would come to terms with it when her time ran out.

She was jarred from her thoughts by a loud knock at the door and hurried inside to open it. But instead of finding Joe as she had expected, she was greeted by four smiling male faces. Richie stepped forward through the open door into Stevie's room. The three men with him followed his lead.

'This is Dave Gordon,' began Richie. 'He plays the guitar; Brad Dennison is our drummer and Allen Lee Taggert here does keyboard.'

123

Stevie looked from one face to the other, smiling.

'Well, Miss Stevie,' began Allen Lee as he brushed his long shaggy blond hair off his forehead, 'it is very nice to meet you and we are mighty pleased to have you join us on this tour. Aren't we, boys?'

They nodded.

'Thank you,' replied Stevie, trying to hide her amusement at the somewhat formal greeting that was so at odds with the youthful and scraggly appearance of the young man who delivered it.

'Joe says you're the reporter that wrote all about you and him in Denver.' This was from Dave, the tallest of the group.

Stevie nodded, overwhelmed by the presence of these four men, who ranged in age from mid-twenties to early thirties.

'Hope you won't take offense, Stevie. But all of us hope that what you write won't set Joe on edge again,' said Dave, the expression in his dark eyes serious.

'He was mad as he could be when he read those stories in the paper about him,' added Brad seriously, shaking his head. Then he looked up as if he just remembered something. 'Of course, they were about you, uh, too.'

'Well, yes, I . . .' began Stevie, prepared to defend what she had written.

'You see,' said Richie by way of explanation, 'Joe always takes what they say about him in the newspapers too personal. We always have to remind him that what some reporters write isn't necessarily the truth, and if they only knew him . . .' Richie blushed and let his words fade, realizing too late just how well Stevie had

124

gotten to know his brother in the short time they had spent together.

In spite of their words, the faces were open and friendly and Stevie decided that she liked them all. At least she knew what was on their minds. She also knew they were loyal to Joe.

'I'll try to keep that in mind when I'm writing future columns,' she replied drily.

A half-hour later Joe called her room, asking if she'd like to go for a drive along the beach before it got dark, and Stevie accepted his invitation with enthusiasm. Since she had never traveled, she was eager to see as much as she could.

They drove down Highway 90 from Biloxi Bay on one end to Bay St Louis on the other, a distance of not quite thirty miles. From the beach, several barrier islands out in the Gulf were clearly visible. Across from the beach, sheltered by huge, spreading oaks, were beautiful old homes.

'Many of these were built before the Civil War as summer homes by wealthy businessmen from New Orleans,' explained Joe, slowing the car so Stevie could see past the rows of picket and iron fences that were as charming and distinctive as the houses behind them. 'They would bring their families here to escape the epidemics of yellow fever that plagued New Orleans year after year.'

Here, too, side-by-side with the traditional white painted wood homes and dark green shutters, were soft pastels and tin roofs, reflecting the island influence of the Caribbean.

'I feel like I'm in another world,' she remarked softly, shifting her gaze from the scenery around her toward Joe.

'You are,' he replied.

When they returned to the hotel, Stevie and Joe were met in the lobby by Richie and Allen Lee. They grinned at her rapid and enthusiastic description of all that she had seen on that late afternoon drive.

'You forgot the lighthouse,' prompted Joe.

'Oh,' she continued breathlessly, 'there's this lighthouse in the middle of the highway. A real lighthouse. And Joe stopped the car so I could go over and read the plaque next to it.' Then she began to tell them about all the historical markers she had seen.

When she had finally run out of breath, Allen Lee said, 'We're all going out to get something to eat later tonight, then on to a club to hear a local group play. Want to come along, Miss Stevie?'

She was on the verge of declining their invitation when Joe spoke up. 'No,' he answered for her. 'Stevie has had enough excitement for one day. I'm sure she's tired and she probably wants to have dinner and turn in early.'

Stevie spun around, her eyes flashing at Joe's attempt to arrange her evening. 'On the contrary,' she replied gaily, ignoring Joe's dark look, 'it sounds like fun. Just let me know what time and I'll meet you in the lobby.'

'Why did you do that, Stevie?' asked Joe after they had left Richie and Allen Lee in the lobby and gone to her room.

'Like I said, it sounds like fun,' she answered with a cheerfulness that she had summoned for Joe's benefit.

The truth was that she was tired. It had been a long day; if it hadn't been for his attempt to arrange her evening, she would have gladly called it quits early. She went to her bag and pulled out a pair of jeans and a black turtleneck sweater.

'You don't know what you're letting yourself in for,' said Joe irritably. 'These guys always hit the hot spots their first night in town to look for girls. Within a couple of hours they are usually paired up with someone for the night. Where would that leave you, Stevie?'

'Looking for someone to pair up with, I suppose,' she answered flippantly, deliberately making light of his warning. 'Look, Joe, I don't need you to watch over me.'

'Suit yourself,' he said as he turned and left the room. *Damn. I can't turn her loose with the guys and I can't tag along as her watchdog.* Besides, it was obvious that Stevie didn't want him along.

Later that night, the members of the band along with Stevie were seated at a long table at The Roundup, a nightclub on the beach. The music was country and loud, and Stevie was surprised that she actually recognized several of the songs the band had played. The crowd was made up of both couples and singles. Several members of the local band recognized Richie and insisted on making their presence known. Richie, Dave, Brad and Allen Lee obliged by signing autographs for anyone who asked, but Joe's absence dampened the crowd's enthusiasm and, after a while, they all returned to their respective tables.

Dave ordered beer all around and as Stevie began to relax, she forgot about the smell of stale beer and the blue haze of cigarette smoke that hung over the heads of the dancers. By the time the next round of beer arrived, she had decided that maybe, just maybe, country music had some merit. She hadn't had this much fun in a long time.

When Brad asked her to dance to a slow ballad, Stevie was about to refuse until she saw Joe making his way across the crowded club toward their table. *So, he couldn't stay away after all.*

Quickly she stood and followed Brad to the dance floor, while across the room a crowd gathered around Joe. A few minutes' later, she noticed Jeannie standing very close to him. Jealousy flashed through her. She pushed it aside. It was none of her business who he spent time with. She looked away, but at every turn, she looked over Brad's shoulder and found Joe's eyes following her. Deliberately she pulled back away from Brad and gave him one of her brightest smiles. He smiled in return, then pulled Stevie closer in his arms.

When the music was over, Brad dropped his arm from Stevie's back and led her by the hand toward their table. 'I thought you were too tired to go out,' said Stevie lightly to Joe as she and Brad rejoined the group.

'I was,' drawled Joe, 'but Jeannie convinced me I was missing a good time.'

I'll just bet she did.

Jeannie said nothing as she fiddled with a fiery strand of hair, but there was no mistaking her message as she moved closer to Joe. The feline look on her face announced that she had marked him as her territory and was now standing guard.

Brad had just pulled out a chair for Stevie when Richie asked her to dance. The tempo of the music was faster now and Stevie looked at the dancers on the floor. 'I'm not sure I can do that,' she said giggling.

'I'll teach you,' said Richie with a grin as he reached for Stevie's hand. 'I'll bet you're a fast learner.'

Joe pushed his hat off his forehead and leaned back in his chair lazily. 'A real fast learner,' he commented with sarcasm. 'And once she learns something she certainly knows how to use it.' The tone of his voice was a contradiction to the smile on his face.

Stevie turned slightly, giving Joe her best 'drop dead' look, but the words out of her mouth were as sweet and smooth as whipped cream. 'You really look tired, Joe. And I know that you really didn't come here because of Jeannie. I'm sure you can see Jeannie just any ol' time you want. You came because you wanted to know what I was doing. Now you know, so why don't you go on back to the hotel and maybe I'll see you later on.' The last few words were low and held the hint of something more to come.

'Come on, Stevie,' urged Richie as he tugged at her arm. Out on the dance floor Stevie felt like she had four feet as she tried to follow Richie's lead. Each time she moved in the wrong direction she dissolved into laughter. When the music ended, Stevie turned in the direction of their table, but Richie caught her hand and pulled her toward him. The song was a slow one.

'I do much better with this kind of music,' she said, laughing.

'I usually do too,' agreed Richie, 'but I'm not usually dancing with a girl who has my brother falling all over his cowboy boots to get to her.'

Stevie pulled back to look at Richie, his words suddenly too important to be lost in the noise around them. 'Did you read the columns I wrote, Richie?'

He nodded.

'Then you should know that Joe is not falling over himself to get to me. He had no intention of ever seeing me again when he left Denver.'

'He told you that?'

'Yes,' answered Stevie.

Richie shook his head. 'Why do you think he went back to Denver to get you and take you on tour with us, Stevie? If you hadn't written about the two of you in the newspaper, he still would have found a reason to come after you.'

Stevie smiled up at him, suddenly feeling warm all over.

Richie looked down into her glowing face. His expression changed now, the teasing all gone. 'How much has Joe told you about himself?'

'Not much,' admitted Stevie.

'I thought not,' Richie muttered. His brown eyes that were so much like his brother's were suddenly serious. 'Go home, Stevie. Joe is a good guy, but in the end you'll only be hurt. He can't give you what you want.'

'How do you know what I want?' asked Stevie, feeling breathless and suddenly uneasy at Richie's words. But the song had ended. Richie turned away from her, tugging at her hand as he lead her back to their table.

The color in her cheeks was high and from a few feet away Stevie's eyes seemed to sparkle. She was thankful that in the darkened corner no one could see the glimmer of doubt that Richie's words had brought to her eyes. At the table she sat down to catch her breath, deliberately ignoring Joe and Jeannie. The waitress delivered another round of drinks, but before Stevie could take more than a couple of sips, Dave pulled her out of her chair to dance with him. She started to protest, but anything was better than Joe's piercing scrutiny and Jeannie's dagger-like glances.

Joe scooted further down in his chair, his feet propped on the rung of the chair opposite him, his scowl more pronounced. Jeannie frowned. This was not going at all like she had planned. 'Let's dance, Joe,' she said sweetly, deliberately moving so that her breast rested against his forearm.

Joe shook his head and spoke without looking in her direction. 'I'm not in the mood. Get one of the other guys. After all, they can't all dance with Stevie at once.'

'Come on, Jeannie,' said Allen Lee, rising gallantly and holding out his hand for her.

Whether out of deference for Stevie or because they couldn't seem to connect, none of the band members had paired up with anyone by midnight. Joe felt foolish. His dire predictions to Stevie earlier about the mating habits of his band had not materialized.

Except for Richie's warning, Stevie was having a wonderful time. She had even gotten through of a few of the simpler dances. And the more fun Stevie seemed to have, the more taciturn Joe seemed to become, and the more clinging Jeannie seemed to do.

131

From across the room the first few notes of 'Crazy', the song made famous by Patsy Cline, hung briefly in the air then drifted from the stage through the smoky blue haze to their corner when Brad stood, intent on asking Stevie to dance again.

'Not this time,' Joe said to Brad in a low voice as he got to his feet slowly, deliberately, and took Stevie's small hand in his larger, roughened one. 'This dance is mine,' he said. His stride as he led her away from the group was deceptively relaxed.

On the dance floor Stevie stood motionless in front of him, her face tilted upward, her blue eyes fixed on his. All night she had known this moment would come, and she had dreaded its coming. Taking both of her hands in his, Joe lifted them and placed them around his neck. Then he wrapped his arms around her waist, pulling her tight against him and began to move. She had danced a thousand dances in her life with many partners, but never had they been as sexy, or the message so clear. Together, the man and the music cast their spell.

Stevie wanted to speak, to tell him this was not part of their agreement, to tell him that she had been warned to stay away from him, but she was powerless to stop the languid, heavy heat that spread to every part of her body. When she finally found the strength to pull back and look into his eyes, she found them heavy with desire. Stevie lowered her lashes and rested her head against his shoulder. He pulled her closer now and rested his lips against her soft hair, inhaling her fragrance.

Neither spoke. Silent and swaying, they were caught up in the melody and the lyrics that said so much. Each time their bodies brushed together it was a caress. Now

132

Joe's lips moved from Stevie's hair to her temple. It wasn't quite a kiss, it was more possessive than that – like a brand. And this time it was Joe who pulled away just enough to see Stevie's face, wanting to see her reaction, knowing that he was in control. But her expression was unreadable, her eyes dreamy, far away. Joe's arms tightened around her, nestling her even more intimately against him.

When the music stopped, they stood as they were, wrapped in each other's arms, unwilling to break the spell. Not a word had been spoken. Neither moved until the dancers who streamed on to the floor for the next song forced them apart.

Stevie didn't remember leaving the dance floor and when Joe squeezed her shoulder and whispered, 'Let's go,' she turned, ready to accept his invitation and fully aware of all that his words implied when she was unexpectedly pulled away from him.

'Come on, Stevie,' said Richie lightly. As she forced herself to smile at him, Stevie tilted her head slightly as if to shake off the spell that had been so recently cast.

'You know, don't you?' she asked Richie with a hint of resignation in her voice as he led her away from his brother and back on to the dance floor.

'That you've fallen for Joe? It's written all over your face. I like you, Stevie, but you don't know what kind of a situation you would be getting yourself into.'

How dangerously close she had come to leaving with Joe. And there was no question as to where that would have lead. *I need to stay as far away from Joe Devlin as I can get. Anything else would be foolish.*

* * *

133

Later that night as she lay in bed, Stevie tried to sort out her feelings, but everything was jumbled. She could still see Joe's expression when she had told him she wasn't leaving with him. Had it been surprise or cynical amusement? The raised brow and the half-smile had been accompanied by a slight shrug of his shoulders. But she remembered how hurt she had been after Joe had left her in Denver, and how she had felt tonight when he had held her once more in his arms. If it hadn't been for that brief interval when Richie had pulled her away from Joe, she knew that right this moment she would be in Joe's bed, not here in the dark alone.

Joe Devlin is one of the charmers, she thought. A weaver of magic spells. A man whose eyes promise everything, whose heart gives nothing. Her eyes grew heavy as she drifted off to sleep. In her mind she saw the legions of men who, through the years, had come to see her mother. The charmers, she had dubbed them as a child, as she had watched each of them take what they wanted and leave. But Carole Parker never saw that, and whenever she would hint at a more permanent arrangement the charmer, with a sad smile, would leave, only to be replaced in a few days or a few weeks by someone just like him.

But in the end there is nothing. It was her last thought before she slept.

CHAPTER 12

The loud ring of the phone startled her. It had never been easy for Stevie to wake up in the morning and right now she couldn't remember where she was. She fumbled for the receiver. When she spoke her voice was low and thick. It was Richie calling to remind her that they were all meeting downstairs for breakfast before leaving for rehearsal at the Coliseum.

An hour later, Stevie watched as mounds of food covered the table in front of her. To her, breakfast meant black coffee and an occasional muffin or croissant.

'What's that white stuff? Cream of wheat?' she asked suspiciously as she looked from her plate to the others on the table.

There was laughter all around. 'Grits,' answered Allen Lee. 'I don't suppose you have them in Denver.'

Stevie shook her head and dipped her fork into the white fluffy stuff on her plate. 'But I didn't order this,' she protested.

'You don't have to,' Allen Lee explained. 'In the South, grits are always served with breakfast whether you want them or not. Of course, if you're a Southerner, you always want grits.'

'Oh,' she replied and, as she looked around the table, was suddenly aware that they were all waiting for her to taste them. She took a small spoonful and studied it from all angles.

'You can't eat them plain,' warned Richie, reaching over to her plate. 'Here, you have to put butter on them and a little salt.'

Gingerly she took a small bite and announced that they weren't bad.

'What did you think they were going to taste like, Stevie?' asked Brad.

She made a face. 'Sand,' she replied, as Joe joined them.

He reached for a chair from the empty table behind them and placed it next to her. 'And you can't wrap them up and save them for later,' he whispered. His husky voice at her shoulder sent an unexpected ripple of excitement through her. Stevie blushed and knew he was referring to the muffins she had stashed in her bag that morning they had met.

All around there was laughter and good-natured teasing. From the other end of the table Brad asked, 'What did you think of your first night out with country music?'

'It was fun,' she answered sincerely. 'I'm really glad you invited me to go along.'

'So you've revised your opinion of country music,' said Joe.

'I didn't say that,' replied Stevie, smiling at the group. Then she turned to face Joe. 'It's still loser music.'

From around the table came loud guffaws.

'Haven't you ever known a cheatin' man, Stevie?' asked Richie, his expression half-teasing, half-serious. 'It's what country music is all about.'

Stevie appeared to be giving Richie's question some deliberation. She knew all about cheatin' men. When she turned slightly in her chair, her eyes locked with Joe's. 'It all depends on how you would describe a cheatin' man,' replied Stevie.

From the other side of the table Jeannie murmured, 'Joe seems to be an expert in that area, especially when it works to his advantage.'

Joe cleared his throat, gave Jeannie a silent warning look that she was out of line, and changed the subject. He knew that he and Stevie were under scrutiny by the band. And last night their behavior on the dance floor had only increased their speculation. Joe now wished that he had sent Jeannie back to Nashville. Her presence here was making everyone uncomfortable and her rather pointed remarks about Stevie were becoming a source of embarrassment to them all.

That afternoon, from her seat in the Coliseum, Stevie recorded the confusion around her in her notebook. To the casual observer there seemed to be no organization to the work that was underway. A great deal of energy accompanied by the appropriate gesturing seemed to go into discussions with the sound and light people. Joe was all over, conferring with his production crew, stepping distances off, then undoing what he had just ordered done. Stevie waited several hours to hear the band rehearse, but all she heard were discordant notes as each musician finally tested the sound equipment.

By now she was bored. She slid down into her seat and closed her eyes. A sudden quiet settled over the Coliseum and, just as she straightened, the band began to play. She was surprised when she realized that they were playing something she recognized. She waited for Joe to join them.

In those first few dreadful days after she found who he really was, Stevie purchased several of his CDs. Without realizing it, in the midst of her anger, she began to see him differently. His charisma reached out to her, and she hated it. His music had both excited and soothed her, and she fought it. Now here she was, waiting, like thousands of others would be in just a few hours to hear him.

'That's it. We'll save the rest for tonight.' Joe's voice echoed in the cavernous hall.

Stevie was disappointed. She had waited all day to hear him sing. She had also hoped to have a few minutes alone with him, so that she could ask some questions for her column, but there was no time. All his energy was geared toward tonight's performance. On the way back to the hotel he suggested that she order something from room service before the show. After the show, he explained, they would all have a late dinner together.

If Stevie expected exuberance from the group that evening before the performance, she was mistaken. Instead they were quiet and introspective. After a while, there was a little light bantering, but nothing like their usual behavior. In the hallway outside the

Coliseum's dressing rooms she stood indecisively. Everyone seemed preoccupied and she felt uncomfortable and in the way. Maybe she should go out front to her seat.

Just then a hand reached out of a doorway and grabbed her by the wrist. 'In here,' Joe said, pulling her into his dressing room.

Inside, Stevie looked around with interest. The room was large, but spartan, not at all the kind of accommodations she had expected, and painted a color she could only describe as hospital green. Along one wall there was a dressing table and mirrors that ran the length of the room. On the opposite wall there was a doorway that led to a small bathroom.

'Sit down,' commanded Joe. 'Do you want something to drink?'

'No, thanks,' she said as she pulled her notebook out of her purse. 'Can I ask you some questions while you're getting ready?'

'What kind of questions?' he asked sharply.

Stevie looked up and saw he was watching her from the mirror. 'Well,' she said, taking a deep breath, 'for starters, what are you thinking about now? How does it feel knowing there are eleven thousand people out there waiting for you to step out on stage and entertain them?'

'It feels like hell.'

His answer surprised her. She waited for him to say something else that would indicate he was joking. She had expected him to say it was exciting, or exhilarating, anything but what he had said.

'I'm always nervous,' he continued. 'It never goes away. I have this awful feeling in the pit of my stomach

139

that I'm going to fail. Once I'm on stage it fades, but each time I wonder. I never know if I'm going to be good enough.' Joe had stopped all pretense of getting ready now. He turned from the mirror toward Stevie.

'What happens on stage?' asked Stevie quietly.

Joe smiled wryly. 'It's tough going at first. Sometimes it takes a while to connect with an audience. But when you do, they know it and you know it. And there's no other feeling in the world like it. It's a high that I can't even begin to describe.'

This was a different Joe that she was seeing now. This was Joe Devlin, the performer. 'And afterwards?' she prompted.

Joe stood and began to undo first the buttons on his cuffs, then the front of his shirt. 'I'll tell you about that later,' he said. 'After the show.'

Stevie began to write in her notebook. Tomorrow she would fax her notes to Harry. Right now it was important that she capture the content and the spirit of what Joe had just told her. She was silent for a few minutes and so involved in her writing that she failed to notice that across the room he was changing clothes.

The next question she wanted to ask flew right out of her mind when she looked up and saw him clad only in a pair of skimpy briefs that she could swear were several sizes too small. She watched as if in a trance as he slipped his arms into a black shirt with turquoise and silver piping.

Stevie cleared her throat and looked away. 'Uh, I could, uh, step out,' she offered. Then she muttered something about privacy.

140

From a green vinyl chair, Joe picked up a pair of black jeans and began to pull them on. 'Does this bother you?' he asked, his brown eyes laughing once more.

Stevie coughed; suddenly it was difficult to speak. 'Not if it doesn't bother you,' she managed to croak after a minute. But she lied. Even though she had previously seen much more of him than she had seen tonight, it still bothered her. This was an intimacy of a different type and it was all she could do to keep her eyes from devouring him. When he reached to pull the zipper on his jeans, Stevie, still seated in her chair, her face at crotch level, was unable to tear her eyes away. Everything in her line of vision seemed larger. Well-defined. Muscular.

It wasn't until Joe reached for his belt that she expelled that breath she had been holding.

'Seen enough?' asked Joe with a suggestive grin.

Stevie turned a bright red. Quickly she jumped from her chair, laid her notebook in the seat of the chair she had just vacated and moved toward the door.

I'm going to . . . to get some air,' she finished quickly. Outside in the hallway she leaned against the green cement wall and breathed deeply. *What was I thinking of just now, staring at him like some adolescent who had never seen a man in his underwear!*

You know exactly what you were thinking of.

When she returned a few minutes later, Joe was fully dressed, yet she avoided eye contact. It was easier. 'I'm going out front to my seat,' she said, gathering her purse and her notebook. 'Where shall I meet you after the show?'

141

'Back here,' answered Joe as he adjusted the collar of his shirt. 'Just show the security people your pass and you won't have any trouble. If you do, just ask them to call me.'

After Stevie had left, Joe paced the room nervously. If the Queen of England was sitting in the front row tonight, he wouldn't have been nearly as nervous. The thought of performing in front of Stevie Parker was a lot more unnerving than royalty.

The final minutes dragged. Tonight it seemed as if the opening band had stayed out on stage longer than usual. When the call came to go on stage, Joe rubbed his damp palms up and down the rough denim fabric of his pants. He had done this a hundred times before. There was no reason to be nervous. Except for Stevie, who would be in the audience watching; judging his every move.

Just before they stepped out on stage, Joe turned to the band. 'The last song is changed to "Crazy",' he said unexpectedly.

The band looked from one to the other. Joe never changed anything this late. 'But, Joe . . .' protested Richie, 'we didn't rehearse it this way.'

'I know,' he answered curtly. 'Just do it.'

Rich shrugged and glanced at each of the others.

'Let's get this over with,' Joe said as they ran on stage.

Show time. It was a combination of music and lights, energy and adrenalin. It was excitement. It would soon be romance. Then seduction. And finally sex and sweat.

In the front row Stevie, caught up in the excitement of the cheering whistling crowd, watched and waited for the first sounds to crash through the air around her. The rhythm, which would be reinforced by the clapping of the crowd, would soon reverberate around the walls.

On stage the band was ready, waiting only for the signal from Richie. Joe squinted at the spotlights that momentarily blinded him, looking beyond them into the thousands of faces who had come to hear him sing. Their disappointments and heartbreaks were the very things that he wrote about. The sound from the audience rose and ebbed like waves. They were ready, heated with anticipation.

The deafening applause began even before the first number had ended and it never stopped until they were well into the second song. On stage the lights had dimmed and this time the spotlights bathed Joe in a soft pink hue. He stepped forward, seemingly oblivious of everything but the melody and lyrics of 'Lonely Nights'. It was number two on the charts and climbing.

The crowd quietened as Joe's voice, rich and husky with a timbre that sent chills racing up Stevie's spine, charged the air. The tempo was slow, caressing; the words sad. It was about the woman who had left him, but whose memory continues to haunt him. In the song he begs her to let him go so he can find someone else to love.

At one point Stevie roused herself long enough to look around at the faces of those behind her. What she saw amazed her. There were tears on many of the faces. Honest-to-god tears that ran down the cheeks of young women and older women. And even men. The kind of men who surely had gun racks in the back of their pickups, and mamas who called them Bubba. Or Jimmy Joe. But tonight they were reminded of old loves and lost dreams – things that would never be.

Eleven thousand people including Stevie Parker watched as Joe Devlin cast his spell. She had to admit it was breathtaking. *He* was breathtaking. The magic was back.

When the song ended quietly, gently, there were a few seconds of complete silence. Then the burst of cheers, applause and whistles came from all sides of the Coliseum. At that moment, Joe knew he had connected.

Now the pace was rapid, the lights hot. Up on the stage, sweat ran down the faces and chests of the musicians. It soaked through their shirts. With his charisma Joe drew the audience to him. His energy was electrifying. Even those in the farthest seats knew he sang to them.

He does have style, thought Stevie. *Such style.* From one end of the stage to the other he paced while the spotlights followed. Waving, laughing. Letting his fans know that he was glad they were there, grinning as they sang along.

After two hours of non-stop music Joe stepped forward, his black hat in hand as he blotted the glistening beads of sweat from his forehead with his shirt sleeve.

'Thank you,' he said, breathing hard. 'Country music fans are the greatest fans in the world.'

A roar of agreement was reinforced by stomps and shouts. Joe held up his hand and waited until the noise died down. 'We're going to do one more song before we leave you. This last song reminds me of someone very special who is here tonight.' His voice was husky now, sensual, and every woman in the audience wanted to believe that Joe Devlin was thinking of her.

Behind him, Richie, Dave, Brad and Allen Lee looked from one to another. Joe sounded more sincere than he ever had. Was it showmanship? Maybe. Maybe it was Stevie Parker, but women were always hanging around Joe. Was Stevie that special? Out of the group, only Richie remembered the song that Joe and Stevie had danced to last night, and only Richie knew what heartbreak lay ahead for the woman who was in love with his brother.

It was quiet now, with only a few intermittent shouts and whistles as the first soft notes of 'Crazy' floated through the air followed by Joe's slightly raspy bar-itone. His voice first pierced the heart, then went in search of the soul. His brown eyes went in search of Stevie Parker.

The moment she recognized the song Stevie knew that this song was for her and her alone. The melody and the poignant lyrics drifted across the stage into the audience until they found her and wrapped themselves around her heart.

Joe's eyes found Stevie's, and before he could look away it was too late. Without ever saying a word to her, he had told her everything he was feeling.

Minutes later the applause was thunderous. Stevie stood where she was, rooted to the floor, never wanting this moment to end. From more than twenty feet away Joe Devlin had made love to her with his eyes and his voice. It was a seduction of quite a different kind.

Minutes after the band had left the stage, the house lights came on and Stevie sank weak-kneed into her seat. She was riding an emotional roller coaster, her heart racing to keep up. Of all the things she had expected from Joe, this hadn't been one of them. It was too much. How could he capture her so completely? What would she do when he would leave her again as he was bound to do?

Backstage, Joe and the band retreated to their dressing rooms to change before they faced the fans they knew would be waiting outside for them.

Members of the production crew crowded the halls and spilled into the dressing rooms. Joe looked around, hoping to catch a glimpse of Stevie, but she wasn't anywhere in sight. Afraid that she had encountered difficulty in getting backstage, he asked one of the security people to watch out for her. For the next forty-five minutes he and the band were besieged by fans who had backstage passes. When the last person had left the dressing room and Stevie still hadn't showed, Joe went in search of her.

It was dark on stage, only a few lights glowed over the exits.

'Stevie? Where are you?'

Slowly, Stevie stood and made her way toward the edge of the stage.

'Honey, what are you doing out here in the dark?' Joe asked as he reached down to take her hand and pull her on to the stage.

'Thinking,' she said softly.

'About tonight,' Joe said.

146

Stevie nodded. 'You were wonderful, Joe.' The words were spoken softly. 'I had no idea. Tonight you managed to captivate every woman in the audience.'

'Even you?' he asked seductively.

'Especially me.'

'It wasn't an act, Stevie. That song was for you, no one else.'

Oh Joe, do you have any idea how much I want to believe that?

He reached down and took both of Stevie's hands in his, placed them on his shoulders, then wrapped his arms around her waist and pulled her close just like he had done the night before. Then he swayed slightly as he began to hum the same melody that he had sang to her earlier. But he didn't get far before Stevie, on tiptoes, wound her hands around his neck and pulled his face down to meet her soft, full lips.

'Hey, Joe, where are you?' At the sound of Richie's voice, Joe and Stevie separated quickly.

'Oops,' said Richie as he realized that he had interrupted something private. 'Uh, are y'all ready to go?'

Joe looked down at Stevie and smiled as if they shared a secret. 'Sure,' he said to Richie, and to Stevie he whispered, 'We can finish this later.'

The restaurant was indeed out of the way, on the north side of Biloxi Bay. 'A place the locals visit,' the security guard had told them after the show. 'Not much on atmosphere, but the food is great and nobody will bother you.'

Inside it was decorated with seashells and fishing nets. At each of the long wooden tables lanterns burned.

147

The flooring was wood planking that had once been finished with shellac but now was bare, yellowed and warped. In the corner sat an old jukebox. There was no need to feed it quarters; a push of the button would send it searching for the selection.

'Mr Broussard, the owner, he get tired of everyone wantin' change for the jukebox, so he fix it,' said their waitress as she took their orders. 'Course, he ain't never change no tunes on it, so none of the regulars play it anymore, but y'all are welcome to if you want.'

As soon as they were served, they knew that the security guard had been right about the food. The fried catfish, shrimp and broiled flounder stuffed with crabmeat were hot and plentiful and accompanied by heaping bowls of french fries, hush puppies, and coleslaw.

Stevie was amazed. 'You Southerners are going to die from what you eat,' she said with conviction, 'but I will say you're doing your best to make it as pleasurable as you can.' There was laughter from both sides of the table as they all reached to help themselves.

From the other end of the wooden table, Brad looked up and caught Stevie watching him as he loaded up his plate. In an exaggerated accent he said, 'Singin' and a-pickin' takes a lot of energy, Miss Stevie. And my mamma says I got to keep up my strength. I'm still in my formative years, you know.'

Stevie giggled at this, and as she ate she listened to them discuss their performance. When Jeannie arrived Stevie was sorry to see her. Before her appearance, the atmosphere had been relaxed; now, it was strained. After a few minutes she understood why.

Whether it was part of her job or something she just did, Stevie didn't know as she listened to Jeannie dissect each of their performances. When she got to Joe, he held up his hand as if to say he had heard enough. 'I'm going to play the jukebox,' he said as he pushed away from the table and stood. 'Any requests?'

As soon as he was out of hearing, Jeannie leaned forward toward Dave. 'What about Joe changing to "Crazy" at the last moment?'

'We were surprised,' said Dave, 'but it worked out okay.'

'It's because of Miss Stevie,' volunteered Allen Lee good-naturedly. 'Joe is sweet on her.' He winked at Stevie.

Stevie blushed and shook her head in denial.

Jeannie's eyes narrowed as she regarded Stevie in much the same way a snake sizes up its prey before it strikes.

'I hope you didn't take Joe too seriously tonight,' said Jeannie. The smile on her face did little to hide the venom in her voice. 'He does that very same thing at every performance. He calls it musical intercourse.'

Stevie's eyes widened in disbelief. She looked around the table, waiting for one of them to deny what Jeannie had just told her. But neither Dave, or Brad or Allen Lee could look her in the eye.

Only Richie with his guileless face was truthful with her. 'It's true, Stevie. It *is* part of our regular routine, but Joe picked out that song especially for you. Usually we do something else.'

Now, all the eyes that wouldn't meet hers a few minutes ago were staring at her. Just then there came a blast of music from the ancient jukebox and Joe ambled back toward the table.

'Joe,' Jeannie began in a voice that was deceptively sweet, 'I was just telling Stevie how – '

'– good the local production crew was. It's not often that we get help of that caliber,' finished Richie smoothly. The look he gave Jeannie was threatening. 'Isn't that right, Jeannie?'

Jeannie's lips formed a thin, angry line, but she refused to answer. The look on her face said that she had no intentions of doing anything that would benefit Stevie.

To fill the sudden void, Allen Lee began to recount an incident that happened backstage before the concert. No one at the table mentioned what had just been revealed.

CHAPTER 13

The later the evening grew, the more boisterous the group became. 'How about it, Stevie? Are you ready for another night on the town?' asked Brad.

'Not me, guys. Tonight I'm calling it quits early. As a matter of fact, if anyone is headed toward the hotel, you can drop me off.'

'It's on our way,' volunteered Dave.

'I'll take you back, Stevie,' said Joe quietly from across the table.

'You don't have to do that, Joe,' answered Stevie, anxious to avoid being alone with him. 'I can ride with the guys.'

'I thought we were going out tonight,' said Jeannie petulantly to Joe.

Turning toward Jeannie, Joe cursed inwardly. Ever since Stevie joined them on tour, Jeannie tried even harder to give the appearance of being a twosome. He had said nothing about them going anywhere except to dinner, as a group, after the show. To Jeannie he said, 'You go on without me. There's no reason why you have to cut your evening short. Just remember, we leave early tomorrow

151

morning for Atlanta. I'm calling it a night. C'mon, Stevie.'

Stevie hesitated, not wanting to go with him. 'Really,' she said as she stood. 'That's not necessary. Don't let me interrupt your plans with Jeannie. I can go with . . .' But Joe already had a firm grip on her arm and was guiding her to the door.

'What's going on, Stevie? What happened to change your mind about tonight?' asked Joe as he drove out of the restaurant parking lot and turned on to the dark, tree-lined road that would take them over the bridge across the bay toward the beach and their hotel.

'Nothing happened. I suppose I was overwhelmed. I was caught up in the excitement of the concert.'

Joe glanced over at her, knowing that she was hiding the real reason. But her expression, which was momentarily reflected in the headlights of an oncoming car, revealed nothing.

They drove the rest of the way to the hotel in silence. Pulling into the brightly lit circular drive, Joe turned the car over the the parking attendant. Stevie had started up the steps toward the entrance when Joe caught her by the hand. 'Come with me,' he said, pulling her toward him.

When she didn't protest he lead her away from the hotel, across the road toward the beach. 'Take your shoes off,' he ordered when they had reached the walkway that ran along the beach. 'We can leave them here until we're ready to go back.'

Stevie complied, and they began to walk side by side, not touching. 'I'm used to snow this time of year. It seems strange to know that it's December and I'm barefooted on the beach.'

Under their feet, the sand was soft and still warm. Overhead the moon was full and the water was a sparkling, inky black. The sound of the tide as it gently lapped against the sand was calm and soothing.

'Now tell me what changed things tonight, Stevie. Neither one of us imagined what happened to us during the show.'

The moonlight cast a glow on her face, giving her skin the translucent look of porcelain. She took a deep breath, intent on sticking to her story. 'Now that I've had some time, I realize that tonight was all make-believe.' The words were soft, almost distant, as if she were voicing her thoughts aloud and not speaking to Joe.

'It was more than that, Stevie.'

She sighed. He wasn't buying her excuse. 'How did it feel, Joe, after the concert? You said you would tell me about it.' It was an attempt to side-step his question.

Okay, sweetheart, I'll play the game your way, at least for now. 'It was wonderful, but it only lasts for a short while. It's the same high I feel when I'm performing, then it fades. It sounds strange, but right after a performance a kind of depression sets in.'

'I can believe that,' said Stevie.

He took her hand. She knew he wanted to make love to her, but after learning that his song tonight, which had been so special to her, was just part of the show, she was more determined than ever to stay away from him.

They hadn't gone more than a dozen yards when Joe, still holding her hand, stopped. Stevie turned to face him. 'It wasn't make-believe, Stevie. There is magic between us. I wanted to deny it, to deny there was anything between us, but I couldn't. That's why I came back to Denver for you.' Joe had moved closer to Stevie, and now he released her hand and took her face between both of his hands.

With the tips of his thumbs, he caressed her face, then brushed his lips slowly, gently across hers. Around them the air was suddenly heavy and still. When her lips parted to meet his kiss, he slid his hands down her shoulders and arms to her waist. Within seconds she could feel his touch, his warm sensuous hands caressing her back under her blouse. It took all her willpower to place her hands between them and stop what would surely follow. It took so much strength to say no to him. With a simple kiss he drugged her senses and commanded her passions to follow his lead.

'I . . . I can't do this, Joe.'

Reluctantly, he let her go, knowing that she was right. He had no right to want Stevie as much as he did.

She turned away from him and began retracing their steps along the beach until she came to where they had left their shoes. She reached down and picked them up and started back across the deserted street. Joe followed.

Inside the hotel they rode the elevator in silence. When they came to Joe's room, he opened the door, hoping that she would change her mind and stay with him.

'I meant what I said earlier,' said Stevie, as she turned toward him, tilting her head back as she rested against the door jamb, waiting for his reaction.

He propped his hand against the wall behind her and studied her for a long moment without speaking.

'I'll see you in the morning,' she said as she turned away, unable to bear his scrutiny any longer, but before she had taken a step Joe straightened, reached for her arm and pulled her around to face him.

His voice was low when he spoke. His lips formed a hard straight line as his eyes searched hers. 'Why do things have to be so complicated between us? I thought . . .'

'I know what you thought, Joe, but you were wrong. Just like I was wrong when I assumed that the song you sang tonight was meant for me.'

'It was,' he said quickly.

'Oh, I'm sure it was. Just because I happened to be in the audience. But if I hadn't been there, you would have sang to someone else. It's part of the act.'

'I see. Who told you that?' he asked quietly as he reached out with his fingertips to gently touch her face. His eyes searched hers.

'It doesn't matter,' answered Stevie, turning her face away from his caress. 'It's true, isn't it?'

'It's true that we always do a song like that, and I always introduce it like that,' answered Joe, 'but that song was for you, Stevie. No one else.' His eyes narrowed. 'Something special happened between us tonight.'

It did, for a while. Stevie averted her eyes, unable to stand his intensity. 'It was a lovely song, Joe, but it didn't change anything between us. One of these mornings you would leave me again, in another hotel with another note and enough money to get home. And for you it would be like that song tonight – just a part of the act.' Stevie took a deep breath and pulled her arm out of his grasp and turned toward her room three doors away. 'I couldn't stand it.'

He was still standing in the hall where she left him when he heard the door to her room click shut. Inside his room, Joe sat wearily on the side of the bed and pulled his boots off.

Damn. He laid back, his hands behind his head, his mind crowded with unwelcome thoughts. Tonight he had poured his heart into that song. Surely Stevie had to know that. But that wasn't enough for her. He knew she wanted more. *I can't give her what she wants. I should send her home and let her find somebody else.*

During the night, his disturbing dreams returned. For the first time in several years, Joe saw Kathy standing before him just like she had the night of the accident, laughing at him, taunting him, telling him once more that he would always belong to her, that she would never let him go.

Joe woke suddenly, drenched in perspiration, overcome with guilt. Wearily he sat up, then stood and crossed the room. With a thrashing motion he pushed back the heavy draperies that covered the French doors that led to the balcony. Outside the full moon floated in the sky, casting an eerie glow in the room. Inside, his heart strained to be set free.

Stevie slept fitfully. Rising early the following morning, she showered, dressed, packed her things and went downstairs to fax her column to Harry. Tomorrow the first segment of her on-the-road experience with Joe Devlin and his band would appear in the paper.

156

An hour later aboard the customized bus the group used for touring, Stevie marveled at the interior. It was an excellent example of space planning. It was also a rolling hotel with a kitchen, bath with shower, fold-down beds, television and comfortable lounge chairs.

She plopped in one of the chairs, interested only in getting some sleep. Later she would interview each of the band members. As the countryside rolled by, she was lulled to sleep by the rocking and swaying motion of the big silver bus. It was only when they stopped for lunch somewhere in Alabama that Stevie woke up.

'C'mon, Miss Stevie, we're going for some more of that good Southern cooking that you love so much. Have you ever tasted country-fried steak?' asked Allen Lee.

'No,' she groaned, 'but I bet I'm about to, right?'

'Right,' Allen Lee said as he led the way toward the front of the bus, then stepped down and held his hand out to Stevie.

'Doesn't anyone down here know how to make a great big fresh salad?' Stevie asked when they were seated inside the restaurant.

'Of course they do, but that's for the ladies' garden club meeting. This is real food. Manly food,' explained Allen Lee.

'Substantial,' added Brad.

'Sticks to the ribs.' This was from Dave.

'Okay, okay. I get it, guys,' she said, laughing.

Joe watched from his place across the table when her order was placed before her. A variety of expressions crossed her face. She was first startled by the size of the heaping plate of food the waitress set before her, then dismayed by the gravy that covered everything on the plate including the mashed potatoes and finally, after the first bite, surprised at how good it was.

'You have the makin's to be a honorary Southerner, Miss Stevie,' remarked Allen Lee. 'Don't you think so, Joe?'

Amused, Joe nodded. Stevie, whether she knew it or not, had wrapped the entire band around her little finger. Even Richie was crazy about her. The only one not captivated by Stevie's natural charm was Jeannie, and the more attention Stevie got, the more biting Jeannie's sarcasm.

After lunch they boarded the bus and continued the trip to Atlanta. For the most part the group was quiet as the late afternoon light faded into darkness. Several miles from the exit to the hotel, Richie pointed out a carnival. From the highway they could see the rides and the lights.

'If you've seen one carnival, you've seen them all.' remarked Jeannie. 'Isn't that right, Stevie?'

Stevie shrugged, not answering.

'That's not true,' replied Richie. 'They're all different. Some have better rides than others. What's your favorite ride?' he asked Stevie.

She blushed and didn't answer.

'The ferris wheel? Tilt-a-whirl?' prompted Richie.

At that moment Stevie wished she could crawl under the bus. Out of sight. 'I've never been to a carnival,' she admitted shyly.

'Never been to a carnival?' Richie echoed in amazement.

'No, never,' said Stevie.

'Not even when you were a kid?' he persisted.

She shook her head.

'Okay, Rich, quit badgering Stevie,' Joe ordered teasingly. 'There are lots of people who have never been to a carnival.'

'How about the circus? Ever been to one?' asked Brad curiously.

'Nope,' Stevie answered with a lopsided grin. 'But I've been to the symphony, and I've seen a couple of Broadway plays that came to Denver. And I saw the Pope when he was there. Does that count?'

'That's grown-up stuff. That doesn't count,' Brad decided.

Stevie was thankful when the big sleek bus pulled into the parking lot of the hotel where they would be staying.

Several hours later they all met in the lobby to go to dinner. 'Go on without us, Stevie and I have plans,' Joe said.

Stevie was as bewildered as the rest of them at Joe's announcement. They had no plans that she knew of. 'Come on,' he said as he took her arm and led her through the lobby to a waiting car, leaving Jeannie and the four men to fend for themselves for the evening.

'Where are we going?'

'You'll see.'

After a few wrong turns, Joe pulled into a dirt parking lot.

Stevie didn't move for a moment. Ahead she could see the bright colorful lights of the ferris wheel as it went round and round.

'Well,' said Joe as he came around the car and opened the door for her. 'Don't you want to get out?'

Outside the car she stood as if transfixed, listening to the sounds of the crowd.

'I've never been to a carnival,' she announced excitedly, as if the scene on the bus earlier had never taken place.

'I know,' Joe said with an understanding smile. Reaching for her hand, he lead her through the cool night air toward the entrance.

Inside the gates, crowds milled about them in all directions. Stevie's senses were at once overwhelmed. From all directions came the sounds of music and laughter and shrieks along with the smells of popcorn, peanuts and cotton candy. Her eyes danced with the reflections of lights. She paused, holding tightly to Joe's hand, not knowing which direction to turn.

'What do you want to do first?' asked Joe.

'Ride something, anything. The ferris wheel,' she said excitedly.

A few minutes later, they sat at the top of the wheel, moving slowly downward every few minutes as the ride stopped to let people off and on. Stevie threw both hands in the air. 'Here we are, Joe, sitting side-by-side on top of the world.' Her smile shined as bright as the lights around them.

'That's what so great about carnivals, Stevie. It's make-believe, and for a little while all you have to do is have fun.' When the ferris wheel started its full rotation, picking up speed as it went, Stevie screamed and clutched at Joe's arm.

160

'This is wonderful,' she shouted. It was something she would say again and again as they moved from ride to ride.

Next came the tilt-a-whirl, followed by the bumper cars, where Stevie's car got hit from all sides, time after time, by all the other cars, including Joe's, because she was laughing so hard she failed to maneuver out of the way of the others.

After that came the more sedate carousel, with its ornately carved and festooned animals. Stevie chose a prancing steed with his head thrown back, his nostrils flaring and his front hooves frozen in mid-air as if he might suddenly break away from his circular platform and gallop through the crowd, only to disappear into night. Joe's horse, which pranced next to Stevie's, appeared to be far more satisfied with his role in life. The music was a Viennese waltz, romantic, lilting and lovely, and Stevie was thoroughly captivated by the old-fashioned charm of the carousel.

In the fun house Joe deliberately tormented her by disappearing whenever possible, and reappearing only after she would scream his name. She was both fascinated and fearful of the fun house with its deceiving mirrors that altered not only her size, but her sense of direction, and maze-like walkways that lead to nowhere. When the the tour of the fun house ended at a doorway two-stories off the ground, with the only method of exiting being a giant slide, Stevie balked, afraid of the height.

'I'll go first and I'll be at the bottom to catch you,' Joe promised.

'I don't trust you,' she said warily.

161

'Okay, you go first and when you hit the ground, I'll come down right behind you.'

'But I'm afraid to go by myself,' she confessed, grabbing his arm.

In the end they went down the slide in tandem, with Stevie screaming and Joe laughing all the way.

'Now let's go ride the roller coaster,' he suggested once they were on the ground. Stevie, whose heart was still beating rapidly from her last experience, looked over toward the roller coaster as the chain of cars came roaring by with shrieking passengers, then shook her head. 'Something more sedate, please.'

On the midway, they stopped for cotton candy. After some deliberation, Stevie chose pink. Then they wandered past the rows of booths where carnival barkers called out to them, hoping to entice them to join them in a game of chance.

Joe draped his arm around Stevie's shoulders and pulled her close as they walked side-by-side. 'How about a souvenir?' he asked. 'Something to remember your first carnival?'

'Right here, little lady,' sang the barker. When Stevie smiled and turned his way, he stepped up his pitch. 'This adorable little teddy bear is waiting for for you to take him home.' In the air he waved a small brown bear with a blue polka dot ribbon around his neck. 'Just have your boyfriend here hit the target three times. That's all, three balls, and he's yours. You can do that, can't you? If you can't, sir, I bet the little lady here can. Looks to me like she has a mean right arm!'

They laughed and Joe stepped forward, placing his money on the counter. It took more tries and money than the prize was worth, but Joe finally won the little brown bear. He was determined that Stevie should have something special to remember tonight.

She hugged the bear to her, impulsively reaching up to give Joe a quick kiss.

'What was that for?' he asked, clearly pleased at her actions.

'That was to say thank you for bringing me here, Joe. It's been a wonderful night. I'll never forget this.'

He looked down at Stevie, memorizing the happiness he saw in her eyes, the sweet smile that turned up the corners of her lips, and her pleasure in having the little bear he had won for her. Tonight she had succeeded in making him feel young and carefree once more.

'Well, what do you think?' he asked as they continued down the midway.

'I think I've had a grand adventure,' Stevie sighed. 'And you were so right, Joe. It's such a magical thing.'

When they arrived back at the hotel, Joe reluctantly left her at the door to her room. He wanted to tell her that this magical night didn't have to end just yet. But in his heart he knew the magic would disappear in the harsh light of morning, when he would have to face reality.

In her room, Stevie hugged the little bear tightly. Tonight had been wonderful, something she would never forget. So many times as a child, she had asked her mother to take her to the carnival, but Carole never seemed to have the time. Finally, she had stopped asking.

Until they had seen the lights from the highway, she had almost forgotten about things like carnivals and circuses. The business of being an adult always seemed to be so much more important than any unfulfilled childhood wishes. But tonight, Joe had known how special things like that could be, and she wished that the magic could have gone on forever. But she was wiser now, knowing that her time with him could only be measured in memories.

CHAPTER 14

The next day was filled with preparations for the concert that night. Stevie now knew what to expect, and for the most part she stayed out of everyone's way, making notes and jotting down ideas for another column. What she needed was a fresh approach to tonight's performance.

'Stevie, I want you with me backstage,' Joe said that night when they arrived at the auditorium.

'Really, Joe,' Jeannie protested as she came down the corridor behind him, the jingling of her bracelets announcing her approach. 'You need time to get ready without distractions and interruptions.' She turned and glared at Stevie, leaving no doubt as to whom she considered the purveyor of both. Then she turned back to Joe with an expression that was full of concern, anxious to see his reaction to her suggestion.

Stevie jumped in, quickly agreeing with Jeannie, surprising everyone. 'Jeannie's right, you know. I'm sure this time is important to you. I'm going out front to interview the fans,' she announced, gathering her things. 'Kind of a "man on the street" approach. I'd like to find out who they are, what they think, and try to gauge their enthusiasm as well as their expectations for tonight's concert. It should make a good column.'

'How innovative of you,' muttered Jeannie, her disdain for both the idea and its originator barely concealed.

After Stevie left, Jeannie followed Joe to his dressing room. Perched on the edge of the dressing table, she ran her hands through her unruly red hair, pulling it back off her face. 'Just exactly how long is this going to continue, Joe?' she asked.

'What?' asked Joe, guessing that she was referring to Stevie and her presence on the tour.

Jeannie sighed. 'Well, I could say this exclusive press coverage, but I'm talking about Stevie Parker and you know it. How much longer are we going to have to put up with her? She has disrupted everything, and every time I turn around the two of you have disappeared somewhere by yourselves. Not only has she made a shambles of the schedule I had so carefully worked out for us, she has everyone drooling after her. Especially you.'

'And therein lies the problem,' observed Joe with a wry smile.

'Damn right. This whole tour is a mess, Joe, and all I want to know is how much longer do I have to put up with her?'

'Until I decide to send her back.'

Jeannie opened her mouth to comment, but Joe held up his hand to stop her. 'You have a choice, you know. Tomorrow you can hop a flight back to Nashville. I'm sure Lorraine has some things that require your attention. It was your idea to come along on this tour,

Jeannie, but it's obvious that Stevie's presence is upsetting to you.'

'Of course, it is, but . . .'

'But it's upsetting to you for the wrong reasons,' he concluded.' It's not the schedule, it's Stevie herself that you are jealous of. You and I have nothing going on between us, Jeannie. You know that. I've been very candid with you about maintaining a level of professionalism in our working relationship. And that's all there is. My relationship with Stevie and how I spend my time is my business. Now, I'll leave this decision to you. You can go along with this arrangement, or you can leave tomorrow.'

Jeannie started to protest, but Joe's statement left no room for argument.

'Stevie will be with us until we head home for Christmas,' he continued. 'That was the agreement I made with her editor. He gets an exclusive for his paper, and we get all kinds of publicity that will pay off in ticket sales when we hit Denver this summer.'

She slid off the edge of the counter and walked toward the door. Once there, she spun around. The anger she felt at having her words turned against her by Joe warred with the instincts that told her she was about to cross a line, one from which she could not retreat. She knew, if she wanted to keep this job, she would have to back down now before the situation got any worse. Without uttering a word, she turned and opened the door.

'It's really better for everyone if you go along with the way things are, Jeannie. You, me and the guys make a good team. I'd like to keep things that way,' Joe cautioned.

It took all her self-control not to slam the door behind her, but she knew she would be slamming the door on her career. 'Of course you're right, Joe. I was only upset at having my plans altered.'

'That's understandable. I'm sure you can find a way to get along with Stevie for the duration of this tour.'

Jeannie smiled outwardly, but inside she was seething. 'I'm sure I will,' she answered evenly, closing the dressing-room door behind her, Instead, she would find a way to get even. She always did.

After the performance, Stevie went backstage. Her interviews before the show had yielded some surprisingly good material. What surprised her the most was the number of middle-aged women in the audience. One woman, clearly past fifty, probably summed up the cult-like fascination with Joe Devlin better than anyone. 'He makes me believe in romance again,' she said simply.

While Stevie had been in the audience watching Joe and the band, the woman's words came to mind. How right she was about this handsome, charismatic man. He could almost make her believe in romance again, thought Stevie, except for one thing: she knew it was all an act.

After the show, she declined an invitation to dinner, deciding instead to return to the hotel. 'I'll take you back,' said Joe.

'No,' protested Stevie. 'You go ahead with everyone and have fun. I'm tired and I'm going to turn in early.'

But he insisted, and she was too tired to argue. At the hotel, he unlocked her door for her and pushed it open. 'Aren't you going to invite me in?' he asked.

'Did you think that this was an invitation? That I passed dinner up so you and I could be alone?' She looked up at him, waiting for his reply.

'No,' admitted Joe with his heart-melting smile, 'but since the opportunity has presented itself . . .'

'You decided you would take advantage of it,' she finished.

'Something like that,' he admitted.

Stevie waved him into the room with a sweep of her hand and went to sit on the bed.

'What is it you want to prove, Joe? That you can get me into bed with you again? That you can drive me out of my mind because I want you?'

'That's not bad for starters, honey.' He leaned back against the dresser, his arms crossed. In the mirror behind him was the reflection of his broad shoulders, while his long legs stretched before him.

'And what would it prove? That you're as good at seduction as you ever were, and I'm as foolish as I once was?' asked Stevie, her blue eyes wide and searching.

'It might prove we can't stay away from each other,' he concluded.

'Oh, God, you just don't get it, do you?' Stevie groaned in frustration, then fell back against the pillows. 'It wouldn't prove anything at all, Joe. Nothing. Except that I was a stupid enough to let you make love to me again. It would break my heart when you left me. But you could walk away, and maybe you would feel a little remorse, but not for long. Right?'

'It doesn't have to be that way, Stevie. We could stay together. You could be with me, travel with me.'

'And what would that make me?' she asked bitterly. 'Your live-in? Your lover? Your mistress? That's not how I see myself, Joe. I want more than that.'

Joe straightened and went to Stevie, pulling her up off the bed and into his arms. He kissed her and she could taste his urgency. When he felt her respond, felt the hunger building in her, he pulled away, holding her at arm's length. 'Think it over, Stevie,' he whispered, then suddenly turned and left the room.

Stevie spent the next afternoon informally interviewing Richie, Dave, Brad and Allen Lee. Deliberately, she avoided any contact with Joe. Jeannie stayed toward the front of the bus, out of the way, spending most of her time reading or writing letters.

When Brad sheepishly told her that he had played the trombone in his high school band, Stevie laughed, unable to visualize him in that role.

'What would you have chosen as a career if you hadn't been able to do this?'

Brad leaned back in his chair. 'You promise you won't laugh?'

Stevie nodded.

'I used to be a teacher. Sixth grade,' he confessed. 'That was my regular job until I hooked up with these guys.'

By the time Stevie had asked that same question of the other members of the band, she discovered the this was indeed a diverse group. Dave had always been a musician and had played with a number of other groups. After college, Allen Lee had supported himself by waiting tables. He was also a talented artist.

Richie had an engineering degree, and while it had never crossed Stevie's mind to ask before, she was more than a little surprised to find out that Joe had a degree in finance, and had, for quite a number of years, lead a double life. By day he had worked as an account executive for a large brokerage firm, while he spent his weekends singing in clubs.

Richie snorted. 'Clubs? Right. Add to that smoky dives and dark, out-of-the-way roadhouses, and county fairs; any place that would let us in the door. As long as we didn't have to pay *them*, we would show up.'

Anxious to talk about the good old days, Stevie was bombarded with stories of places they had been and the people they had met.

'But what was it that made the difference?' she asked, eager to know what triggered their success. 'One day you were just like a hundred other groups trying to get a break, the next day you became famous.'

'It didn't happen that way,' explained Richie, 'although we did get a break when we were selected to be the opening act for Darrell Davis. That was the beginning.'

'It was a combination of things that just seemed to fall into place,' Joe contributed from behind Stevie. 'Overnight successes are rarely that.'

'Joe's song, "Lonely Nights", was the beginning,' explained Richie. 'About that same time, people who had never before paid any attention to country music began to listen. "Lonely Nights" is a crossover song – country music that jumped to the pop charts.'

While they talked, Stevie made notes. Some of what they told her she already knew from her own research.

It was their viewpoint that made the rest of it interesting. This group honestly seemed to have a handle on their success, realizing how incredibly fortunate they had been, knowing that everywhere talented people worked and waited, sometimes for a lifetime, and sometimes in vain, for that one lucky break.

'But what is it that makes the difference?' she asked. 'Line up ten talented people. One makes it, nine don't. What is the secret ingredient? We all know that talent plays a part, naturally, but there's something else. Am I right?'

They all nodded, but it was Joe who supplied the words. 'Drive. Determination. Refusing to give up, even when everything goes against you.'

Stevie turned toward Joe and their eyes met.

'Just one of life's lessons, Stevie,' he said quietly.

In the face of her coolness toward Joe, Dave seemed to become more attentive. At first Stevie thought it was just her imagination, but now she didn't think so. Her first impulse was to discourage him, knowing it would lead nowhere. But she liked him, and maybe she was overreacting. Maybe his attention was only a gesture of friendship. Besides, she could tell that Joe found it annoying. At various times when she had been interviewing Dave, Stevie would look up, only to see a scowl on Joe's face.

They arrived in Charlotte, North Carolina, that evening. On the way up to their rooms Stevie had nothing on her mind except a hot shower. In the hallway, when Dave asked if she had plans and she said no, he invited her out for a drink. Why not, thought

Stevie. She liked Dave and a few hours out might be fun.

Over drinks at a small neighborhood bar near the hotel, Dave asked the question that had been on his mind all day. 'Tell me about you and Joe.'

Stevie hesitated, then explained truthfully, 'I'm here because I was assigned to write a series about Joe. You know, the life of a country music entertainer.'

'And?' prompted Dave.

'And he definitely is a sensation,' she concluded.

'Are you speaking professionally or personally?' Dave leaned forward now and waited to hear her answer.

Stevie had now spent enough time with each of the band members to know that beyond their long hair and the country-boy demeanor, they were all intelligent, educated and surprisingly perceptive.

'Both. I can't deny that Joe is impressive, but just for the record, if you are asking, there is nothing between Joe and me.'

The waitress set their drinks on the table. 'What about the newspaper articles you wrote, and what about when Joe dedicated that song to you?' Dave asked.

Stevie shrugged. 'Dave, I spent two days in the company of a new country music sensation and I didn't even know who he was. When I found out, the opportunity to write about it was too good to pass up. I'm a journalist. I'm always looking for a story. As for the song thing, well, you heard Jeannie the other night at dinner. It was all part of the act.'

'But you were taken in by his performance, weren't you? It was written all over your face. If Jeannie hadn't told you, you would . . .'

Stevie laughed, her face flushed with rosy color, and held up her hand. 'Stop, please, Dave. I give up. I was pretty gullible, but then, aren't all women supposed to be taken in by Joe Devlin when he sings like that?'

'I like you, Stevie. You are an honest woman.'

Not really honest, she thought, just clever at side-stepping the truth. Stevie moved the conversation to other topics, and it was only when Dave asked about her plans for Christmas that she was reminded that she would be spending another holiday alone, unless she decided to visit her mother. A sudden sadness washed over her. She always found the holidays to be a depressing time of the year.

When they finished their drinks, they walked back to the hotel. Sometime during the evening Dave had discovered that he was more interested in having Stevie as a friend than anything else. Once he had telegraphed that message to her, they had both relaxed. It was a nice feeling. Outside the door to her room Dave leaned down and kissed Stevie lightly.

Just as she turned to go into her room, she saw Joe coming down the hall. Stevie wondered if he had seen Dave kiss her? It doesn't matter, she thought, as she opened the door. He wouldn't care who kissed me.

She was tired but she wasn't sleepy. Propped up in bed, she flipped the television channels with the remote control, but nothing held her interest. Just as she was about to click it off, there was a knock at the door.

'Room Service.'

Stevie padded across the room to the door and looked though the peephole. With the chain still hooked, she opened the door a crack and said, 'There must be some mistake. I didn't order anything.'

'No, ma'am. Mr Devlin ordered this.'

Stevie felt foolish, holding a conversation through a two-inch opening. 'Oh, well, Mr Devlin's room is down the hall,' she replied.

'Yes, ma'am. But he ordered this for you, Miss Parker.'

As she glanced at her reflection in the mirrored closet doors, she knew her short white silk nightshirt was barely decent. 'Uh, could you please just set it down by the door?'

'Yes, ma'am.'

When the waiter disappeared, Stevie opened the door and stepped out into the hall. With one bare foot behind her propping the door open, she leaned down. On the tray was a bottle of champagne and two glasses. She straightened, tray in hand, balancing herself on one foot and came face to face with Joe. Stevie looked down at the tray, then up at him. Putting two and two together, she said sarcastically, 'What a coincidence, meeting like this. And I suppose you'd like to share this with me.'

He nodded, his eyes full of mischief, and for a moment Stevie's resolve to stay away from him wavered. 'Sorry,' she said finally. 'No deal.' Forgetting that her foot was holding open the door to her room, she swung around, turning her back to him. The moment she heard the click she realized that she was locked out of her room. With the tray still in her hands, she turned once more to face Joe.

An appeal for help was on the tip of her tongue, but before she could utter one word, Joe shrugged. 'Too

175

bad,' he said as he turned and ambled off toward his room.

'Joe, wait,' she called after him. 'I'm locked out.'

Joe paused, glanced back over his shoulder, his eyes traveling over Stevie, making her uncomfortably aware of her scanty attire. Then he smiled regretfully and disappeared into his room. The click of his door closing echoed in the hallway.

With the tray still in her hands, Stevie hurried down the hallway to Joe's room. She rattled the door with her bare foot. 'Joe! Let me in. Please!'

He opened the door a crack. At that moment the elevator doors opened and a couple in their late sixties turned in Stevie's direction.

Stevie quickly set the tray down on the floor. 'Will you let me in?' she hissed through the crack in the door. The couple glanced at her curiously. She turned toward them with an embarrassed shrug. 'I'm locked out,' she explained.

Through a crack in the door came Joe's voice. 'Her room is down the hall, but she keeps chasing after me. Now she wants me to let her into my room for a nightcap – she even brought the champagne,' Joe said to the passing couple as he opened the door wider. 'But it's awfully late and you can see what her intentions are just by the way she's dressed.'

Stevie glared at him while the woman grabbed her husband by the arm and hurried him toward their room. Halfway there the husband turned, smiled, and winked at Joe and Stevie.

'Now see what you've done,' said Stevie with her hands on her hips.

'What?' asked Joe innocently.

'Embarrassed me on purpose in front of those people. Now are you going to let me in or not?'

Joe lounged against the door frame, his arms crossed and looked down at her. 'That depends on why you want to come in.'

'Dammit, Joe,' Stevie said threateningly.

'Okay, okay,' he said. 'I'll let you in if you'll have that drink with me.' Before he could step aside Stevie pushed past him and marched toward the telephone and dialed the front desk.

'What about that drink?' he asked as he brought the champagne in and set it on the table.

'No thanks,' she said as she held the receiver to her ear.

'You promised,' Joe reminded her with a smile while crossing the room toward her.

'I lied,' she said as she waited for the desk to answer.

'No, you didn't.' Joe reached out and took the receiver from her hand. 'A deal is a deal. I want to talk to you.'

Stevie looked around the room as if searching for a way to escape. 'There's nothing to . . .'

'Stevie,' said Joe in a low voice. His fingertips cradled her chin and turned her face toward him. 'Tell me what's wrong? What happened between us?'

'Nothing,' she answered.

'What about the other night? At the concert, and afterwards on stage? You can't deny that something happened.'

'No, I can't.'

'And then?' he prompted.

'Then I came to my senses. I can't go anywhere with you. I can't complicate my life by becoming involved with you, Joe. It would be just like that night in Denver all over again. One morning you'd be gone and I would always wonder what I had done wrong and what was wrong with me. I've spent my entire life asking myself that question. I want a normal life. I'm looking for . . .'

'A relationship?' asked Joe. 'Commitment? Love?'

Stevie was silent for a moment. 'Never mind,' she whispered. 'It has nothing to do with you.'

'I see.' He reached out and took Stevie's hand, tugging until she sat down beside him on the bed. Joe knew exactly what Stevie wanted – marriage, a husband who would be home every night and a couple of kids. What woman didn't want that?

'No, you don't,' she answered and she wished she wasn't so close to him. The impulse to reach out and touch the hair at the nape of his neck was strong.

Joe laid back on the bed and grabbed Stevie, one arm around her waist, then rolled her over on top of him. 'Come with me, Stevie, wherever I go. Stay with me. I promise you won't regret it.'

Now his face was only inches from hers and she wanted to bury her face against his chest and forget everything except the feel and smell of him. 'Joe, please.'

'Please what? What exactly do you want me to do, Stevie?' His breath was warm against her face, his voice was low and sexy.

Please get out of my life. Please don't make me want to love you so much. But it was too late. Joe rolled her onto her back and now his full lips, only inches away from

178

hers, were too much of a temptation. Stevie felt him grow rigid against her thigh and a slow heat began to spread outward from a spot low in her abdomen. As she searched his brown eyes she saw they held a secret, but this time it was a secret they shared. Each of them knew what was about to happen.

Just as Joe slipped his hand under Stevie's silk nightshirt, there was loud knock at the door.

He swore as he rolled on his side, laying still for a moment, then stood and walked across the room.

Stevie jumped up from the bed. Why was she feeling so guilty? With both hands she tried to smooth her tangled hair, but they stilled the moment she recognized Jeannie's voice at the door. Stevie listened intently, but the voices were too low to hear what was being said.

Then Jeannie's voice grew louder. 'Is there someone with you, Joe? Is that why you won't let me in?' Then Jeannie saw Stevie's reflection in the mirror. 'Why is it you have time for her and not for me?' Now her voice was loud and angry.

'That's enough, Jeannie,' commanded Joe.

'That little bitch will cause you more trouble than you know. All she's looking for is a story, but you already know that, and what better to write about than how she was screwing Joe Devlin!'

The blood rushed to Stevie's face as she walked toward the door and deliberately rubbed herself intimately against Joe's torso. 'Hurry up, darling,' she said sweetly.

Jeannie's eyes widened at the sight of Stevie. 'Well, if this isn't getting to be a regular duo. The slut and the

179

star. I always thought you were more discriminating than this, Joe.'

'Don't say anything you might regret, Jeannie. Go on to your room.'

Jeannie's voice was laced with venom when she spoke. 'Tell me, Joe, is she just doing you, or are you sharing her with the whole band? Did you tell her that's how the sluts that chase after you usually end up?'

With one hand Joe pushed Jeannie out the door and slammed it behind her. Then he leaned back and cursed.

'I'm sorry, Stevie,' he said a few moments later as he sank down in an armchair a few feet away from the bed.

Stevie shook her head slightly as she sat on the edge of the rumpled bed, her nightshirt tucked close around her. 'I asked for it. I don't know what made me act like that. I only did it just to antagonize her. Sorry, Joe. I'm just as much at fault for provoking the situation.' Stevie stood and ran her hands down the sides of her night shirt. 'I'm going to my room.'

'No. Let's talk this thing through,' said Joe as he ran his fingers though his dark hair in a gesture of frustration. 'I can't be within two feet of you without wanting to tear your clothes off you and make love to you. I don't know what to do about it, do you, Stevie?'

Stevie shook her head.

He continued. 'You have been a thorn in my side since that day I kissed you in the airport. When things heated up between us I didn't know what to do about it, so I left. It wasn't the honorable thing to do, but I couldn't get involved. I never expected to see you again, but I couldn't get you off my mind. Then you decided to tell the world about your days and nights with Joe Devlin. I still can't believe you did that. Why, Stevie?'

Stevie looked up at the ceiling, then down at her hands. 'I wanted to get back at you. When I found out who you were, it made things even more painful. It hurt when you left me at that hotel. You paid me off, Joe, and that was the final insult.

'I was worried about you,' said Joe in his defense. 'I didn't pay you off.'

'Then why did you leave me all that money? It . . . it made the whole thing seem cheap. It made me feel dirty.'

'I'm sorry, Stevie. I was worried about you, and I didn't want to leave you without some assurance that you could get home okay.'

Stevie searched his eyes and knew that he was telling the truth. She managed to nod, afraid to trust herself to speak. Joe stood and walked toward the windows that looked out over the lights of the city. Then he turned back toward her. His voice was ragged, the words forced. 'As much as I want to, I can't give you what you want, honey.'

A hot rush of tears threatened to give her away. Her throat closed making it painful to swallow. She blinked, hoping to hide the tears. 'You don't know what I want, Joe.' It hurt to speak.

'Believe me, I do,' answered Joe soberly. 'God, I know exactly what you want. A guy who will always be there for you at night when you go to sleep and in the morning when you wake up. Someone who will take care of you and never leave you. Someone you can love,

181

that will always love you in return. That's not me, Stevie,' he whispered.

'Look at what kind of life I lead. I'm on the road constantly. Me and the guys, we live like gypsies. That's not the kind of life I could ask anyone to share. I'm withdrawing my invitation to you to go with me. But that's not all, honey. I don't have the right to ask you for anything.'

Stevie's heart skipped a beat, then there followed a heavy sadness that seemed to weigh her down.

'I can't keep you with me, Stevie, and I know that's not what you want. You want to get married, and you should. But not to me.' Inside Joe felt his guts wrench at his words. 'I'm not the guy for you, honey.' This last was barely a whisper.

Stevie stood, trying valiantly to keep her pride intact.

'Was I so obvious, Joe?' Now her eyes glistened with tears.

'No, babe. It was me. I knew what you needed right from the beginning. I'm just not it. It's why I left you in Denver, Stevie. I felt so damn guilty. I should have never made love to you.'

'Then why did you come back and insist that I go on tour with you?' she asked softly.

Because I couldn't get you off my mind, and now I'm afraid I won't be able to get you out of my heart. Out loud he replied, 'I was angry about the articles in the newspaper. I felt like I'd been duped.' Joe paused, then added, 'And I wanted you with me. It was selfish of me. I thought maybe we could at least have this time together.'

'For how long, Joe?'

He shook his head. 'I don't know, honey.' Joe cursed the hand that fate had dealt him.

'And when it was over?'

'I would send you away.'

Stevie nodded as if to affirm something she had known all along. Then she reached for the phone and dialed the front desk. She drew a deep breath then said in an unsteady voice, 'This is Stevie Parker in 412. I've locked myself out of my room. Could you please send someone up right away to let me in?'

At the doorway she turned. Her heart felt like it would burst from the pain. *Say something, Joe. Tell me not to go. Tell me you love me*. Stevie wanted to be able to tell Joe that it was okay, that she understood, that it was preposterous to think that someone as famous as he would love a nobody like her. Most of all she wanted to tell him that she could settle for whatever time they could spend together. But the truth was, she couldn't stand the thought of having him leave her.

'I have to go now,' she said with quiet dignity. *Before I tell you that I love you with all my heart and soul*. Dimly she heard the door click behind her as she pulled it shut. It was as if she had closed a chapter in her life.

Numbly she moved down the hall toward her room. Within minutes someone from housekeeping appeared and unlocked the door for her. A few minutes later Stevie crawled into bed, cold and shivering. She would survive. She knew she would, but just for tonight she would give into all the hurt she felt. With her knees pulled up against her chest, she curled into a ball. Slowly, like bright glistening crystals, tears spilled from her blue eyes and ran slowly down her cheeks and into her hair.

In his room Joe cursed himself for handling things so poorly. He hadn't meant to hurt her like that. *My God, the look on her face!* It would haunt him for a long, long time.

Damn. Why couldn't she be like all those other women who just wanted to have a good time while they could, then move on to someone else?

Joe grabbed his jacket off the back of the chair and slung it over his shoulder. From the nightstand he picked up the keys to his rental car and switched off the lights. He needed a drink and some noise. Anything that would keep him from seeing the look on Stevie's face.

Outside the night air was cold and damp, the wind biting. But Joe didn't feel any of those things as he got into the car and drove away, wanting to put as much distance as possible between him and Stevie.

CHAPTER 15

Daylight followed a sleepless night, and for Stevie the arrival of morning did not make things better. How could she continue to travel with Joe with the way things were? She showered and dressed slowly as she wrestled with her troubled thoughts. Finally, when she could stand it no longer, she dialed Harry's office.

'I'm coming back,' she said flatly when he answered.

'Stevie, you can't. The response to this feature has been terrific. Newsstand sales are on the rise. You can't stop now.'

'I have to, Harry. It's . . .' She hesitated, not knowing exactly what to say. Then she took a deep breath. 'It's more than I can handle.'

'The assignment? The traveling? What is it?' he asked.

Stevie held the receiver away from her ear. How could she answer Harry without telling him the truth? 'I'm not feeling well.'

'Aw, Stevie, I'm really sorry, but it will pass. You'll feel better tomorrow. Can't you at least stick this out a few more days?' On the other end of the line Harry

Conklin ran his bony fingers through his thinning salt-and-pepper hair, adjusted his glasses higher on the bridge of his nose, and muttered something about loyalty.

'Harry, don't you dare try and make me feel guilty over this. You're the one who set this whole thing in motion, and you're not out of trouble yet,' warned Stevie.

'Just a few more days, Stevie, until the end of the week. You'll be coming home soon for Christmas.'

Her anger at Harry's actions had faded days ago and Stevie knew she would try to do what he asked. If it hadn't been for him, she wouldn't have this job.

When Harry had hired her as a staff writer he had taken a chance. Over the years he had interviewed so many young journalism graduates who were searching for the glamour they associated with working for a major newspaper. The hard work, long hours and tedious assignments always surprised them. Most of them couldn't hack it.

At the interview Harry was sure that Stevie Parker had always dreamed of being like Lois Lane, dashing from one story to another. It was there, in her eyes. He even understood it, having once been young and new to the business. He had even suffered from a similar malady. But he saw ambition, energy and enthusiasm there also, and her writing was good. Operating on not much more than gut instinct, he hired her. In the end he knew that was the only thing that counted.

Stevie knew that Harry had believed in her when no one else did, and because of that he would always have her loyalty. For his sake, she would try to make it through the next few days.

'Okay, Harry, I'll try,' she sighed.

The rest of the day was easy. Since the group was scheduled to appear that night, they would not be traveling again until tomorrow morning. All Stevie had to do to avoid Joe was to stay in her room. Later, as she read over her notes from the previous day, she decided she had enough information from the interviews she did on the bus with the band to do a feature on them. It would provide her with her next day's column.

The ring of the phone startled her. She hesitated before answering it, then realized that she could not hide forever. Reluctantly, she reached for the receiver.

'Stevie, we're in the lobby waiting. Are you on your way?' asked Richie.

'I . . . uh, sorry, Richie. I should have called you.' Again she used the same excuse she had used with Harry and wished she could think of something more original. 'I'm not feeling too well. I think I'll stay here in my room and work.'

'Is there anything I can get you?' asked Richie.

'No, thanks,' replied Stevie.

Stevie managed to piece together enough information to fax back to the paper, using much of what she had gotten yesterday in her interviews. That she was able to concentrate long enough to write anything was a miracle to her. Her feelings kept getting in the way.

She wanted to run, yet she wanted to stay. She wanted to cut all ties with Joe, but how could she

187

when she wanted to be with him every minute of every day? She wanted to put him completely out of her mind and her heart, but she wondered if she would ever feel this way about anyone again. How, she pondered, could love inspire such inconsistencies and such extremes? How would she ever survive the pain?

Late that afternoon she heard the group as they returned from rehearsal. Soon there was a tentative knock at her door. Stevie hesitated, then she was both disappointed and relieved when she opened the door to see Dave standing there. Deep down she wanted Joe to come to her and make things right between them.

'Richie said you were sick.' He was concerned.

Stevie chewed on her lower lip as she mumbled, 'Uh, not sick, exactly. I don't feel well.' Her voice trailed off. She was a lousy liar.

'Oh.' Dave hesitated, then stood there for a moment longer. Suddenly his face turned red. He was obviously embarrassed now and it took Stevie a moment to realize exactly how he had misinterpreted what she had just said.

She stammered as she realized that her words had caused him to believe that her problems were of the monthly female variety. Quickly she protested, 'Oh, no, Dave. You don't understand. It's not that . . . not what you think. It's nothing,' she finished lamely.

He stood there for a moment, embarrassed at his mistake, then he said awkwardly, 'Well, okay. I'll see you later, Stevie.'

Blushing, Stevie nodded and closed the door. Without a doubt, every member of the band would now think that she was suffering from cramps. It was all she could do to keep from banging her head against the door in frustration. She paced the room for a while, then grabbed a magazine. Forcing herself to relax, she laid across the bed, hoping to read until dinner.

It was dark in the room when a loud knock sounded at the door. Stevie squinted at her watch, but it was too dark to read the dial on her watch. Disoriented, she made her way to the door and opened it slightly.

'I've been calling you for the past half-hour,' said Joe irritably as he pushed the door open and walked across the room and switched on the light. 'Why didn't you answer?'

Stevie, still groggy, shook her head. 'I didn't hear the phone ring. What time it is?'

'It's a little past midnight. I hurried back to the hotel after the show to see about you.' answered Joe. 'How could you not hear the phone?'

Stevie shrugged. 'I'm a heavy sleeper.'

'Dave and Richie said you were ill.'

'I feel fine.'

'Stevie, you don't have to be embarrassed because you're not feeling well.'

Stevie blushed. 'Look, Joe, I know what you think, but I feel fine.'

'Dave didn't think so.'

'Dave misunderstood me,' said Stevie irritably. 'I don't have cramps or anything else wrong with me for that matter. It's not even the right time of the month.'

'Then why didn't you come to the concert tonight?' There was just the slightest inflection in his voice that hinted he might have missed her.

'I didn't want to see you.' Stevie bit her lower lip.

'Have you had any dinner?' asked Joe brusquely.

At her negative response, Joe replied, 'Neither have I. I'll order from room service.'

At this Stevie came fully awake. 'Oh, no, you don't. I don't know what you think you're doing, Joe Devlin, but I can't take any more of this. One night you tell me there can't be anything between us, that I should find someone else, and the next you're ordering room service in anticipation of a nice cozy evening together. Well, no deal. If you're looking for a quick score, you're in the wrong room. Jeannie is in room 527. I'm sure you'll be more than welcome there.'

Stevie paused for a breath and Joe took a step toward her. 'That was a cheap shot, Parker.'

'Stay away, Devlin,' she said, involuntarily stepping backward. 'Let's just keep some distance between us. Like a zillion miles.'

Joe stopped where he was and studied the expression on her face, the look in her eyes. In spite of her words, he saw the hurt reflected there. And what would be gained by pursuing her further? He already knew he was powerless to give her what she wanted. What she deserved.

He straightened suddenly and when he spoke his voice was quiet and strangely gentle. 'Don't worry, Stevie. I won't bother you again. I just came to see if you were okay.'

'I'm doing great, Joe. Really great,' she said sarcastically as she followed him to the door.

Joe paused and turned back to her. 'Did anybody ever tell you that you have a big mouth considering how small you are?'

'Lots of people,' she replied with the sharpness that was her defense. 'It's part of who I am.'

'I don't think so, Stevie,' he concluded seriously as he reached out with one hand and gently smoothed her hair away from her face then slowly moved to cup her small chin in his palm. 'I think you use it just to keep from being hurt.'

Afraid of what his touch would do to her, Stevie turned her face away, breaking the fragile intimacy of the moment. 'Well, thanks so much for sharing that bit of down-home philosophy.' Her voice was brittle.

Joe stepped back and raised his hand in a mock salute as he left the room. 'Anytime, ma'am.'

The next day things remained at an impasse. Joe and Stevie were polite whenever others were around, but they tried to avoid any situation that would place them together. By the following morning Stevie had serious doubts that she could make it through another day. She was just thankful that Jeannie had decided to return to Nashville that morning. At least she wouldn't have to endure anymore of her barbs.

By the end of the first week the tension between Joe and Stevie had escalated. As they headed north toward Virginia, it was beginning to affect everyone. Today the entire band had been irritable and short-tempered. When a silly argument between Brad and Allen Lee became heated over which teams had played in Super Bowl XVI and nearly escalated into a brawl, Joe abruptly shouted to the driver to pull over to the side of the road.

When the heaving home-on-wheels was silent and still, Joe announced that the next person who started an argument for any reason was guaranteed to become eligible to collect unemployment.

There was silence until Richie said, 'C'mon, Joe. You and Stevie are responsible for all this. Nobody can have any fun because they're afraid of saying the wrong thing. Everybody is on edge. Two days of this silent-treatment crap between the two of you is enough. It's getting on all our nerves.'

'Whatever is between Stevie and me is none of your business,' replied Joe tersely to his brother.

From her seat Stevie watched Joe anxiously.

'Besides, Stevie and I are getting along just fine. It's you guys that can't seem to get it together. Isn't that right, Stevie?' For the first time that day Joe sought Stevie out, speaking directly to her.

Stevie swallowed and nodded, and as she did so she realized that her presence was making things miserable for every one except maybe Joe. He had successfully ignored her since that night in her room in Charlotte.

When they pulled into the hotel parking lot in Richmond, relief swept through the bus. Standing and stretching, the men began collecting their things, then filed off the bus into the hotel.

Joe was about to follow them when he turned and saw Stevie still sitting in her seat. 'End of the line,' he said, nodding toward the door of the bus.

'No pun intended, I assume?' asked Stevie. This time there was no sarcasm. There was only a trace of wistfulness in her blue eyes.

Joe stood very still. His heart might tell him how much he needed Stevie, but his conscience would not let him forget that he could never have her. Then suddenly he smiled that warm, caring smile that was his trademark, the one that was capable of sending thousands of women into near frenzy night after night. 'None at all.' His voice was almost a caress.

Stevie stood. 'But it *is* the end of the line for us, isn't it, Joe?' Her question was hardly more than a whisper.

Joe held his hand out for her. Looking down, his smile faded. The laughter was gone from his brown eyes. 'I wish it could be different for us, Stevie.'

She could only nod. 'I'm leaving for Denver in the morning.'

This time Joe nodded in understanding, knowing that her departure was inevitable. 'I'll drive you to the airport.'

'No, I'll take a taxi. I don't think I can say goodbye to you.' Her voice was shaky.

As she turned and made her way toward the exit she heard him say, 'I'll miss you, Stevie.'

And I may never get over you, Joe. Slowly she walked across the parking lot toward the hotel, her head down. *Not for as long as I live.*

'Well, yippie-ky-yo-ky-yea!' said Bill Schaeffer the following Monday in an exaggerated western drawl as he tipped his imaginary Stetson. 'Howdy, ma'am.'

It was Stevie's first day back at work and she was on her way down the hall to get coffee. She was feeling fragile this morning and not at all in the mood to be teased. 'That's not funny, Bill,' she said without breaking her stride.

'Weren't you supposed to be gone another week?' he asked.

Stevie didn't answer.

From across the room, another photographer called out to her. 'Hey, Stevie! Can you do the Cotton-eyed Joe yet?'

Stevie ignored him and turned toward Harry's office. Without knocking, Stevie walked in and shut the door behind her. With both hands behind her, she gripped the door knob.

Harry looked up in surprise.

'I'm not writing another word about Joe Devlin,' she announced. 'If you try to make me, I'll quit. Have you got that, Harry? No more story. *Nada*. Nothing.' Stevie stood for a moment longer, her breath shallow, her face flushed. Then she turned and walked out of the office, closing the door behind her.

Harry leaned back in his chair and stared at the door. What was that all about?

CHAPTER 16

From Richmond the band went on to Pittsburgh. It was their last stop before Christmas. Immediately after their performance there they disbanded, with Brad heading to Nashville, Dave to Delight, Arkansas, and Allen Lee to Memphis. In January they would all meet again in Cincinnati.

An hour's drive from Atlanta, in Piney Creek, a place too small to appear on any map, Ellen and Charlie Devlin waited in anticipation of the arrival of their two sons for the Christmas holidays.

Richie and Joe had been home less than twenty-four hours when Ellen first noticed that Joe was quieter than usual. Of her five children, it was Joe, her second-born, that she worried about the most. Charlie would tell her that she was silly to worry about him. He was, after all, the most successful of all their children. But Ellen would answer that it was that very reason, plus a few others, that caused her to worry.

Joe was the most thoughtful of all her children. Even when he was growing up, he would befriend the child that no one else liked. As one of the most popular kids in school, he thought it was his responsibility to choose for his team the kid who would most likely be the last one to be picked. Once he dedicated himself to a cause, no matter how unpopular, he would always see it through.

Ellen had seen changes in him in the past and most of these could be attributed to Kathy's accident. It was as if all happiness had been stolen from him that night. During this visit home he seemed more withdrawn, as if he had something serious on his mind.

'Jeannie called earlier for Joe,' Ellen announced one morning as she tipped the coffee pot to refill Charlie's cup.

'Hmm,' answered Charlie from behind the morning paper.

'Charlie, hon, I want you to listen to me,' Ellen demanded, returning the glass container to the coffee maker. 'Jeannie is very concerned about Joe. We got to talking and she told me that he had a girl traveling with him on this last tour. Jeannie says it's bad for Joe's image; it could seriously hurt him.'

Charlie laid his paper down and lifted his cup. 'Joe is a grown man, and as far as anyone outside this family knows, he is also a single man. If he had a girl with him, then that's his business. So far he's managed his career pretty well without our help.'

'Jeannie said . . .' began Ellen.

Charlie swallowed and replaced the cup in its saucer with a clank. 'Ellen, honey, Jeannie Williams has been chasing after Joe since the day he hired her. She's bound to be a little disturbed if Joe has some girl hanging around him.' Charlie picked up his paper again and began to read.

Ellen was silent for a moment then said, 'I wonder if what Jeannie told me is true.'

Carefully Charlie folded the newspaper and set it beside his coffee, resigned to the fact that he would have to hear Ellen out before he could get back to reading the sports section.

Seeing that she had her husband's full attention, she scooted her chair closer to the kitchen table, leaned forward, then proceeded with enthusiasm. 'This girl, according to Jeannie, works for a newspaper. Jeannie says that she either tape records or writes down everything that Joe and the rest of the band says and does,' said Ellen, warming to her subject. 'And she's writing an exposé about what they do out on the road. That could ruin Joe's reputation.'

'How?' asked Charlie, genuinely interested. He had never cared much for Jeannie, but this could be interesting, now that she might have some competition. It was obvious to everyone, except maybe for Joe, that Jeannie was out to ensnare him and his money for herself.

'Well, you know, Joe is so clean-cut, the thought of him hanging out with some girl who's common as dirt . . .' Ellen shook her head.

'How do you know that?' asked Charlie.

Ellen halted, giving him a quizzical look. 'What?'

'That she's common as dirt?'

'Well, just look what she's doing, Charlie, traveling with a bunch of men all over the countryside. It's scandalous, and I plan to talk to Joe about this.'

Charlie turned his face away to hide his smile. Ellen had a blind spot when it came to her children. When she had first found out about about groupies, she was horrified. Camp followers, she had promptly called them, then she made Joe and Richie promise that they would never take up with those kind of women. And to this day, she would have sworn on a stack of Bibles that they never had.

Charlie, on the other hand, knew better. It might not be a regular thing, but Joe and Richie were human. It happened. Without conferring, Charlie and Ellen each made a mental note to ask Joe more about this girl.

On Christmas Eve afternoon, Ellen was busy preparing dinner for that night when Joe appeared in the kitchen, his arms full of packages. The smell of baking ham basted with brown sugar and covered with pineapple was enough to remind him that he had skipped lunch that day. After setting his gifts on the big round oak table, he opened the oven to check out its contents.

'Get out of there, Joe,' scolded his mother gently.

'How long before it's ready, Mom?'

'Not until all the family is here. Find something else to eat.' Joe grabbed a piece of pie from the refrigerator and took it to the table.

'When you finish, there are plenty of things that need to be done between now and dinner.'

'I know,' replied Joe. 'Look at all this stuff. I hate wrapping gifts and I know you're too busy. Do you think Connie will help me?' Connie, at twenty, was the baby of the family and still in college.

'You'll have to ask her, honey. If all else fails, try bribery. Connie is always broke.'

Trying her best to appear casual as she wiped her hands on a dish towel, Ellen then smoothed her light brown hair off her forehead with her wrist and said,

'You haven't said much about the tour this time. Did you have any problems?'

Joe looked up in surprise. His mother hardly ever questioned him about his career, except to find out where he was going and make sure he and Richie promised to call at least once a week. She was proud of them, he knew that, but to her he was still her Joe, not a celebrity. His job, she would explain to her neighbors, was to entertain people. To her it wasn't much different than that of his brother Gary, who was an accountant, or his sister Grace, who was a computer programmer. They just had different talents.

'No, it was pretty routine,' he answered.

Ellen reached for a glass bowl on the top shelf of the cabinet.

'Here, let me get that for you,' said Joe as he took his plate to the counter. Reaching over his mother's head, he pulled the bowl from the shelf.

Ellen rinsed and dried it. 'Jeannie mentioned that you had a girl traveling with you for part of the time.'

Joe looked up. He expected to see a look of disapproval on his mother's face, but she was bent over now, peering into the open refrigerator, her face hidden.

'Not exactly a girl – a woman, a reporter from Denver. Old enough to go traveling on her own,' he answered.

'Hmm, weren't you just in Denver a few weeks ago?' This was from the recesses of the refrigerator.

Joe's eyes narrowed. Her act didn't fool him at all. His mother was on a search-and-destroy mission, and he could tell that once she got hold of a few facts she wasn't going to let go. 'You know I was, Mom. Look, I've got to go find Connie.' Joe stood up to leave.

'I'm not going to pry, Joey.' Ellen laughed, aware that he was on to her. 'Not like I usually do, that is. Unless, of course, you want to talk about it.'

How many times had he heard that line before? 'There's nothing to talk about,' said Joe. 'Her name is Stevie Parker and her paper sent her to write a story about us, and when she finished she went home.'

'She's not one of those camp followers, is she, Joe?'

Joe shook his head, unable to conceal his amusement at his mother's use of the old-fashioned term. 'Group-ies, Mom,' he corrected. 'That's what they call them now, and everybody has them. Even pro athletes. Especially baseball players. They even travel from city when the team travels.'

'Just like camp followers,' murmured Ellen, as if to say 'I told you so'. 'Well, you've been awfully quiet since you've been here. Does it have anything to do with this girl?'

Instead of answering his mother's question, he crossed the kitchen to her, then stooped and planted a kiss on her cheek. 'You're prying, Ma. I've got to go – last-minute stuff.' He grabbed his packages as he passed the table.

'If you don't tell me, Joe, Richie will.' Her voice came floating sweetly across the kitchen.

'Not this time, he won't,' Joe answered confidently. 'I found out that bribery works with him, too.' He was bluffing. Richie had been telling on him since he was old enough to talk. Sometimes Joe wondered why he ever let Richie be a part of the band. With him around there were no secrets from the family.

Christmas Eve and Christmas Day passed quickly enough with all of the Devlins at home. Two grandchildren, aged three and five, provided the adults with the opportunity to play Santa. It was during dinner when Joe looked around the dining room table at his family, then his brother Gary and his wife Susan and their two boys, that Joe felt a sudden sadness wash over him. Gary was thirty-four, two years older than Joe. *I should be sitting here like Gary with my wife and babies. But I'll never have that chance again.*

That night after dinner, Joe reached for the phone and dialed Stevie's number. After four rings her answering machine picked it up. The recording that instructed the caller to leave a message was brief and to the point, and when Joe heard the beep, he hung up. He had wanted to tell Stevie that he missed her, that he had wanted to hear her voice. Most of all he wanted her to know that he wished she was here beside him. But none of those things could be said to an answering machine.

It wasn't until the day after Christmas that Ellen had a chance to ask Richie about Stevie. Connie was visiting a friend and Charlie had gone to the Post Office.

'Why so interested?' Richie asked with a grin.

'Well, Jeannie said that this girl was writing stories about the band for the Denver newspaper, and Jeannie seemed to think that it wasn't going to do Joe's image any good. I was just wondering what you think?'

'Mom, I think that Jeannie has ambitions that involve wearing a diamond ring and becoming more than Joe's manager, and she's not shy about letting everyone know it. When Stevie joined the tour, Jeannie just about went into orbit.

'Just between you and me, I think that there is something between Joe and Stevie. I think he loves her and and I know that she's in love with him.'

For the first time Ellen felt a surge of hope for her troubled son. 'How do you know, Richie?'

He grinned at his mom, then wrapped his arm around her shoulders and gave her a quick hug. 'She told me. Well, not exactly word for word, but if you could see them together, you wouldn't have any doubt that she's the right girl for Joe. None at all.'

The week that followed was cold and rainy. Being indoors so much was getting on Joe's nerves and he had not been able to completely shake the melancholy feeling that had descended over him on Christmas Day, so he began to look for little projects around the house that he could do to help out. When Joe's mother suggested that he help his father fix the leak under the kitchen sink, Joe reluctantly agreed. Plumbing was not his idea of a project. More like a major repair job.

'Why don't you call John Paxton to fix this thing, Dad?' Joe knew next to nothing about fixing leaks and since his father hadn't made any progress in the last half-hour, Joe suspected he didn't either.

'John Paxton is a plumber, Joe. Do you have any idea how much money John charges these days just to walk in the front door?' Without waiting for an answer, Charlie continued. 'Bout as much as that high-priced entertainment lawyer that works for you in Nashville.'

'I'll pay for it,' offered Joe, hoping his father would admit defeat before he made the problem worse.

'You save your money, son. One of these days you might decide to settle down and not travel all the time.'

This produced a smile. His mom and dad hadn't changed at all. They were as cautious and conservative as ever, but as Joe looked around the big, cozy kitchen he couldn't help but think that his parents had done okay for themselves, even with five kids to raise.

Ellen never brought up the subject of Stevie again to Joe, but Charlie did that afternoon from his prone position on the kitchen floor. He pulled his head out from beneath the kitchen cabinet and peered up at Joe. 'Have you given it any thought?'

Joe, who was seated on the floor next to the metal box of tools, looked at him blankly.

'Straightening things out, I mean,' his father explained. There was no need to ask his father what he was referring to. This was a difficult subject for Joe, and Charlie knew it. But at least twice a year one of his parents instigated a conversation like this. They always referred to it as 'straightening things out'.

'Nope,' replied Joe, hoping that this would end the conversation. But of course it wouldn't. Eventually his father would mention Kathy.

'Well, you're thirty-two, Joe. Don't want to wait too long before you settle down and start a family.' Then without missing a beat Charlie stuck his head under the sink again and continued the conversation. 'Your mother mentioned you had a girl on tour with you – from Denver, I think she said. Did you meet her when you were there?'

Joe took a deep breath and ran his hand through his dark hair. 'You are not very subtle, Dad, and neither is Mom.'

Accompanied by the sound of a pair of channel locks clanking erratically against metal pipes, Charlie ignored Joe's remark and continued. 'According to your mother, it's not a good idea to be traveling around the country with those kind of women – bad business. Next thing you know, she'll be slapping you with a paternity suit. That's what they do, Joe.' Then he muttered, 'What kind of a woman travels around the countryside with a bunch of guys anyway?'

Joe wasn't sure if he was expected to answer that question or not, but he leaned his head back against the kitchen cabinet and said with a devilish grin, 'The dangerous kind.'

Using his shoulders to push himself forward, Charlie scooted out from beneath the sink, his face flushed, his words punctuated with the silver channel locks that he held in his right hand. 'Mary Nell Roberts is still single, Joe. You could do a lot worse, you know. Nice girl, from a nice family.'

Joe liked Mary Nell. They had gone to school together, but they had never been more than friends. His dad didn't seem to understand that he could have his choice of almost any woman he wanted. Except one, he thought.

'We could ask Mary Nell over for dinner on Saturday, New Year's Eve. That is, if she isn't busy,' suggested Charlie.

'Dad, you forget. I'm not exactly in a position to think seriously about anyone, and I don't want you to ask Mary Nell over.'

Joe paused, then added, 'If you want to have someone over for dinner, ask one of those dangerous women, like the one that was on the tour with me. Mom calls them camp followers.'

'Watch out for those kind, Joe. I know all about those kind of women. Believe me, I speak from experience.' Charlie's head disappeared under the sink again.

Joe almost laughed out loud. Right now, the sight of his dad did little to lend credibility to his words. 'Aww, Dad, camp followers? You?' he began teasingly, but Charlie interrupted him, this time crawling out from beneath the sink and sitting up straight.

'Not camp followers. That's your mother's term and she got it from her grandmother, who was still living World War I long after it was over. I'm talking about dangerous women.'

When he had replaced the channel locks in the tool box, Charlie said, 'I'm serious. They're the worst kind. I ought to know. I got caught by one.'

Joe looked blank for a moment then, with an incredulous look on his face, he asked, 'Mom? You mean my mother? Hardly a dangerous woman!'

Charlie nodded, grinning. 'She was!'

Joe burst out laughing, certain his father was teasing.

'Oh, I know,' said Charlie holding up his hand as if taking an oath. 'You don't see her that way, but you know how tenacious she can be. And remember,' he said, with a grin that was so much like his son's and a lecherous expression that was almost comical, 'she wasn't always your mother.'

Charlie leaned back against the cabinet. 'We met when she was nineteen. Her folks had just moved here, and since she was the new girl in town she was kind of mysterious and aloof. I was single and twenty-four and not in any hurry to settle down, but I have to admit that she did catch my eye.

'In those days marriage was the farthest thing from my mind. I just wanted to date Ellen, but when I asked her out she turned me down. Said she knew what kind of a man I was and exactly what I was after.'

Joe wasn't one hundred percent sure, but he could have sworn his father actually blushed.

Charlie continued. 'Finally, we went to a dance together and I really fell for her, but she wouldn't have anything to do with me after that. Kind of strange, though, now that I look back. I kept running into her every place I went.'

With a grin Charlie said, 'I tell you, Joe, it about drove me wild. Every place I went, there she was. Just as pretty as you please, smiling and ladylike on the outside, and conniving and devilish on the inside. Ellen was a dangerous woman and I *knew* it. I knew she wanted to get married, that she was just playing hard to get, and she knew I had no intention of getting serious.'

'What changed your mind?' asked Joe curiously. For the first time he could actually envision his father and mother as they must have been when they were young, as people, not just parents.

'Well, it was as plain as the nose on your face that she was more than a little interested in me. And it was just as plain that I wasn't going to get anywhere with her, at least not where I wanted to be.' Charlie rolled his eyes. 'So six months later I married her.'

Joe laughed heartily.

'Now, about that dangerous woman from Denver,' said Charlie with a chuckle. 'Maybe your mama ought to call her and invite her for dinner Saturday night. Richie says . . .' What Richie had told his parents was that he thought Joe was in love with Stevie, but was too stubborn to do anything about it.

Joe stood up. 'Richie has a big mouth, Dad, and if you haven't finished fixing that leak in an hour I'm calling John Paxton to come over.'

Charlie got to his feet. His voice was earnest now. 'Joe, you know your mom and I only want you to be happy.'

'I know, but this is my life, Dad.'

'Then live it to the fullest, son. In spite of all your success, you're still living under the shadow of what happened to Kathy. Don't continue to live a lie, Joe. What happened was not your fault, and you cannot spend the rest of your life feeling guilty over it.'

Joe squeezed his eyes shut in pain at the mention of Kathy's name. For seven long years he had carried his burden of guilt. 'I don't want to talk about this now,' Joe said tersely.

Charlie rested his hand on his son's shoulder. 'I know, but Richie says . . .'

'Dammit, I don't care what Richie says and neither should you,' snapped Joe.

Charlie could feel the tension in his son's shoulders. 'Sit down for a moment, Joey,' he said, unconsciously using the childhood endearment and the same tone he used when Joe was little and someone or something had hurt him. 'You can't let what happened with Kathy interfere with your chance for happiness. You can't change the past, and it was not your fault, Joe.

'Now Richie says . . .' began Charlie, then held up his hand to silence Joe before he could protest. 'Richie says this girl from Denver is very special.'

Joe stood and walked toward the kitchen door. 'She is,' he said quietly.

'But Kathy still has control of you, doesn't she, Joe? Even after all this time?' The question hung heavily in the air between them.

Without answering, Joe snatched his keys from the kitchen counter and went out into the gray, wet afternoon.

In spite of the the overcast sky and the cold winter temperatures, the trees were still surprisingly green. As he peered through the rain-washed windshield, the wipers beat a rhythm all their own that had nothing to do with the accelerated beat of his heart.

Why couldn't everyone just leave him alone? He didn't want to think about Kathy. But without warning the glistening scene before him vanished and was replaced by her angry face and bitter words. Helplessly, he was plunged back seven years to the night that changed his life forever.

CHAPTER 17

The set had ended and Joe had stepped outside to get away from the smell of cigarette smoke and stale beer. The Neon Rose was no better or worse than a hundred other places he had played. They all smelled the same. From the parking lot he could here the sounds of the crowd and the Allan Jackson tape that was playing while the band was on its break.

'Joe?'

He turned, startled. 'Kathy? What are you doing here?'

'I surprised you, didn't I?'

Joe sighed. 'Kathy, you can't keep following me around like this.'

'What are you hiding from me, Joe? What are you so afraid to have me find out?'

'I'm not hiding anything. Tonight I asked you if you wanted to come with me, but you said no. You shouldn't be driving around this late at night by yourself. It's dangerous.'

'Do you worry about me, Joe?'

'Kathy, I just told you . . .'

209

'Why don't you just admit that you don't love me, Joe?' She hurled the accusation at him.

Joe rubbed his hands over his eyes. 'Not now, Kathy. Please. We can talk later.' The wind sent a chill through Joe in spite of the leather jacket he was wearing. He didn't know how many more of these scenes he could handle.

Her face was taut, her deep brown eyes narrowed like dark slits in her pale skin. 'When will that be – when you get damn good and ready to come home?'

'Look, I have to get back inside. My break is over,' said Joe. 'Now come on inside with me or go on home. It's too cold for you to be out here.' Since this was the only place he had been hired to perform in several weeks, he couldn't afford to mess up. It wasn't Nashville, not yet, but right now it would have to do.

The blinking sign that spelled The Neon Rose cast a sickly pink glow over the puddles of water that were scattered across the parking lot, testimonials to an earlier rain. Kathy reached into the pocket of her jacket and drew out a pack of cigarettes. The wind whipped strands of her long, dark hair across her face as she tried to strike a match.

'Here,' Joe said, taking the cigarette and matches from her and hunching his shoulders against the wind to light the cigarette for her.

'I want you to come home with me now,' demanded Kathy as she took the lit cigarette back from him and inhaled deeply.

'Don't ask me to do that. You know how much this job means to me. I'll be through here in another hour, then I'll be home.'

Without warning Kathy began to scream at him. 'You won't, you won't! You'll be with some other woman! I know it!'

'Kathy. Kathy, please don't do this,' pleaded Joe.

'Don't lie to me, Joe. I know you're cheating on me.'

Joe shook his head and looked over his shoulder to see if anyone had overheard them. 'I've never cheated on you, Kathy. Why do you say these things?'

She was sobbing now. 'You're lying again. If you aren't lying, then tell me why you never say you love me?'

Joe winced at her question. That part was true. He didn't love her, but he had done his best to conceal it. He had seen Kathy like this before and usually he was able to calm her down, reassure her. But she was getting worse. Her charges were unwarranted and her behavior irrational. Any chance the marriage might have had had long ago been destroyed.

They had met when he was playing at a club she and her friends frequented on the outskirts of Knoxville. It had been on a break much like this that she had followed him outside. In the space of that fifteen minutes, Kathy Harrison had decided that she wanted Joe Devlin. That had been a year ago.

Shortly after that she began to show up at every club he played. She made it clear that she was there only because of him. She was beautiful, desirable and available. It was a combination that Joe found impossible to resist. A month later she began traveling with him, and when Kathy had told him she was pregnant, they were married.

Immediately after the wedding she began to change, her behavior becoming more and more erratic. She was insanely jealous and her accusations bordered on the bizarre. At first it was only accusations, but then she had taken to following Joe everywhere, certain that he was meeting other women. For the first few months, Joe attributed all this to the fact that she was pregnant, and that these outbursts were due to the hormonal changes in her body.

They had been married three months when it soon became obvious than her condition was caused by something far more serious than pregnancy. On the night he had come home to their apartment and found her hysterical, Joe knew that Kathy was seriously ill. He begged her to get help. He would go with her, he promised. She refused, screaming that he was the one who was making her crazy.

'Please, Kathy,' he had pleaded. 'If you don't want to do this for yourself, do it for the sake of our baby!'

She laughed then, an eerie, mocking sound he had never forgotten. Then her voice was low. 'There is no baby.'

He felt like a knife had sliced through his heart. He searched her tear-stained face. She is truly ill, he thought, and she was lying about the baby just to hurt him.

He reached out and gently began to smooth her damp hair away from her temples. 'Don't hurt our baby, Kathy,' he pleaded in a controlled voice. 'Let me take you to see the doctor. We can get help; we'll work though this thing together. I promise.'

She had looked up at him then, her dark eyes flat and void as if nothing lay behind them. The hysteria was gone, had disappeared so quickly he might almost believe it was something he had only imagined. When she had spoken, it was with an expressionless calm. 'I shouldn't have told you, Joe. I should have let you go on believing there was a baby. I'm not pregnant. I never was.'

'But why . . .?' he began, then swallowed down the hurt that threatened to overwhelm him. 'Why did you tell me that you were going to have a baby?'

'Because I knew it was the only way I was ever going to get you to marry me.' Her voice was filled with despair.

Joe had always thought that the truth had a special sound, a ring all its own, and once the words were spoken they seemed to hang in the air with an unmistakable clarity. At last, the truth was there between him and Kathy.

She was beautiful and sexy with her dark hair and eyes and her smoky voice. But he had never loved her. When she had told him she was pregnant, he had married her out of a sense of responsibility. Without the knowledge that she was going to have a baby, he would have never considered it.

Joe sank down next to Kathy, stunned at a lie of this magnitude, unable to fathom what kind of person would do something so ugly and deceitful. What kind of a person? His wife. And while it was true he had never loved her, he had never thought of not believing her.

Now, standing in the parking lot, Joe closed his eyes for a moment, erasing the ugly memory, then said, 'I have to go inside now, Kathy. Come in with me. You can sit close to the stage and watch me. Then when I finish we'll go home together.'

'You just want me to see the other women you sleep with,' she said bitterly.

Exhaling, Joe reached out for her, hoping to sooth her fears. 'I want you with me. No one else. Let's go inside, Kath.'

They walked a few steps, his arm around her sloped shoulders, and Joe began to breath easier. *Maybe the worst is over.*

Suddenly Kathy pulled away from his grasp and began crying hysterically. 'You'll leave me here and go off with someone else! I know how cruel you can be, and I can't stand to have you torment me any more!' She turned and ran across the wet pavement, weaving in and out between the parked cars. Joe ran after her, but before he could reach her she was already inside her car.

He grabbed for the door handle, but it was locked. Tires screeched against the pavement as she threw the car into reverse, backed out of the lot, then turned on to the dark, narrow road and sped away.

He sprinted toward his truck, ready to follow her.

From across the way, the manager of the club stuck his head out the door. 'Hey, Devlin, am I paying you to stand in the parking lot all night or come in here and entertain my customers?'

Joe stood, indecisive. Surely Kathy would go on home. Tomorrow this thing would blow over. It always did. At least until the next time. He shoved his hands in his jacket pockets and turned back toward the club.

Everything was dark when Joe left the club later and crossed the parking lot to his truck. The sign over the doorway had been turned off. He hated going home, but

214

he knew he had to. He only hoped that Kathy was asleep by now. Somehow I've got get help for her, he thought. She can't keep going like this.

There was no traffic on the deserted road and the headlights reflected the dense growth of trees on each side of him. Ahead the road curved sharply to the right and when he rounded it he was pulled from his reverie by the blue-and-red flashing lights ahead.

He slowed to a stop and as he did a state patrolman wearing an orange safety vest approached. Behind the officer Joe could see several wreckers with their yellow lights parked along the side of the road. At right angles to the wreckers were an ambulance and fire truck.

'Someone lost control going around this curve, probably because of the slick roads.' said the officer. 'Went over the side into the ravine.'

Kathy! The terrible thought came unbidden.

'What about the driver?' asked Joe, the pulse at his temple beating rapidly.

No. No, she would be home by now.

'They're bringing her up now, but they've been working to free her for about an hour. She's alive, but her injuries look serious,' replied the officer.

She was so angry when she left. Please, God, please don't let it be her.

'Say, are you all right?' asked the officer. Even in the glow of his flashlight, the officer could see that Joe was suddenly pale, his forehead beaded with sweat.

Please, God, please don't let it be her.

For a moment he leaned forward, his head resting against the rim of the steering wheel. 'What kind of car?' he managed to ask.

'Do you know the driver?' asked the officer cautiously.

Joe struggled to speak and when he did his voice was hoarse. 'My wife came this way a little over an hour ago. She was driving a white Ford.'

Just then several paramedics pushed their way through the thick brush that lined the side of the road. In the glare of his headlights Joe could see they were carrying a stretcher.

He flung the door open and scrambled from the pickup.

'Wait just a minute, sir,' the officer cautioned. But Joe pushed past him, intent on finding out if the injured driver was Kathy. He reached her just as the paramedics were loading the ambulance.

Oh, God. Oh, God.

Joe couldn't breathe. She lay there before him, covered in blood, her face illuminated by the garish flashing lights. Later, all he would recall about that moment was praying. The woman before him looked like a fragile, pretty doll that had been broken and brutally torn apart.

From a long way away he could hear someone calling him, then he felt a hand on his arm shaking him.

'Sir, is that your wife? Sir? The driver's license in her purse says her name is Katherine Devlin.'

The officer beside him repeated the question several times before Joe turned toward him, his eyes blank with shock. He nodded. 'Is she going to be all right?'

'Is this her husband?' the paramedic standing nearby asked the officer.

The officer nodded.

'Then you'd better come with us,' said the paramedic. 'Your wife's condition is critical.'

The next seventy-two hours were a nightmare. Kathy's mother arrived at the hospital, and it was evident from the way she treated Joe that she blamed him for the accident. Kathy's father and mother divorced when Kathy was only four, and no one knew where her father was. Joe's parents arrived along with Gary to be with him, and while he was grateful for their support, he felt that this was his burden to bear alone, not theirs. If it hadn't been for his selfishness, none of this would have happened. *Why couldn't he have just gone home with her when she asked?*

The news, when it came, was devastating. Kathy would live, explained the doctor, but the damage was irreparable. Because of severe injuries to the spinal cord, she was paralyzed. She would never be able to walk again. They knew that there had been injury to her brain, but it was impossible to determine how much damage had been done. The doctor didn't know whether she would ever comprehend or speak again, or be able to communicate in any way. Only intensive therapy and time would provide those answers.

Kathy's mother began to scream hysterically, refusing to take any comfort from Joe or his mother. 'You hated her!' she screamed at Joe. 'She called me almost every day to tell me how you treated her. Why didn't you just kill her instead of leaving her like this?'

Joe remembered beating the wall with his fists until his brother Gary pulled him away, then leaning against his father and mother, crying, for the injustice that

Kathy had suffered and for his helplessness in the face of it.

With effort, Joe pulled his thoughts back to the present. It had begun to rain again. He peered through the windshield anxiously, not knowing that what caused his vision to blur was not just the splattering of the rain against the glass, but also the tears that filled his eyes. With the back of his hand he swiped at his eyes, surprised. He had stopped crying over Kathy a long time ago. His constant guilt was reminder enough of what he had done.

In an effort to shake off his depression Joe forced himself to think about his plans for the coming year. A new beginning. A chance to begin a new cycle. New goals to achieve, new music to write, new songs to record. He thought about the tour that would begin soon. It would be good to get back to work.

Many times during the past week he had wanted to call Stevie, but each time he picked up the phone he realized there was nothing to be gained by dredging up those memories. She, too, was part of the past. He had nothing to offer her. But, dammit, the truth was that he still wanted Stevie with a ferociousness that alarmed him.

CHAPTER 18

At the last minute Stevie accepted Bill's invitation to go skiing in Vail on Christmas. But the day passed in a haze and she seemed to be moving in slow motion. The happy voices around her seemed too far away to be understood, sounding like so much din and hollow. Meaningless.

The town itself was decked out for the holidays with tiny shimmering white lights and huge red-ribboned evergreen wreaths everywhere. She tried her best, but she couldn't seem to get into the spirit of the day, so she was relieved when late that afternoon Bill suggested they head for home.

Stevie gave the ski rack on the back of Bill's Jeep a last check and was about to climb into the car when she heard a familiar voice behind her.

'Stevie? Is that you?'

She turned and, as she did so, she knew who she would see. 'Hello, Michael.' He hadn't changed at all. Behind his sunglasses he was still incredibly, perfectly handsome.

'You're looking well,' he said. 'Here for the holiday week?'

'No, just the day.' To Stevie her voice sounded far away, as if she was in a tunnel. This was the first time she had seen Michael since . . . well, that Christmas Eve a year ago. He hadn't changed a bit, she thought, as she took in his designer ski wear.

'How have you been, Stevie?'

She saw Bill approaching the Jeep from the driver's side and Stevie, without answering, turned to him, grateful for the diversion. 'Ready?' she asked. Then she turned back to Michael. 'Uh, I'm with a friend. The car's all loaded. Goodbye, Michael.'

'Goodbye, Stevie.' He turned and walked away. After a few steps, he turned. 'Happy New Year, Stevie.'

Stevie pretended she didn't hear him as she yanked open the door to the white four-wheel drive.

Yeah. Happy New Year.

The drive back was quiet. Most people were staying in Vail for the holiday week so the usual traffic delays on the drive back to Denver through the Eisenhower Tunnel were absent.

'Aren't you going to tell me who that was?' asked Bill after they were on the highway.

Stevie sighed. 'That was Michael Baldwin.'

'The ex-boyfriend?'

'Yes, indeed,' she answered, hoping that Bill would refrain from asking her any more questions. 'I know it was rude of me not to have introduced you, but honestly, Bill, I was anxious to get away.'

'No problem,' replied Bill with his usual good nature.

Stevie reached out and punched him playfully in the shoulder. 'Thanks, pal.'

Back in the city, the Christmas lights and decorations looked lonely and forlorn. Maybe she was destined to spend every Christmas like this. While it was true that there were worse ways to wait out the holiday, all Stevie really ever wanted was to experience a normal Christmas, spent with family over a big dinner in a house filled with love and laughter; the kind of Christmas other children seemed to have when she was growing up.

She leaned back in her seat, stretching her legs. Last Christmas she had been with Michael, at least for part of the time. Now it seemed so long ago. And for a while she had thought that with Michael her dreams of having a home and family might actually come true.

They had been seeing each other for four months, and it all seemed so right, so perfect. Along with a group of friends, she and Michael had gone to his home in Aspen for Christmas. While everyone else had been there for several days, Stevie, who had had to work, didn't arrive until the day before Christmas Eve. On the drive up, she had been excited, certain then that Michael was going to propose to her. Ah, Michael.

What a fool I was, but no bigger fool than I've been over Joe. Bad luck is all I ever seem to have when it comes to men.

In the beginning Stevie had been swept off her feet by Michael Baldwin's lavish attention. They had met at the wedding of Beth's sister, Sharon. It was a sparkling affair with three hundred guests in the ballroom of the Brown Palace Hotel. A fairy-tale wedding, and it was there that Stevie thought she had met her fairy-tale prince.

Everything about Michael was perfect: his finely sculpted aristocratic features, the blond hair that fell casually over his forehead, his natural elegance. Looking back at this meeting, Stevie acknowledged that even in the beginning, in spite of his obvious physical attributes, she was just as attracted to Michael's wealth as the man himself.

To Stevie, Michael Paul Baldwin represented everything she had ever hoped to attain, as well as her complete disdain of everything she had left behind. His attention to her was not only flattering, it was breathtaking.

'You'll hear from him,' Beth had said with confidence the day after the wedding. 'Michael couldn't keep his eyes off you, and while every other woman was gushing and clingy, you remained amazingly unimpressed. I have to hand it to you, Parker. You were damn cool.'

Stevie had blushed. While her demeanor that night wasn't exactly what Beth thought – her aloofness was actually due to an unexpected bout of shyness – it was still high praise. 'I wouldn't even know what to say to him if I did see him again.'

'Just ask him something about himself, or something about the stock market. He's a broker. They love to talk about themselves and their careers. Daddy says the Baldwins didn't need another doctor or lawyer in the family, they just needed someone to manage their millions. And that's what Michael does. He manages the family fortune as well as his own.'

'Does he have one?' Stevie had asked.

'A fortune? You bet. From his grandmother when he turned twenty-five, plus he's the sole heir to Baldwin Industries.' Beth had sighed. 'Not my type, you understand, much to my mother's dismay, but a girl could do a lot worse. Personally, I like real men. Men who sweat.'

Stevie had recalled Beth's last two boyfriends, both of

whom had worn black leather jackets, ridden motor-cycles, and sweated profusely. She wrinkled her nose in distaste. 'I remember.'

Beth had been right about Michael, though. He had called Stevie the following weekend. It was as though once they had found each other they couldn't spend enough time together. Only the demands of Michael's career and hers kept Stevie from spending all her time with him. Careful, cautious Stevie Parker had jumped into this relationship with both feet, certain that she had met the one man who would ultimately change her life.

As the months passed, Beth couldn't help but notice the dramatic changes in Stevie. It had seemed to Beth that Stevie couldn't begin a sentence anymore without prefacing it with 'Michael says'. Beth's outspoken, irreverent, and sometimes mouthy, former roommate had seemed to be without an opinion of her own.

And on the occasions that Beth had been around Stevie and Michael when they were together, Michael had always seemed to find fault with some aspect of Stevie's appearance in front of others. He was never downright rude, that was not his style, but it was enough to destroy Stevie's fragile self-confidence. Beth had known that his criticism upset Stevie, since she always went to such great lengths to please him.

'Michael wants me to spend Christmas with him,' Stevie had announced to Beth one day over lunch.

'Christmas at the Baldwins. Now that should be some turkey dinner,' Beth speculated.

'Oh, it isn't going to be dinner at his parents,' explained Stevie. 'It's going to be just the two of us and some friends at his home in Aspen.'

Beth spoke, choosing her words carefully, hoping her inquiry would sound casual. 'Has Michael ever mentioned introducing you to his parents?'

'Well, sure, I . . .' Stevie had hesitated, then lowered her eyes. 'When the time is right, he will,' she had said with more certainty than she felt and wished that Beth hadn't asked that question.

Since the holidays were coming up, Stevie had also assumed that it would be an appropriate time for Michael to introduce her to his parents, but when she had asked him about it, Michael had answered her with a vague reference to his parents' busy holiday schedule. That was the first time that Stevie had had some doubt that maybe Michael wasn't as serious about her as she thought he was.

It had snowed all day on the twenty-third, making the drive to Aspen slow, but Christmas Eve had been crystal clear. The sunlight had caused the snow to glitter, its brightness enough to cause Stevie to squint as she crunched the snow beneath her feet. Overhead the sky had been a vivid blue. She had been gone most of the morning and part of the afternoon, anxious to finish her shopping for Michael in town.

At the front door to his three-story timber and glass home, which was anchored on a mountainside overlooking the town, she stomped on the cedar planks beneath her feet to loosen the snow that clung to her boots. Inside she pulled them off, then took off her coat and gloves. The house had been quiet, so she had assumed that everyone else had either gone to the slopes or had followed her lead and gone into Aspen. Down the hall she knocked on the door to Michael's bedroom.

Preoccupied with her thoughts of the evening that lay ahead, she pushed the door open then halted, frozen at the sight before her. For a moment it hadn't seemed real, but it was Michael's labored breathing she heard, and it was his naked body she saw moving.

'Oh, God!' she had sobbed.

Michael had moved away from his partner. There was no shock, no reaction to Stevie's presence, no indication of remorse. Unhurriedly, he had rolled to his back, his head propped against the headboard, naked except for the sheet he had remembered to pull across the lower part of his body. The look on his face was one of derision as he watched the array of emotions that crossed Stevie's face: shock, anger, betrayal, then pain.

'Why couldn't you have told me?' she cried. 'Didn't I mean anything to you? Anything at all?'

With one hand Michael reached for a cigarette from the package on the night table. Through the blue haze of smoke that curled its way upward he smiled a cold, cynical smile. She was so pathetically transparent.

Panic and a terrible ache assaulted her as she realized that he was not the least bit shaken that she had discovered him in bed like this. Rather, it was as if he and the dark-haired young man who lay next to him shared a private joke. That Stevie had found them together like this was a source of amusement!

Somewhere down deep Stevie had always suspected that Michael harbored a ruthless and sadistic streak, but she had never guessed that he would destroy something she considered so special. Her mind raced wildly. Had there been clues all along? Should she have guessed?

225

How could she? Nothing in the months that she had known him had given her any indication that he lived a secret life. Nothing in her entire life had prepared her for the shock of seeing him like this. For God's sake, she had been in love with him!

'Surely you didn't think that you were the only one, did you, Stevie?' Michael had paused, giving her an opportunity to reply. When none was forthcoming he continued. 'Don't be naïve. This doesn't have to be the end of things, you know. Let me explain,' he had finally said in a bored tone, but by then Stevie had turned away and was running down the hall, toward the front door. Tears ran unchecked down her cheeks.

She had heard him call, then heard the derisive laughter that followed. Outside Stevie ran to her car like she was being chased by demons. She knew all about those kinds of explanations. For years she had heard them from her mother who had wanted so badly to believe both the lies and the men that told them. Carole would even make plans around them, always telling Stevie how her life was going to change. But they were all lies. Fancy, fabricated, sometimes elaborately so, but in the end, always lies.

During the remainder of the drive home, Stevie tried to shake off her melancholy mood, reminding herself that it did no good to castigate herself over the past. It was dark when Bill dropped her off at her apartment.

She took a hot shower and put on a pair of sweat pants and a sweatshirt. In an effort to combat her loneliness, she turned the TV. On the counter that separated the kitchen from the living room, the light on her answering machine glowed steadily, mocking her with its absence of messages. Not even one Merry Christmas wish. Somewhere down deep she had been certain that Joe would call.

On Christmas Eve Stevie had dialed her mother's number but there had been no answer, and it had been too early to call this morning before she left with Bill, so now she reached for the phone. But when Carole Parker answered, Stevie cringed. It would have been better if she had called her mother earlier. Mornings were always better.

'Hello?' repeated Carole. Her voice was slow and thick with a huskiness that is only acquired after years of steady drinking and smoking.

'Hi, Carole. It's me.'

'Stevie?'

'Yeah. How are you?' Her attempt at cheerfulness was feeble.

'I'm okay.' Carole didn't ask how Stevie was. She never did.

'Well, Merry Christmas.' Suddenly Stevie was embarrassed, wishing she could end this call now.

'Oh, yeah. Merry Christmas.' Carole's voice faded as if she just remembered what day it was.

'Did you get the packages I sent?' asked Stevie.

'Umm, yes, I got 'em, Stevie. Thanks.'

'Did you like the robe? Did it fit?' Stevie had spent several of her lunch hours shopping for just the right color and size. She had finally settled on a soft flowered print with ecru lace on the collar and cuffs.

'It's nice, Stevie. Uh, Stevie . . .?'

Stevie shut her eyes tight. She knew what was coming and, just once, she desperately wished it wouldn't.

'Could you send me some money? I haven't felt too good lately. I've missed a lot of work and you know those stingy bastards won't pay me if I call in sick.'

Stevie wanted to remind her mother that she was lucky she still had a job, considering her excessive absenteeism, but she bit her tongue. Instead she sighed. 'I'll mail you some money tomorrow.'

'I'll pay you back,' promised Carole. 'When I get on my feet.'

'Sure.' Her mother always said that when she asked for money, but she never did. It didn't matter to Stevie if she never saw the money. She just wanted her mother to be healthy and self-sufficient.

In the background Stevie heard a man's voice. Another man, another night, thought Stevie sadly. Was it someone Carole knew, she wondered, or was it another stranger she had picked up at the bar? There had been a time when Stevie had wondered if going to bed with a man would help to ease the pain of loneliness. Now she knew it did, but only until the next morning.

'I've got to go now, Stevie,' Carole whispered dramatically into the phone. 'Uh, I've got someone here. A friend.'

'Yeah, I know. Merry Christmas, Carole.' Stevie sat for a moment, the receiver still in hand, not able to remember when she had no longer felt it necessary to call her 'Mother', and saddened over the way things were between them. She grieved for all the things they had missed.

She replaced the receiver and went into the kitchen to make a cup of tea. Without meaning to, her thoughts drifted to Joe. Most days she knew she had done the right thing by not staying with him. Tonight she fervently wished that things had turned out differently. It was Christmas night and she was alone. After a while Stevie began to feel drowsy and scooted down on the sofa. *I seem to do that a lot lately*. In a few minutes she was sound asleep.

Since many of the people at the paper had taken the week between Christmas and New Year's Day off, the office was unusually quiet on Monday. The next day was much the same except for the fact that Stevie was not feeling well. Each night since she had returned home from the tour she had gone to bed early, her energy depleted. On Wednesday she mentioned it to Beth. Beth, whose office was also downtown, was an account executive with Kohl and Garrison, a large advertising agency. Whenever their schedules allowed, they had lunch together.

'I think I'm coming down with something,' complained Stevie as she pushed her salad around the plate. 'I haven't slept good since I've been back to work, but I can't seem to stay awake either.'

Beth listened while Stevie went on to describe her other symptoms. 'That must have been some tour, Stevie. Are you sure it was strictly business between you and Joe Devlin?'

'You know me, Beth. Always busy, professional to a fault, dedicated to my career and all that,' Stevie quipped with a wry smile.

Beth leaned forward with a knowing smile on her face, ignoring Stevie's glib answer. 'Any chance you're pregnant?' she asked bluntly.

Stevie stared at her, a blank look on her face.

Beth continued. 'All those symptoms you just described, that's exactly how my sister Sharon felt when she found out she was pregnant.'

Stevie blushed and stammered. 'That's ridiculous. Of course I'm not pregnant. I'm sure I'm fighting the flu. I . . . I couldn't be pregnant,' she concluded with more confidence than she felt.

'Well,' said Beth with a shake of her shiny dark hair, 'You should certainly know.'

Was it possible?

Quickly Stevie did some quick calculations and was shocked to realize that her period was almost two weeks late. Why hadn't she realized that before? She had been so busy denying that she was having cramps to everyone when they were on tour that she hadn't realized that the time for that was actually due.

The one and only time she and Joe had made love things had happened so quickly. Their encounter had been so intense, so unexpected that she just hadn't . . . Joe hadn't . . . No precautions. They hadn't even talked about it. *Oh, dear God, you wouldn't let this happen to me, would you?*

For the remainder of the afternoon Stevie had difficulty concentrating. Finally she left work early, pleading a headache. On her way home she stopped at Dynan's Pharmacy and bought a home pregnancy test.

At home she set the package on the counter, then she took off her coat and hung it in the closet. First she eyed the pink and blue package as if she was a fighter sizing up an opponent. Then she slowly walked around it as if she were gearing up to do battle with it. Then, changing tactics, she turned her back on it, ignoring its presence altogether.

But in the end the cleverly designed package won. Stevie could no longer ignore its presence. Admitting defeat and an overwhelming desire to reassure herself that what Beth had suggested could not possibly be true, Stevie tore open the box and read the instructions. She set the package down, unable to concentrate, yet unable to wait any longer.

A few minutes later with the results before her, she reread the instructions, certain she had done something wrong. There must be some mistake, she thought, as she scanned the piece of paper in her shaky hands, but the words blurred because of the tears in her eyes. She slid down slowly to sit on the edge of the bathtub, bracing her shoulder against the wall, stunned by the knowledge that she was pregnant.

Still shaken by her discovery, Stevie repeated the test the following morning with the same result. Then she called in sick. At noon she was still in her pajamas. Now she was past feeling sorry for herself, she was just plain angry at herself and Joe. It was his fault as much as hers.

All those years of telling herself that she would never be like her mother, and just look at the predicament she was in. At least her mother had acquired a veneer of respectability through her short-lived marriage.

Stevie picked up the phone, then put it down without dialing. A few minutes later she picked it up again, only this time she dialed the number Joe had given her before she had left the tour. If you ever need me, he had told her.

When Stevie heard a woman answer she almost hung up.

No, the voice at the other end had said, Joe wasn't there but if she would leave a number he would call her back.

When the phone rang that evening Stevie answered, expecting to hear Joe's voice.

'Is this Stevie?' Stevie didn't recognize the woman's voice. 'This is Ellen Devlin, Joe's mother.'

She was stunned. 'How are you, Mrs Devlin?' she managed to inquire politely after a few moments.

'I'm fine, thank you. I wanted you to know that Joe isn't going to be home until late tonight, but I know he'd love to see you. And we'd all like very much to meet you.'

Joe would love to see her? They would all like to meet her? 'That's very kind of you, Mrs Devlin, maybe one of these days . . .'

'Could you come to dinner on Saturday night, Stevie, New Year's Eve?' Ellen waited for an answer, shrugging her shoulders at Richie who was standing nearby, then said, 'Stevie?'

Once more Stevie was silent. *This is a very strange conversation.* Maybe she should shake her head to clear it or something. 'Mrs Devlin?'

'Yes, dear?'

'I, uh . . . I live in Denver, in Colorado, so it's very kind of you to invite me to dinner, but you're in Georgia, and it's . . . a long way from here.' Stevie did a quick mental calculation. It was at least fifteen hundred miles, maybe more, between the two cities.

'Yes, dear, I know,' answered Joe's mother matter-of-factly, 'but we've got it all worked out and it would be such a lovely surprise for Joe.'

I'm sure it would, thought Stevie with irony. *And I have a lovely little surprise of my own.*

Ellen continued. 'You see, Joe thinks I'm going to invite Mary Nell Roberts.'

'Who?' asked Stevie bewildered.

'Mary Nell. She's a friend of Joe's. She's crazy about him, of course; so is Joe's manager, Jeannie. Jeannie Williams. Do you know Jeannie?' asked Ellen. Without giving Stevie a chance to answer she continued. 'Of course you do. You were on the tour together. But she's around Joe all the time. It's different with Mary Nell. Joe just can't wait to see her whenever he's home.' Ellen turned and winked at Richie. This was one of those times when a small extension of the truth was justified.

Oh, he can't, can he?

'Actually,' continued Ellen, 'they have a very special relationship, but here I am rambling on again. I'm sure Joe has told you all about Mary Nell.'

Not a word.

'Of course, Joe has told us all about you, too, and we'd love to meet you.'

From a few feet away, Richie rolled his eyes and grinned at his mother. What a conniving woman she was.

But before Stevie could answer, Ellen said, 'Richie has already made all the arrangements for your plane ticket and he will pick you up at the airport in Atlanta and drive you here to Piney Creek.'

Stevie was on the verge of telling Mrs Devlin that she never wanted to see Joe again, but when she considered her present dilemma, she knew she would have to face him sooner or later. Why not in front of his family? 'I'd love to come to dinner, Mrs Devlin. Thank you so much for inviting me.' *Instead of Mary Bell. Nell. Whatever her name is*, she added silently.

Joe's mother handed the phone to Richie so he could make arrangements to meet Stevie. When Stevie had first joined the tour, Richie had felt an obligation to warn her that Joe would break her heart, only because he had been certain that Joe would never care enough about anyone to change his life. But now Richie believed that Stevie was the only person who could give his brother the kind of happiness he deserved. He only hoped that he and his mother were doing the right thing by bringing Stevie here. When would his stubborn brother realize that the two of them belonged together?

'Hi,' Beth said cheerfully the next morning. She was standing at Stevie's front door, holding a bakery box in her hands. 'I called you at work, but they said you weren't coming in today, that you were sick. Why didn't you call me? I would have come over to see about you. I brought some doughnuts. Got any coffee? I'll make us a pot. You just go sit down.'

Stevie groaned and gestured toward the refrigerator. 'The coffee is in the freezer. Stays fresher there.'

'You don't look sick,' said Beth over the bar that separated the living room and the small kitchen. 'You just look tired.'

'How come you're not at work?' Stevie asked crossly.

'Oh, I went in, made a few phone calls only to find that no one else is in their office today. Most places are closing early this afternoon. I called you to see if you wanted to go shopping. They are practically giving stuff away at the after-Christmas sales. It's a great time to stock up on next year's Christmas gifts.'

'Ugh,' said Stevie. 'I can't bear the thought of going inside a store, at least not for a few months. It takes a while for me to get over the trauma of the holidays, and it usually takes my budget a lot longer than that.'

'Speaking of holidays, what are your plans for New Year's Eve?' Beth, ignoring Stevie's mood, carried the coffee and doughnuts into the living room and sat in the chair while Stevie huddled on the sofa, eyeing the doughnuts with distaste. For the past week, the sight of anything chocolate had made her stomach roll.

Stevie took a sip from her steaming cup before replying. There was no easy way to share her news with her best friend. 'I'm going to be out of town for New Year's weekend,' she said.

Beth reached for a chocolate doughnut, then paused at Stevie's announcement, her eyes widening. 'Really? Where?' she asked.

'I've been invited to visit Joe's family for the weekend,' Stevie answered cautiously, but before she could explain the unusual circumstances, Beth jumped up, doughnut in hand and reached to hug Stevie.

'Oh, Stevie, that's wonderful.'

'I'm not so sure of that,' replied Stevie. 'You see, Joe doesn't know I'm coming.'

'But I thought you said . . .'

'Oh, I did. I'm going to visit his family. His mother called me last night to invite me. My visit is going to be a surprise to Joe.'

'Oh.' Beth waited now, sure that there was more to this story.

Stevie looked down at her hands. 'I also have another surprise for Joe, and to tell you the truth, Beth, I don't know what his reaction will be.' Stevie took a deep breath. 'You see, I'm pregnant. It was just the oddest coincidence that Joe's mother called last night. But I thought that this would be as good a way as any to tell Joe.'

Beth reached out to her friend and hugged her. 'Oh, Stevie. Are you sure?'

Stevie nodded.

'Are you okay?' Beth asked.

Stevie managed a weak smile. 'I'm not sure. I do know that I'll feel a lot better after this weekend, once I tell Joe.'

Beth studied Stevie, not wanting to pry, but unable to keep from asking. 'What do you think his reaction will be?'

Stevie leaned back against the cushion of the sofa and sighed. 'I don't know, Beth. And to tell you the truth, I'm scared to death to find out. I do know that he doesn't want any kind of entanglements. He made that very clear on the tour. My prospects are not very good.'

'Uh, is that when all this happened?' asked Beth curiously. 'On tour?'

'No,' said Stevie. 'Actually nothing happened between us on the tour. This is the result of the night we

236

spent together during the blizzard. Ironically, it seems that television personality Gretchen Kirsh accurately predicted my fate that day on her show.'

'A baby. Wow!' exclaimed Beth with a grin as she plopped back against the sofa pillows.

Yeah. Wow.

Stevie uncurled her feet from the sofa and stood. 'Get a refill on your coffee, Beth. While you're here you can help me go through my closet and decide what to take on my trip. Exactly what is the proper attire to announce that one is in "the family way"?' For the first time in two days Stevie smiled.

Beth joined in, lightening the moment. 'Come this way, my dear. I'm sure you have the perfect outfit.'

While she packed her bag later that night, Stevie was victim to the feelings of both dread and excitement. She dreaded telling Joe she was pregnant, and at the same time she was excited at the prospect of seeing him again. All this from a woman who not forty-eight hours ago never wanted to see him again.

What do you hope to change?

Carefully she folded a blouse and placed it in her suitcase.

He won't change his mind about you.

Stevie took a pair of jeans out of the closet and folded them.

You're a fool. He doesn't love you.

Next she packed a pair of sneakers.

But you love him and now you're going to have his baby. And after all, this is just as much his problem as it is yours, right?

Now Stevie stood with her hands on her hips.

Do you intend to tell him so?

Damn right.

Hah! For a girl who's so smart, you're really dumb about men. Do you think he's going to marry you?

Stevie had no answer. As she finished her packing, she wondered if Joe had any idea she was coming to visit. She was sure about one thing though. If he was expecting Mary Bell what's-her-name, he was certainly in for the surprise of his life.

CHAPTER 19

The plane was a half-hour late, but when Stevie walked from the jetway into the crowded terminal Richie was there waiting. With one hand he took her bag, with the other he gave her a quick hug.

The drive from the Atlanta airport to the Devlin home in the little community of Piney Creek took just a little over an hour. The conversation was mostly about the band, then about the Devlin family. It wasn't until Richie turned off the interstate that Stevie asked the question that had been uppermost in her thoughts.

'Does Joe know I'm here?'

'No,' answered Richie truthfully.

'Why didn't you tell him?'

'Because he's too stubborn for his own good. We all believe Joe really cares about you.'

'We?' Stevie asked with smiling skepticism.

Richie's face turned red. 'Ah, I should have said me. Besides, Mom and Dad wanted to meet you.' Richie glanced toward her. 'We thought that if you were here with the family, Joe would realize what he's missing.'

Impulsively, she reached out and placed her hand on Richie's arm. 'You're one of the good guys, Richie.'

'Yeah,' he said, embarrassed but pleased at her words.

'But it won't work,' added Stevie, shaking her head.

'Why not?'

'It's complicated,' answered Stevie.

'Then why did you come all this way?' asked Richie bewildered.

With a wry smile Stevie said, 'Because your mom asked me to dinner instead of Mary Bell.'

'Nell,' corrected Richie.

'Whatever.'

Richie chuckled as he made a left. Piney Creek wasn't even a town. More like the crossing of two county highways, the town was made up of a small grocery store and post office combination, a Texaco station that had been recently remodeled to accommodate a mini-mart, a hardware store that sold almost everything, a dairy bar that doubled as a drive-in restaurant as well as the local gathering place, and two churches.

'This is even smaller than the town I grew up in. What do you do when you want a pizza?' asked Stevie.

Richie laughed. 'We get in the car and drive back toward the interstate.'

'Has your family always lived here?' Stevie asked with interest as they drove down the main street.

'Yes.'

'That must be nice,' Stevie remarked wistfully. 'To have all your family close by.'

About a half-mile from town, Richie turned into the driveway of the Devlin home. The big white two-story house had dark green shutters and a porch that extended all across the front, then wrapped around one

240

side of the house. Large trees hovered protectively all around. Stevie's first thought was that the house looked safe and welcoming, like it had been there forever.

'I wish you'd stay here at the house with us, Stevie. Mom will be disappointed.'

'Thanks, Rich. I know your mother was sincere about the invitation to stay here at the house, but I think it's better if I stay at one of the motels near the highway. I'm not sure how things will go between Joe and me, and I don't want anyone to be uncomfortable.'

Richie got out of the car and walked around to open the door for Stevie. Together they walked up the steps to the front porch. Reaching around her, he opened the front door with a little push.

Stevie hesitated, taking a deep breath. She wasn't at all sure that she had done the right thing by coming here. Joe had made it clear he didn't want to be tied down. What would happen when she told him she was pregnant? Would he feel obligated to marry her?

As soon as she heard the car in the driveway Ellen Devlin rushed to take the cake she had just made out of the oven, pulled at the dish towel she had tied around her waist as a makeshift apron, and took a swipe at her hair to smooth it back into place.

She was far more nervous at the thought of meeting Stevie than she would like to admit. She was even more apprehensive at what Joe would think about all this. Not even to Charlie did she confide her fears. Ellen and Charlie were not in the habit of interfering in the lives of their grown children, but in Joe's case Ellen had decided drastic action was in order.

Joe, the most successful of all their children, was also the unhappiest. When he had first introduced Kathy to the family they had all been pleasant to her. None of them ever dreamed that, for whatever the reason, Joe and Kathy would ever marry. But when they did, in true Devlin fashion they accepted Kathy as one of their own.

But being nice to Kathy became increasingly difficult as the problems between she and Joe multiplied. At family gatherings Kathy was surly, often directing bitter, hurtful barbs towards Joe. Finally, Joe began refusing invitations from his family, using a variety of excuses for his absence. To his credit, he never admitted that he and Kathy were having problems. But instinctively Ellen knew when things began to go wrong for her son. If it hadn't been for the accident, Ellen had no doubt that Kathy and Joe would have separated before the year was out. As it was, Joe had been the one holding things together.

True to form, the family still banded together. Even though an uneasy truce between Joe and Kathy's mother had been declared, Joe tried never to visit Kathy on the same days as her mother. When Joe was out of town, each of the family took turns visiting her.

Now, after seven long years, Joe was still trapped in a loveless marriage, held there by his guilt over his wife's accident. While some might consider her interference wrong, Ellen was determined that her son have his chance at happiness. She was willing to risk his displeasure to find out if Stevie Parker was the right woman for him.

Hesitantly Stevie stepped inside the large living room. There were two matching sofas covered in a soft cream-and-rose fabric. A coffee table, flanked by two wing back chairs, sat near the fireplace. The room was light and open and welcoming. It only took Stevie a few minutes after she had met Joe's parents to decide that the room's decor accurately reflected their personalities.

'Stevie, I've baked a cake and there's a fresh pot of coffee,' said Ellen as she signaled for Stevie to follow her.

'Hey! What about me?' asked Richie as he set Stevie's bag down in the hall.

'Come on,' said Ellen to Richie as she reached up to hug him, 'but you'll have to eat your cake in the living room. This is the only chance I'll have to talk with Stevie before dinner.'

'Bribe me with two pieces and I might leave you two alone.'

In the kitchen, the aroma of freshly baked cake with rich chocolate icing was enough to send Stevie's stomach into a spin. She swallowed and prayed she wouldn't be ill. Pregnancy had definitely turned her taste buds upside down. Chocolate cake had once been her favorite dessert and now the smell of chocolate bothered her more than anything else.

'Just a very small piece, Mrs Devlin. I had lunch on the plane.' Stevie struggled to smile through the waves of nausea that assaulted her. As she toyed with the cake and sipped at her coffee, knowing that she would soon have to give up anything with caffeine, Stevie was thankful that Ellen was too busy talking to notice that she had hardly touched her cake.

They were midway through the second cup when Stevie felt her stomach lurch. *Breathe deeply. It will pass.* Her hand was shaking when she set her cup in the saucer.

'Are you all right, Stevie?' asked Ellen.

Stevie nodded. 'I had a bout with the flu a while ago, and I'm still a little shaky.'

Even though Stevie was curious about the Devlin family and asked a lot of questions, Ellen never felt that she was prying. In almost every instance except one Ellen was able to answer Stevie's questions truthfully.

'What do you think Joe's reaction will be when he finds out I'm here?' asked Stevie.

'Well now, Stevie, that's hard to say, but from all the nice things that have been said about you, my guess is that he's going to be very pleased.'

Or plenty pissed, thought Stevie. The chances were fifty-fifty, and right now Stevie would bet her last dime on pissed. Either Ellen Devlin was hell-bent on playing matchmaker, or she didn't know her son at all.

Within a half-hour Ellen had decided that Stevie was just what Joe needed. She was smart and spunky, and kind and generous, and it was obvious that she was in love with Joe. It was there in her eyes. If Joe couldn't see it, then he needed a push in the right direction. And that's what mothers were for.

'Tell me the real reason you invited me here, Mrs Devlin.'

'Please, call me Ellen.'

Stevie leaned forward, her elbows on the table. 'Okay, Ellen,' she said with a grin, 'it's time to tell the truth.'

'Well, you see, Richie told us about you.'

'Joe didn't mention me?' Stevie asked curiously.

'Not until I asked him. Then he told me about your newspaper sending you on tour with the band.'

'Is that all? All he said?'

Ellen nodded.

'Oh.' Disappointment clouded Stevie's eyes.

'Was there something else he should have said about you?' Ellen inquired with a smile.

'Well, maybe not to his mother,' Stevie teased.

'Is there more to tell?' Ellen asked hopefully.

This time it was Stevie's turn to sigh. 'I'm afraid so.'

But before Stevie could say more, a dark-haired girl wearing jeans and a sweatshirt came crashing through the back door like she was being chased.

'Oops,' she said, skidding to a halt. Connie looked from her mother to Stevie, then said, 'I have this awful feeling I've just interrupted something.'

'You did,' said Ellen.

'Sorry,' Connie said to her mother then introduced herself to Stevie, pulled a chair up to the table and helped herself to a piece of cake.

At that moment, Ellen could have gladly strangled her youngest daughter. Her timing was terrible. Stevie had been on the verge of confiding in her. Now the opportunity was lost.

The Devlin family, or at least the part of the family Stevie had met, made her feel welcome. Later in the living room, Connie remarked, 'Joe is really going to be surprised to see you here.'

'I know,' answered Stevie.

'Mom's never invited any of Joe's, uh, friends home before except . . .'

245

'Mary Nell Roberts?' finished Stevie.

Connie leaned forward now, her legs tucked under her on the sofa. 'How do you know that?' she asked.

'Your mother told me over the phone. She said Joe and Mary Nell have a special relationship.'

'They've known each other a long time,' admitted Connie. She wanted to tell Stevie that her mother had been trying to get Joe romantically interested in Mary Nell for years, but dutifully following her mother's instructions, Connie would let Stevie assume there was something between Joe and Mary Nell.

It would certainly be exciting to see what would happen when Joe found Stevie seated at the dinner table instead of Mary Nell. At least *this* family dinner wouldn't be boring.

In the kitchen Charlie Devlin kissed his wife lightly on the back of the neck.

'What was that for?' she asked with a smile.

'That was for being brave enough to invite a girl home that you think your son is interested in.'

'Oh, he's interested all right,' said Ellen with confidence. 'And she's interested back.'

'She's just a little bitty thing,' said Charlie. 'How old do you think she is?'

'Richie says Stevie is twenty-eight,' said Ellen.

'Well, she looks like she's Connie's age. What do you think of her?'

Ellen turned away from the sink to face Charlie, her eyes dancing with mischief. 'I think our boy Joe is in for a big surprise.'

'And a hell of a New Year,' added Charlie with a wink.

* * *

246

A few minutes after everyone arrived that evening for dinner, Ellen looked around her kitchen at her children and their families who had, one by one, drifted into the kitchen. 'I don't know why I bother to set the dining-room table,' she confided to Stevie. 'This rowdy bunch would be happier eating in the kitchen.'

Stevie laughed and nodded. 'Well, they do look happy to be here. Maybe it's because –' Just then the back door opened and Joe walked in. Stevie's heart stopped at the sight of him, then resumed its beat in double time. He looked so rugged in his denim jacket with the collar turned up. Drops of rain glistened in his dark hair.

'Looks like we're in for another storm,' he began. His voice drifted off as he caught sight of Stevie standing next to his mother in the middle of the Devlin kitchen, looking for all the world like she belonged there.

Suddenly the Devlin family members were silent, their eyes fixed on Joe. 'What's going on here?' he asked, his brown eyes traveling around the room until they returned to Stevie.

'It's a Happy New Year, Uncle Joe. Don't you know that?' The adults laughed, grateful that three-year-old Brian had answered Joe's question. Joe grinned and ruffled his nephew's hair.

'We get to stay up as late as we want tonight, 'cause a new year is coming,' explained Tommy, who was five.

Stevie attempted a weak smile.

Richie was the next to speak. 'Mom called Stevie and invited her to dinner.'

Joe turned toward his mother who shrugged, smiled and turned her back toward him to stir something on

247

the stove. Then he looked toward Stevie. 'And you just rushed right over.' His humor was overlaid with sarcasm.

'I heard your mother was an excellent cook,' said Stevie with a bravado she didn't feel. There was scattered laughter and the atmosphere in the kitchen was on its way back to normal.

Joe crossed the room with long strides and took Stevie's arm. He was in the process of ushering her into the empty dining room when Ellen announced, 'We'll be ready for dinner in about five minutes, everyone. Stevie, would you and Connie mind helping me here for a few minutes?'

Joe scowled, and left the kitchen to hang up his coat and wash up before dinner.

'What is going on here?' he asked Richie in the upstairs hallway. 'What is she doing here?'

'I don't know, Joe. It's something Mom cooked up. Last week she was asking a lot of questions about Stevie and . . .' Richie shrugged, giving Joe his best, don't-ask-me-I-didn't-have-anything-to-do-with-it look.

Downstairs a few minutes later Ellen said, 'Well, I think everything is ready. Please show Stevie to the table, Joe.' Then she signaled to the rest of the family to follow them.

'Stevie, sit here, please,' instructed Ellen, 'and Joe, here.' She indicated the chair next to Stevie.

'I think I'll sit over here instead,' announced Joe as he walked to the opposite side of the table. 'I don't want to miss anything.'

Ellen shot Charlie a look that pleaded for him to say something, but Charlie just shrugged his shoulders in amusement.

248

'Then I'll sit next to the guest of honor,' said Richie, quickly slipping into the empty chair beside Stevie.

From his place across the table Joe watched her interact with his family. It was obvious that she had already made friends with his sister, Connie, and was on her way to charming the rest of the family as well.

Joe knew he had overreacted when he had discovered her in the kitchen, but seeing her with his family was more of a shock than he would admit. Stevie Parker had caused him to wage silent war with himself. She had forced him to deal with his guilt over Kathy; guilt he had never been able to resolve.

From across the table he studied her. Her expressions were animated as she conversed with his parents and brothers and sisters, but when her eyes met his they became guarded, wary. She wasn't here on a whim, he decided. Stevie was here for a reason and he was determined to find out exactly what was so important that she flew halfway across the country to see him.

In spite of her animation and her seemingly genuine interest in his family, Joe noticed that Stevie had eaten only a few bites of her dinner, pushing her food around her plate with her fork. Evidently she wasn't quite as relaxed as she would like him to believe, but when Gary's wife, Susan, asked how she and Joe met, Joe silently applauded the utterly fascinating and highly creative story Stevie told. There was just enough truth to it to make it believable. When she finished she dared a look at him. He nodded in approval.

Stevie's nervousness was increasing by the minute. Soon the pretext of dinner would be over and she would have to face Joe. She knew he was waiting, patiently biding his time until they could be alone. It was like waiting for the other shoe to drop. When Grace and her husband asked her about skiing in Colorado, she was visibly relieved.

Over coffee and dessert Stevie's eyes met Joe's, seeking some measure to gauge what he might be thinking, what he might be feeling, but there were no clues. His eyes revealed nothing, his expression, while still not overly welcoming, was not quite as formidable as it had been in the beginning.

Finally when everyone was in the living room, Joe, standing close behind Stevie, whispered, 'Where are you staying tonight?'

Before Stevie could answer, Richie, who was nearby, answered, 'Mom and Dad invited her to stay here, but Stevie insisted on staying at a motel. I thought you, uh, or one of us could drive her there later.'

Joe turned back to Stevie, but Gary and Grace were talking with her. He was like a caged animal. Every time he suggested that maybe Stevie was ready to leave, someone in the family protested that it was too early. 'We have to ring in the New Year, Joe,' said Connie with a devilish smile, looking at her watch and unwittingly aiding Ellen in her attempts to keep Joe and Stevie apart as long as possible.

At midnight, he reached out for her, pulling her close. Then he kissed her. 'Happy New Year,' he said in a husky voice. The room might as well have been empty, for they were both oblivious to the sound of laughter and the horns and the confetti that Connie was scattering over every one.

'Happy New Year, Joe.' Their eyes held until she was pulled away by Richie for a hug and a kiss.

Less than an hour later Stevie had thanked Ellen and Charlie and apprehensively followed Joe out to his truck. During the drive to the motel they were both silent until they neared the interstate. 'Any one of these places is okay,' said Stevie, indicating the rows of moderately priced motels that lined the access roads that ran on either side of the highway. But Joe bypassed them and instead pulled into the drive that led to the elegant and expensive Southern Inn. Stevie looked up, surprised. 'I don't think I can afford this, Joe,' she said quietly.

Without looking at her he answered, 'I can.'

'But I don't want you to pay . . .' Before Stevie could finish Joe was already out of the truck, unloading her bag. Reluctantly she followed him into the lobby and within minutes they were on their way up to her room.

CHAPTER 20

On the second floor Joe slid the plastic card through the scanner, then pushed the door open for Stevie. Inside she switched on a lamp, feeling like she was on her way to a destiny that was out of control. The time for telling had arrived. She could no longer guess at the outcome.

She prayed that he would take her in his arms and tell her that everything would be okay, that the future was theirs to share. But she knew the odds of that happening were not in her favor. If nothing else, Joe had been brutally honest about not wanting to be involved in a relationship.

Sorry, Joe. This is going to require a little more involvement than previously thought.

She turned when she heard him set her bag on the floor. As he straightened his eyes riveted hers and suddenly her courage fled. 'I . . . maybe it was a mistake to come here, but I have something to tell you and it seemed like a good –' She never finished.

Joe took her by the shoulders and brought her to him roughly. His lips caught hers in a hard, searing kiss. His strong arms wrapped around her while his hands moved lower to pull her tight against him. The kiss seemed endless and when Joe ever so slightly lessened the pressure of his lips against hers, Stevie almost moaned with disappointment.

'Why are you here?' he whispered fiercely. 'Don't you know you're driving me crazy? Each time I think I'm strong enough to walk away from you, I find out just how wrong I am. Do you know what you do to me, Stevie?'

But Stevie never had the opportunity to answer before his tongue began its slow sensual assault. This time she did moan. His breath was hot and moist against her skin, and Stevie, who had rehearsed this moment in her mind so many times, never had a chance.

She was completely caught up in her response to Joe's sensual onslaught, giving up any pretense of resistance, only to drown in physical sensations. Deep in the pit of her stomach was that signal that preceded the hot rush of passion that raced through her, leaving her weak and wanting. Stevie, who had never been made love to in this heated, demanding way, was powerless to protest. All she could think of how much she wanted to feel his naked body against hers.

And Joe, who, from the minute he had laid eyes on her, had wanted to yank her out of his mother's kitchen and take her someplace where he could make love to her, had exercised all the control he could muster. Through an interminable dinner and the drive to the hotel that had followed, he had wanted nothing more than to take Stevie in his arms. Now that he had her, he wasn't about to slow up enough for her to change her mind.

With sure hands he reached for the buttons at her throat and skillfully undid each one. His lips never left her, never ceased to demand until he had her blouse around her waist and her bra unfastened and thrown aside. Stevie fumbled with the buttons on his shirt. With both hands she pulled at the garment freeing it from his pants.

Now Joe tugged at her skirt with one hand while he expertly pushed her panties and hose down with the other until she was completely free of them.

Without warning he lifted her and carried her across the room, then set her on the edge of the desk, spreading her legs and positioning himself between them. With his mouth he caressed first one breast then the other. Then his tongue, never moving from her sweet, soft skin, began to trace a circular pattern downward. Realizing his destination, she started to protest, but the words never reached her lips. Never before had she experienced the heat she felt now. Never before had she wanted to be made love to with this demanding urgency.

When Joe was free of his clothing, Stevie greedily ran her hands and mouth over him, inciting in him the same urgency he had given her. She strained toward him, seeking the force and weight of him that would soon fill her. He groaned, and pushed her hands away. He could wait no longer. With a swift, sure motion Joe drove into her, then stilled as he heard her gasp. 'Oh, baby,' he whispered. 'Stevie, honey, I didn't mean to hurt you.'

When she shook her head to signal she was okay, Joe hesitated a moment longer then began to thrust again, matching his rhythm to the primeval beat that sounded between them. When Stevie met his thrusts, the need increased, urging them to move together harder, faster until finally they found unbearable pleasure and release.

Breathing unevenly, Stevie held on to Joe desperately, needing the heat of his body against her, feeling like some part of her soul had reached out and touched his and joined them at the very center of their being. With her arms wrapped around him Stevie nestled her head against his broad chest.

Joe straightened and caressed her hair. At last she had found a place where she was loved and safe. For tonight it was enough just to be here with him.

Joe clasped her to him and felt as if he would drown if he let go of her, wishing that he didn't need her so, hating that she had the power to keep him coming back to her. It was as if he knew from the beginning that their souls were destined to meet and fuse forever in an exploding passion. Sweetly, Joe pushed Stevie's damp hair from her forehead and kissed her there. He wanted this moment to last forever.

Later, after opening a bottle of champagne and toasting the New Year, they made love again, this time with less urgency. Joe slept for a while, then roused and pulled Stevie closer to him. She had not forgotten the reason why she was here, but tomorrow was soon enough to tell Joe that she was pregnant. For once in her life she knew that things would be okay; Joe loved her as much as she loved him. After tonight nothing could destroy the bond between them.

The next morning Joe opened his eyes slowly and looked around. He had spent so many nights in so many hotels that it no longer bothered him to wake up in a strange place. He turned his head and looked down at Stevie. Her mussed curls fanned out over his shoulder. Her naked body was nestled against him and the feel of her was enough to arouse him once more. As he turned toward her, Stevie opened her eyes slowly and smiled. How she could manage to look angelic and wanton at the same time was a puzzle to Joe. But right now all he cared about was the urgent need he had to possess her once more.

'Your family is going to know where you were last night,' Stevie announced over the breakfast tray that room service had delivered a few minutes earlier. She was seated in the middle of the bed, wearing Joe's shirt, watching him as he ate heartily from the tray. She was enjoying the sight of his torso, bare above the sheets, immensely. It would be wonderful to wake up like this every morning.

He looked up at her, his eyes filled with mirth. 'So what?'

'So, it's embarrassing,' she replied primly, taking a sip of her juice. 'They'll know we did it.'

Joe laughed out loud. 'Then why did you come down here, Stevie? You knew this would happen sooner or later. You know we can't keep our hands off each other.'

'And now so does everyone else,' muttered Stevie. *Now. Tell him about the baby now.*

'Joe,' began Stevie, 'there's something I have to tell –'

'I know,' he interrupted as he sat the tray aside, his tone suddenly serious. 'My family is hoping I'll change my lifestyle, and when Richie told them about you, they decided it was time to get us together. Just a few days ago my dad gave me a lecture about the fact that I was thirty-two and I should think about settling down.'

The pulse in Stevie's temple throbbed as she listened to his words. Her life, her future, hung suspended by a thread of hope as she waited for his next words. More than anything she wanted to know that he loved her, that he wanted to marry her. She wanted so badly to hear those words before she had to tell him that she was pregnant. Once he knew that, he would feel obligated to marry her.

She knew that he would act responsibly. He would want to make things right. After all, it was his baby. But down deep she wanted him to say that he wanted to spend his life with *her*. Not because he had to, but because he wanted to.

Breathlessly, she waited for him to say more. She wanted to prompt him, to shake him, but instead, she sat motionless. Waiting.

'Those are the things I should do, Stevie, with you. I should marry you and settle down.' His brown eyes met her. Gone was the teasing light. He pinned her with that serious, intense gaze as if he could see clear through to her soul.

An alarm went off in Stevie's head. Something in his tone warned her. The words were right so far, but something unspoken lay between them.

'I can't deny what I feel for you, Stevie, and I sure as hell can't deny the sexual attraction between us.'

Stevie waited.

Oh, God, please let him love me. Please let this one thing in my life go right. I'll never ask for anything else.

'I love you, Stevie.'

'Oh, Joe . . .' she said as she expelled the breath she had been holding. Then she unclenched her hands and held her arms out to him, her face lit with the glow of a thousand candles.

Instantly Joe realized his mistake. He caught her hands and pulled them down before they reached him. He held them there firmly. 'No, Stevie, honey, please wait.'

Suddenly Stevie's face lost its incandescence as she searched his eyes. He took a deep breath, then continued. 'I love you, Stevie, but this is not going anywhere. I *can't* marry you.' The words pierced his heart as he saw her lovely face crumple, her dreams crushed. His own pain was so great that he couldn't even imagine what she was going through.

Stevie sat motionless. Time had stopped. In that moment she knew what death was like.

Oh, God, did you just turn your back on me the day I was born?

Her blue eyes were wide now with pain and fear. She wanted to ask him why, but she couldn't speak.

He moved to the side of the bed and began to dress. 'It has nothing to do with how I feel about you. It's me. It's something that happened a long time ago. Something I can't change.' He stood now and turned to face her. His voice drifted into a whisper. 'I'm married.'

First there was stunned silence, followed by doubt and disbelief.

Married?

Then she wanted to scream, to hit him, to make him feel her pain. To tell him he was a rotten bastard for not telling her the truth. For making her love him.

258

'Married,' she echoed aloud. 'I see.' The words sounded very far away, almost as if they belonged to someone else.

'No, no, you don't, Stevie. I never wanted to hurt you.'

With as much dignity as she could muster, Stevie rose from the bed. 'Why didn't you tell me?' Tears clouded her eyes as she walked away.

'I wanted to, Stevie.'

Then she turned back toward him, her head bowed, and without warning the words slipped past her. They were no more than a whisper. 'I'm pregnant.'

For a moment, Joe's eyes widened, but when she raised her face to his, his expression had turned hard and unyielding. He moved closer until he towered over her. Deliberately he hardened his heart against the sadness in her face. He had heard these deceitful words before, and he wouldn't make the same mistake twice. When he spoke, his voice carried all the bitterness he had harbored for so many years. 'That's what they all say, babe, in the end.'

The words were precise and searing and they cut through Stevie like white-hot steel.

CHAPTER 21

For what must have been the hundredth time, Richie took his eyes from the road and glanced over at Stevie. He couldn't ever remember feeling so bad, and he wasn't even sure exactly what had happened between Stevie and Joe. He only knew that things had not worked out between them, and he felt responsible.

Maybe it had been wrong for the Devlin family to bring Stevie here, but for the first time in years, they had honestly believed that they were doing the right thing for Joe. If he couldn't find the way to happiness on his own, the least they could do was point him in the right direction. But it had backfired so miserably, and in the end, all they had done was to hurt Stevie.

In her mind Stevie replayed the scene that had taken place only a few hours ago. She had told Joe about the baby and he hadn't believed her. He thought she was lying, a last-ditch effort on her part to ensnare him. With time, she might get over this, but she would never forget the look of disgust on his face.

Damn you, Joe Devlin.

When Richie could no longer stand the silence in the car, he spoke softly. 'I'm sorry, Stevie. For the way things turned out.'

Stevie swallowed and attempted a small smile. Her voice was shaky. 'It's okay, Richie. You have no reason to be sorry. You even tried to warn me about Joe. Remember that night in Gulfport? You told me not to get serious over your brother.' Her voice cracked and she had to take a deep breath before she could go on. 'And I told you in the beginning that things between Joe and me were complicated.'

I just didn't know how complicated.

'I might have even listened to your warning, Richie, except for one thing. It was already too late. I thought that Joe's reluctance to have a relationship was because he didn't believe in marriage. Boy, was I wrong about that.' Stevie locked her fingers together, then brought them to her lips. 'But what I don't understand is why you and your family wanted me to come down here?'

'Geez, Stevie.' Richie rubbed his hand across his chin. 'That's complicated, too. Joe's marriage is sort of a family secret, something we never talk about. The publicity, well, it just wouldn't be good for anybody, not for Joe and not for Kathy. The marriage has been over for a long time. It was a terrible mistake to begin with, but he wouldn't do anything about it.'

'Why not?'

'It's a long story, but we all want something better for Joe. He's been miserable for a such a long time. Even now he still feels guilty over what happened, and he never wanted the details of his marriage to get out to the press – Oh, boy!' said Richie, remembering that Stevie

261

was a reporter. 'Me and my big mouth. You wouldn't write about this, would you? I know you've been hurt by Joe, but . . .'

'Tell me about Joe's marriage,' said Stevie quietly. But Richie refused to say more than what he had already let slip. And no matter how hard she pried, she could not get him to say anything else.

Stevie was silent. More than anything she wanted to Richie to turn the car around so that she could confront Joe and ask him all the questions she had been too shocked to ask. She wanted to pound her fists against him to express the complete hopelessness she felt, to call him all the rotten names she could think of.

But she did none of these things. Instead she turned her tear-streaked face toward the window, resting her head against the cold glass, and watched the green and brown blur of the countryside as she sped farther and farther away from the man who had broken her heart.

Inside the airport Richie wanted to stay with her until her flight was called, but Stevie refused his offer. When he handed her bag over to her, the look on his face was one of such pure misery that Stevie felt compelled to say something. 'I know you feel bad for me,' she began. 'I'm truly hurt that Joe wasn't honest with me, but I won't use anything you said against him. I just want to get back to Denver and get on with my life.' She reached up and hugged Richie briefly, then kissed him on the cheek. 'Tell your mom I understand what she tried to do. I don't want her to feel any worse than she already does.'

On the flight home, Stevie tried to think, to plan for the future, but all she could think of was Joe's harsh words, over and over. Why had that been such a surprise to her? Because they had made hot, shattering love to each other? Because their need for one another had been so great? All along he had told her he didn't want to get involved, and she hadn't believed him. She had foolishly believed that love could conquer any obstacle. Except this one. Joe Devlin was a married man.

The following week Stevie went back to work. There were dark smudges under her eyes and her face was drawn. Her nausea was persistent now, sometimes lasting the entire day. Instead of gaining weight she lost it. Harry noticed the change, but when he questioned her she explained that she had not quite bounced back from the flu she had a while ago.

As she slipped back into a daily routine she was able to manage the days. It was the nights that were painful.

When Stevie was two months pregnant she went to the doctor, who confirmed what she already knew. There was no question in her mind about what she would do about this baby. It was hers and she would love it fiercely. Nobody had wanted her, but for her baby it would be different. Not only would she provide for it, but she had enough love inside her to be a good mother. They would be a family, and she would do every thing in her power to compensate for the absence of a father.

At home that evening Stevie put a frozen dinner into the microwave and set the timer. When it was ready, she carried the plastic tray to the table, then sorted though her mail while she ate her solitary meal. When she spotted the envelope addressed to her in Joe's clear, bold handwriting, she pushed her dinner away and reached for it.

In her haste, the envelope slipped from her shaking fingers and fluttered to the floor. This was the first time she had heard from him since she had returned home. Her heart beat heavily, as though it could pound its way right through her chest, as she bent down to retrieved the envelope.

Inside was a single sheet of paper and a check. Without warning hot tears rushed to her eyes. With the back of her hand she swiped at the tears, but the words before her were blurred as she read.

Dear Stevie,

Please use this check for anything that you need for yourself or the baby. I've made arrangements for this amount to be sent to you each month from now on. You won't have to worry about anything, including your medical bills. I will take care of everything.

Stevie, if I could take back all the things I said that hurt you, I would. If I could have kept from loving you, I would have done that too, and maybe this would have never happened. I should have at least had the decency to tell you the truth, but it's too late for that. God, how I wish things could have been different for us.

Sighing, Stevie leaned her head back against the sofa. After a minute she looked at the check in her hands, not knowing whether to laugh or cry at the irony of it all. It was more than three times as much as her take-home pay each month. Well, she thought wryly, if you're going to get knocked up, it certainly pays to pick someone who is rich.

Feeling suddenly tired, she rose from the sofa slowly and crossed the room to her desk. She dropped the check into an envelope and addressed it to Joe. Tomorrow she would put it in the mail. Joe Devlin could keep his guilt money. She refused to be paid off just so he could soothe his conscience.

For two days the envelope with Stevie's return address had remained unopened on Joe's desk. All along he had known what it contained, yet he had hoped for something more, some sign of forgiveness, something to vindicate his actions.

Once he had come to his senses, he felt terrible about the way he had treated Stevie. She wasn't Kathy. She was nothing like her. And Stevie would never lie to get what she wanted. It would have been so simple in the beginning if he had told the truth.

'I'm married.' Two words that, if said out loud, would have kept him and Stevie out of this terrible mess. In his heart, Joe knew that if he had told her the truth, Stevie would have walked away from him and never looked back, no matter how powerful the attraction. He also knew that was the very reason he had kept silent.

He had tried to leave her, but each time he kept going back. He had even warned her that he wasn't the man for her, and she had listened, heeded his warning, and walked away. And she might have even stayed away if it hadn't been for his family. Now there was a baby. His

265

baby. Joe rested his head in his hands, and drew a deep breath. *Dear God. What am I going to do?*

He should have known that Stevie would be too stubborn to accept anything from him. Carefully, he laid the envelope aside.

Joe was caught in a crossfire. He had successfully pushed Stevie out of his life. It was what he intended to do all along. Avoid any emotional involvement at all cost. But thought of living without her made him miserable. Stevie was pregnant with his child while Kathy, his wife, his responsibility, lay helpless in a nursing home with no chance of recovery.

How could he abandon her? How could a man make a choice like that? Why should he ever have to?

These questions haunted Joe. They swam around in his head, they churned in his gut, and at night, when all was quiet, they caused him intense pain. His desire for happiness and his love for Stevie warred with his sense of responsibility and duty toward Kathy.

When Stevie had told him that she was pregnant, he felt crushed by the weight of his responsibilities. He felt like he was once again being manipulated. Kathy had done that to him; first with the lie about being pregnant, then with her outrageous accusations of infidelity. Now he was caught between a woman who had imprisoned him with guilt and a woman he loved with all his being.

Night after sleepless night, he wrestled with his conscience. He knew that only he had the power to set himself free from guilt. But did he have that right? And if he decided that he did have that right, did he have the strength to carry it through?

The band met again in Cincinnati on January fifteenth. Things were still strained between Joe and Richie. Joe had never explained what had happened that New Year's Day to Richie, and Richie could not quite bring himself to forgive Joe for the misery he had inflicted on Stevie. No matter what the cause, or who was at fault, Stevie was kind and loving. She deserved better treatment.

So Joe remained distant not only from his brother but from Dave and Brad and Allen Lee. Gone was the easy camaraderie that they had always shared. The only time that things seemed to click was when they were on stage. The music becoming a catharsis, bringing them together and easing Joe's heartache. Each performance, he continued to dedicate a song to 'a special lady', but his heart wasn't in it. His eyes would scan the crowd, foolishly imagining he would see Stevie there.

'You are not the same group you were before Christmas,' remarked Jeannie critically after the performance in Cincinnati. They were on their way to Cleveland. 'You play like five guys who get together once a week to practice in someone's garage. What happened over the holidays? Did you get rusty? Did you forget who you are?'

Brad, Dave, Allen Lee and Richie shrugged. Only Joe looked as though he hadn't heard her. 'Excuse me,' he said, rising.

'Joe, where are you going? We need to discuss this.' asked Jeannie.

When Joe didn't answer, Jeannie jumped up and followed him toward the back of the bus. When he sat on the edge of one of the beds, she joined him.

'What's gotten into you, Joe?' she asked. 'Did I miss something by staying in Nashville over the holidays?'

'No, you didn't miss anything,' he answered. 'I'm just tired. The break wasn't long enough.'

'Look, we've got some time in Cleveland before the show. Why don't I arrange for a car, and you can get away for a while. It might do you good.'

The next day Jeannie had a rental car delivered to the hotel. When Joe came downstairs, she was waiting by the car, keys in hand.

'Thanks, Jeannie,' Joe said, reaching for the keys.

'Not so fast,' she replied, jerking her hand out of his reach. 'I'm going with you.'

Joe was about to protest, then decided against it. Lately he had criticized everything Jeannie had said or done. Maybe he needed to lighten up a little. If he was truthful, he would have to admit that it was nothing Jeannie did, but instead his complete preoccupation with Stevie. He had to find a way to resolve things.

'Where do you want to go?' he asked once they were in the car.

'I heard about an out-of-the-way restaurant about a half-hour from here. I though we could have lunch, share some wine, and, well, who knows where things might lead? After all, it's a beautiful day, even for January,' Jeannie teased as she leaned toward Joe, placing her hand on his thigh.

'I know.'

'What?' asked Jeannie, startled at his abruptness.

'I know where things would lead, or at least where you would like them to lead.'

She laughed nervously. She had meant to be more subtle. All along she had known that subtlety was not her strong point. With some guys it didn't matter. The more aggressive she was, the better they liked it. But Joe wasn't like that. No matter how hard she tried, she couldn't seem to find the right approach with him. Today, however, she sensed that his mood was different. He seemed to be more receptive to her. 'Can't blame a girl for trying, can you?'

Or a guy for being lonely. 'So where is this place?'

Jeannie sat back against the seat, feeling smug and once more in control as she gave him directions.

From the highway they turned on to a two-laned county road that curled through the countryside where the most remarkable scenery were the small farms that neatly lined both sides of the road. When they came to an intersection, they turned east and within minutes Joe pulled up in front of the Plum Tree Inn.

The restaurant was small, dark, and cosy with candlelight and leaded glass windows that looked over grounds that were bordered by thick woods and a winding stream. The food, which was French, was delicious, and the wine, also French, impeccable. Joe could feel the tension easing out of him.

'Aren't you glad we came out this way?' asked Jeannie softly, leaning forward.

Joe nodded. 'It's just what I needed, Jeannie. I almost hate to see the afternoon end.'

'It doesn't have to end, Joe. This is an inn. We could get a room and . . . stay.'

Joe leaned back in his chair, closing his eyes. Why not? He tried to envision him and Jeannie together, but neither the image or the excitement materialized. Instead, he saw Stevie's face. Wearily, Joe straightened. He might be lonely, but he could not replace one woman with another. He had ruined Stevie's life by not telling her the truth; he wasn't about to repeat the same mistake twice.

He leaned forward. 'Jeannie, this has been a wonderful afternoon and I want to keep it that way. It's time for us to get back.' He reached for his wallet, pulling out his credit card. When the bill had been settled, he escorted Jeannie out into the afternoon light.

'There will be other times, Joe. I can wait.'

After opening the car door for her, he came around the car and slid behind the wheel and said, 'People move on, Jeannie, believe me. Some dreams just never materialize. You are a beautiful woman; the thought of sharing an afternoon with you should be tempting. But you should be making this offer to someone else.'

'You can't tell me you didn't expect this,' she said.

'I expected it,' he replied thoughtfully, 'in fact, I would have to be blind not to see it coming. I just didn't anticipate that something else would get in the way.'

Jeannie studied Joe's profile and had the oddest feeling that even though he was sitting right here next to her, he might as well have been a million miles away. It was then that the irony of the situation struck her. She had arranged this getaway so she could have Joe all to herself, her sole intent: a seduction. She was in the right place with the right man, but she, unfortunately, was not the right woman.

As far as he was concerned, this afternoon had been nothing more than an experiment. Oh, he had been ripe for a seduction, all right. She could sense these kinds of things about a man. He had had every intention of going through with it. But his conscience got in the way.

One of these days, you'll have to reckon with me, Joe Devlin. When you least expect it.

Meanwhile, the tour went on. His thoughts were never far from Stevie, and it seemed the harder he looked for answers, the more complicated the questions became. After many wretched days and tortuous nights, Joe knew he had to see Kathy. Perhaps the answers he was seeking had been there with her all along. Taking advantage of a break in their schedule, Joe flew home.

In the beginning, immediately following the accident, he had been a frequent visitor at the nursing home, always bringing Kathy a little gift, something bright and cheerful. He would spend hours talking to her or reading to her. Each time he had searched for some spark, some sign that she recognized him, but there had been none.

Kathy's eyes had remained unresponsive and flat, almost as if her brain had decided it was no longer responsible for the care of the body that housed it. While she still had the use of her hands, their movement was uncoordinated and uncontrolled. After prolonged therapy, the doctors had determined that her condition would never improve, but instead would continue to deteriorate over a period of time.

On each visit, Joe continued to look for some response, some acknowledgement that she recognized something of the world around her. If he hadn't been so desperate in his determination to see improvement in her condition, he would have long ago admitted that there was no reason for hope. When he had first received the bleak prognosis, he had wept openly. He mourned her suffering, and the fact that he had never loved her.

Anyone unaware of the nature of the work that was done at Parkside might assume it was a college campus. The faded red of the brick was partially covered by the abundant ivy that climbed the walls, and the walkways were flanked by manicured hedges. The grounds were meticulously landscaped; beginning in early spring, flowers in their neatly tended beds began to bloom. It was there, in a room on the ground floor with a full view of the gardens, that Kathy Devlin had stayed for the past seven years.

Last year, when Joe's career suddenly took off, as a precaution he had had the records at the hospital changed. To protect her from the prying eyes of the press, she was now listed under her maiden name: Katherine Lee Harrison.

This morning, the sun glistened on the damp grass. Even though it was still January, the air was crisp, hinting at the promise of spring. Joe sat on the curved concrete bench, his dark head bent, his shoulders slumped, his elbows resting on his knees. After spending time with her doctor and some of the hospital staff, he needed a few minutes of solitude.

He had no idea what he would say to Kathy, or what his decision would be. He only knew that the time had come to see her again.

While he waited for the attendant to bring her out onto the terrace, he tried to think, to reason, but his mind refused to cooperate. He had tried to apply logic to his problem, from every conceivable angle, and it had led him here to this moment, to this place. Now he knew this was a decision that could only be made by the heart.

When the attendant left, Joe moved closer to Kathy's wheelchair, then reached out and tucked the blanket that covered her legs closer around her. As he sat quietly, studying her, it was hard for him to believe that this was the same woman he had wed. Her skin was sallow now, and her hair dark and lank. Only her restless hands showed any sign of life.

His heart beat rapidly as he reached to still her hands. Taking both of them into his, he whispered, 'Kathy? Kathy, it's me. Joe.' He paused, swallowing hard, before he asked the question he had asked each time he came to see her. 'Do you remember me, Kath?' He waited, searching for any sign that there was recognition or understanding behind the eyes that remained fixed, staring straight ahead.

He reached out to her, gently framing her fragile face with his hands. And in that moment he knew the awful truth.

When he spoke again, his voice was low and shaky, the thick lump in his throat making it difficult to speak. 'I wish there was some other way to do this, to make this easier for you and for me, but there isn't.' Joe tilted his head back, his eyes fixed on the blue sky above, filled with tears. 'I tried, Kath. God knows I have tried.'

He turned away, looking to control his emotions. After a few minutes of silence he continued. 'I have something important to tell you, Kathy. I only hope that you will forgive me. Since the accident, I have never known if you can understand me or not. I don't know if you can hear what I've come to say to you, but I've got to try once more.'

He took a deep breath. 'I hate everything that happened between us and I would give anything, anything, to make you well again. You have to believe that, Kathy.' Joe paused, his eyes never leaving her face. 'But now something has happened in my life that's very important. Now I've got to do what's right for me. It's time for me to begin again.' He swallowed hard, hating his words, hating himself, yet knowing that this was his salvation.

'I'll never abandon you, Kath. You will never be alone. I'll always take care of you, but it's been seven years since the accident and nothing has changed for us.'

Oh, God, this is so hard.

'But now it's time for me to put my life back together, to go forward and meet my future.' Joe rested his elbows on his knees and buried his face in his hands. When he raised his head he looked into Kathy's eyes, but they remained blank and unseeing.

He stood, looking out over the velvet lawn and wondered how each perfect day could follow one after the other, oblivious to all the things that were imperfect in the world. Then he leaned over and kissed her softly on the cheek and smoothed her hair back off her forehead. 'Goodbye, Kathy,' he whispered, then straightened and signaled to the attendant just inside the door.

Joe turned away and walked slowly toward his car. Tears spilled from his eyes, but this time he made no attempt to wipe them away. Today, for the first time in seven lonely years, he would leave his guilt behind. He had done everything in his power to help Kathy. He would never stop helping her, but it was time to begin again.

The following morning Joe called a lawyer he knew in Atlanta, someone he trusted who was not connected with anyone in the music business, and instructed him to set up a trust fund for Kathy's care. He also instructed him to do whatever was necessary to begin proceedings for a dissolution of marriage. The entire affair was to be handled as quickly and discreetly as possible. So far, Joe had been able to protect Kathy from the prying eyes of the press. He intended to keep things that way.

It should have been easy to tell his family of his decision, but it was almost as difficult as the decision itself. It wasn't that he feared their censure over the divorce, for that would not be the case. But he did fear that they would censure Stevie over her condition, and him for his abdication of responsibility.

Joe and Charlie were seated at the big kitchen table that evening, while Ellen finished loading the dishwasher. All afternoon, Joe had wrestled with how to tell them about the divorce. It wasn't that they wouldn't understand, because they would. And he knew they liked Stevie, so that was not the problem. The problem was his impending fatherhood. How would they feel about that?

He took a deep breath. 'Uh . . . I know that you have been wondering about Stevie and me.'

Ellen came over to the table and sat down. Charlie looked up and nodded. Privately, they had speculated about what had happened that New Year's, but they had agreed not to bring it up unless Joe did.

Joe ran his hands over his face. 'This is such a mess! There is no easy way to tell you this. Stevie is pregnant. I'm going to be a father.' There. It was said.

Joe looked from his mother to his father, waiting for their reaction, for them to say something, but they remained silent. He did notice, however, that Ellen had reached out for Charlie's hand and was holding it tightly.

Joe cleared his throat nervously.

Ellen's lower lip quivered and Charlie blinked rapidly. Then Ellen went to sit next to Joe, putting her arms around him.

'This is a difficult situation for you, Joey,' said Charlie.

'It is,' said Joe, sadly. 'I wanted to talk to you about this sooner. I just didn't know what to do. What *I* should do.'

'And now you know?' asked Ellen softly.

'Now, I know. Stevie and I have created something wonderful together. This baby needs me.'

'And what about Stevie?' asked Ellen.

Joe turned to his mother with a wry smile. 'Stevie doesn't want anything to do with me. I've sent her money and every month she's returned it.'

'Have you talked with her?' Ellen asked.

'No, not since New Year's Day. Not since I told her I couldn't marry her.'

'Which brings us to the heart of the problem,' observed Charlie.

276

'It does,' admitted Joe, 'but getting this far hasn't been easy. I went to see Kathy.' Joe looked up and his eyes seemed to focus on something far away. He could see her clearly, he could still feel the pain. 'I realized something while I was there. That there had never been anything between us. And if she hadn't had that terrible accident, there would have been nothing between us now. What Kathy did in the beginning, the lie she told, was an act of complete selfishness. I know now that she had other problems. I tried to help her, but I didn't realize how ill she was until it was too late. In spite of all that happened between us, I still care about her and I have an obligation to her. I always will.'

Joe breathed deeply.' But now I have other obligations, so I . . . I've started divorce proceedings.'

Tears ran down Ellen's face. 'When are you going to tell Stevie?' she asked, knowing how her son must have wrestled with his decision, and how Stevie must have felt when she found out about Joe.

'When the time is right,' he replied softly.

For the most part Stevie was resigned to becoming a single mother. She was determined to do a better job raising her child than her mother had done with her. Soon she would have to tell her mother about the baby, but she wasn't ready for the questions she would have to answer, or the litany her mother would recite of wrongs that men could do. Including an illegitimate child. Stevie knew about all those wrongs and still she had let her heart rule her head.

As the months passed, Stevie realized that sooner or later she would have to move to a larger place, but right

277

now she would stay where she was. Since she didn't have an extra bedroom to use as a nursery, she compromised by painting her bedroom a pale sunny yellow, and hanging new curtains. In one corner of the room, a baby bed and a matching chest waited in their cartons to be assembled. Next to that was a mobile and several pictures. A baby quilt and pillow, carefully wrapped in tissue, waited in the closet.

On the day she first felt the baby move, she had decided it was time to tell her mother she was pregnant. That Saturday, Stevie called Carole and asked if she could come home for a visit. Even though it was early in April, it still snowed that afternoon; when Stevie arrived in Eagle, several hours late, it was already dark.

'I thought you changed your mind,' said Carole as she opened the door against the biting wind.

'No,' said Stevie, brushing the snow from her coat and stomping her feet to shake the snow off her boots. 'It was just slow going. It's snowing hard out toward the highway and at times it was difficult to see the lights of the car in front of me.'

Inside the trailer it was warm. Stevie shrugged out of her coat, and carried it and her small canvas bag back to the bedroom. When she returned to the kitchen, Carole was pouring boiling water into two white ceramic mugs.

'Instant coffee?'

Stevie declined and opted for hot chocolate instead. She looked around the trailer, noting that nothing had changed since the last time she was here. Everything still looked dingy.

'Do you want something to eat?' asked Carole.

'No, thanks. I stopped for a hamburger just before I got on the highway.'

For the first fifteen minutes they exchanged, if not pleasantries, small talk. The opening she had been waiting for came when Carole asked her what had made her decide to visit.

'I have some news.'

Stevie took a deep breath, but before she could speak Carole said in a flat disinterested voice, 'You're either getting married, or you're pregnant, or both.'

Deflated, Stevie looked at her mother and wished for the thousandth time that she knew what made her tick. Where was the romance in her soul, the zest for living, the love she should have had for her only child?

'Only one of the above, and it doesn't involve a band of gold,' Stevie answered, resorting to sarcasm.

Carole was silent for a minute, then reached for the pot of water on the stove and refilled their cups. 'What are you going to do about it?'

'Do?' asked Stevie. '*Do*?' she repeated, her voice rising. 'As in, "Do I plan to terminate the pregnancy?"'

Carole nodded, her expression unchanged.

Stevie laughed derisively. 'I should have known that would be your first question. Well, I'm not going to *do* anything, Carole. I'm going to have this baby.'

'What about the father? Have you told him?' Carole reached for a pack of cigarettes and a lighter.

'He's not going to marry me, if that's what you're asking. It's a long story,' said Stevie with a sigh.

Carole placed the cigarette between her lips and inhaled deeply. 'It usually is. Who is he?'

'He's . . . nobody. Just a guy I met on vacation,' answered Stevie. It was partly true. She would never tell her mother that the baby's father was rich.

'What about money?' asked Carole. 'Will he help you out?'

Stevie nodded. 'He's already made arrangements,' she answered truthfully. She would not tell her mother that she had refused every attempt of Joe's to help. Carole would never understand that.

'How far along are you?' asked Carole, letting her eyes stray down to Stevie's midriff. But her bulky sweater revealed nothing.

'Four and a half months. The baby is due in August.'

Stevie waited then for some words of encouragement that would be supportive of her decision, some offer of help, some sign of affection, but she waited in vain. The words when they did come were harsh and unyielding.

'Well, I hope you're not planning to come back here when you have this kid. This is your problem, Stevie. I dealt with mine a long time ago.'

Stevie swallowed, fighting down the hurt she felt. What had she expected? A sudden rush of maternal concern after twenty-eight years? An offer of moral support? How many times would she set herself up for failure before she would realize that Carole cared nothing for her? Nothing at all.

Stevie pushed her chair back from the kitchen table and stood. 'Don't worry, I won't bring my problems or my responsibilities home to you. It is my decision to have this baby, and it was made out of the desperate need to have someone of my own. I love this baby and I will care for it without your help. I don't know why I

always think that someday things might change between us, *Mother* –' Stevie took a deep shaky breath
'– but they never will, will they?'

Carole averted her eyes from her daughter and ran
the long red fingernail of her index finger around and
around the rim of the coffee cup. 'No,' she answered.
And in that single word was all the blame she had
always laid on Stevie for screwing up her life.

Stevie straightened her small shoulders, her pride
still intact. 'I'll leave early in the morning. I'll try not to
wake you.'

For just a split second she waited, as that childish
need to have her mother to say something caring
surfaced. Then she sighed and walked toward the
bedroom.

CHAPTER 22

Long before Stevie told her mother about her pregnancy, she had confided in Harry Conklin. While he had been supportive, he had also been shocked – speechless, even.

'You, Stevie?'

Stevie had shrugged and replied, 'Me, Harry.'

'Well, I'm . . . I'm . . .'

'Surprised?' supplied Stevie.

'Dumbfounded is more like it.'

'I know you have too much class to ask, Harry, so I'll just get this over with. The father and I are not getting married.'

'I see.' Harry leaned back in his chair and digested the news. He was of a generation to whom the term 'single mother' hadn't existed. It was a concept that, no matter how open-minded he tried to be, still eluded him. As the parent of four grown children, he knew how tough it was to raise a family. He also knew how many times one small child could zap the energy of two adults. He couldn't imagine going it alone, day after day. And Stevie – Stevie of all people – she was so sensible.

Harry reached deep into his memory, calling up long-ago emotions when he had been a younger man and he had first met his wife. He had been so intense, so focused. And nothing could have kept him from falling in love. He had been very lucky. Things had worked out. But, he reasoned, Stevie hadn't been as lucky, and times were different. So, if there wasn't going to be a wedding, she didn't have many options.

Stevie waited for his next question, but Harry didn't have to ask who the father was. He knew, and he had a pretty good idea when the baby was due.

'Is there anything you need, Stevie?' he asked quietly. 'Are you doing okay?'

She smiled for the first time in a while. 'I am now,' she answered, grateful for his support.

Harry cleared his throat. 'Good,' he said gruffly. 'Now get back to work.'

When Kevin Moore nearly skidded around the corner near her desk a few weeks later, she knew he needed a favor. Breathlessly, he leaned over her computer.

'You're fogging up my screen, Kevin,' she complained.

'Sorry. Listen, Stevie, I need your help. Will you go over to the courthouse for me and sit in on the Longstreet hearing?'

Stevie groaned. 'Kevin . . .'

'Just this once, Stevie, please?'

'And what are you going to be doing while I'm at the courthouse?'

'My wife's car won't start and I have to pick up the kids at school.'

'Well, that's better than your last excuse. Okay, I'll do it, but just this once. Oh, and make sure you clear this with Harry.'

'Thanks, Stevie, you're a pal.'

Stevie glanced at her watch. Court resumed at one o'clock. She had plenty of time to grab some lunch and walk the six blocks to the courthouse.

Outside it was a beautiful day. After a long winter, spring had finally arrived in Denver. The walk to the courthouse was invigorating; once there, she hated to go inside. Like many public buildings, the corridors were dark and poorly lighted. When she found the right courtroom, she slipped inside. Seated in the back, she pulled out a notebook and began to takes notes.

Stevie had to admit that the Longstreet case was more interesting than most, and it was one that she had followed. She had actually met Worth Longstreet once at a charity fundraiser she had attended with Beth. He was a handsome man in his early fifties. Everything about him was expensive and well-groomed.

Longstreet was a socially prominent and well-respected physician who was on trial for the murder of his second, and much younger, wife. What made the case even more tragic was that the wife had been three months' pregnant when she was killed.

It was Longstreet's contention that an intruder broke into their house late at night while he and his wife were sleeping, tied him up and killed his wife. There was only one problem with his story, thought Stevie, as she listened to the court proceedings.

The next day, Kevin thanked her for filling in for him.

'What would you say if I followed this trial all the way through?' she asked.

'It's fine with me, Stevie, but why the sudden change of heart?'

'I don't know, Kevin. There was something about Longstreet . . . maybe it was his complete lack of emotion while the prosecutor delivered his opening statement.'

For the next week Stevie continued to cover the trial. She was especially interested when Longstreet decided to testify on his own behalf.

'He's guilty as sin,' she had reported back to Harry the next morning. 'His delivery was too smooth. This was not a man who was distraught over the death of his young and beautiful wife and the child she was carrying.'

'Well,' Harry had said with a sarcasm that Stevie decided to ignore, 'I guess I needn't send you back to the courthouse today since you've got it all figured out.'

Stevie nodded in agreement. 'There's only one problem,' she had confided.

'And that is?' Harry had asked.

'The prosecution has only circumstantial evidence and they haven't yet established a motive.'

'I see,' Harry had said. 'Which means exactly what, Stevie?'

'It means I have to figure out the motive behind the murder. The prosecution has already established opportunity.'

'Lord help the judicial system,' Harry muttered. 'Go,

Stevie, just make sure we have enough for a column for tomorrow's paper.

'No problem,' she assured him.

Stevie had covered every angle she could think of. She had talked to the police, studied the hearings each day, and while she knew nothing more than she had at the beginning, she was still convinced that Worth Longstreet was guilty.

As it turned out, it was a remark that Beth had made regarding the oddity of a man the age and importance of Worth Longstreet suddenly wanting to become a father that triggered Stevie's imagination.

The following day, she had pondered that remark and became more convinced than ever that perhaps his wife's pregnancy was significant. She had begun by digging into his personal background, then into his professional life.

'Maybe he was too busy building a successful career,' suggested Beth later.

'Umm, I don't think so. He's been practicing for over twenty years. Besides I talked to his first wife. She told me that when they were married she wanted a family, but he never wanted to be tied down.'

'Well, maybe it was a mid-life crisis. Perhaps he had decided that he wanted a child to carry on the family name,' said Beth.

'Well, whatever the reason, said Stevie, 'the pregnancy wasn't planned. Doctor Longstreet had booked himself and his wife on a cruise in June. She would have been seven months' pregnant by then. Not an ideal time to travel.'

* * *

'I've got it,' she announced to Harry one afternoon. 'Well, motive at least. The prosecution will have to go back and do more digging for the hard evidence.'

Harry sat back in his chair, prepared to listen to Stevie's latest attempts at playing detective.

'Worth Longstreet's wife was carrying someone else's child. He couldn't have been the father because he couldn't have children. The knowledge that she had cheated on him drove him to murder.'

'Stevie, are you sure?' asked Harry, suddenly attentive.

'Here it is, Harry. See for yourself.' Stevie handed Harry a handful of documents. 'Longstreet had a vasectomy while he was still married to his first wife, but I doubt she knew about it. Among the medical profession, it is an accepted practice to render professional services such as this at no charge. So there was no medical insurance involved, nothing to draw any attention. At any rate, it would have been a minor procedure.'

'How did you find out about it?' asked Harry.

'I went to the hospital and asked a lot of questions. I found a nurse who remembered that he had once been treated by a colleague. She had a friend who worked at his clinic. Bingo!'

'So you think Worth Longstreet actually killed his wife in a fit of jealousy?'

'Not exactly,' she replied. 'A man like Longstreet would never do something like that.'

'But I thought you said . . .'

'Yes, I did,' she explained to Harry. 'But what I meant was that Longstreet is responsible for his wife's death. A man like him would never dirty his hands. He hired someone to do it. That's why there is no physical evidence linking him to the crime.'

When Stevie presented what she had uncovered to Harry, it was enough to justify the story that appeared in the paper the following day.

When other newspapers across the country picked up the story, Harry said, 'Sometimes you amaze me, Stevie.'

'Yeah,' she replied with a grin. 'Sometimes I even amaze myself.'

It was Lorraine Fisher, Joe's secretary, who first brought the story to Joe's attention. 'Isn't that something? Like right out of a movie. I knew all along that Stevie Parker had guts. Knew it the first time I took that message she left for you.' When Joe didn't respond, Lorraine went on. 'Do you remember that message, Joe?'

'I remember,' he said drily. 'Let me see that, please, and keep any further comments you're about to make to yourself.'

Lorraine smiled, trying her best to appear innocent, and surrendered the newspaper.

Joe took it into his office and sat at his desk. Along with the story about the prominent Denver doctor who had been found guilty of conspiracy to commit murder was a picture of Stevie and the story of how she had uncovered facts that had helped to convict him.

Joe stared at it for a very long time, then reached for the phone and dialed her number. He longed to hear her voice, to have her reassure him that she was okay and that the baby was okay. But what would he say to her?

Congratulations? Nice work? I think about you every minute of every day? I'm miserable without you? I'll never be the same until we're together again?

He hung up before completing his call.

That evening Jeannie took the elevator to Joe's Nashville apartment. After that afternoon in Cleveland, she had never again been as obvious in her attempts to change their relationship. That whole episode still rankled. But she would bide her time. Now that Stevie Parker was out of the picture, she would be able to turn things around.

'Hi,' said Joe as he opened his door. 'I'm almost ready, just need to re-do this tie.' Tonight they were on their way to a dinner meeting with the management of MultiSound. He turned and walked back through the living room toward the bedroom, and Jeannie couldn't help but admire what Joe Devlin did for a tuxedo. There might be fifteen men all dressed in the same identical attire tonight, but Joe would stand out from all of them.

One of the things that Jeannie Williams found intriguing about Joe Devlin was that he was as comfortable in formal dress, surrounded by a roomful of tuxedo-clad recording executives, as he was in jeans while shooting pool in a neighborhood bar. 'Want me to tie it for you?' called Jeannie sweetly.

'No, thanks,' he said from behind the door. 'I think I've – got it. But you can get my copy of the agreement out of my briefcase. I've made some notes in the margin that I want you to look over.'

Jeannie looked around, then spotted the briefcase on the floor next to a chair. Deftly, she flipped the top open, and began to look through the contents. She located the papers and was in the act of closing the case when she noticed the return address of an unfamiliar law firm on a large envelope. She reached inside and pulled the envelope out. It was from Atlanta. Why had Joe contacted a law firm other than the one in Nashville they always used? Was he trying to negotiate a deal behind her back?

Looking toward the closed bedroom door, she reached inside the envelope. What she saw caused her mouth to drop open with surprise. It was a petition for divorce! John Joseph Devlin was petitioning for a dissolution of his marriage to Katherine Lee Harrison Devlin.

Stunned, she read it again, then quickly scanned the rest of the pages, but the only information of any value was that Katherine Devlin was currently a resident of Jasper County, Georgia. Tomorrow she would make some inquiries.

'Hey, Jeannie, does this look straight?' Joe called from down the hall.

Jeannie jumped and hastily returned the envelope and its contents to the briefcase.

'Here,' she said with a smile, standing as he came into the living room, 'let me take a look.' With her long manicured nails, she ran her hands up the lapels of his tuxedo, then playfully straightened his black tie. 'You look like a million dollars,' she said in a sultry voice.

And what I just found out about you, darling, could be worth at least that much and more.

When her condition had become obvious, there was so much speculation at work about the baby's father that Stevie was tempted to quit and try her hand at freelance writing. But the regular paycheck was more important to her than her pride. Carefully she monitored her spending and put as much money into her savings account as possible. It would see her through her maternity leave when, after her vacation and sick leave had been used, she would be without an income until she could return to work.

If she had put her pride aside and accepted the monthly checks that continued to arrive from Joe, finances would not have been a problem. But each time his check arrived she returned it. It was only his letters, always a single page in length, that she kept. They always included his schedule for the month and a few phone numbers in case she needed to reach him, and always a request to accept the check he had enclosed.

Against her better judgement, Stevie followed Joe's career. It was difficult not to, since his picture and his music seemed to be everywhere. His popularity continued to grow. Sometimes she loved him and sometimes she hated him, but at no time could she put him out of her mind. What a lopsided thing love could be.

'No one ever told me that it would be so uncomfortable to be pregnant in the summer,' Stevie said to Bill as they entered the air-conditioned building and made their way toward the elevator. With her forearm she took a quick swipe at the drooping curls that stuck to her forehead. It was early June and she still had almost two and a half months to go until her due date.

'Would it have stopped you?' asked Bill with a sly grin.

Stevie shot him a look that said that she didn't appreciate his attempt at humor. 'You know what I mean,' she replied.

Bill reached out and grabbed Stevie by the shoulder and gave her a teasing shake. 'You are going to survive this, Stevie, and when it is all over I'll have a beautiful nephew or niece.'

Even though Bill Schaeffer was no relation to Stevie, he had appointed himself the baby's official uncle, just as Beth would become its aunt. Stevie welcomed his genuine interest. They were friends and would never be more, but Bill was someone she could trust and the only person besides Beth Carr who knew for a fact that Joe Devlin was the father of her baby.

'See you later,' said Bill as he and Stevie stepped out of the elevator. 'Got to get back to work.'

'Thanks for lunch,' she said. Bill had bought hot dogs and cokes from a street vendor, then they had found a shady spot and empty bench on the Sixteenth Street Mall. It was the perfect place for people watching.

Stevie had just settled herself in front of her computer when Tom Harris, an assistant sports editor and a man she had never liked, stopped by her desk.

'Have you heard that Joe Devlin is going to be in town in a couple of weeks? He's doing a concert at

McNichols Arena,' Tom said with a hint of smugness in his voice.

Stevie kept her eyes fixed on her computer screen. 'Really? Are you planning to go?' she asked offhandedly.

Tom was caught off guard. He had been needling Stevie since her condition became visible. In the past he had asked her out several times, but each time she refused. Now it irritated the hell out of him that no one seemed to know who Stevie Parker, Miss Too-good-for-him, was fooling around with. He suspected it might be Devlin.

'Uh, no,' he replied, not quite as sure of himself as he had been a few minutes ago. 'Actually, I thought you might be going.'

'No,' answered Stevie carefully, looking up at him for the first time, 'I don't like country music. You'll have to excuse me, Tom. I have to finish this. Harry's waiting for it.'

'Yeah, sure,' Tom mumbled as he shrugged and turned away.

Stevie looked back down at her computer and allowed herself the tiniest of smiles. Then she resumed typing. Today alone, at least five of her co-workers had asked her if she knew Joe was going to be in town. When she had seen the press release then heard the announcement on the radio she told herself it didn't matter, but it did. All of a sudden he wasn't going to be hundreds or even thousands of miles away. Joe would be here in Denver. Hardly anyone had missed the opportunity to make her aware of that.

She could tell herself that she was over and done with him, but every time she felt her baby move she was reminded of him. She knew that when her child was born she would look into that tiny face and be reminded of Joe every day for the rest of her life.

His latest album was at the top of the charts, and each time she heard him sing it was like a caress, soft and loving. And in her mind she would see his handsome face and the laughing eyes that seemed to know all her secrets. Then she would remember the last time they had made love and the hurtful accusation that had followed.

During the next two weeks there was a media blitz to promote the concert. Without warning she would see his face on television and hear his voice on the radio. The worst was the night she had seen a clip from the Biloxi concert on TV. It was the segment of Joe singing 'Crazy'. Her eyes had clouded with tears. Other times she wondered what was wrong with her. Why couldn't she forget him?

By the night of the first concert, Stevie was frazzled. If she had to tell one more person that no, she had not heard from Joe and no, she was not going to the concert, she would scream. Just knowing that he was within reach had unnerved her. But Joe had not attempted to contact her. He might as well have been a thousand miles away.

What did you expect?

I thought maybe . . .

On the way home from work, Stevie stopped by the grocery store and did some shopping. The grocery, usually crowded at that time, looked deserted. They are all at the concert, decided Stevie.

All those women who should be home fixing dinner for their husbands are out tonight, fantasizing over Joe Devlin's every word and every smile. Just like me. But when it's over they, at least, have sense enough to go home and get on with their lives. I never even knew when the show was over.

At home she shoved the plastic container of salad that would be her dinner in the refrigerator and put her groceries away. When she had finished, she played back the messages on her answering machine and scanned her mail.

Then she flipped on TV and watched the news. During *Entertainment Tonight* she ate her salad. By 9:00 p.m. she had washed her hair, painted her nails and was in bed reading. At 10:30 she turned out the light. Her phone never rang.

Saturday was warm and sunny and, after a morning spent running errands, Stevie decided to give her car a thorough cleaning. Dressed in a pair of denim shorts and an old pink shirt that used to be baggy but now stretched over her extended belly, she marched toward her car with determination. She had no idea where this sudden burst of energy had come from, but today it seemed therapeutic. She wanted to keep busy.

She didn't want to think about Joe; she didn't want to dwell on the fact that he was here in town and hadn't wanted to see her. That was her emotional response. Intellectually, she knew that any contact with him was futile. He was married. Off limits. And it was over.

Armed with an assortment of cleaners, Stevie opened the car door and scooted across the front seat to begin work. When she straightened from her bent-over position after cleaning the dashboard and both door panels, she had a kink in her back along with several smudges on her face. Her hair had escaped the black hair band she was wearing and fell forward over her forehead. Needing to stretch, she opened the car door on the passenger side and pushed herself out and up. She was still not big, considering how far along she was, but balancing her extra weight had become increasingly difficult.

At seven months into her pregnancy, Stevie looked more like she was hiding a basketball under her shirt than a baby. With both hands on her hips she stood back from the car and bent from the waist, first to the right, then to the left, stretching as she admired the job she had done.

With one hand she pulled her hair band out and ran her fingers through her hair. Then she replaced the hair band, pushing her hair back off her forehead, and patted her tummy. 'We do good work, baby,' she said in a soft voice. 'Maybe we could go into business together.'

'You wouldn't need another partner, would you?' asked a deep, amused voice behind her.

Stevie whirled around at the sound, her eyes wide open and disbelieving. No more than ten feet away, leaning against the fender of a red four-wheel drive, was Joe Devlin. The tan shirt he wore was open at the throat, the cuffs folded back to reveal powerful forearms. His long legs were encased in jeans and his feet, crossed at the ankles, were clad in a pair of Nikes. His baseball cap was pushed back off his forehead to reveal the humor in his brown eyes. The grin on his face was tentative as he waited for Stevie to say something.

Joe watched the expressions that crossed her face, intent on gauging her reaction to his sudden appearance. It had been almost six months since that New Year's Day, and he had come to see her, to ask her to marry him. He was free now; his divorce final only a few days ago.

Stevie, who had been alternately cursing and dreaming about this man since the moment she met him, was completely speechless. With faltering steps she backed up toward her car. When she felt the warm metal against the the backs of her legs, she placed both hands behind her on the fender. It was something to cling to. When he had first spoken, her eyes had locked with his. Now she couldn't seem to look away.

'Aren't you going to tell me how glad you are to see me?' asked Joe.

Stevie shook her head from side to side.

'You've changed,' Joe said pointedly as his eyes traveled down to her protruding stomach.

'It is that obvious?' Stevie asked with sarcasm. 'What are you doing here, Joe?' she asked defensively.

Joe smiled. 'I did a concert here last night. Surely you read about it.'

'I know that,' said Stevie. She let go of the fender long enough to gesture at the ground. 'I mean, what are you doing *here*?'

Now the smile had faded and his voice was serious as he answered, 'I came here to see you, Stevie, and my baby.'

'Great,' she said. 'Well, now that you've seen us you can put your conscience to rest, stuff your money back in your pocket, and be on your way. The baby and I are just fine.'

Joe shook his head. 'I don't think I can do that, Stevie.'

'Why not? You certainly didn't have any trouble with it the last time I saw you.'

Joe unfolded his arms, pushed himself off the fender of his car, and crossed the pavement slowly toward her.

Defiantly, she crossed her arms across her breasts. When Joe was no more than a few feet away from her Stevie warned him, 'Stay away from me, Joe Devlin.'

But Joe continued to close in on her until he was only inches away.

She straightened, letting her arms fall at her sides. 'Don't touch me,' she said nervously.

Joe grinned and her heart stalled. How could any one man have this effect on her? Stevie tried to back away, but she was trapped against the car.

Joe reached both arms straight out and rested them on her shoulders; his hands dangling loosely behind her.

'I'm warning you, Joe,' she said unsteadily.

But Joe wasn't listening. His right hand had moved from her shoulder to the hollow just below her ear. With the roughened pad of his thumb he slowly massaged the soft, sensitive skin there.

A little shiver raced through her. His touch was too much for her to handle and she jerked away from him. 'Stop it, Joe,' she said irritably. 'Leave me alone. I've gotten along fine without you. This is no time to change things.'

'But you want me, Stevie.' His word were even, factual.

Stevie shut her eyes tightly. Oh, God, how she wanted him, in spite of everything. 'No,' she lied.

'Does it matter that I love you and want to be with you?'

Stevie hesitated, considering his words, knowing how long she had waited for this. 'No.' She lied again.

Don't do this, Joe. Please.

'What about the baby?'

'The baby is just fine. I can take care of it. Of us,' she corrected. 'Quit wasting your time trying to salvage something that was never meant to be. And,' she added, 'please don't send any more checks. I won't take a dime of your money.'

Joe took a step back and shook his head mockingly. 'You're a hard woman, Stevie Parker.'

'And you're a cheatin' man, Joe Devlin.' Her words were bitter as she stepped around Joe and began to walk away.

Without turning Joe reached back with one hand and caught Stevie by the arm, pulling her back to face him. 'What is that supposed to mean?' he asked, his voice low and hard.

Anger radiated from Stevie's blue eyes. 'Figure it out, cowboy. You're the one who's married. No wonder you couldn't come to terms with any kind of a commitment.'

Joe flinched at her words. He wanted to correct her, to tell her that he was free now, that he had come to ask her to marry him, but her words stopped him. Slowly he uncurled his fingers from her arm.

'Why didn't you tell me the truth, Joe?'

Joe looked around uncomfortably as a car pulled into the space next to Stevie's. 'Look, can we discuss this inside?'

'No.'

'Then get in my car and let's go some place where we can talk,' said Joe.

But Stevie didn't want to go anywhere with Joe. His magnetism was too great.

'Okay,' said Joe, shrugging his shoulders. 'You win this round, Stevie, but the next round belongs to me. We'll talk later. I'll send a limo to pick you up tonight and bring you to the concert.'

Before she could protest, the baby kicked her hard several times in a row. Joe's eyes followed hers downward as the little basketball-shaped bulge under her T-shirt began to move side to side of its own accord.

'What's going on?' asked Joe.

'Evidently the baby is trying to send me a message.'

Joe watched in fascination as the baby moved again. 'Can I feel it?'

Stevie watched his face and her earlier anger faded. 'You could, if I let you,' she answered softly, 'but the truth is that I want to stay as far away from you as possible.'

'Why?' asked Joe softly.

'You know why,' said Stevie, her determination wavering. 'It's . . . it's this thing you do to me. It's silly, considering how shabbily you've treated me, but you are a charmer, Joe. I'll give you that.'

'Then let me charm you into coming to the show tonight,' he said smiling.

'I don't go out with married men,' she replied evenly.

'Cut it out, Stevie. Just meet me tonight. I'll make all the arrangements. What can happen with twelve thousand people around?'

Stevie thought back to that night in Biloxi when she thought Joe was singing just to her. 'You'd be surprised,' she answered.

He watched as a variety of emotions fluttered across her small face. Then, without warning, he leaned down and kissed her softly. It took her completely by surprise. Slowly he backed away from her. 'Things aren't always the way they seem to be, honey. See you tonight,' he said confidently as he got into the four-wheel drive.

Joe had started the engine, shifted into reverse and was backing out when Stevie approached the car. He braked and waited.

'I won't be there tonight,' she repeated firmly. 'You're married, and I'm through tormenting myself over you. There is nothing between us, Joe.' She stepped back. Her eyes glistened with the hint of tears.

Joe's expression was serious. 'We have a baby, Stevie. And because of that we'll never be through with one another.' He turned his face away from her and backed the car out onto the street. Without looking back, he drove away.

Promptly at seven that evening, the limousine arrived just as Joe had promised, but Stevie sent the driver on his way. No matter how much she loved Joe, the truth was that he was married to another woman. To continue to see him would cause her nothing but heartbreak.

Across town at McNichols Arena, Joe paced nervously in his dressing room. 'Are you sure she's not here?' he asked Richie again.

Richie nodded. 'They are probably tied up in traffic. Just relax. She'll be here,' said Richie with a confidence that was far from what he was feeling. 'It's almost time,' he said, nodding toward the door. The strains of the opening group's final number could be heard echoing through the hallway.

To Joe, the concert seemed to move in slow motion. He wished he could walk off the stage and leave the band to finish the show. But he had to remember that he owed everything to the people who came to see him perform. He tried his best to avoid looking at the empty seat he had reserved for Stevie in the first row. Each time he did, his heart was full of pain. He had wanted Stevie there tonight, wanted her to hear 'Each Night Without You', the song he had written the night after they had last made love.

He looked past the spotlights into the thousands of faces before him and began to sing what he had written. The words came from deep within his soul, the music from his heart, causing many in the audience to cry unashamedly as they sang the words of loneliness and heartbreak right along with him.

After she had sent the limousine driver on his way, Stevie had been too restless to stay home so she called Bill and Beth to see if they wanted to go to the movies. Inside the dark theater Stevie sat, unable to follow the plot of the film. Her mind was on Joe.

'How about some ice cream?' asked Bill on the way home.

'I think I'm fat enough, but I have no willpower. Ice cream sounds great,' Stevie confessed.

'I never turn down ice cream, especially if you're treating, Bill,' said Beth.

They stopped at the Dolly Madison store on Evans Avenue, near the University of Denver campus.

'I love this place,' Stevie announced while she waited for a double dip of strawberries and cream on a sugar cone. 'Look at it. The high ceilings, the wooden floors, the soda fountain. I bet it hasn't changed a bit since the Forties. Just imagine a juke box over there where the big freezer case is, then close your eyes. You can almost hear the music.'

'What song is playing?' Bill asked.

'"Stardust".'

'You're such a romantic, Stevie,' said Beth.

Yeah, and look where it got me.

It was after midnight when they took Beth home. A few minutes later they arrived at Stevie's apartment. Bill walked Stevie to the door, and she had just pulled her keys out of her purse when she realized that the door was already unlocked.

'Bill, I locked this door when we left. I think there's someone inside,' whispered Stevie as she stepped back. Bill reached out to push the door open and just as he did Stevie heard Joe's voice.

'Where the hell have you been all night?' he bellowed from her bedroom.

'What are you doing here?' demanded Stevie, stepping inside. Bill followed.

'Waiting for you. You didn't answer me. Where have you been?' Joe walked into the living room.

'I don't have to answer you,' said Stevie defensively, 'but just so you'll know, I've been out. With Bill.'

'Uh, Stevie,' said Bill tentatively, peering around her. 'Is everything okay here?'

Stevie stepped aside and turned toward Bill and nodded. 'Bill, this is Joe Devlin.'

There was a distinct challenge in Joe's stance while Bill suddenly adopted the role of Stevie's protector. When Joe suddenly crossed the room to shake Bill's hand, the tension between the two men evaporated.

After a few moments, Stevie turned to Bill, 'Thanks for the nice evening. I'll see you tomorrow.'

'Are you sure you're going to be okay?' Bill nodded toward Joe.

'I'll be just fine.' Stevie smiled at Bill's chivalrous attempt to protect her. He had the heart of a lion, brave and fearless, but at five-eight Bill would hardly be a match for Joe. She closed the door and still gripping the knob, she turned to face Joe. But he was in the kitchen bent over, looking in her refrigerator.

'Let's see. We have some wine or beer, or how about coffee? What'll you have?' Joe straightened just as Stevie pushed past him and jerked the refrigerator door out of his hand and pushed it shut.

'Anything I want,' she answered, 'and what I want is for you to get out. Just how did you get in here anyway?'

'The manager let me in,' answered Joe.

'I ought to sue the management for that,' said Stevie.

'Aw, Stevie,' said Joe grinning. 'It wasn't her fault. I really had to work to convince her it would be okay.'

'Well, what finally did the trick?' asked Stevie sarcastically, her hands on her hips. 'Was it your devastating charm?'

Joe leaned against the door frame. 'That and two passes to tomorrow night's concert.'

Stevie rolled her eyes. 'I should have known. You have no principles when it comes to getting your way with women, Joe. None at all.'

'Shameful, isn't it?' said Joe as he poured two glasses of wine. 'Of course, you could have prevented this by coming to the concert tonight.' He held out the glass to her, but before she could take it he pulled it back. 'Wait. I don't think you're supposed to have any alcohol in your condition.'

'Mind your own business,' said Stevie as she took the wine glass from him. She hadn't had any alcohol since she found out she was pregnant, and she wasn't about to start now. But she wasn't going to let Joe tell her what she could or couldn't have.

'What were you doing in my bedroom? Snooping?' asked Stevie as she walked the short distance down the hall. At the doorway she stopped. On the bedroom floor were the assembly instructions and all the pieces to the baby's bed. The empty carton had been propped up against the wall.

Stevie seemed to be at a loss for words. 'I could ask you about all this,' she said after a few moments, 'but since you haven't answered any of my questions . . .' She looked up at Joe. Her eyes were wide and questioning. Her chin quivered.

Joe leaned down and kissed her lightly, then grabbed her by the hand. 'Come on, honey. You can read the instructions for me. Let's get this baby bed put together. This little guy will be here before you know it and he won't have a place to sleep. You know, Stevie, you need a bigger place. It's going to be too crowded here.'

With a gentle tug, he pulled Stevie to the floor with him. 'Where do you suppose this goes?' he asked as he reached for a screwdriver. 'Here,' he said as he pushed the sheet of instructions toward her. 'See if you can help me figure this out.'

Stevie swallowed. 'I . . .' she began.

'Wait, I've got it,' said Joe with a smile as he reached across the floor for another part. Then he paused and looked over at her. 'This is a nice bed. Our baby should feel safe and warm here. What do you think, Stevie, is it a boy or a girl?'

The sight of Joe Devlin sitting cross-legged in the middle of her bedroom floor putting together a bed for their baby was just too much for Stevie. 'What are you doing to me?' she asked in a soft, plaintive voice. 'It doesn't matter about this bed. You won't be around to see it. You're married, Joe. Go home to your wife.'

Her heart was racing. 'You know, I waited so long for you to say you loved me. I never dreamed there was any reason we couldn't be married.' She took a deep breath.

Joe reached out to take her in his arms, to tell her that they could get married, now, tomorrow, next week, whenever she wanted, any place she wanted, but before he could tell her why he was here or even touch her Stevie continued. 'Maybe you never really lied to me, but you never told the truth, either.

'All my life I've watched men lie to my mother, and I've watched her believe their lies because she wanted

306

so badly for them to be true. I'm not like her, Joe. I can't let myself believe in you. Not any more. I want you to leave.' Stevie was breathing hard now, and in her throat she tasted bitterness.

As Joe listened to her words, something inside him turned cold. When he had made his decision to seek a divorce, it had been one of the most difficult things he had ever had to do. Since then he had waited many months, purposely staying away from Stevie until he was free to ask her to marry him.

He had always loved her, from the very beginning. And now all he had to do was to tell her that he was free. But her words sliced through him. He hadn't expected this to be easy. After all, he had left her to face things alone and she was bitter and hurt. But neither had he expected this. It had never occurred to him that she wouldn't welcome him back into her life. But now he looked at her face and knew that she meant what she had said.

Joe unfolded his long legs and stood among the scattered parts on the floor. Then he reached down to pick up his hat off the floor and dusted it off against the legs of his jeans. He reached a hand out to Stevie and helped her to her feet. He kept her hand in his for just a moment, then released it.

When he reached the front door he turned and looked back. Stevie was standing in the bedroom doorway and the light behind her cast a halo that outlined her swollen shape. Joe pulled the door shut behind him with one hand. With the other he settled his hat low over his eyes. If he never saw Stevie Parker again he would always remember how beautiful she looked, and how close he had come to the happiness he so desperately wanted.

CHAPTER 23

'My God, Stevie, what happened between you and Joe last night?'

Stevie sat up in bed with the phone against her ear and pushed her hair out of her eyes. She couldn't tell what time it was, but it seemed like the middle of the night.

'Who . . .?'

'This is Richie. Joe came back here last night and practically beat down the door to my room. Then he kept me up most of the night talking about you, about his life. I don't think I've ever seen him that upset,' said Richie hurriedly.

'Richie. Richie, wait. No matter how much you want things to work out between me and Joe, they're not going to,' said Stevie with certainty.

'Why the hell not?'

'Because he doesn't love me,' answered Stevie, her voice quavering.

'Dammit, Stevie, just what do you want? Joe's life has been a living hell. Of course he loves you. Didn't he tell you? It was only because of you that he finally made the decision to get a divorce.' Richie's words hung in the air.

Stevie was stunned. 'Divorce?' she repeated in a whisper. 'Joe is divorced?'

'Yes,' said Richie impatiently. 'And it was probably the most painful thing that he has ever had to do.'

'Because he cared for her,' said Stevie, flatly.

'Geez, Stevie!' Richie took a deep breath to counter-act his frustration. 'No, I mean yes. Shit. Of course he cares for her. It was because of the way things were between him and Kathy.'

Stevie was silent, digesting what Richie had just told her. 'Then why didn't he tell me last night, Richie?'

'He never told you.' It was a statement. 'Just exactly what went on between you two last night?'

Stevie fell back against the pillows and sighed. 'I said some terrible things I didn't mean. I told him I couldn't trust him, and I didn't want him in my life.'

This time it was Richie's turn to be silent. Finally, he said, 'You two are a couple of screw-ups, you know that?'

Stevie nodded at the phone, but Richie didn't have to hear the words to know that she agreed with his assessment of their behaviour. 'I've got to see Joe,' she said. 'Where are you?'

'I'm at the hotel, but I think you should wait until tonight before you try to see him. Give him some time to think things over. Why don't you come to the show tonight?' said Richie.

'Tell me where to meet you.'

Richie ran his hand through his hair as he gave her directions. 'I'll leave a pass for you at the box office. It will get you backstage, but you'll have to show security some ID.'

A few minutes later Stevie hung up. Had she ruined everything? Now she had to figure out how she was going to get Joe to listen to her. 'Okay, baby,' she said as she patted her protruding stomach, 'we're about to find out if you inherited any of your father's talent for showbiz. Let's hope so, or this could be our swan song.'

That night in the hallway outside Joe's dressing room, Stevie waited nervously. Here the music from the stage had a strange tinny sound, thin and disjointed. The security guard had let her go as far as the door to Joe's dressing room, but no farther. He had been kind enough to get her a folding chair, but she couldn't sit still so she paced the gray concrete floor. What if Joe wouldn't accept her apology? What if he brushed right past her and didn't even acknowledge her presence?

Suddenly the music stopped and the roar of the crowd slithered backstage through the maze of hallways until Stevie finally realized that the concert was over. Joe and the band members would be leaving the stage for their dressing rooms. She panicked. Her palms were sweaty and she was so sure she was about to be sick that she bent over, her hands folded over her stomach.

Voices and laughter echoed down the hall. The sounds were louder now, more rambunctious. He was on his way. Frantically Stevie looked for a place to hide. She couldn't face Joe now. Especially now that she thought she might be sick.

'Are you alright, ma'am?' asked the security guard as he leaned over to unlock the door to Joe's dressing room.

Stevie spun around, frightened by the unexpected sound of his voice. Her eyes were wide when she shook her head. 'No,' she pleaded. 'I think I'm going to be sick.'

Now it was the guard's turn to panic. 'There's a ladies' room down that way,' he offered, gesturing down the hallway toward the stage.

Stevie shook her head, bringing her hand to her mouth. She needed a place to hide. Now. 'I can't make it,' she said, feigning weakness.

The guard looked from right to left and then did the only thing he could think of. He let Stevie into the dressing room. 'The bathroom is over there,' he said quickly, 'And for God's sake, please don't tell anyone how you got in here. I could lose my job.'

Stevie turned and waved weakly as she shut the bathroom door behind her. Inside, she closed the lid on the toilet and sat down. If she had lied to the guard about being sick just a few minutes ago, she wasn't lying now. Why hadn't she thought this out instead of rushing head first into this? Stevie looked down at her stomach, protruding under the tailored beige blouse and slacks she wore. She should have considered the consequences of her actions a long time ago.

The noise from the hallway spilled into the large dressing room. A dozen voices, mostly male, mingled, the sounds punctuated with laughter and occasional shouts.

'Hey, Joe,' shouted Allen Lee, 'I thought that woman in the front row was going to tear your pants off, then go for your shorts.

'If she had been six inches closer, she could have done some serious damage,' replied Joe, laughing.

'Nah,' said Richie, 'She would have to get a lot closer than that!' The laughter was loud and bawdy.

From her place inside the bathroom Stevie could hear the group as they entered the dressing room, then the tinkling sound of ice being dropped into glasses. She stood now and crept over to the door, opening it just enough to allow her to see into the room beyond. Most of the faces there were recognizable, including Jeannie's. Why did *she* have to be here?

Stevie's face flushed at the thought of being discovered like this. Somehow she had to get herself out of here. The small tiled room was windowless and there was no place to hide except the shower stall. It was then that she remembered that Joe and the band would leave the dressing room soon to sign autographs for the fans who were waiting outside for them. She would leave then. No one even had to know she was here. She only hoped no one needed to use the bathroom.

But that hope was short lived. Stevie jumped at the sound of the doorknob turning. The door opened slightly, a face appeared briefly, then the door was pulled shut again. She sat up straight but before she could decide whether she should hide or not, the door opened again.

'Stevie! What are you doing here?' hissed Allen Lee as he quickly shut the door behind him. 'And what the hell happened to you?' he added, as his eyes fixed on her altered shape for the first time. The members of the band hadn't seen Stevie since before Christmas.

Stevie opened her mouth to answer, but Allen Lee waved his hand in the air. 'Never mind,' he said, looking her over. 'I think I've got this figured for myself. You've come to see Joe and *that* is the reason.' He inclined his head toward her stomach.

'Allen Lee,' she said, tugging at the sleeve of his shirt, 'you've got to help me. I did come here to see Joe, but I can't go through with this. Not in front of all those people. You have got to make sure that no one comes in here. Then, when Joe and the guys leave, I can get out of here.'

'Not a chance, Stevie. You and Joe belong together. All the guys know it, so why don't you two?'

Just then there was a knock at the bathroom door. 'Hey, man! You gonna be in there all night?' asked the voice on the other side. Quickly, Allen Lee opened the door and pulled the intruder inside to join them.

'Stevie, what are you doing here?' asked Brad. Then he saw the bulge under Stevie's blouse. 'Oh,' he said, blushing, as if that one word explained everything.

'Well, stop staring at her like you never saw a pregnant lady before,' admonished Allen Lee in a loud whisper, 'and go tell Richie to get rid of all those people out there. Stevie is here to see Joe. Privately.'

Brad nodded, still staring at Stevie until Allen Lee gave him a shove. 'Now!'

'What do I say?' Brad asked as an afterthought.

'You'll think of something,' said Allen Lee as he opened the door and pushed Brad out.

A few minutes later Richie eased through the bathroom door to join Allen Lee and Stevie. 'I've been looking all over for you, Stevie. Where have you been?' he asked anxiously.

'Shh!' This came from Allen Lee.

Richie shot him a look that said he should mind his own business. 'I've always considered myself a good detective, but honestly,' he continued, 'I never thought to look for you in here. Stevie, what the hell are you doing?'

The sound that escaped Stevie was a cross between a sigh and a moan as she hid her head in her hands and considered the absurdity of her situation. 'You have to get me out of here, Richie,' she pleaded.

'Clear it out, guys.' The deep voice from behind them echoed, bouncing from wall to wall, from ceiling to floor.

Richie jumped. Allen Lee moved protectively toward Stevie. Stevie's head jerked up and she could feel the blood rush to her face.

Reluctantly, Richie and Allen Lee made their way through the doorway. Once they were out of the way there was room in the bathroom for Joe. Leaning against the wall in his black shirt and jeans with his hat pushed back off his forehead, he seemed taller and more imposing than ever.

Slowly, Stevie pushed herself to her feet. Before Joe could speak, she asked. 'How did you know . . .?'

'Brad. He's a lousy liar.'

'I . . . I don't even know what I'm doing here,' said Stevie, shaking her head and wishing that it really was possible to die of embarrassment. 'I let Richie talk me into coming here tonight, then when I got here I knew I couldn't face you.' Her eyes were suspiciously bright and her small chin was quivering slightly.

Joe looked down at her heart-shaped face and her glistening blue eyes and his heart melted. All he wanted to do was to hold her in his arms, but it was too soon for that. He wasn't about to let her off that easily. Not after the hell she had put him through last night. 'So you hid in my bathroom. Why are you here, Stevie?' His expression had softened, but Stevie was too nervous to notice.

It was difficult to breathe this close to him. She swallowed. 'I came to tell you that I didn't mean what I said last night and . . .'

'And . . .?' repeated Joe.

He is not going to make this easy on me.

But Stevie didn't see the slight crinkling at the corners of his brown eyes as they watched her. Nor did she know that Joe was holding his breath because what she would say next was so damn important to him.

Stevie took a deep breath. 'I love you, Joe. I love you so much that you're all I think about. I . . .' Stevie's voice drifted away.

Joe tilted the brim of his hat forward, straightened his long frame, then reached out for her hand. He pulled her from the bathroom back through the dressing room and out into the hallway.

Halfway down the hall he stopped, suddenly, released her hand and turned toward her. Stevie waited. She had expected Joe to do something; take her in his arms, kiss her, walk away and leave her, anything. Instead, he reached for the crown of his hat with his fingertips, lifted it slightly, then resettled it so the brim of his hat rode lower over his eyes.

For a few brief moments while he scrutinized her, time had ceased to move. Without taking his eyes from her Joe held out his hand, palm upward. And Stevie, her eyes wide, her heart trusting, placed her small hand in his. Joe turned and led her toward the backstage exit. She blinked, bewildered, as she was pulled along behind him. Since her declaration of love, Joe had not uttered one word.

Outside the auditorium the other members of the band waited. Jeannie started toward Joe as he came through the door, then stopped abruptly when she saw Stevie. 'Well, well, just look who's here again.' She looked Stevie over, then added, 'And we certainly don't have to ask what you've been up to lately.' The words were barbed, designed to hurt.

They did.

'Jeannie!' hissed Richie. 'Shut up.'

Joe sent a glaring look toward Jeannie as he passed her by. 'I'll catch up with you later,' he said to Richie as he and Stevie walked across the parking lot toward her car.

A few minutes later Joe pulled into a brightly lit all-night café that specialized in serving breakfast twenty-four hours a day.

'Two coffees, make one de-caf,' Joe said to the waitress as he and Stevie slid into opposite sides of the aqua vinyl-covered booth. If the waitress had recognized him, she didn't let on, or maybe she was just too tired to care. When the two steaming cups were placed before them, Joe thanked her and then focused his attention on Stevie.

Stevie looked around. Only a few other tables were occupied. The quiet hum of voices and the smell of frying bacon was somehow soothing. Of all the places he could have taken her, this had to be the least romantic.

As if he read her thoughts, he said, 'This is neutral territory.'

'Oh.' Maybe it was better this way. Bright lights and people. A guarantee that there would be no scenes.

Joe picked up the thick white mug and drank. 'My divorce was final a few days ago,' he said quietly as he set the cup down on the beige formica tabletop.

Stevie waited, not trusting herself to speak, holding her breath at Joe's words.

'I went to see you last night to tell you that, and to ask you to marry me.' He watched her face carefully.

Stevie bit her bottom lip. She could feel her chin quivering. She had waited so long to hear those words and now that she had, she couldn't respond.

Joe waited but Stevie only stared at him. Then he cleared his throat and looked away. Unable to stand her silence any longer, he said, 'Well?'

This time it was Stevie's turn to clear her throat. All this would have been so much easier if he had only taken her in his arms. But here in this restaurant it all seemed so impersonal as if they were discussing someone other than themselves.

'Umm, ah . . .' Stevie stopped then began again. 'There's something you should know. I have lousy luck, Joe.'

Joe nodded in understanding.

'No, it's more than that,' she protested. 'It's really bad. Did I ever tell you that?' Stevie fought the urge to laugh hysterically. 'You see, my mother didn't want me when I was born and for eighteen years she ignored me until I finally got the message and left home. Then there was Michael, my boyfriend. My only real boyfriend.

317

After a few months I thought we were headed down the aisle, but instead he dumped me for . . . for someone else.'

Stevie rested her forehead in her hands, then peeked up at Joe. 'Oh, what the hell. You might as well know the truth,' she continued in a conversational tone. 'He dumped me for a guy.' Stevie's attempted laugh was ragged. 'Well, let me tell you, that did a lot for my self-confidence.'

Taking a deep breath, Stevie continued. 'I've had years and years of bad luck. Then my vacation was canceled because of a blizzard. So instead of going to Florida, I met you. Only I didn't know who you were, and I certainly didn't know you were married, so I slept with you and now . . . well, you know the rest. Now how's that for luck?'

Stevie paused and rolled her eyes. 'Yesterday I said some nasty things to you and probably ruined my one shot at the real thing. Real happiness. You see, Joe, I figured that out because ever since I told you that I love you in the hallway back there, you haven't said anything that would make this any easier for me.'

Her breathing was shallow now and she finding it harder and harder to bear Joe's scrutiny. 'Now I don't suppose there's any chance that . . . that you still want to marry me, is there, Joe?' The words came out in a rush.

'Yes.' Joe's tone was straightforward.

'Yes?' Stevie's eyes widened. 'Yes? Are you sure you're not just saying that because you feel obli-gated? Or sorry for me? Because of this?' Her eyes traveled down to the roundness beneath her breasts.

'Because if you do – feel obligated, I mean – we can just forget about this whole marriage deal. I can just add it to my bad luck list.'

'I feel obligated,' Joe said finally, 'because I love you, Stevie. Before I met you, it didn't matter to me whether I was married or not. I never really believed that I would meet anyone who could make that big a difference in my life. The existence of a marriage gave me a reason to avoid any kind of relationship. Then I met you and I let guilt get in my way. A shrink would have had a great time analyzing that.'

He paused and rubbed the base of his neck with his hand, flexing his shoulders, stretching as he did so. 'I want to tell you about Kathy and me.' This was said in a tone so casual that it took a few seconds for it to sink in.

Stevie wanted to refuse to listen, she didn't want to know anything about the woman who had first laid claim to Joe, who would always be a presence in their lives. But the look in his eyes pleaded with her to hear him out.

He began to speak, slowly at first, then the story seemed to tumble out as if it had been locked away too long. In the glare of the overhead lights he recounted the time he and Kathy had lived together and their hasty marriage when he thought she was pregnant. Even though Joe tried to keep his voice steady, Stevie heard the underlying bitterness when he told how he had discovered Kathy had lied to him about having a child.

In a low voice he continued, describing her growing paranoia and jealously; the times she had accused him of being unfaithful; their argument in the club parking lot the night of her accident.

319

It was only when he spoke of the accident that his voice broke with emotion. Stevie reached across the table and placed her hand on his.

'She's been in a nursing home ever since.' Joe finished and looked away, swallowing the emotion that hovered so close to the surface.

'Oh, Joe, how terrible. For both of you,' Stevie whispered softly.

'She doesn't know me, Stevie. She hasn't known anyone or anything since the accident. It's been seven years. I was so overwhelmed with guilt and remorse that I vowed I would never leave her. I punished myself for so many years, even after I met you and knew without a doubt that I loved you. By that time I had convinced myself that I didn't deserve to be happy. First, I punished myself, then I punished you by telling you that I couldn't marry you.'

Joe leaned forward grasping Stevie's hands in his. 'I went a little crazy that morning when you told me about the baby. My first thought was that you were trying to trap me, just like Kathy had.

'It wasn't until after you had left that I realized that you weren't anything like that. How could you be? You wouldn't even keep the money I sent.' Joe shook his head. 'It was then that I knew I could free myself. I had always had the power, but it was one of the most difficult things I have ever had to do.'

'Oh, Joe, I never knew. I just thought that . . .'

'That I didn't love you,' finished Joe. 'But I do. I love you so much that I think I'll go crazy if I can't have you.'

'Joe,' said Stevie with a wide smile as she leaned forward, 'what are we doing here? Why did you bring me to this place?'

Joe grinned for the first time. 'Because it wasn't romantic. I needed to know how you felt about things, about me, and I didn't want any outside influences. I never meant to hurt you, Stevie. I just couldn't face the truth. Last night you said you couldn't trust me. I brought you here to find out if we could start again.'

The look in her eyes gave Joe was his answer and as soon as he saw it he jumped up, tossed some money on the table and grabbed Stevie by the hand, pulling her along with him. Outside, the glass doors had barely closed behind them when he pulled Stevie toward him, placing his hands on each side of her stomach. 'I love our baby, Stevie, and I'll always regret what I said to you when you told me you were pregnant.'

As if in response, the baby kicked and Stevie laughed as her stomach changed shapes under her blouse. Joe watched in amazement as he felt the surprisingly strong thumps under his hands. 'Is he always like this?' asked Joe.

She nodded. 'What do you expect with such strong-willed parents?'

He wrapped his arms around her and pulled her close, then leaned down to kiss her. 'Let's go home,' he said as he raised his head a few minutes later.

CHAPTER 24

As they rode through the dark deserted streets, Joe kept glancing toward Stevie as if to reassure himself that she was really here beside him.

'You're not going to change your mind, are you? When you've had time to think things over?' asked Stevie with uncertainty.

'Not a chance,' said Joe, as he pulled her closer.

Stevie snuggled against his shoulder then pulled back. 'Uh, Joe, there's . . . there's something I have to tell you. It's about getting married.'

Joe pulled her against him once more and kissed her hair. 'I know,' he said smiling down at her.

'You do?'

'Sure. I've been reading all these books on pregnancy and I know that it might not be comfortable for you if we make love.'

Stevie's eyes widened in surprise and she pushed against his shoulder in an effort to sit up straighter. 'Oh,' she said as she digested this information. 'You've been reading about pregnancy?'

'Uh huh,' he said with a grin.

'And it said that sex, uh, might . . .'

Joe nodded. 'It said that sometimes it might require some . . . innovation. But it's okay, Stevie, I just want us to be together,' he said reassuringly.

It was quiet in the car for a few seconds then Stevie asked, 'Uh, did this book say anything about, uh, what is the best way to find out about, uh, how to, you know, innovate?'

'Nope.'

'Oh.' Stevie was silent for a minute. 'Well, how do you suppose we could find out?'

At this, Joe burst out laughing. 'I'm sure you'll figure something out once we reach the hotel.'

'Yeah,' said Stevie with a mischievous grin. 'I'm sure I will.' Pregnancy had done nothing to lessen her desire for this man beside her. Briefly, she wondered if this was normal, then decided that nature probably controlled these things, and she was more than willing to cooperate.

'I may even help,' said Joe teasingly.

'Yeah,' said Stevie as she nestled against his broad shoulder. 'I'll just bet you will. But that wasn't what I was going to tell you.'

'It wasn't?' This time it was Joe's turn to look surprised.

'Nope,' she said, trying her best to look serious. 'It's about getting married. I wanted to tell you that I've always dreamed of having this big wedding. *Big*, Joe. Elaborate. You know, at least six or seven bridesmaids, a flower girl and a ring bearer. And of course I'd wear a long white dress with a lace veil, nothing too fancy, but lots of beads and sequins and pearls. And a long train. A cathedral-length train. After all, I'm only going to do this once in my life.'

There was stunned silence. Joe was caught completely off guard. Even though he had given marriage a lot of thought, never had he given any thought to the actual wedding. And if he had, his interpretation would have been very different than what Stevie had just described.

'But, Stevie,' he began a few moments later, ready to point out the obvious. His protest was interrupted when Stevie began to laugh, a clear sparkling sound.

'You were kidding about the big wedding, weren't you? I mean, all the publicity . . .' he asked.

'Well,' she said, her tone serious. Then she giggled. 'Couldn't you just see it, Joe? I'd need a dress with a ten-foot train just to balance out the size of my tummy.'

'I'll give you anything you want, Stevie, including a big wedding,' said Joe seriously.

'I know you would.' All the teasing was gone now. 'But all I want is you,' she said as they turned into the driveway of the hotel where he was staying.

Inside the lights had been dimmed and the lobby was deserted except for the skeleton staff that manned the desk. Across the room a few hardy guests sat behind tall plants in the lobby bar. Joe and Stevie had almost reached the double glass-doors that would lead past the atrium and pool to his room when a loud, brassy voice shattered the quiet.

'Did she manage to convince you that you were the father of her kid, or did she threaten to bring a paternity suit against you?'

Recognizing Jeannie's voice, Joe halted and swore, then pulled Stevie close to his side. Without turning around he reached into his pocket and extracted his room key. 'Room 319,' he said, as he held it out to Stevie. 'Go on up and wait for me.'

Stevie shook her head, wanting to stay with him.

'Go on,' he said tersely. 'I'll be up in a minute.'

Stevie glanced behind her at the redheaded woman

324

who sat at the bar, then looked worriedly at Joe. He opened the glass door for Stevie and gave her shoulder a reassuring squeeze, then a gentle push.

With a rage that threatened to explode at any moment, Joe made his way across the lobby toward the bar. From her slurred words, it was obvious that Jeannie had been drinking heavily.

From her place at the bar, Jeannie flashed him a feline smile. 'We can get our lawyers on this, honey. By the time we get through with her, that little bitch will wish she never met you.'

'Get up,' Joe said through clenched jaws when he reached her.

Jeannie stood unsteadily then ran her hand down the front of his shirt in a gesture that was meant to be possessive. Joe pushed her hand away. Her touch, which had once seemed appealing, now disgusted him.

Silently he escorted her from the lobby. Outside her room he left her. 'I'll talk to you in the morning after you've had a chance to sober up.'

Jeannie fumbled with the key to her room. She knew Joe was angry with her, but she didn't care. Always resourceful, she had found out all the details of Joe's divorce. Once he became aware of that, she was confident he would do whatever she wanted. Inside her room she stood unsteadily in front of the mirror, fluffed her red hair and studied her reflection as she removed her heavy silver earrings and the bracelets she always wore. She had no intention of letting go of Joe Devlin.

'I'm sorry, babe,' Joe whispered when Stevie opened the door to him a few minutes later. 'I hate that you heard that.'

'She's drunk,' said Stevie, needing some way to excuse the the hurtful words. 'And jealous.'

'She'll get over it,' said Joe with a certainty he didn't feel.

'No, she won't get over this, Joe. Maybe if she and I had met under different circumstances that would be true. But you slept with her. And even though it was before you and I met, it changes everything.'

'Jeannie is a professional and as the manager of this group she makes a lot of money. It's too good a deal to mess up. She may not like the fact that we're together, but she'll put it aside and get on with business as usual. But I don't want to talk about her any more,' said Joe as wrapped his arms around Stevie, then guided her backwards across the room until her knees touched the edge of the bed. With care, he lowered her onto the bed and began to nuzzle her neck while he unbuttoned her blouse.

'What *do* you want to talk about?' she asked breathlessly, all too aware of the sensations he was causing.

'Nothing,' he said, silencing her with a kiss. When he helped her slip out of her blouse, he laid down on the bed beside her, propping his head on his hand and pulling her on her side so he could see her better. In silence he stared at her as she lay there in her lacy bra and slacks.

Suddenly Stevie was embarrassed to have him look at her misshapen body. Her sensuality seemed strangely at odds with her pregnancy and she was embarrassed by her desire for him. 'Don't,' she whispered when he reached over and gently traced a pattern on her breast.

Joe's hand stilled.

Then she pushed at his chest with one hand. 'Don't look at me like that.'

'Why not?' he asked lazily.

'I . . . I'm fat.'

'You're beautiful,' said Joe in a low voice.

'No,' she said, struggling to sit up. 'It's okay, Joe.' She ran her hand through the ends of her hair. 'You're the first person who has seen me like this. It just feels strange.' She took a breath. 'And I guess I got caught up in . . . well, you know.' Stevie waited for him to say something and when he didn't she turned to look at him where he still lay propped on his elbow.

'No, I don't know,' said Joe, his voice sounding slightly raspy, his eyes fixed on hers. 'Is this about being afraid to make love, or being afraid that I will be turned off by what I see?' Without waiting for her answer, Joe pulled her down on the bed beside him again and turned her toward him. With one hand under her chin he tilted her face upward, forcing her to meet his gaze. 'Because if this is about not wanting to make love because it would be unpleasant or uncomfortable for you, that's okay,' he whispered. 'We don't have to do anything but lay here together. But if it's because you think I'm not turned on by you, that's definitely not true.' At the same time he rolled toward her and covered her lips with his, Joe reached for Stevie's hand and guided it to the one part of his body that gave witness to his words.

The knowledge that Joe still found her desirable in spite of her pregnancy thrilled Stevie. At first his lovemaking was cautious and tender, and it became obvious to Stevie that he was unsure of himself, afraid of hurting her. Wanting to let him know that she wasn't that fragile, she whispered, 'Honey, if something doesn't seem right, I'll tell you, but otherwise, except for a slight frontal protrusion, everything else is just like it used to be.' Stevie giggled then at what she had just said.

'What are you laughing at?' asked Joe with narrowed eyes as he rolled on to his back, taking her with him so that now she was straddling him.

Stevie propped her hands on his wide shoulders and leaned down to nibble on his lower lip. 'Well,' she said, 'it just occurred to me that if anyone should know how to handle a slight frontal protrusion, it should be you. But maybe I'm wrong. Everybody knows you cowboys are all talk and no action.'

'Well, little missy,' he drawled in his best imitation of John Wayne, 'I'll guess I'll just have to show you how dangerous my slight frontal protrusion can be for gal like you.'

Stevie ran her tongue lightly over his lower lip. 'Any time you're ready, cowboy,' she whispered.

Jeanne slept late the following morning and it wasn't until she went down to lunch that she learned of Joe's announcement to the band that morning that he was going to marry Stevie. Inflamed with jealousy, she went in search of Joe. She found him with Richie outside the hotel near the tour bus.

'I need to talk to you,' she said, pulling him away from Richie.

'Let me guess,' said Joe with a hint of sarcasm. 'You came to apologize for the ugly things you said to Stevie last night.'

Jeannie ignored his remarks. She had an agenda of her own and it didn't include apologies. 'I just heard about your plans to marry Stevie. Are you crazy? Women like her are all over the place just waiting to snag someone like you. The first thing they do is get themselves knocked up, then they come after you for a huge settlement.'

'Gosh,' said Joe sarcastically. 'And here I thought you were going to congratulate me.'

Richie snickered.

At the sound, Joe turned toward his brother. 'I'll meet you inside,' he said. The tone of his voice made it clear that this was an order.

Jeannie smiled at Joe and moved toward him. 'Wise up, Joe. Dump her before the media gets a hold of this.'

'Jeannie,' he warned, 'you are on dangerous ground. This is none of your business.'

'Yes, it is,' she insisted, rushing on, her green eyes glittering. 'I helped make you a star, Joe. If it wasn't for me, you would still be knocking on doors in Nashville and crooning in some dump for anybody who would give you a few nights' work. We're a team and we're good together – in bed and out. It can be that way again, Joe. Just give us a chance.'

'Our relationship is nothing more than professional, Jeannie. I made that clear a long time ago when I told you that I had made a mistake that night with you. Stevie and I are getting married. If that bothers you, then maybe you should look around for other career opportunities.'

'That was nasty, Joe.'

'It's the way things are,' he replied truthfully.

Jeannie looked pointedly down at her long red nails then ran her fingertips lightly along the side of Joe's face, watching him intently from beneath her lashes.

He flinched at her touch.

When she spoke her voice was both cunning and sweet. 'It would be too bad, wouldn't it, Joe, if the media got a hold of the nasty details of this affair. Especially your *divorce*.'

Joe stiffened, clenching his fists.

Jeannie smiled up at him, obviously pleased with his reaction. Her voice was softer now, resembling a purr. 'It would be so sensational, wouldn't it? Big star leaves his poor paralyzed wife of seven years for the other woman, a tramp who is pregnant with his bastard.'

Joe was silent, shocked at what he had just heard. 'How did you . . . how did you know about the divorce?' Joe asked incredulously when he could finally speak.

'I didn't know. Not until that night we went to dinner with the record company people.' Her green eyes reflected her satisfaction. At that moment Jeannie was sure she had the upper hand. She was definitely in control of things. It was always easier to get what you wanted when the deck was stacked in your favor.

Then, with a sickening feeling, Joe remembered that evening in his apartment when he and Jeannie were on their way to dinner with the MultiSound people. He had asked her to look over his notes on the agreement. He had forgotten the divorce petition, which had been in his briefcase along with his other papers.

'The rest was easy once I knew your wife's maiden name. I called in a few favors and wow! It seems I'm privy to facts about you that very few know.'

Joe stared at the hateful woman before him and realized that she was someone he didn't know. This was not the business manager he had always trusted. This was a woman consumed with rage and jealousy.

'Your fans are so traditional, Joe,' she continued in a conciliatory tone. 'They believe in going to church on Sundays followed by dinner at Mom's house. Then there's the bowling league on Thursday night. Never mind that those same fans go out on Saturday night, get drunk and screw around on their husbands or wives. They still go to church on Sunday and bowl on Thursday. Do you honestly think they'll forgive you for this? It really doesn't matter what *they* do, Joe. It's what their heroes do that counts.'

She waited for a reaction. Some sign that she had gotten through to him. 'Ditch her, Joe, and I won't say a word. You can trust me.' She studied him carefully, assessing the damage her words had done. His jaw was clenched, his eyes narrowed. I have him right where I wanted him, thought Jeannie smugly. By the balls, and he knows it.

But his words shocked her. 'You're fired. Get your things together. Richie can arrange for a plane ticket back to Nashville or any place you want, but I want you out of here today.'

The smile of satisfaction that had hovered on her lips as she delivered her ultimatum died and was replaced with an ugly sneer. The threat she issued was vicious. 'I'll ruin you, Joe, and I'll make sure that bitch's life is miserable. I'll see to it that you're on the cover of every sleazy tabloid in this country. Then we'll see what your God-fearing fans think of you then.'

Joe turned and walked away, leaving her alone in the hotel parking lot.

331

'You are going to regret this, Devlin,' she called after him. 'I'll get even with you. Just wait and see.' Her voice was shrill now, her eyes blazing.

Joe kept walking toward the hotel. If she had been a man, he would have beat the shit out of her the moment she had opened her mouth. Right now all he wanted was to find a wall to drive his fist through.

'She's bluffing,' said Richie later as they were loading up to leave.

'No, I don't think so,' said Joe as he ran his hand over his chin. 'I think Jeannie will do it just to get even with me for marrying Stevie.'

'Are you going to tell Stevie?' asked Richie.

Joe shook his head affirmatively. 'I have to. She'll find out about it sooner or later. Besides, we've already had too many secrets between us.'

'What about you? And the band? How much will this kind of publicity hurt us?' asked Richie.

'I don't know. I'm not worried, though. We'll survive, but I don't want Stevie to have to go through this. She doesn't deserve it.'

'Neither do you,' said Richie as he grabbed Joe briefly by the shoulder in an unexpected display of sibling loyalty.

Joe shrugged, then let his broad shoulders slump as he rested his head in his hands. 'I don't know if all this is worth it, Rich. I guess success does have its price, but sometimes the wrong people have to pay.'

CHAPTER 25

'What about Carole?' asked Beth as she helped Stevie pack the last of her dishes. Tomorrow all her things except for her clothes and the baby's furniture and clothing would be put in storage until she and Joe decided where they would be living permanently.

'I haven't told her yet,' said Stevie while she wadded up more newspaper and stuffed it into the carton.

'Look, Stevie, I know that you had a bad experience with Carole when you told her about the baby, but this will be different. Surely she'll be happy to know that you're getting married? Believe me, mothers are ecstatic about that kind of news. Mine certainly would be. Just call her. You're running out of time,' pointed out Beth.

'I know. I will,' said Stevie.

'When?'

'Tonight. I promise.' Stevie squeezed her eyes shut for a moment, knowing that it was so much easier to make this promise than it would be to actually follow through on it.

'I could have been a movie star, you know.' The words slid into each other. When there was no response,

Carole Parker propped herself up on her elbow, deliberately dragging her tangled blond hair across the chest of the man that shared her bed. His eyes were closed. 'Did you hear me?'

Without seeming to move he answered with a sparse grunt, but it was enough to satisfy her.

'I was even named after a movie star.' This was accentuated by the random pattern her scarlet nails drew through his chest hair.

The grunt was repeated, but this time it was not what Carole wanted to hear.

'Don't you want to know which movie star?'

He reached out and pulled her so she lay half across him. 'Darlin', I already found out everything about you I wanna know. This ain't gonna be no long-term thing, you know. I gotta be back on the road tomorrow.'

'It's Carole Lombard. Carole with an e,' she explained, ignoring him. 'She was married to Clark Gable.'

It was always the same. She used to mind that, dreading the parting that would come the next morning and the inevitable promise of 'I'll call you'. Now she didn't mind so much. What mattered was that after a night out she didn't come home alone.

'Is that your phone I hear?'

Carole shifted and looked toward the closed door of the bedroom. 'Probably,' she replied, snuggling once more against his warmth. The last thing she wanted was to move.

'Don't you think you ought to find out whose calling? I'll still be here when you get back.'

'Okay, okay,' mumbled Carole as she climbed from the rumpled bed and pulled a faded lavender robe around her. On her way out she looked over her shoulder at the man who lay waiting for her. In the dark it was almost impossible to make out his features, and for a split second she couldn't remember his name. Sometimes it didn't matter. Sometimes the names they gave her were not even their real ones.

With both hands Carole pushed her hair back from her face, feeling a dull ache at her temples that would become a full-blown headache by morning.

In the dim light of the stainless steel hood that hung over the stove in the compact kitchen, she reached for the phone that hung on the wall near the kitchen table.

'Hello,' Carole sighed into the phone.

'Hi, it's me. Did I wake you? I know it's late, but I have some news,' Stevie announced.

'Couldn't it have waited until tomorrow, Stevie?' Carole inquired irritably.

Stevie took a deep breath. She hadn't heard from her mother for several months, since the weekend she had told her about the baby. When would she learn that Carole had no interest in her or her child?

'I suppose so . . . No,' Stevie said firmly, unwilling to be put off. 'It can't wait. I'm leaving town in just a few days. I'm going to be married next week. I, uh, I just wanted you to know. This is really short notice, Carole, but I would really like it if you would come to the wedding. It's going to be in Joe's hometown in Georgia. I'll get you a plane ticket and some money for clothes. It would mean so . . .'

335

'I won't be able to make it, Stevie,' Carole said stiffly.

It was impossible for Stevie to stifle the small 'Oh' that escaped her lips.

'Well,' said Carole after a few seconds of silence, 'it's very late, Stevie.'

'Yes, yes it is,' Stevie agreed softly as she heard the click on the other end of the line. It wouldn't be until much later that night that she would realize that Carole hadn't asked her who she was marrying, or where she would be living.

Stevie stood at the window, long after she had hung up the phone, staring as if in a trance into the darkness. For years she had tried, honestly tried, to foster an emotional bond between her and her mother, but she had never succeeded. Why Carole remained distant and uncaring of her was a mystery. What Stevie did know about her mother, she had learned in bits and pieces throughout the years.

At seventeen, Carole's only goal in life had been to get to Hollywood, and she had been sure that she was destined to be in movies. Everyone in Eagle had told her so: her mother, her high-school drama teacher, all her friends, even Frank Parker, the twenty-five-year-old rodeo cowboy she had met that summer at Cheyenne Frontier Days. When she married him after knowing him only a week, he promised her he would take her to Hollywood just as soon as he could get the money together.

A year later, with so many towns and rodeos behind them that she had lost count, Carole was having trouble keeping her dream alive. The more she talked about

Hollywood, the more distant Frank became. When she told him she was pregnant, he left her at a motel in Wichita Falls, telling her he would be back in a few hours. But she never saw or heard from Frank again.

Motherhood brought no joy. Her daughter Stevie brought no joy. Over the years Stevie had wrestled with her mother's indifference, wondering what it was about her that irritated her mother to the point of withholding any form of love and affection. Stevie had no way of knowing that every time Carole looked at her, she was reminded of her youthful dreams and the very reason Frank Parker had left her.

Through the years Carole had always blamed Stevie for her inability to find a husband. What man wanted to take on the responsibility of someone else's child? Carole and Stevie didn't argue, but neither did they get along. They just simply stayed out of one another's way as much as possible. It was as if their lives ran along parallel lines, never touching, never crossing. Things never changed even as Stevie got older. If anything, Stevie's growing up seemed to remove Carole's obligation to perform even the most basic role of parenting. At times Stevie's longing for affection was overwhelming.

In the kitchen Stevie poured a glass of milk, then carried it with her to the bedroom, careful of the moving boxes that were scattered randomly throughout the apartment. Protectively, she cradled the child within her with one hand, and re-avowed her love for the life that she carried.

337

No matter how hard she tried, Stevie would never be able to erase the memories of her lonely childhood. She would always remember the narrow muddy road that ran in front of their trailer and the huge puddle of stagnant water that was always there in the winter when the snow melted, then turned to mud in June and would finally dry up July when the hot, dry winds blew across the barren fields. The smell of garbage rotting in the hot sun, overflowing the confines of the huge blue metal bins was as real to her now as it had been when she had lived there. At night the sound of the howling wind sometimes invaded her dreams.

In miles Eagle, Wyoming, was less than a hundred from Denver. For Stevie, it was another lifetime.

It was with mixed emotions that Stevie resigned her position at the paper. It had been at the center of her life for so many years.

'I'm going to miss you, Stevie,' said Harry as he hugged her. Everyone in her department had gotten together and had a going-away party for her.

'Well, you were responsible for almost everything that's happened to me in the past seven months. Except for this,' she said, smiling as she patted her tummy proudly.

The next morning Bill and Beth took her to the airport, refusing to leave until she had boarded the plane. 'Don't look so sad,' she said to the two of them. 'I'll see you in a few days at the wedding. Just don't disappoint me.'

Just then her flight was called. Bill picked up her bag and walked her toward the gateway. 'You know, Bill,' she said, 'I don't think I've traveled as much in my entire life as I have since I met Joe. Traipsing from one end of the country to the other is a way of life for him. Leaving Wyoming to go off to college at Fort Collins was a big deal for me. I've come a long way since then.'

Bill hugged her then handed her the bag. When he spoke the concern in his eyes was evident. 'Will it work, Stevie? Joe is gone all the time, and after the baby is born you won't be able to travel with him.'

Stevie reached up and touched Bill's cheek. 'You are such a dear friend, Bill. We'll make things work. We love each other too much not to. I'll see you at the wedding and don't forget your impending uncle-hood.'

She turned to Beth. Beth knew how alone she had always been and how much she longed to be a part of a family. The words that she had wanted to say to thank her for her loyalty and friendship stuck in her throat, but her eyes managed to say it all.

'Be happy, Stevie.' Beth could hardly speak. So much was riding on the man who was taking her friend away to a new life.

Bill removed his glasses and surreptitiously swiped at the moisture that had gathered in his eyes. I'll miss you, pal, he thought, as he watched her board her flight.

If she had planned it all herself, Jeannie couldn't have asked for more perfect timing. Her contact with the various tabloids had paid off handsomely in more ways than one. Not only had she been the one responsible for the nasty stories about Joe, she had also been well-compensated for her dirty work. With a copy of *The US Gazette* spread out in front of her, Jeannie leaned back satisfied. She might be unemployed, but she had enough money to last until she found another job.

The pictures of Katherine Devlin had been remarkably easy to get. Jeannie and a photographer, posing as Katherine's cousins from out of town, had gotten all the pictures they needed. The attendant had even agreed to stand behind Katherine in one photo.

When it was all done, Joe Devlin looked to all the world like a selfish, heartless bastard while Stevie became 'the other woman'. And the story of his infidelity appeared everywhere, even in Piney Creek, Georgia, where people read *The US Gazette* as well as all the other papers of its ilk.

No one in Piney Creek could remember anything as exciting as seeing one of their own on the front page of a newspaper, except that time Jackson Birdwell, the owner of the Texaco station at the center of town, put a bullet through his own toe when he tried to stop a thief from robbing him. That made the front page of *The Atlanta Constitution*. They even had a picture of Jackson in the hospital with his foot all bandaged.

But this was different. This was Joe Devlin, the most famous person to ever come out of Piney Creek, and this wasn't the Atlanta paper. This was trashy gossip. All in all, it was just plain scandalous.

Public opinion was divided, with half of the town sympathetic toward Joe's decision and the other half condemning. But they all agreed that that Miss Stevie that Joe had brought home to marry seemed like a nice girl, even if she was in 'the family way'. After all, she came from a big city and people who lived in cities had different values than the residents of Piney Creek.

Joe and the band were in Amarillo when the papers first appeared on the stands. He had time, at least, to call Stevie and tell her that Jeannie had indeed made good on her threat. Even forewarned, everyone had been shocked at what they saw and read. It was ugly and distorted, but it was still true.

'It will blow over, honey,' he assured Stevie. 'In a few days they'll find something more sensational and our indiscretions will be, if not forgotten, at least put aside in favor of someone else's sins.

'I hope Jeannie got a lot of money for this,' continued Joe, 'because when it gets around that she was responsible for leaking this story to the press, she won't be able to get a job in the country music industry. No one will touch her. They'll figure that if she did it to me, she'll do it to them.'

'Will you tell anyone that she was responsible for this?' asked Stevie.

'No,' said Joe. 'I won't have to. This is a big industry but it still regards itself as a family, Stevie. We all take care of one another, and most of us know each other, having met and worked together either on the way up or the way down. Somehow, someone will find out that this was Jeannie's doing.'

'Are you going to be okay, Joe?'

'Not until I see you again in a few days, honey, I won't.'

Stevie smiled and hung up the phone. They could weather this storm of bad publicity together. In less than a week she would become Mrs John Joseph Devlin. Maybe her luck *had* changed.

CHAPTER 26

Joe could not understand Stevie's refusal to call her mother and invite her to the wedding. 'Just explain it to me, honey,' he said patiently as they sat at the table in his parents' kitchen.

'I can't,' she said, her blue eyes wide with a hint of pleading. 'You wouldn't understand.'

'How can you get married and not have your mother at the wedding?'

Stevie sighed wearily, crossed her arms on the table and rested her head on them. 'Please, Joe. I don't even know how to explain it to you. Even if I asked her, she wouldn't come.'

'How do you know?'

'Dammit, Joe, I know,' snapped Stevie.

I called her before I left Denver. I wanted her to know I was going to be married.

'I'll ask her, then,' said Joe decisively.

'Ask, who?' said Ellen, cheerfully as she opened the back door, a sack of groceries in her arms.

'Stevie's mother, to come to the wedding,' explained Joe. 'She won't ask her, so I'm going to.'

'Oh my goodness,' said Ellen nervously. All day, she

343

had wrestled with whether or not she should tell Stevie about her mother. Now that Joe was pressuring Stevie, she had to tell her. 'In all the confusion and all the arrangements, I completely forgot.'

'Forgot what?' asked Joe as he rose to take the groceries from his mother.

Ellen pushed her hair out of her eyes and dabbed at the beads of moisture that had gathered on her brow. 'Your mother called, Stevie, this morning. Said she got your number from your friend Bill at the paper.'

Stevie raised her head now.

'You didn't tell your mother where she could reach you?' Joe asked incredulously.

'What did she say?' asked Stevie quietly, trying to hide the anxiety she felt.

Ellen frowned. 'Well, naturally I invited her to come for a visit so we could get to know each other, and to stay here at the house with us for the wedding.' She looked toward Stevie anxiously, and wished there was some way she could soften her next words. Instead she went to Stevie and rested her hand on her shoulder. 'But she said she wouldn't be able to make it.'

'Why?' asked Joe, completely missing the silent communication between his mother and Stevie. 'Is she sick or something?'

Stevie ignored Joe's question and rubbed the heels of her hands against her eyes, wishing she could erase the pain she felt. She hated to ask, but she had to know. She turned toward Ellen, her eyes wide. When she spoke it was barely a whisper. 'What else did she say?'

Ellen slipped into the chair next to Stevie, put her arm around her shoulder and sent a warning glance toward Joe to keep quiet. 'She saw the write-up about you and Joe in the magazines at the checkout line in the grocery store.' Ellen sighed, then continued. 'She said that you didn't tell her that the father of your child was a rich and famous star. But she was really glad because . . .' Ellen paused, and took a breath '. . . when he got tired of you and left she wouldn't have to worry about you and your child coming back to live with her.'

Stevie lowered her head and closed her eyes. *Why does it still have to hurt so much after all these years?* She inhaled raggedly. 'Only she didn't quite say it like that, did she, Ellen? Not exactly in those words.'

Joe started toward Stevie, intent on taking her in his arms, ready to ease the hurt she must be feeling, wondering what kind of a mother would treat her daughter that way, but Ellen shook her head firmly, stopping him.

'No, honey,' Ellen answered softly, 'she didn't say it quite like that.'

Joe cursed under his breath.

Stevie pushed away from the table and stood, unable to speak. With her eyes still downcast, she opened the back door and went outside. The air was as heavy and hot as it had been that morning. The sky was a deepening dusty pink. Soon it would be dark.

Inside Joe stood and started to follow her, but Ellen stopped him. 'Give her some time, Joey. She needs to be alone.'

Stevie walked away from the house down the drive to the path that led to the creek. It had been worn permanently bare of grass by the Devlin kids over

345

the years and was now a ribbon of red Georgia clay that cut through the forest of towering majestic pines.

Joe found her a half-hour later sitting on the grass next to the creek. Without speaking he eased his long frame on to the ground next to her, then reached for a slender tree branch that lay on the grass. With it, he drew imaginary figures in the grass.

'This is one of my favourite places,' he said softly. 'I used to come here when I was a kid and I needed to be alone. I've made some of my most important decisions here.'

'Like what?' she asked, grateful that he didn't immediately initiate a conversation about her mother.

'Like whether or not I should tell my dad that I wasn't sure I wanted to play football in high school. That I didn't want to be an engineer like him, or go to college at Georgia Tech. Stuff like that. What about you?'

Stevie tried to smile, but didn't quite make it. 'I didn't need a place like this,' she explained solemnly. 'There weren't a lot of decisions for me to make, and when there were, I made them.'

She took a deep breath, remembering.

When she was a junior in high school, Stevie got a job stacking groceries at Safeway and announced to her mother one evening after work that as soon as she graduated she was leaving home for college.

Carole had shrugged her shoulders and refused to look up at her daughter. 'Where do you think you're going to get the money?' she had asked as she sat at the kitchen table applying a second coat of red nail polish to her long nails.

346

Stevie ran her hands through her curly blonde hair, then studied the tips of her scuffed tennis shoes. 'I've got a job, I'll save my money,' she had answered defensively, 'and Mrs Davis, my English teacher, says my grades are good enough to get a scholarship.'

Carole had shrugged again. 'Suit yourself.' She didn't care much what Stevie did as long as it didn't interfere with her. If Stevie moved out when she graduated, so much the better. The trailer was too crowded.

It was after Stevie's announcement of her intentions to attend college that Carole had become more withdrawn, and she had begun to drink more than usual. Stevie had wanted to help, but she didn't know how; the barriers between them were too great.

Stevie had no way of knowing that her mother, at thirty-five, had given up. Carole had finally realized that no one out there was going to give her a better life; no one was going to sweep her off her feet; that having an *e* on the end of her name didn't mean a thing.

After a few minutes of silence Joe said, 'I'm sorry, Stevie.'

She nodded, putting her memories aside, knowing that he was not only sorry for having pushed her about inviting her mother, but he was sorry for her pain.

'I've tried so hard to understand her, Joe, to figure out why she doesn't love me, but I can't. Am I going to be that kind of mother?'

'Oh no, honey, no.' Joe wrapped his arm around her shoulders and pulled her toward him.

'It's all I know.'

'That's not true, Stevie. You have a great capacity for love, for sharing. I don't know what makes your mother

347

like she is, but I do know that you are nothing like her.' Joe stood and pulled Stevie to her feet then he kissed her lightly. 'Let's go home, honey. Mom will be worried about you.'

Stevie nodded. 'She will, won't she?' Her expression was serious.

He smiled and took her hand to help her on her feet. 'She worries about all the Devlin kids, and now that includes you.'

Since Stevie had no family or friends nearby, Ellen, Grace and Connie decided to host a surprise bridal shower for her. Beth would be arriving just in time to attend, and the guest list was no problem since almost everyone in Piney Creek had been invited to the wedding.

'Nothing but a bunch of silly women,' muttered Charlie, as he helped Ellen rearrange the furniture in the living room.

'You wouldn't want to see Stevie cheated out of a shower, would you, Charlie?' asked Ellen as she surveyed this latest arrangement.

'Of course not,' answered Charlie. 'I just don't understand why you couldn't have had it over at the church hall.'

Ellen ignored his grumbling. 'Grace can help me finish this. Will you pick up the cake at Morton's before two o'clock?'

'I'll go right now,' volunteered Charlie, 'before you decide to move the sofa again.'

The shower was indeed a surprise and Stevie was touched at the generosity of her soon-to-be family and their friends. Only two of the invited guests had declined, and Ellen knew it was because they disapproved of Joe and Stevie. But then, those two disapproved of almost everything that went on in Piney Creek.

After the guests had left, the Devlin women along with Beth and Stevie sat in the living room surrounded by wrapping paper, ribbons and gifts.

'I still can't believe all this,' said Stevie. 'Everyone was so nice, and the gifts are lovely.'

Grace and Connie stood and began to gather up the empty plates. 'Here,' said Beth, rising, 'I'll help.'

'Well,' said Ellen, 'I think everyone had a good time.'

'Especially Mary Nell,' added Stevie.

Ellen laughed. 'I suppose I should apologize for that. It was only a little white lie.'

'It was a real whopper, Mom,' said Connie as she started to stuff the wrapping paper into a plastic trash bag. 'She made me go along with it, Stevie. I wanted to tell you the truth about Joe and Mary Nell, but Mom wouldn't let me. She said we needed her as leverage.'

'I forgive you, although I have to tell you it worked. I stewed about Joe and this Mary Nell person all the way down here. And the only reason I'm letting the two of you off the hook is because things worked out between Joe and me. Besides, I like Mary Nell. She's sweet, and she told me that Joe had been her friend since the first grade, and that she hadn't seen him in over a year. Privately, she also told me that she's dating Chad Conners.'

Ellen and Connie looked at each other, then back at Stevie. In unison they asked, 'Who is Chad Conners?'

Stevie stood and stretched slowly. Then turned toward Beth and Grace and winked. 'I don't know,' she said with a studied innocence. 'All she said was that he . . . Beth, didn't she say he was from Los Angeles?'

Beth could hardly keep a straight face. She knew that Stevie was making all this up just to get back at Ellen and Connie for the Mary Nell story, and that by this evening whatever she told them would be all over Piney Creek.

'She showed me his picture,' said Beth.

'He's very good looking,' added Stevie.

'I think he's on one of those soap operas, you know, *All My Children*, or is it *Days Of Our Lives*?' Beth looked toward Stevie, appropriately puzzled.

'That's right,' Stevie said. 'They met in Atlanta at some charity fund raiser.'

'I do know he's rich,' volunteered Beth.

'Very rich,' confirmed Stevie with a nod. 'Old family money, from the Boston Conners, I believe.'

Connie squealed. 'Mary Nell? Our Mary Nell?'

'Engaged to an actor on a daytime soap?' repeated Ellen incredulously.

Stevie shrugged, then studied her fingernails. 'It seems she wasn't interested in Joe after all.'

'Bad, bad girls,' chided Grace, giggling, after Ellen had gone to use the phone, and Connie had decided to run over to a friend's house. 'But the two of them deserved it. And the two of you are so good at this.'

'Very good,' agreed Beth with a laugh.

Grace gave Stevie a quick hug. 'Welcome to the family, Stevie. You'll do just fine as one of this rowdy bunch.'

Joe and Stevie were married on a warm Saturday afternoon in early July in the Piney Creek Community Church, where the Devlin family had always attended services. With its single steeple and white clapboard siding, it looked much the same as it did thirty-six years earlier when Joe's parents had been married there.

Inside the church, the sun radiated brightly through the stained-glass windows, casting a kaleidoscopic pattern of colors across the heavily waxed pine floors. In the front row sat a smiling Ellen Devlin along with Joe's brothers and sisters. Behind them were assorted aunts, uncles and cousins. Bill Schaeffer watched the proceedings, happy that Stevie had been so warmly received into her new family.

Across the aisle sat Brad, Dave and Allen Lee, their faces shining like beacons, believing that they had a part in bringing Joe and Stevie together.

Behind them sat Lorraine Fisher and her husband, Tommy. From Stevie's very first phone call to Joe's office, Lorraine had suspected that Joe had finally met his match. After meeting Stevie, she was positive.

Stevie wore a tea-length ivory silk dress, adorned only with a lace collar and the string of pearls that Joe had given her as a wedding present, and carried a small bouquet of pale pink roses and ivory gardenias.

Joe wore a traditional dark suit, and Stevie thought she had never in all her life seen a more handsome man. Beth, dressed in pale frothy pink, was her maid of honor while Charlie Devlin was his son's best man.

After the ceremony, there was a reception in the adjoining church hall. It was there that Joe proudly presented his new bride to all his family and friends.

Nearby stood the smiling Reverend Morris Johnson, who had conducted the ceremony even though he hadn't been too keen on the idea in the beginning.

'After all,' he had said to Stevie and Joe when they had first met with him, as he adjusted the rimless glasses he had worn since he was a young graduate of divinity studies, 'the bride is seven-and-a-half months pregnant, and then there is that scandalous newspaper thing.'

But then he mumbled something about if God could forgive, so could he. But no circuses in his church, he admonished. No Hollywood shindigs that would rob the marriage vows of their sanctity. Joe might be famous, but the media was not to disturb this solemn occasion.

And they didn't. Joe, who had always tried to maintain good relations with the press, even through this turbulent time, solved that problem by inviting the newspaper and television people to a wedding reception later that evening at the Sheraton in Atlanta. While the champagne flowed and the lavish buffet was constantly replenished, he and Stevie answered all their questions and allowed them to take all the pictures of them and their family that they wanted.

Stevie wanted to hide every time there was the flash of a camera, but Joe held her firmly by his side. 'I feel like everyone is looking at me,' Stevie said shyly.

'They are,' Joe said, grinning.

'But I'm so . . . fat, and so obviously pregnant,' she moaned.

'Obviously. Yes, you are, obviously, and you're beautiful. Now let's dance.' Joe leaned down and kissed her as more cameras flashed.

The questions from the press, which had flown furiously toward them in the beginning, had now begun to diminish.

'In direct proportion,' observed Richie with a silly smile, 'to the number of bottles of champagne consumed.'

Later that night, when they were alone in their room, Stevie was more nervous than she had ever been around Joe. This was it. This was real. Their first time together as man and wife. It didn't matter that they had made love before, that she carried his child. This mattered, this was the beginning of their life together, and she worried that he would be disappointed with her.

From her bag she took the delicate pink silk and lace gown and robe that Beth had given her and clutched it to her. When she had changed, she joined Joe in the bedroom of their suite.

'Do you think that you can handle a champagne toast?' he asked in a husky voice as he let his eyes roam possessively over her.

She attempted a self-conscious smile, suddenly nervous at his intimate perusal.

'Come here, Stevie.'

She went to him, walking into his strong arms.

'I love you, Mrs Devlin.'

'All of me?' she asked shyly.

'All of you. And I can't wait to get my hands on you.'

'All of me?' she repeated with a smile.

'Let me show you exactly what I have in mind,' he said seriously as he untied her robe. And when his lips touched her in all the secret places that only he knew, setting her on fire, Stevie's heart soared. She needn't have worried so. This was Joe, the stranger she had fallen in love with after only one kiss; the man who could excite her, infuriate her, and take her places she never knew existed; the man who taught her what it was to love, and to be loved.

And Joe, who had been no less nervous, was consumed with a passion that seemed to intensify each time he and Stevie were together. He was truly a man in love. For the very first time.

Their honeymoon was short, only four days. Neither Stevie or Joe had wanted to waste any of their precious time together traveling, so they stayed there in Atlanta and spent their nights making love and their days sightseeing. But it ended too soon when Joe had to leave to fulfill his concert commitments.

'I promise you another honeymoon, later, after the baby is born – anywhere you want to go,' he said as he prepared to leave.

'I'll be home as soon as I can, then we can look for a place to live. But for now, until the baby comes, I don't want to leave you alone. Are you sure you don't mind staying with my folks?' Joe asked that morning.

Stevie shook her head. 'You just don't understand how wonderful it is for me to actually have a family around,' she said.

Charlie and Ellen delighted in spoiling Stevie, and Stevie, who had never before been on the receiving end of this kind of treatment, glowed with happiness.

Joe came home twice in the next two weeks, but he could only stay for two days each time. He had rearranged as much of his schedule as possible so he could be home with Stevie in August when the baby was due. But he still had concert commitments and those dates had been arranged as much as a year in advance. About those he could do nothing, but hoped that their baby would be considerate of its parents in choosing its arrival time.

'Stevie,' Ellen called through the screen door one morning late in July, 'I'm going down to the church this afternoon to take some things for the rummage sale on Saturday. Would you like to go?'

It was already hot and humid outside, even though it was early. Stevie, who had given up drinking coffee, not out of deference to her condition but because it was just too hot, was sitting on the front steps drinking a cold glass of orange juice. She was about to refuse on the grounds that she wasn't feeling particularly energetic, when a violent pain ripped through her lower back. She screamed, knocking over the glass of juice and sending it crashing against the concrete steps of the porch.

Ellen came running from the living room and out the screen door, sending it slamming back against the walls of the house. 'Oh, my God! Charlie!' she screamed, as she took one look, then bent down and took a gasping Stevie in her arms.

'The baby!' panted Stevie. *Don't panic!*

Charlie rounded the corner of the porch then and, seeing Ellen and Stevie, said, 'I'll call the doctor, then I'll try to reach Joe.'

'It's too early,' said Stevie, panting between pains as Charlie helped her into the back seat car a few minutes later.

'It's okay,' said Ellen beside her. 'Babies arrive on their time schedule, not on ours.'

'But it's a whole month early,' protested Stevie from behind clenched teeth.

'I know, honey,' said Ellen as she smoothed Stevie's hair. 'Just try to relax in between the contractions. We'll get you to the hospital as soon as possible.' Over Stevie's head she exchanged worried glances with Charlie. She had no medical training, but she had had lots of practical experience. Ellen had given birth to five children and never had she had a labor that had begun with such intense pain. It was not a good sign. In the car, Ellen timed the contractions. They hadn't gotten any closer together, but neither had they lessened in their intensity.

Even though Charlie had the air conditioning on, it felt to Stevie like it was a hundred and twenty degrees inside the car.

'Did you get hold of Joe?' she asked Charlie worriedly through clenched teeth. 'Is he on his way?'

Charlie glanced up at the rear view mirror, a worried look on his face as his eyes met Ellen's. 'He said to tell you he loves you and he'll be here as fast as he can,' lied Charlie. The truth was that he had reached Richie, but no one knew where Joe was. The last time anyone had seen him was last night after the concert.

'Good,' whimpered Stevie. She could feel another contraction building. 'I love him, too.'

Ellen smiled at this. Stevie was like another daughter to them and she was especially cherished by all the Devlins because of the happiness she had brought to

Joe.

The nearest community hospital was a half-hour away, and as Charlie sped down the highway, he prayed that Stevie and the baby would be okay. And that Joe would get here in time. Charlie calculated that even if Richie found Joe and got him on the next flight from Memphis, he couldn't possibly get to the hospital before noon.

But Richie couldn't find Joe. Some two hours later, Richie was just coming off the elevator when he saw his brother about to get on the elevator next to his. 'Where the hell have you been?' Richie shouted. Without waiting for an answer, Richie grabbed Joe by the arm. 'Stevie's in labor, you've got to get home right away. The next flight leaves in forty-five minutes. Go grab some clothes and let's go.'

For a moment Joe was still, then Richie's words sunk in.

'Oh, shit!'

When they were on the expressway a short time later, Richie looked over at his brother. 'Man. You look like something the cat drug home.'

Joe rubbed his hand anxiously over his cheeks and chin, the stubble there scratching his hand. 'Yeah. What did Dad say? It's too early for the baby. It's not due for another month,' he observed worriedly.

'I imagine that's what Stevie thought about two hours ago.' Richie clamped his lips together in an effort to keep his temper under control. He could never remember being this angry with his brother.

Joe sat up straight. 'Two hours? She's been in labor

357

two hours?'

Richie glanced at his watch. 'Going on three, if she hasn't already had the baby. You don't hear too well after being out all night, do you? I told you that in the lobby.'

'Is she okay? God, I would never forgive myself if anything happened to Stevie or the baby.'

Richie's anger faded at Joe's remorse. 'Dad sounded worried, Joe. Her pains were really severe. And just where the hell were you, Daddy Dearest?'

Joe rested his head in his hands. 'I met up with Tommy Mac and Perk and those guys. You remember Perk Hanson?'

Richie remembered. Perk Hanson and Tommy Mac Baker were hard-core country music boys, at least fifteen years older than Joe, with faces that were lined with the evidence of their hard living and hard drinking.

'They came backstage after the show. Hadn't seen them in a long time and they insisted we all go out for a drink, so I did.'

'And what took you so long to get home?' asked Richie

'Geez, Rich, I don't know. One drink led to another and another, you know how those guys are,' moaned Joe. His raging headache was a testimonial to the amount of alcohol he had consumed the night before and the fact that he hadn't yet been to bed.

'I know how *they* are, but you hardly drink,' Richie reminded him.

'Well, I did last night. Time sort of got away from me. We got to catching up on things and swapping stories. They kept ordering rounds of drinks and I ended up rip-roarin' drunk right along with those guys.'

'Man,' said Richie, shaking his head, 'I've never been a father, but any jackass knows that a baby never arrives when it's supposed to. They're either early or late. You should have been where you were supposed to be. But that still doesn't answer my question, Joe. Where were you all night?'

Joe groaned. 'A couple of girls that Perk knew showed up so he invited them to join us at the table. Later, we all wound up going to another club, then another.'

'Well, that's swell, big brother, really swell. You never did that kind of stuff, Joe, even when the rest of the guys did,' said Richie reproachfully. 'What possessed you to go off the deep end this time?'

Joe leaned back against the seat and squeezed his eyes shut. His eyelids felt like they were lined with sandpaper. 'It gets worse, Rich,' he said with a groan.

Richie looked over at him.

'Jeannie came into the bar where we were. She was there with Jack Toller. Trying to line herself up with a new job, I imagine.' Joe took a deep breath. 'Anyway, she saw one of those girls hanging all over me.'

Richie cursed.

'My sentiments exactly,' said Joe.

'Do you think she'll say anything?'

Joe raised his head. 'She'll pee in her pants if she doesn't.'

CHAPTER 27

At the airport Joe managed to shave and change his clothes in the men's room before his plane left for Atlanta.

When he arrived at the hospital, he sprinted down the hallway to find Stevie and his parents.

He met his dad coming out of Stevie's room. 'How is she?' Joe asked breathlessly.'

'Go in and find out for yourself,' said Charlie as he stepped aside and gestured for Joe to enter the room. Outside he was brimming with happiness that Stevie and the baby were all right. Inside he was fighting the urge to knock his son on his ass for not being there when Stevie needed him. But Ellen had made him promise not to spoil this day. No matter where Joe had been, Ellen was sure he had some perfectly good explanation.

Inside the room, the sun streamed through the window and fell across the most beautiful sight Joe thought he would ever see. Stevie was sitting propped up in bed in a hospital gown, looking tired but more radiant than he had ever seen her. In her arms was a tiny bundle wrapped in a pink blanket.

Joe crossed the room quickly. 'Stevie, honey, I am so sorry I wasn't here with you.'

Stevie smiled up at him. 'You missed the greatest performance of my life, Joe. Meet your new daughter. She was early, and she's a little bitty thing, but she's absolutely beautiful, isn't she?'

'Like her mother,' said Joe in a whisper. Gingerly he sat on the edge of the bed while Stevie handed him the baby. From beneath the blanket his tiny daughter stared at him with the bluest eyes he had ever seen. With hands that seemed ten times larger than they should, he adjusted the tiny knit cap on the baby's head. He leaned over to kiss his daughter, then Stevie, and his heart was overflowing with love. And from that moment on, he knew he had everything a man could ever want.

In all the excitement of becoming a new parents and the media attention the newly arrived Ellen Elizabeth Devlin received, the question of Joe's whereabouts the morning Stevie went into labor no longer seemed important.

All during her pregnancy Stevie had wondered what it would be like to have a baby, a part of her that would always be hers to love and cherish. The reality was that she couldn't even begin to fathom the depth of her feelings for this child. She had no idea that her love for their baby, and the desire to protect her, would be this *intense*, this *consuming*. Never, never, she vowed, would her child ever feel unloved and unwanted.

Joe was completely at ease caring for Elizabeth, seeming to know what all her needs were. Stevie, on the other hand, was overwhelmed. 'What if I do something wrong? What if I don't feed her enough, or I feed her too much?' she moaned. 'I'm almost afraid to pick her up because I might hurt her.'

'Just relax, honey,' he told her. 'Babies are more resilient than you think they are. If you're anxious, she senses that. You need to make her feel safe and content.'

'How do you know these things, Joe?' asked Stevie wide-eyed. Today was the first day home from the hospital, and they were in the downstairs bedroom of the Devlin home. It would be their home for a while.

He laughed. 'I have three younger brothers and sisters, or have you forgotten?'

'Oh.'

'Stevie, honey, you'll be okay and so will Elizabeth. You've never been around babies and you're just nervous. Now, here, you hold her.' Stevie opened her arms to receive her daughter.

'She's so beautiful, Joe. We are so lucky.'

Joe nodded, suddenly unable to speak because of the lump in his throat as he gazed at the precious little girl that Stevie held. He was the lucky one. He had never imagined this kind of happiness.

When Elizabeth was two weeks old, Joe had to resume touring, promising Stevie he would return home as often as possible until she and the baby could travel with him.

The night before he left, they were lying in bed while Elizabeth was sleeping soundly in the lacy white bassinet next to them.

'I'm going to miss you,' whispered Joe. 'I wish I didn't have to leave you and Elizabeth ever again.'

Stevie smiled lazily and reached out to touch his face. 'Me, too, but I knew that was part of the deal when I got you.'

Joe reached toward the table next to the bed and took a small white envelope from the drawer. 'I have a present for you.'

Stevie scooted up in bed, pushing the pillows against the headboard. 'A present? For me?'

'I think you'll like this.'

Stevie opened the envelope. Joe had cut out the picture of a traditional white two-story house from a magazine and glued it on a card. 'It's your new home, Stevie.'

She was speechless. Just when she thought things couldn't be any better, Joe had done something else wonderful.

'That's just a picture I cut out,' he explained seriously. 'The real house can be anything you want it to be.'

'Oh, Joe, a real home. I've never lived in a house, you know,' she whispered, awed by his generosity.

'I know, honey. Beth told me.'

He had also given Stevie her choice of where they would make their home. 'Anywhere, any city you want,' he had said.

It didn't take but a few seconds for Stevie to make her decision. 'Piney Creek is our home,' she had said. 'I want Elizabeth to grow up surrounded by all her family. All our family.'

It was settled. As soon as Stevie felt up to overseeing the numerous details and making the necessary decisions that went into building a new house, they would begin construction on twenty wooded acres near Piney Creek.

The next morning was hectic as Joe finished packing. 'But what am I going to do when you're gone, Joe?' Stevie asked with a hint of panic in her voice.

He turned, all pretense of packing ceased, and leaned over to kiss her firmly and unhurriedly. 'You are going to miss me like crazy,' he murmured.

She did, feeling suddenly lost, like the other half of her was incomplete.

A month later, Joe was both pleased and apprehensive when he was asked to appear in an interview with Beverly Simmons on her nationally televised show. Beverly, a network-news veteran of many years, was a sharp interviewer known especially for her straightforward, often unexpected, needling questions. She was also notorious for taking a simple remark out of context, using it like a razor, and slashing her guests until her audience could almost smell blood. Yet, to be asked to appear on her show was a hallmark of success that would automatically move Joe from the status of country music entertainer to star.

At the same time, Joe reminded Stevie one night as he cradled Elizabeth in one arm and held her bottle with the other hand, he had to consider the kind of questions that Beverly would ask. She was certain to bring up Kathy. That's old news, Stevie had assured him. In the end, they both agreed that this opportunity was too important to turn down, so Joe agreed to do the show.

The interview would take place in two weeks in Piney Creek.

The director picked the Devlins' big front porch as the site for the interview. It would, he thought, capture some of the essence of what country music is all about. The area around the house was roped off to keep the neighbors back out of the way while the lights and camera equipment were moved into position. After being introduced to Beverly and her crew, Stevie, holding Elizabeth against her shoulder, stood along with Charlie and Ellen off to the side and watched as they went to work.

'Here's how it works, Joe,' Beverly explained the day of the interview. 'This is all done in one take unless there is some technical problem, or unless we really screw up. You don't know what questions I'm going to ask and I have no idea what your answers will be. That's what makes for a good interview. Are you ready?'

'Ready,' he said and took a deep breath.

Beverly Simmons was a relaxed, friendly woman in her late forties, meticulously groomed and at least fifteen pounds overweight. Instead of detracting from her appearance, the extra pounds gave her a certain wholesome, almost maternal, credibility. But the moment the camera started shooting, she became a different person. Gone was the friendly demeanor. A consummate professional was at work.

Joe, to his credit, appeared relaxed and answered all Beverly's questions with humor, charm and honesty. Stevie held her breath when Beverly asked the questions they both knew would come. 'Tell me about your first marriage, and why you kept it a secret until recently.'

'Kathy and I were married for almost eight years,' answered Joe, meeting Beverly's eyes directly. 'Seven of those years she spent in a home that provides full-time nursing care. She is paralyzed and not able to do anything for herself.' He then went on to explain how Kathy's condition was the result of an automobile accident.

'Then how could you divorce her?' asked Beverly with astonishment, her voice strident. 'How could you leave your wife like that? So helpless?'

Joe was no longer aware of the people around as he concentrated on Beverly's question. He took a deep breath before he attempted to answer her. 'It was a very difficult and painful decision,' said Joe quietly. 'I'm not even sure I can explain it. I agonized over it for a very long time, years before I met Stevie. You have to understand, Beverly, that Kathy doesn't recognize me. She hasn't known anyone since the accident. She cannot function in even the simplest way; she has suffered permanent brain damage.'

Joe shut his eyes before continuing and when he opened them, they glistened with unshed tears. 'And that is never, never going to change. I'm thirty-two years old. I have my whole life ahead of me.'

Joe paused, looking down at his hands. When he looked up again the camera was positioned so that he was looking directly into it. The pain in his eyes was clearly evident. The truth was there for all the world to see. His voice was husky with suppressed emotion. 'How could I do that to Kathy?' he repeated. 'Truthfully, I never thought I could.'

'So you got your divorce and you married Stevie Parker, a journalist whom you had met in Denver.'

'Yes,' said Joe.

'And when you married her, she was seven-and-a-half months pregnant with your child.'

Joe nodded. 'That's not the way things happen for most people, and I wish it could have been different. But I did the very best I could to protect and care for Kathy. I still do the best that I can for her. She will always have whatever she needs. I'll always take care of her.

'But now I am so fortunate to have Stevie and our baby. For the first time in a long time I have someone to love and someone who loves me.'

Beverly Simmons smiled, genuinely disarmed by Joe's good looks, his natural charm and his heart-wrenching honesty. But it didn't stop her from her doing what she excelled at: peeling away the slick covering of the people she interviewed to expose the raw layers underneath.

'Before your marriage, you fired your manager, Jeannie Williams.'

'We terminated our association,' clarified Joe cautiously.

'Was it because she had found out about your secret marriage, and had threatened to tell your story to the tabloids?' asked Beverly leaning forward, her tone confidential.

'It was because we disagreed over the direction my career was going to take,' said Joe firmly

'But you and this woman had at one time, before you met Stevie, been intimate?'

'Yes,' admitted Joe.

'And is the reason that Jeannie Williams is no longer employed by you, because your wife found out about the affair and couldn't stand to have Miss Williams around?' she asked quickly.

Joe leaned forward, his displeasure at her question evident. But before he could reply, she quickly resumed her questioning and the professional façade slipped back in place. 'Someone told me that you were not present for the birth of your daughter. Is that true?'

Joe stiffened slightly at the question and a nagging feeling settled over him. Beverly was just trying to get him rattled by putting him on the defensive. He had done enough interviews to know that controversy drives the ratings up. It would make a better show.

'That's true,' answered Joe. 'The baby was born a few weeks early and I was in Memphis doing a concert. I arrived about a half-hour after Elizabeth was born.'

'There have been reports that you were seen out at a club the night before your wife went into labor, with a group of people. One of them was a woman who appeared to be particularly friendly with you.'

Joe opened his mouth and was prepared to tell Beverly that the people he was with were old friends, and things were not like she had made them sound, when Beverly said sharply, 'Tell me, Joe, do you have sex with other women besides your wife when you are out on the road?' The question was delivered in staccato fashion.

Joe clenched his jaw, furious that Beverly Simmons would assume that she had a right to ask him these kind of questions. Yet he shouldn't have been surprised. It was obvious that Jeannie Williams, while she probably would have had no direct contact with Beverly, had been at hard at work behind the scenes. 'I am faithful to Stevie,' answered Joe in a carefully controlled voice. 'I love her and I will always be faithful to her.'

'But were you in that club the night before your wife went into labor? And was there a woman there with you?' The questions were fired at him again.

'I was there with some friends that I hadn't seen in a long time. Two women that they knew joined them, and one was sitting next to me. It was one of the few times in my life when I had too much to drink.'

Joe desperately wanted to look over at Stevie, to see what she must be thinking, but he dared not break eye contact with Beverly. To do so would be tantamount to an admission of wrongdoing.

'Isn't it true that you left that night with the woman from the club and didn't return to your hotel until the next morning, long after your wife was in labor?'

Joe's gut contracted. This was sounding more like a cross-examination than an interview, but he was too far into it to stop it now. Realizing that to deny it would serve no purpose, he answered. 'I was with my friends when we left and went on to another club and then another. The two women went along. Other than staying out all night, nothing happened. I returned to my hotel early the next morning.'

He took a deep breath. 'Not being there when our baby was born is something I will regret for the rest of my life. I feel like I failed Stevie when she needed me the most.'

True to her style, Beverly abruptly changed her line of questioning and Joe breathed easier. He still had to face Stevie, but the worst part was over. As soon as the filming was over he looked over where Stevie had been earlier, but she was no longer there.

At the conclusion of the interview Beverly shook hands with Joe, and it reminded Joe of what it felt like to be the loser in a tennis match. Relaxed now, Beverly had once more reverted to her real personality.

'You're quite a guy, Joe.' she said with genuine admiration. 'For the longest time I didn't know who you were or why all these people who never before liked country music were suddenly fans of yours. Then I bought some of your tapes and watched some of your videos, and I knew.

'It's not the song that you sell, it's the promise of love. We all dream about it and we all want it, but the most incredible part of it is that, when you perform, what we see up there is really *you*, not just an act. And that makes believers out of all of us.'

Joe smiled wryly. 'Thanks, Beverly, for the nice words. After the number you did on me just now, I'm grateful I don't have too many fans like you. Right now I have to go find my wife and explain what millions of viewers are going to see and hear in a few weeks.'

A few minutes later, Joe found Stevie down by the creek. 'I didn't do too good, did I, Stevie?' he said as he leaned against the trunk of the big oak, propping one foot behind him. 'Maybe I'm not ready to play in the big leagues.'

Stevie turned toward him, her eyes blazing. 'Oh, you're ready all right, Joe. You can lie and cheat just like the rest of them.'

'It was wrong of me, Stevie, not to tell you, but I didn't mean to let things get out of hand. Nothing happened.'

'How can you say that? Even if nothing happened that night, something happened the next day. I was in labor with our baby, Joe, and no one knew where you were. I remember your dad telling me in the car on the way to the hospital that you were on your way. I was so frightened and I needed you so much. And what about today? How many millions of people are going to know how little regard my husband has for me and our child?'

'That's not true, Stevie.'

'I think it is. And tell me, Joe, how do you suppose Beverly Simmons knew about this? Did the network have someone following you, or is this just something you do all the time?'

Joe left his spot against the tree and came toward Stevie. 'Jeannie was there. She saw me and she must have heard later that I had signed to do this interview.'

He reached out for Stevie, but she pulled away. 'Well, if Jeannie knew, and Beverly knew, why the hell didn't I know, Joe? Why didn't you tell me? Did you think I would never find out?'

'Stevie, I never cheated on you. I never would. I was just hanging out with some old friends. It was a dumb thing that I did.'

'Am I supposed to believe that? You're no different than those men that used to lie to my mother. The difference is that she wanted to believe their lies. All my life someone has lied to me. First there was my mother. I thought that, because I belonged to her, she was supposed to love me. Well, that was a lie. Then there was Michael. My whole relationship with him was built on a lie. Well, this time I'm not buying it.'

Suddenly Joe was reminded of the night of Kathy's accident when she hurled her bitter accusations of unfaithfulness at him. And he could feel his anger at the unfairness of it surge through him. He hadn't deliberately set out to hurt Stevie. 'I don't care what you believe,' he replied bitterly. 'Marriages should be built on trust. When you decide to trust me, then we can put this behind us. Until then, I'll be going back on the road. Call me when you're ready to talk.' Joe turned and began to walk up the path to the house.

From behind him, through the trees that lined the path, came Stevie's answer. The old, practiced sarcasm slipping easily into place. 'Don't hold your breath waiting for the phone to ring.'

CHAPTER 28

The sound of the applause was still ringing in their ears as they made their way backstage.

'Good music tonight, guys,' said Joe as they crowded into his dressing room. It was there that they dissected the performance, unwinding until it was time to greet the fans outside who were waiting to see them.

From an ice chest Richie dispensed cold beer.

'I can remember playing some places where all I got paid at the end of the evening was all the beer I could drink,' said Allen Lee.

'Must have been all the free milk you could drink,' teased Dave, ''cause we all know you were too young for anything else.'

'We were better tonight, didn't you think so?' asked Richie.

Joe nodded, knowing that some of that was due to his attitude, which was a little more relaxed than it had been over the past few days. He and Stevie would work their problems out, he was certain of that. It would just take time.

'Hey, Rich, pass me one of those,' called Joe over the din of voices that echoed in the room.

Richie was about to reach into the chest when there was a knock at the door.

'Go away, please!' yelled Richie, laughing. 'We need a break.'

'This is Security. I have a message for Mr Devlin.'

Suddenly the room was quiet.

'Your family is trying to reach you. You need to call home as soon as possible.'

Richie and Joe's eyes met and together they stood. Without being asked Brad, Dave and Allen Lee stood and left the room.

With shaking hands Joe dialed the number. His mind raced in turmoil. Stevie answered the phone.

'Are you all right? Is Elizabeth okay?' Joe asked quickly when Stevie answered the phone.

'We're all okay here, Joe, but Kathy's mother called about an hour ago from Parkside and spoke with Ellen. Kathy is much worse, Joe. Mrs Harrison wants you to come as quickly as possible. The doctors don't think Kathy will make it through tomorrow.'

'Tell her I'll be on the first flight out of here in the morning.'

'I will,' promised Stevie.

Joe and Richie stayed up most of the night talking. By dawn Joe was at the airport to catch the first flight leaving for Atlanta.

Two hours later Stevie met him at the airport. They spoke very little during the drive to Parkside.

An early-morning quiet had not yet been disturbed when they entered the hospital. The staff was just beginning their morning routine. Joe turned to

374

Stevie. 'This must all seem very strange to you,' he said.

She wanted to reach out to him, to tell him that she had insisted on going to meet him, that she knew how difficult this was for him, and this was one time when he shouldn't have to make choices about whose feelings to consider. It was Kathy and her mother who needed him now.

'I'll wait here,' volunteered Stevie, when they had entered the lobby. 'When Ellen and Charlie get here, I'm going home to stay with Elizabeth.'

Joe nodded with understanding, then rushed down the hall to the room that had become so familiar over the years. At the doorway, he paused. Frances Harrison was asleep, slumped in a chair next to her daughter's bed. Worry had etched lines in her face, leaving her looking much older than her actual years.

Joe's eyes traveled to the bed, which seemed to swallow Kathy's slight form. If anything, she looked more frail than she had the last time he had seen her. Her face, always thin, seemed drawn. Silently, he made his way across the room to Kathy's side. Gently he reached out and took her hand.

Mrs Harrison stirred, then her eyes opened. 'Oh, I didn't know you were here, Joe.'

'I just arrived, Frances. I knocked, but you didn't hear me.'

Frances sat up straight in her chair. 'Thank you for coming on such short notice.' Things had been strained between Joe and Kathy's mother since the accident. Most of their conversations since had been stilted and centered around Kathy and the arrangements for her care.

'How is she?' asked Joe, his eyes moving to Kathy.

Frances Harrison attempted to straighten her wrinkled clothes and smooth her hair that had once been as dark as her daughter's, but was now streaked with gray. 'It was a very bad night, Joe. Her lungs have weakened considerably. It's . . . she's not good. I don't know whether to pray that she survives, or hope that she doesn't linger.' From someone else that would have been a harsh statement, but Frances Harrison had suffered as well as grieved for her daughter.

She stood then, looking around the room, before letting her eyes settle on her former son-in-law. 'It has been such a long time, hasn't it, Joe?' she asked quietly.

'Yes, it has, Frances,' he replied, knowing that she was referring to Kathy's condition.

Joe released Kathy's hand and went to stand by the window. Outside, the gardens were still in bloom in spite of the withering heat. It was fall now, but only by the calendar.

'I wanted to call you, Frances, so many times, to tell you how sorry I was.'

'I never gave you much of a chance, did I, Joe?'

Joe shrugged. 'People do what their heart tells them.'

'But I didn't listen to mine,' Frances confessed. 'I let the desire to see you suffer because of Kathy's injuries overrule everything else. That's a terrible way to live, Joe. It ate away at whatever decency I might have had left in me. I know that you weren't responsible for her accident.

'I had such hopes for her in the beginning when the two of you married. I thought that at last she had found something, that elusive thing that would finally make her happy. But she was ill, Joe and getting worse. When the doctor told me that she was never going to get any better, I needed someone to blame. And that was you.'

'Frances, you needn't – '

'No,' she interrupted, 'let me finish. You were good to Kathy. I know that. But she would make up these terrible stories, and I couldn't face the fact that my only child was sick, so I listened to her, and I believed her. That way, I didn't have to face the truth.

'When all those magazines wrote about you leaving Kathy for another woman, I had even more reason to hate you, but a funny thing happened. For once I stopped thinking about my problems and I tried to put myself in your place, to ask myself what I would have done if I was married to someone I didn't love, and then . . .'

'Frances – '

'No, it's all right, Joe. I know that you cared for her even though you were never in love with her, and I doubt that she was in love with you. I think she might have been in love with the idea of what you might later become.'

Frances drew herself up, standing straight, and took a deep breath, then said, 'You have a baby now.'

'Yes.' His reply was barely audible.

'And you're happy?' she asked gazing into his brown eyes, as she sought both forgiveness and the truth.

'Yes, I am.'

'That's good, Joe.' She sighed. 'Now I think if you don't mind, I'd like to get some coffee. Would you care for some?'

'You go ahead, Frances. I'll stay here with Kathy.'

She nodded, then left the room.

377

Along with Frances, Joe remained at Kathy's side for the next twelve hours until, silently and peacefully, she drew her final breath.

In spite of the heat, the day of the funeral was appropriately gray, interrupted by sporadic showers that did not freshen the air, but only made it more oppressive. Appropriately, Stevie remained at home with Elizabeth, while the rest of the family attended the service.

Joe had already made his peace with Kathy. For him the hospital vigil and now the funeral were formalities, rites of sorrow that must be enacted, not only because society expected it, but because Frances Harrison needed them to mourn the passing of her only child.

'He could at least call and ask about Elizabeth,' Stevie said irritably to Ellen a few mornings later as they sat on the steps of the wide front porch. With the back of her hand she wiped away the perspiration that had gathered on her upper lip. On her lap she jiggled a happy, gurgling Elizabeth.

'If I remember right, he did,' said Ellen matter-of-factly. 'Yesterday and the day before. I'm sure he's going to call again today, too.'

Stevie stood and laid the baby down on a quilt she had spread out. 'I'm going to get another iced tea. Want one?' asked Stevie as she deliberately ignored Ellen's reminder.

'No, thanks,' said Ellen.

Now that her mother had put her down, Elizabeth started to cry.

'Here,' said Ellen. 'I'll take her. Go ahead and get your tea. Come here, sweetie. Your grandmother could

378

hold you and love you all day long,' she said as she reached for the baby, bringing her close to her heart.

Ellen was right, of course, thought Stevie as she opened the screen door. Joe had called, but she was still hurt and had been distant to him so the conversation was brief. *He shouldn't have been out that night. And at the very least he should have told me about it.*

The time they had spent together when Joe had been home for the funeral had been brief, and the atmosphere had been strained. In the midst of her new family, Stevie had suddenly felt like an outsider. It had nothing to do with the family's treatment of her, which was always warm and sincere. But it did have everything to do with a family that rallied around its son and brother, his loss, and a part of his life that she hadn't shared.

Stevie had deliberately chosen to remain aloof from the proceedings. Instinctively, she knew that her presence would only disturb the delicate balance between Joe and Frances Harrison.

When Joe had to leave again, she had wanted to stop him, to tell him that they needed more time together. He had been pleasant to her while he was home and, on the surface, even affectionate, but there was a wedge between them that hadn't been there before his revelations on the Beverly Simmons interview.

When Stevie returned with her tea, she sat on the front porch steps, leaning back against the white column. 'It must be thirty degrees hotter out here than inside.'

'I know,' agreed Ellen. 'Ask anyone from the South what man's greatest invention is and every one of them will tell you that it's air conditioning.'

Ellen continued talking softly to Elizabeth while Stevie drank her tea. 'Stevie,' said Ellen after a few minutes. 'I don't mean to pry, but . . .'

'But that's what you do best, Mom,' said Connie cheerfully as she pushed the front door open to join them on the porch.

'I do not!' protested Ellen. 'And don't you have some place to go?' she said teasingly to her youngest child.

'No, ma'am,' said Connie, her brown eyes wide as she settled herself on the steps between her mother and Stevie.

'Well, find some place, honey.' It was said sweetly, but it was the same message Ellen had delivered for years to all of her kids when she wanted to speak privately to one of their siblings.

'Oops, guess I do,' said Connie as she jumped up. 'Watch out for her, Stevie. *We* all do.'

'My goodness,' said Ellen playfully to Stevie, 'you bring babies into the world, feed and clothe them, love them, buy them cars, send them to school, and all you get in return is a bunch of kids who think they know everything.'

After considering her words, Ellen had to laugh, this time at herself. 'And why shouldn't they? They knew enough to get you to give them all those things in the first place.'

'Uh-oh, Stevie. If I were you I'd get out of here while I still could,' said Connie. Then she leaned down and gave her mother a hug. 'Bye. I'll be back later.'

Ellen winked at Stevie and continued her rhythmic pats against Elizabeth's back. 'Connie is right, you know.' Then her expression became serious. 'What about you and Joe? You can't keep going like this, honey.'

Stevie looked out over the green expanse of lawn and the trees beyond. 'Oh, Ellen. I don't know what I should do. I feel so betrayed. I can't understand why Joe wouldn't tell me about that night, why he would even do something like that. Didn't he think that I would find out?'

'Maybe,' said Ellen, 'but knowing Joe as I do, I believe that he was ashamed of his actions and disappointed in himself. It's very possible, Stevie, that with all the excitement surrounding Elizabeth's birth, he felt that telling you about his night out would serve no purpose.'

Stevie shrugged her shoulders. 'Maybe.'

'Joe loves you, Stevie, and whether you know it or not, his decision to leave Kathy cost him a lot emotionally. Don't let something so insignificant as a case of bad judgement come between the two of you. Trust is the most important thing in a marriage. You trusted Joe to be truthful with you and he failed. Joe trusted you to understand that he was sorry for what he did. So far, both of you have failed this first test.'

Ellen reached out and squeezed Stevie's hand briefly. 'Start again, Stevie. Call him. Get used to loving and being loved, and realize that both of you will make lots of mistakes through the years. That doesn't mean that you no longer love each other.'

Stevie leaned her head back against the carved wood column. 'I don't know what to say to him,' she sighed. 'I guess I don't know very much at all about love, but I'm trying to learn.'

'Do you miss him?' asked Ellen gently.

Stevie nodded.

'Then that's all you have to say to him.'

Stevie was silent for a moment as she pushed her damp hair off her forehead. 'I don't think I want to tell him that over the phone,' she said.

'Then go to him, surprise him. I'll tell Richie you're coming.' Ellen glanced at her watch. 'Go upstairs and pack. You have plenty of time to catch a flight.'

'It seems to me I did this once before,' said Stevie sheepishly.

'Did it work?' asked Ellen with a smile.

'Yep. Joe proposed.' Stevie paused as if thinking back on that night. 'I'll do it,' she said with conviction. 'But wait, what about Elizabeth?'

'Leave Elizabeth with us. Charlie and I can spoil her rotten. You stay as long as you want, honey. The baby will be fine.'

Stevie arrived in New Orleans that evening and took a taxi to the hotel. Joe and the band had already left for the arena. She dressed carefully in a deep sapphire blue silk dress that clung to her newly returned curves. The blue accentuated her eyes and made her hair look like shimmering twists of gold. Dangling rhinestone earrings added the sparkle she needed.

'I don't think I can get any closer,' said the taxi driver some two hours later as he made a left four blocks from the University of New Orleans Lakefront Arena where, in just a few minutes, Joe would be performing.

'Yes, you can,' said Stevie as she followed the instructions Richie had given her. 'Just turn where I tell you.'

From the hallway backstage, Stevie could hear Joe on stage along with the cheers of the crowd. The security guard who met her at the entrance escorted her through the maze of halls. Passing an office door, Stevie saw her reflection and was pleased. This concert tonight was an important social event, part of a special charity effort to raise funds for medical care for children.

Even though she tried to appear calm, she was still nervous. Richie thought her idea to surprise Joe was terrific. And Richie, always her willing accomplice and a born matchmaker at heart, took care of everything on his end. All Stevie had to do was show up tonight.

Well, here I am, about to make a fool out of myself again.

Her heart was beating and her knees were weak as she climbed the steps to the stage. She stood off to one side where she could see Joe but still remain out of sight. Instead of his usual western attire, he was dressed in a tuxedo polished off by a glistening white shirt, black boots and what had become his trademark: the black Stetson.

As the crowd cheered the finish of a song, Richie, standing behind and to the side of Joe, acknowledged Stevie's presence with a thumbs-up signal. Now Joe was talking to the crowd, setting the mood for their next song, but before he could begin Richie slipped the strap of his guitar over his head, laid it down and stepped forward. Joe, sensing the movement near him, turned and looked toward Richie questioningly. Richie grinned and waved at the audience.

'Would you like to say something, Rich?' asked Joe. Richie nodded.

Joe grinned at the audience. 'Folks, this is my brother, Richard Devlin', as he made a sweeping gesture with his hand, then stepped away from the microphone.

Brad, Dave and Allen Lee all snickered at the introduction. They all knew how much Richie loathed being called Richard.

Richie grinned at his older brother. 'Thanks, Joe,' he said, 'for that fine and very formal introduction, but my friends call me Richie.' Applause and whistles echoed. For just a moment longer Richie stood there with a silly look on his face, looking out over the audience. The audience responded with scattered laughter and applause as if they, too, were anxious to be surprised.

Joe stood off to the side, his hat pushed back off his forehead, his expression amused. This was not the first time Richie had decided to do something impromptu in the middle of a performance, and the audience always loved it. With his boyish face and his natural charisma, Richie always managed to charm as he entertained.

'You know, folks, Joe is always doing something nice for us, so we,' Richie gestured to include the rest of the band, 'decided to do something nice for Joe.'

The crowd clapped and whistled, signaling their approval. When the noise died down, Richie turned and gave the signal for them to begin playing. The song was 'Crazy'. Joe's expression changed so subtly that only the group on stage realized that he was not pleased with what they had done. They hadn't played that song since that night in Biloxi when he sang it to Stevie.

The first few notes lingered in the air.

Offstage, Stevie heard the music and was stunned. She hadn't expected Richie to do this. It was too much and too many feelings assaulted her, making her remember the night Joe sang that song; all the times she had spent with him, all the reasons she loved him. From her place offstage she saw Richie wave to her, her signal to join them onstage, but she remained where she was, her feet frozen to the floor.

Approximately thirty feet away from where Stevie stood, Joe stepped forward and joined Richie. Even though he smiled at the audience, he spoke through clenched teeth so that only Richie could hear. 'What's going on here? Why are you doing this?'

Richie smiled back. 'Ahh, things are not going well, big brother. She was supposed come out on stage, but I guess she got stage fright.'

'Who?' demanded Joe.

'Stevie.'

'Stevie is here?' asked Joe with astonishment.

'She was a few minutes ago.'

Joe walked toward the microphone. 'I'll be right back, folks,' he said as he waved his hat. He signaled to the band to keep playing. If the look on Joe's face was any indication of his mood, Richie knew that they would all get an earful after this performance. With long strides Joe crossed the stage and disappeared behind the curtain. He looked to his right and found Stevie, standing back out of the way.

When she saw him, her heart raced.

The sight of her was breathtaking.

'I'm the one who is crazy, Joe,' she said, taking a step forward. 'I didn't know about the song and when I heard it, it made me remember everything. About us.'

'Is that what you came here to tell me?' Now Joe was standing in front of her, his hands resting lightly on her waist. Stevie swallowed. Here, he seemed bigger than life.

'I came to tell you that I love you and that I want us to be together. Always. I miss you, Joe.'

Joe's eyes crinkled at the corners as his face broke out into a wide grin, then he kissed Stevie quickly. 'Let's go,' he said excitedly as he grabbed her hand. From the stage, the melody of the song that had meant so much to them seemed to surround them.

Seconds later, Joe rejoined the group on the stage, this time bringing Stevie with him. He had her hand gripped firmly in his, determined that she wouldn't get away from him. At the sight of Joe and Stevie, the fans began to stomp their feet and cheer. When he passed in front of Richie, Joe said, 'I'll settle things with you later.'

He stepped to the microphone. 'Ladies and gentlemen, my brother Richie did have a wonderful surprise for me. And here she is.' He bowed slightly to Stevie. 'I'd like for you to meet my wife, Stevie Devlin.' He tugged at her hand and pulled her forward. Throughout the arena the applause was enthusiastic and welcoming.

Then his eyes turned serious and his voice was husky as he continued, speaking both to Stevie and his fans. 'If you've ever been in love, you know that love is sometimes painful.' The noise lessened. The audience grew quiet. 'It's what I write about and it's what I sing about. There was a time when I thought I would never have this kind of love and the hurt was so great that I didn't know if I could survive.'

Joe turned toward Stevie and took both her hands in his. 'Then I met Stevie and knew I'd found what I'd been looking for all my life. Sometimes it's difficult to put what I feel into words, so I wrote a song just so I could tell Stevie all about it. It's called "Nobody's Baby".' Joe turned toward Stevie and, with one hand under her chin, leaned down to kiss her lightly. Then he straightened, picked up his guitar and strummed the opening chords. 'This is for you,' he said to her in a husky voice.

In the near silence he began to sing, his voice marked by that slightly raspy quality that had become so familiar to millions. His tone conveyed intimacy, his words tenderness. And anyone who was watching that night was touched by what they saw. Joe's eyes were serious, his smile loving as he sang the words he had written the night following their parting.

In the quiet just before dawn I remember all the
nights we've shared

Behind him the band joined in, their accompaniment rounding out the haunting melody.

And I reach for you but you're not there

Stevie looked up at Joe as she felt the words and the music he had written wrap themselves around her heart and soul.

Let me kiss away your tears and love you
through the night
Let me hold you safe from all your fears

Joe's voice rang clear now while Richie and Brad joined in on the chorus, singing harmony.

You're nobody's baby but mine, only mine
I grieve when we're apart, for my soul cannot
soar without my heart

There were many in the audience who didn't bother to wipe away the tears that had gathered in their eyes. Instead they savored the the words and the melody that had somehow reached out and touched them. When the song ended and the last note lingered in the air, there was a moment of silence before the audience recovered and sent its roar of approval toward the stage.

Up on the stage, Joe laid his guitar down and pulled Stevie into his arms, giving her a kiss that sent shock waves all the way down to her toes. 'I love you, Stevie,' he said as he raised his head and looked into her eyes. Then together they turned and waved at the crowd.

From his side, Stevie smiled up at this wonderful man with the laughing brown eyes and knew that this was as close to heaven as she would ever be.

'Something tells me that life with you is just going to be one surprise after another, babe,' said Joe with a grin as they ran offstage.

When they were clear of the stage, Stevie stopped, pulling Joe toward her for another kiss. 'You have no idea,' she murmured as his lips closed warmly over hers.

None at all, cowboy.

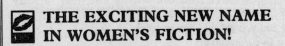# THE EXCITING NEW NAME IN WOMEN'S FICTION!

PLEASE HELP ME TO HELP YOU!

Dear *Scarlet* Reader,

Last month we began our super Prize Draw, which means that **you could win 6 months' worth of free Scarlets!** Just return your completed questionnaire to us (see addresses at end of questionnaire) before 31 July 1997 and you will automatically be entered in the draw that takes place on that day. If you are lucky enough to be one of the first two names out of the hat we will send you four new Scarlet romances every month for six months, and for each of twenty runners up there will be a sassy *Scarlet* T-shirt.

So don't delay – return your form straight away!*

Sally Cooper

Editor-in-Chief, *Scarlet*

QUESTIONNAIRE

Please tick the appropriate boxes to indicate your answers

1 Where did you get this Scarlet title?
Bought in supermarket ☐
Bought at my local bookstore ☐ Bought at chain bookstore ☐
Bought at book exchange or used bookstore ☐
Borrowed from a friend ☐
Other (please indicate) _____

2 Did you enjoy reading it?
A lot ☐   A little ☐   Not at all ☐

3 What did you particularly like about this book?
Believable characters ☐   Easy to read ☐
Good value for money ☐   Enjoyable locations ☐
Interesting story ☐   Modern setting ☐
Other _____

4 What did you particularly dislike about this book?
_____

5 Would you buy another Scarlet book?
Yes ☐   No ☐

6 What other kinds of book do you enjoy reading?
Horror ☐   Puzzle books ☐   Historical fiction ☐
General fiction ☐   Crime/Detective ☐   Cookery ☐
Other (please indicate) _____

7 Which magazines do you enjoy reading?
1. _____
2. _____
3. _____

And now a little about you –
8 How old are you?
Under 25 ☐   25–34 ☐   35–44 ☐
45–54 ☐   55–64 ☐   over 65 ☐

cont.

9 What is your marital status?
   Single ☐   Married/living with partner ☐
   Widowed ☐   Separated/divorced ☐

10 What is your current occupation?
   Employed full-time ☐   Employed part-time ☐
   Student ☐   Housewife full-time ☐
   Unemployed ☐   Retired ☐

11 Do you have children? If so, how many and how old are they?
   _____
   _____

12 What is your annual household income?

under $15,000	☐	or	£10,000	☐
$15–25,000	☐	or	£10–20,000	☐
$25–35,000	☐	or	£20–30,000	☐
$35–50,000	☐	or	£30–40,000	☐
over $50,000	☐	or	£40,000	☐

Miss/Mrs/Ms _____
Address _____
_____
_____

Thank you for completing this questionnaire. Now tear it out – put
it in an envelope and send it to:

Sally Cooper, Editor-in-Chief

USA/Can. address	*UK address/No stamp required*
SCARLET c/o London Bridge	SCARLET
85 River Rock Drive	FREEPOST LON 3335
Suite 202	LONDON W8 4BR
Buffalo	*Please use block capitals for*
NY 14207	*address*
USA	

NOBAB/4/97

Scarlet **titles coming next month:**

CAROUSEL   Michelle Reynolds
When Penny Farthing takes a job as housekeeper/nanny to
Ben Carmichael and his sons, she's looking for a quiet life.
Penny thinks she'll quite like living in the country and she
knows she'll love the little boys she's caring for . . . what she
doesn't expect is to fall in love with her boss!

BLACK VELVET   Patricia Wilson
Another SCARLET novel from this best-selling author!
Helen Stewart is *not* impressed when she meets Dan Forrest
– she's sure he's drunk, so she dumps him unceremoniously
at his hotel! Dan isn't drunk, he has flu, so their relationship
doesn't get off to the best start. Dan, though, soon wants
Helen more than he's ever wanted any other woman . . . but
is she involved in *murder*?

CHANGE OF HEART   Julie Garratt
Ten years ago headstrong Serena Corder was involved with
Holt Blackwood, but she left home because she resented her
father's attempts to control her life. Now a very different
Serena is back and the attraction she feels for Holt is as
strong as ever. But do they have a future together . . .
especially as she wears another man's ring!

A CIRCLE IN TIME   Jean Walton
Margie Seymour is about to lose her beloved ranch, when
she finds an injured man on her property. He tells her not
only that he is from the 1800s, but that *he*, not she, owns the
ranch! It's not long before feisty Margie Seymour is playing
havoc with Jake's good intentions of returning to his own
time as soon as he can!